MW00781671

7 FREE PRELUDES

AT

FreeFantasyFiction.com

STONE OF RUIN

STONE & RUIN

Z.S. DIAMANTI

GOLDEN
GRIFFIN

For Aiden,
You've brought more joy to my life
than you know.

LAND OF **KELVUR**

CRAE WASTES

SEA

FELL KEEP

VENTOH

DUSKWOOD

DORANTOWN

EASTERN KNOLLS

LAKE KNOLL

THE PALISADE

AIDEN'S DELL

THE SHOALS

FOREST OF WIRRA

ANTALON

ELAIN'S SHOULDER

LAKE TORI

TALVIN

GOLREL

LAKE NEL

LORNASH POINT

FAR

FAR COVE

EANT

ZORS

ZOR LEDI

ZOR TOREIS

ZOR VELNIS

ZOR PLEDIR

ZOR LANTI

LOD MORAZ

LOD ZIM

LOD KELPIO

LOD POIN

LOD LAKE

LOD MIETO

LERIAN SEA

CHAPTER ONE

THE ROAD TO RUIN

E very muscle in Karnak's imposing body tensed at a loud *crack!* in the nearby woods. The blood in his veins pumped in great waves, its warmth creeping into his neck. The orc gripped his battle axe, making his green knuckles whiten. He sniffed the air, hoping to smell some hint of their enemies, but the moisture hung thick, bathing everything around with the scent of wet earth. When nothing else happened, Karnak rolled the tension out of his shoulders.

A snowflake melted as it landed on his muscular arm. The orc leaned back against the wooden barrier, holding his axe to the side, as he raised a hand to catch another drifting flake. *A late flurry,* he thought. Spring was showing its telltale signs, so the cold wasn't unbearable. The orc was grateful for the slow change in season. He'd take the cooler weather as long as the land of Kelvur would give it to them.

Karnak looked to the dwarf sitting against another barrier. The dwarf's black beard bristled as he noticed the light dusting beginning to fall. A wide grin emerged behind Coal's bushy beard. A low roll of excited whispers grew from the barricaded warriors all around. Karnak's lips parted around his tusks as he also smiled.

When the wicked sorcerer Jaernok Tur had swooped upon the city of Ventohl with his new army like a swarm of wasps, they captured the city in hours. Karnak and the Javelin warriors—or those who survived the attack—barely escaped. Many did not. At first, they thought nothing would stop Jaernok Tur's army from hunting them down; but winter hit hard only a few days later, and encounters with the sorcerer's forces ceased.

With spring coming, Karnak had led a group of Javelin warriors from Dorantown to barricade the road to Ventohl. The defenders had only been there two weeks, but they'd witnessed the seasons shifting. Soft snow had segued to stinging rain in intermittent torrents that left their surroundings boggy. Karnak wondered when Jaernok Tur's inevitable wave of destruction would fall upon them. They assumed that the reprieve granted to them by winter would be mirrored with an equal measure of relentless attacks come spring.

Another *crack!*

The group fell silent, eyeing the forest on either side of the road. Karnak shifted his gaze, and a young warrior raised a hand and whispered, "Sorry!"

Karnak growled under his breath and squeezed his battle axe tighter in his fist. He drew in the damp air, filling his lungs, in an attempt to slow his racing heart. Karnak pressed his eyes closed, listening for another noise. The orc cursed the trees of Duskwood and their incessant creaking in the wind. None of the warriors knew whether the sorcerer's legions would make a move in cooler temperatures. The scouts they'd sent to Ventohl always came back with little information, none willing to risk getting too close.

An awkward guttural noise from the trees caught Karnak's attention, but when he peered through the shadows, he saw nothing—including the warrior who'd been there a moment ago.

"Coal," Karnak whispered to the dwarf.

Coal didn't speak but crouched to a ready position, bringing his war hammer to bear before him. The dwarf nodded his readiness. Karnak moved along the barricade toward the trees and peered through the dim, searching for the young warrior.

Another *crack!* halted him in his tracks.

"Wretchli—," a Javelin warrior hollered before his warning was cut short.

The warriors on the road swayed uncertainly. The ones Karnak had positioned in the woods on either side of the road were supposed to flank any attackers, but it seemed they were the ones being flanked.

Suddenly, a young woman wearing brown leathers burst from the forest undergrowth, her eyes terror-widened. She looked at Karnak and opened her mouth. Before she uttered a word, her face shifted from terror to confusion as a black spear erupted from her midsection. She tottered and fell to the side, revealing the killer behind her.

A man-sized creature stood fifteen feet away with a wicked grin on his gnarled face. His eyes were orange flames in his skull. His blackened skin could hardly be called that as it barely contained the creature's smoky innards. Smoke swirled around him as though it kept his disfigured form together. As Karnak gathered his wits, the creature let out an ear-piercing screech.

"Wretchlings! To arms!" Karnak roared as he ran down the embankment and heaved his axe down into the creature's shoulder. As the blade sliced through the thin exterior of the monster, streams of smoke billowed from its body. The wretchling fell instantly.

Metal on metal clanged along the road and through the forest. Karnak turned as Coal's hammer slammed into a shorter wretchling brandishing a jagged black dagger. The creature flipped backward, landing hard on the ground before the dwarf brought his hammer down on its head. The wretchling exploded into a cloud of putrid black smoke.

"I guess they're back," Coal huffed.

Karnak growled his reply and ran off to take on another of the dark monsters. He found one of their few griffin guardians parrying a particularly quick wretchling that wielded two swords. The guardian held his own, parrying, striking, and parrying again. Karnak heaved his axe, hurtling it through the air. It tore through the wretchling like a water skin, as smoke spewed from the crumpling creature. Its orange flame eyes extinguished, and the monster lay dead.

The guardian nodded his thanks and turned to find another opponent, but a black arrow struck him, and he fell to his knee. Karnak ran toward the guardian's side, but another arrow landed its mark, putting the guardian down before the orc reached him. Karnak whirled on his feet, finding a smug wretchling staring wickedly at him.

Karnak moved slowly toward his axe, stuck in the pile of what used to be a wretchling. His eyes never left the creature that stared unrelentingly at him. *Why does he not take the shot?* Karnak wondered.

The wretchling's gaze was unnerving. When the creature took a step to the side, Karnak prepared to dive. He wasn't sure he could dodge an arrow if the wretchling loosed it from his bow, but the orc would not die easily. Instead of loosing an arrow, the creature merely stepped behind a tree.

Karnak dove anyway, rolling over his axe and lifting it before him. When he caught sight of the wretchling again, the creature was farther away, still leering at the orc and stepping slowly. Karnak nudged the guardian that lay unmoving next to him.

The man was gone. A snarl worked its way from the orc's throat to his lips, his tusks grinding to the side.

Coal blasted another wretchling, sending spurts of smoke spiraling away. "Karnak!" the dwarf yelled. "What are you doing?"

Karnak turned to the dwarf after the monster disappeared behind another tree. "That wretchling. Did you see it? It's strange."

When they'd fought the dark creatures in Ventohl, the wretchlings—the mindless and murderous drove of what used to be the sorcerer's geldrin army—came at the heroes in Ventohl like a legion from the depths of Malkra. They seemed unthinking and savage.

This one is ... different. Karnak jumped to his feet and barreled through the trees.

"Karnak! Wait!" Coal hollered as he charged after the orc.

Karnak ran as fast as his legs could propel his big body. A glimpse of the wretchling off to the side slowed him before the creature disappeared behind another tree. *Where ... are you?* Karnak thought. He strained his eyes, scanning the trees. *There!* He dashed away, just as Coal caught up to him.

"Boehlen's Beard," the dwarf grumbled. "Where are you going?"

The soggy ground squished under the orc's heavy footfalls as he stormed along. He slid to a stop as he rounded a copse of trees that opened into a small clearing. Karnak immediately recognized his error as the creature slithered up the side of a young dragon and perched on top.

Karnak ducked behind a tree as the dragon sprayed flames at the orc. The wet trees erupted into an inferno as though they were dry kindling.

"What in Finlestia?" Coal shouted as he dove beside the orc.

Karnak spun around the burning tree and glared at the creature that had drawn him to that spot. "It's a varlek," Karnak said. "One of Jaernok Tur's generals."

Only one spy had been brave enough to close in on Ventohl and look inside its broken walls—an elf mage by the name of Lanryn. He, of course, had superior eyesight and hearing and, with his magic tricks, had gathered more information about the new army than any others. He'd only seen the wretchlings once in all his trips—enough to spur them to set up the barricade on the road.

"And this varlek has a dragon." Coal pointed out the obvious surprise.

The varlek smirked smugly at the orc as the dragon wafted its wide wings and lifted them into the air. The creature released a wild howl. The noises of the battle behind them ceased almost instantly. The varlek nodded to the orc and the dwarf, who stood dumbfounded at the edge of the clearing, before he turned the dragon to fly back toward Ventohl.

They watched the young dragon fly away until it passed the tree line beyond their vision. Karnak released a low growl.

"Another dragon," Coal grumbled, shaking his head.

"I have the feeling this was only a test," Karnak said.

"What?"

"We have to get back to Dorantown. They stand little chance against a dragon. We need to get everyone out of there."

"Maker, help us," Coal whispered.

The orc agreed. *Maker, help us, indeed.*

Chapter Two

Little Falconer

M errick stepped lightly over a fallen log. His footfalls were not silent like an elf's, but they were almost inaudible for a human. He brushed against a wide oak as he knelt to the ground.

Tracks!

The huntsman pulled his shoulder-length brown hair out of his face and tucked it behind his ear. Squinting, he scanned the trees, looking for other signs of his prey. He saw a broken leaf a short distance away and smirked.

Got you.

He meandered to the tree and looked around. Anyone who saw him would think he was either baffled or lost. He stepped around the large tree as though he were beginning his search again.

Merrick pressed close to the tree, hidden under a wide branch. The huntsman was an adept climber. How many times had he climbed the trees of the forest outside of Tamaria when he was growing up? Countless. This tree was no different.

He smelled the fresh wood as he gripped another branch above his head. Merrick jerked his hand back, realizing he'd grabbed a handful of sap. *That won't wash off so easily*, he thought with displeasure. He rolled his eyes and continued his climb.

Something in the tree above him moved the branches as it crawled to a new position.

Probably trying to see where I got off to, Merrick mused.

Silent as a cat, he climbed until he reached a large branch where he could crouch and peer around the trunk of the enormous tree.

There you are, he thought.

He maneuvered himself around the tree's trunk, keeping his feet as close to the trunk as possible to avoid shaking the branches. He held tightly to a branch above him and leaned out as far as he could. He extended one finger and tapped the halfling on the head. "Found you!"

Kippin emitted a terrified squeak and nearly jumped out of his skin. He wobbled for a second as though he might fall from the giant tree. His arms waved wildly as he tried to balance himself. Merrick grabbed the little halfling by the front of his tunic, holding him fast.

"You scared me half to death," the halfling said.

Merrick laughed, amused with himself. "You almost had me that time, Kippin," he said as he shimmied into a comfortable seat on the wide branch.

"What gave me away?" Kippin asked, his round lips pursing with disappointment.

"You got lazy when you were walking."

"I did not," the little halfling argued. "I wanted you to see those tracks going in that direction," he added, pointing toward the distance.

"Ah, but you broke several leaves and tiny branches near the bottom, trying to get up the tree without leaving more tracks in the mud," Merrick said calmly. He removed an apple from his satchel and cut a slice with his knife. The huntsman extended

8

the apple slice to the young halfling who took it reluctantly and perched beside him on the branch.

"But I couldn't reach the other side without you seeing my tracks going around the tree," the halfling said through a bite of apple.

"Then you chose the wrong tree," the huntsman stated matter-of-factly. "Clever to give me footprints leading in one direction, but you have to make sure there are enough exposed roots on the tree for you to skirt it and climb without leaving a trace."

Kippin looked down at his apple slice in defeat, picking at the yellow skin.

Merrick cut another slice and offered it to Kippin, who quickly shoved the rest of his first slice in his mouth and took the new one. Merrick smiled.

"You'll get the hang of it," the huntsman encouraged. "Soon enough, I won't be able to find you, and I'll be sick with worry."

Kippin looked up, a smile tugging at the corner of his mouth. "If I could do that, then no one would be able to find me."

Merrick laughed and said, "Well, I'm sure there are people who track much better than I do. But hopefully you'll be able to hide from the wretchlings when they come back."

The huntsman's face turned serious, and he looked across the forest from their high perch. The trees swayed peacefully, paying no mind to the troubles of men. Kippin pulled the rest of the apple out of the distracted man's hand and took a big bite, filling his cheeks like a squirrel.

A pang of regret stabbed Merrick—not regret that he'd taken Kippin under his wing. Quite the contrary. He loved Kippin, and over the past several months, he and Kippin and Ralowyn had become a unique family. Merrick regretted that he had to teach the young halfling how to survive a brutal world.

"Come on," he said after a long while. "We can't go home empty-handed. Ralowyn will be wondering why we were gone so long."

He winked at Kippin as he helped the halfling to a lower branch before descending himself.

Merrick knelt silently to the ground, placing his knees in the duff of the forest floor. He summoned Kippin to his side with a hand gesture. The halfling padded to him and leaned over the huntsman's shoulder.

"What is it?" Kippin asked curiously.

"Rabbit trail," Merrick replied. "See how the duff is trampled and the grasses are curved around the trail? Hares run through here. They're likely headed to some water in a nearby meadow."

"Ralowyn would be happy with some rabbit for stew," Kippin suggested.

"I think she would." Merrick chuckled quietly. "I'll show you how to set a trap for them."

They spent the next hour finding more rabbit trails and setting up slip snares to catch their quarry. The huntsman demonstrated how to tie the knot so the loop would tighten when something ran through it. After setting a few, Kippin was tying them like he'd been doing it since he was born. The halfling still looked to Merrick after each knot, beaming under the man's winks of approval.

Quietly, they exited the area, searching for the meadow. The sun warmed the woods through the verdant canopy, causing the smell of fresh spring to touch their noses. Merrick felt very much at home in the far reaches of Duskwood. He had always been drawn to the wild.

When his father, Grell, a master huntsman of Tamaria, first took him out as a boy to hunt, his heart soared. Merrick found himself in a distant land, teaching a young halfling to do the same. Fate had swept him into an unexpected situation, but watching Kippin climb over a fallen log, Merrick was certain he wouldn't trade his circumstances for anything.

The sudden wail of a bird of prey froze the huntsman in his tracks. Kippin heard it, too, and turned to Merrick with wide eyes. The man placed a finger to his lips, urging quiet movement. Merrick stepped on top of the fallen log and balanced as he tiptoed along its length. He stepped on tree roots whenever possible to keep his movements silent.

Finally, he ducked low, alongside another massive log on the edge of a blooming meadow. *Yes,* he thought excitedly. Kippin sidled next to the man, placing a small hand on the huntsman's shoulder. Merrick signaled for him not to speak. He pointed to his eyes and then across the meadow, indicating they were attempting to spot the bird.

He scanned the sky for the bird but saw nothing. His eyes navigated the tree line for signs of a nest, though he saw no distinguishable markers. Merrick bit his lip as he thought. Kippin's face scrunched as he looked at the huntsman, clearly hanging on to the man's every move. Suddenly, Merrick grinned. He tapped his nose and jutted a thumb to the side before rising to his feet.

They maneuvered stealthily around the edge of the meadow until Merrick found a spot with a wider vantage of the open haven in the middle of the dense forest. They sat quietly, watching and waiting.

And then they saw it.

A young falcon glided high above, his wings outstretched, almost motionless. Kippin's mouth gaped as Merrick pointed to the falcon. The halfling's little hand squeezed the wool of the huntsman's cloak in his excitement.

Merrick eyed the small bird. It had to be young. He guessed it was a male due to its brilliant spots and grey back, but he couldn't be sure at that distance. Plus, falcons in Kelvur could be different than those in Tarrine.

The man glanced out of the corner of his eye at Kippin. The halfling's wonder at the sight of the bird stirred something within the huntsman. He tapped the little halfling's hand and signaled for Kippin to follow him.

Once they were some distance away, Merrick turned to him and whispered, "We're going to catch that falcon."

They spent the majority of that day gathering supplies to trap the falcon. Merrick trimmed flexible yew branches, while Kippin gathered sticks of specific sizes. When Merrick was satisfied with the cleaned yew branches, he attached them to a net they'd brought from Dorantown.

Kippin watched Merrick closely as he went about the intentional work. The huntsman flexed the branches several times to make sure the net would snap just right. Happy with the results, he showed Kippin how to tie the sticks he had gathered to form a cage wall. The young halfling enjoyed tying knots, and Merrick gladly taught him new ones for the project.

They worked in relative silence, Kippin breaking it with a whisper here or there for Merrick's approval on a task. The halfling tied knots diligently, his tongue sticking out the side of his mouth in concentration.

Eventually, they had everything prepared, and the evening twilight was falling. Merrick quietly led Kippin to the snare traps they'd set earlier for rabbits.

Kippin's face lit up when they found the first captured hare. At the sight of Merrick's disappointed look, the halfling shifted his own. They gathered the dead rabbit, and Merrick tucked it away in his satchel while Kippin reset the trap.

When they found another rabbit still alive in one of their snares, the halfling stowed his elation, awaiting the huntsman's reaction. Merrick nodded vigorously to the cage Kippin carried, a wide grin on his face. Merrick grabbed the rabbit and gently placed the creature into the cage. The man's excitement surprised the halfling into motion. Kippin closed the open side and coiled the string around some of the other sticks, locking it in place.

The halfling beamed at the man, and Merrick tapped a finger to his amused lips to remind Kippin to stay quiet.

They returned to their makeshift camp where Kippin whispered excitedly, "How do you know how to do all these things?"

Merrick smiled as he pulled a wrapped loaf of bread from his bag. As he ripped it apart for them to share, he said, "A few years back, an elf from Vandor came to my hometown, Tamaria. I went to the market to sell meats and furs, and when I arrived, crowds of people were gathering around this elf to watch his spectacle."

"Was he a magician?" Kippin asked through a mouthful of bread.

"No." Merrick chuckled, shaking his head. "He had a falcon, and he was displaying the wondrous things he'd taught the bird to do. Like many people, I was transfixed by the bird. But when the show was over and others left, I stayed. I had to know how he was able to work with the bird."

"Did he tell you?" Kippin asked, scooting closer to the huntsman to see him in the moonlight.

"He did." Merrick nodded, handing the halfling more from his own piece of bread. "His name was Antoril, and he taught me that falcons could be used for hunting. He taught me how to catch and train my first falcon. He also taught me how to work with her, an art called falconry."

Kippin chewed on the word—or maybe just the excessive bite of bread in his mouth. "Is that how you caught Valurwind?" the halfling asked, amazed.

"No," the huntsman said, suppressing a laugh. He pulled a beautifully carved figurine of a falcon from his pocket. The smooth stone was cool in the evening, and the crystalline accents glinted in the moonlight. "She is a falcon set apart. She is the queen of falcons. I don't know how someone catches an astral falcon, but we sure are glad they did. Right?"

"Sure are," Kippin said, after gulping down a bite.

Merrick rubbed the figurine. Valurwind had saved his life plenty in the past. When the wretchlings swarmed the castle of Ventohl, he'd called upon the astral falcon. Like always, mist formed and morphed into the giant bird, whose spots and colors looked more like stars in the sky than the normal patterns of her smaller cousins. When the retreat was sounded, Valurwind had carried Merrick, Ralowyn, and Kippin to safety.

"What was your falcon's name?" Kippin asked curiously.

"Her name was Rora," Merrick said, a hint of sadness in his words. It struck him that he hadn't mentioned her to Kippin. "She was as brave as Valurwind, only much smaller."

"Rora is a pretty name."

"It is. In elvish, it means 'heart.' Even though she was small, she had a big heart. Just like someone else I know," Merrick added with a wink.

Kippin brimmed with pride at the compliment.

"Alright," the huntsman said, gathering up his things. "We won't have a fire tonight. We don't want the falcon to get spooked by the smell of smoke. Let's climb up that tree. It has a nice wide branch we can sleep on."

"Sleep in a tree?" Kippin asked, bewildered.

"Don't worry. I won't let you fall out. It's going to be cold, so we're going to sleep close tonight anyway. We'll get up early tomorrow to set our trap."

In short order, they were comfortably nestled in the tree. The rabbit slept soundly in the cage, hanging from a nearby branch. Kippin shivered into Merrick's side. When the huntsman wrapped his cloak around the little halfling, they both warmed up quickly. Merrick smiled as he brushed the curly locks away from Kippin's already snoring face.

The huntsman nudged Kippin until he woke. The little halfling wiped the drool on his face and blinked the night away.

"We have to set our trap for the falcon," Merrick whispered.

The notion perked the halfling up, and he looked around crazily, trying to get his bearings. "I'm ready," he said unconvincingly.

They walked in silence to the meadow where they'd seen the falcon the day before. There, they set out the cage with the rabbit inside, placing a few tasty leaves in it for the creature to munch on. Merrick bent the yew branches attached to the net and slotted a pin that was tied to a long rope. He ushered Kippin toward the underbrush where they could hide, unraveling the rope as they went.

When they were finally in a position to watch for the falcon and still be hidden, Merrick extended the rope to Kippin. The halfling's eyes widened, and he shook his head. Merrick smiled and nodded as he pushed the rope into Kippin's hands.

Silently, Merrick motioned for Kippin to be patient. The huntsman made a bunny with his fingers and fluttered his other hand like a bird flying down on top of it. As soon as the bird hand descended on the bunny hand, both hands transformed to pull an invisible rope.

Kippin nervously nodded his understanding.

They sat for hours as the morning grew long. The sun crept into the sky, and the bugs and daytime critters emerged. The tall flowers of the meadow danced in the light breeze, but the pair had seen no sign of the falcon. Kippin turned to Merrick countless times, but the huntsman merely raised a hand to remind the halfling to stay patient.

Eventually, Kippin's belly rumbled so loudly that Merrick heard it. The man smirked and figured that was the end of their hunt for the falcon. He looked up to the sky as he inhaled deeply. Just then, he saw the bird.

The way Merrick flinched and threw a staying hand toward the halfling made Kippin tense. The huntsman pointed to the falcon high above. The bird hovered for a long while, seemingly very interested in their caged rabbit. Merrick wasn't sure if the falcon sensed them or not. He hoped the bird didn't.

Even though it wasn't particularly hot, a bead of sweat worked its way down the huntsman's brow. How long had he been holding his breath?

He glanced at Kippin. The halfling was on his knees, itching and ready to pull the rope. They watched as the young falcon lowered itself, getting a better look at the rabbit.

Finally, the falcon dropped on the cage.

"Now!" Merrick urged.

Kippin pulled the rope with all his might.

The rope plucked the pin from its secure place and sent the yew branches flipping over the cage, wrapping the falcon in the attached netting. The bird fluttered its wings, unsure what was happening, but quickly fell still.

Kippin leaped to his feet and stared in disbelief. Merrick stood as well. He turned and lifted the halfling into his arms.

"You did it," he said. "You got him!"

When Merrick set Kippin back on the ground, the young halfling's bare feet padded across the forest floor as he ran to the net. He inspected the scene in utter shock.

He turned toward Merrick and lifted one fist high above his head, shouting in a victorious tone that emphasized each word. "I am a falconer!"

Merrick laughed at the little man's display. "Yes, you are."

Kippin bounced on his feet several times, unable to contain his excitement. As Merrick approached, the halfling glanced between the huntsman and their trap. His lips pursed, and his brows crinkled.

"What do we do now?" he asked sheepishly.

Merrick chuckled and said, "Let me show you."

CHAPTER THREE

SCARS

T he high winds blew fiercely across the ridge of the Scar Cliffs in Calrok. Smarlo patted Klovur on the neck as she twitched, her muscles tightening in anticipation. She wasn't the largest wyvern, nor was she considered one of the fiercest, but she was fast. And whether other orcs could tell or not, Smarlo knew she prided herself on that fact.

Most Tarrinians looked at wyverns and assumed them great, unthinking beasts. Many saw them as smaller, weaker dragons with only two legs, unable to spit fire. The orcs in the squadrons around Drelek who worked closely with the creatures knew better. Every wyvern had its own temperaments, quirks, and skills. Riders had to learn such details about their wyverns and work with them in tandem to become effective warriors.

"Easy girl," Smarlo whispered to Klovur, as he stroked the scales of her neck.

Klovur's shoulder blades and wing bones rolled a couple times as she clung tighter to the stony cliffside. The waters of the Gant Sea crashed upon the massive rocks at the bottom of the steep drop.

"Whoa, Galbrish. Hold. Hold," Lehra cooed several paces away.

Galbrish was a large wyvern male. Smarlo found it humorous that Lehra, a small human woman, rode him. Galbrish's rider, an orc named Jinlo, died during the battle in the mines to defend Calrok from the invaders that rose from the Underrock.

The Griffin Guard had flown all the way to the orc city to join them in their fight. Lehra had lost her griffin defending the orcs' home. While griffins were finicky when it came to riders, wyverns didn't require a special bonding process. Wyverns and their riders developed their bonds and trust in one another as they worked together.

Smarlo and the other leaders decided that guardians, who were already well-trained in flying tactics and practices, could potentially learn the art of wyvern riding. Lehra and Jeh were the two guardians chosen for the honor. They had lost their griffins but were not too injured to begin training soon after the battle. Thus far, they had not disappointed and had proven adept flyers.

While flying with wyverns differed from flying with griffins, many of the flight tactics and practices were similar. The guardians took to it like they'd been doing it their entire lives, which Smarlo learned was not far from the truth. Most guardians started their training at the age of eleven. Their eagerness to learn and take on every challenge the Scar Squadron threw at them quickly gained the guardians much favor with the rest of the group.

As several riders high atop the Scar Cliffs readied their wyverns to race, Smarlo decided he could still teach them a thing or two.

The orc mage leaned closer to Klovur's back, and the wyvern tensed harder. Several orcs, sitting atop their wyverns on the cliff's edge to watch, shouted encouragements to the competitors.

Smarlo looked down the line of wyverns and riders readying themselves—five in total.

Belguv, commander of the Scar Squadron, drifted out on the wind ahead of them. His wyvern flapped its leathery wings several times to find a comfortable breeze on which to float. Belguv raised a hand and shouted, "Racers, ready!"

Oh, we're ready, Smarlo thought, gripping tightly to Klovur.

"Go!" Belguv shouted.

The five wyverns and their riders dropped from the cliffside, accompanied by the cheers of their fellow squadron mates. The rushing wind *whooshed* past them as they plummeted. Smarlo used all his strength to keep from being peeled away from Klovur. He tilted his head, pressing himself as tightly to her scaly body as possible. He couldn't see, but he didn't need to. He trusted that at the last moment, just before they crashed into the rocks like the waves, Klovur would pull them out of their dive, and they'd be off.

And so, she did.

When Smarlo was able to look around, he saw where they fell in order. A couple of the teams were ahead of them, including Galbrish and Lehra. Galbrish's great weight made him drop like a giant boulder falling from a high peak. The wyvern's mass and wingspan wouldn't help them, though, as they weaved between mighty rock pillars that shot high into the sky from the sea floor.

An enormous wave slammed against one of the stone pillars, spraying mist and foam onto the riders. Galbrish flicked his powerful wings, sending water droplets flying in beautiful arcs of refracted light. Klovur dashed through them, scattering the array. While Galbrish's turns around each pillar were clunky and slow, Klovur navigated the weaves with ease and precision. Smarlo smirked as they zipped past Lehra and her big wyvern.

Smarlo and Klovur passed the last pillar and entered the straight shot out to the sea. Tark, the youngest orc in Scar Squadron, was still ahead on his wyvern. Smarlo grinned.

They'd raced before. While Tark and his wyvern were fast, and their bond still growing, Smarlo and Klovur had beaten them in their previous encounters. They needed to make up some ground, though.

Klovur stretched her leathery wings and banked the duo around the far reach of the Scar Cliffs where the rock face fell away into open sea. The next task in the race was to tap the top of one of the guard towers near the docks. It was a test of a rider's ability to make delicate maneuvers at great speeds. A rider had to slow enough for their wyvern to tap the roof without causing damage but also keep up their momentum for the steep climb to the top of the Scar Cliffs.

Smarlo and Klovur slowly gained on Tark and his wyvern as they flew over the bay toward the tower. That leg of the race would make or break the young orc. If Tark managed the maneuver with ease, Smarlo and Klovur would be hard-pressed to overtake them in the climb.

An orc in the tower, part of the city watch, braced himself. Smarlo was certain the watch hated when the riders raced, and their annoyance amused him. Tark's wyvern beat his wings to make its attempt on the tower. The orc inside gripped the railing as he was wind-whipped by the wyvern's powerful wings.

Tark and his wyvern shot into the air, having tapped the roof of the tower.

Pretty good, Smarlo mused. "Let's show them what we've got, Klovur," he shouted.

Klovur, showing seemingly little effort, tapped the roof of the tower and beat her wings furiously into the climb. For every wyvern, the climb through the sky to the top of the Scar Cliffs seemed a complete drag compared to the speed with which they started the race. Klovur powered through, her wings taking long draws as though she swam through the sky.

Tark peeked back over his shoulder, and his eyes widened before he turned forward and leaned tighter to his wyvern. Smarlo gritted his teeth, his small tusks producing a wicked grin. They had caught up.

As the two wyverns climbed, Klovur slowly edged ahead. Cheers from above resounded as the wyverns snipped at each other, exhausted from the effort and not entirely comfortable with the close flying. As they approached the edge of the cliff, orcs shouted encouragement to Tark, as though it would spur the young orc on. In the end, Klovur landed on the clifftop just before her opponent.

The orcs erupted—several of them cheering in ecstasy, others wailing in dismay. Smarlo laughed as several orcs tossed pouches of coins to others, obviously paying for lost bets.

"Almost had me that time, Tark," Smarlo commented.

"If Sarntik grows any more, we'll have you," Tark said.

"I wouldn't bet on it," Smarlo replied, as he shot Tark a wry look and caught a pouch of coins tossed to him by Belguv.

As the others arrived, the orcs cheered again, many shouting encouraging words to Lehra and Jeh, who had flown with great effort.

Smarlo, overwhelmed with joy, glanced around at everyone gathered atop the Scar Cliffs. Moments like those made him believe the world wasn't all bad ... even if wicked sorcerers from Kelvur wanted to destroy them.

"Oh, good," Tanessa said, as she brought a pot to the table. "I was wondering if you were going to make it. It's getting dark."

The orc woman smiled warmly as her orcling ran to greet Smarlo at the door. Smarlo lifted the little tyke high above him. Gernot playfully tugged the orc mage's ears. Smarlo tickled the orcling's round belly and then set him on his feet.

"I was at the cliffs. We had a race to end our training day this evening."

"Oh, did Tark beat you this time?" Tanessa asked, lowering a loaf of grain bread to the table as they sat.

"No." Smarlo snickered and crinkled his nose into a funny face at Gernot who was already stuffing a piece of torn bread into his mouth. "He's getting fast though. Sarntik may be able to take Klovur in a few months."

They fell silent as Tanessa dished out a bowl of turkey soup for each of them. The steam's aroma wafted into Smarlo's nose, signaling to his stomach that he was ravenously hungry. "Thank you," he said. "This looks great. Right, Gernot?" He spooned at the soup, moving the rice and vegetables around to gather a bite with turkey.

"Thank you," Gernot chimed as he slurped from his spoon.

They fell back into silence, the only noises being those of the little orcling devouring his supper. Smarlo had been coming to the house every evening for dinner. He couldn't explain it, but he felt beholden to them, as though it was his responsibility to be there for Tanessa and Gernot while Karnak was across the sea. The evenings had been pleasant for the past several months through the winter, but as spring drew near and Smarlo's inevitable departure loomed on the horizon, there had been more painful silences.

When Tanessa returned from tucking Gernot into bed shortly after supper, Smarlo handed a steaming mug to the orc woman and poured one for himself. They'd taken to sitting with their tea in the tall-backed chairs near the hearth each night. Smarlo spent much of the time staring into the swirling red rooibos tea, while Tanessa worked herself up to ask the questions that plagued her throughout the day.

Though Smarlo had one of the magical Shells of Callencia, which allowed him to communicate with their allies across the sea, he didn't know Karnak's every move in Kelvur. The orc mage gave her updates on her husband whenever he had them, but many of their discussions of late surrounded Smarlo's upcoming trip with the Scar Squadron. They planned to head south to Kane Harbor and cross the sea with members of the Griffin Guard, the garvawk warriors of Galium, and some of the Riders of Loralith. It was to be the greatest combined force Tarrine had ever sent out.

"When does Deklahn arrive?" Tanessa asked about the king's personal mage adviser.

"He should be here in the next couple of days," Smarlo said. "We received an owl from Ruk with a message just this morning. King Genjak is not entirely enthusiastic about the Scar Squadron crossing the Gant Sea. But he understands that Calrok has had the most interaction with our allied forces and we're best equipped to work alongside them in such an unprecedented mission."

Smarlo scratched at his green ear as Tanessa quietly sipped her tea. The scarred tip of his ear, only half the length of his other one, nagged at him sometimes.

"Does it still bother you?" Tanessa asked, noticing his discomfort.

"The scar itches sometimes," Smarlo admitted. Half his long ear had been cut off during the battle in Calrok's deep mines. Over the past several months as it healed, he'd sometimes felt like his ear was still whole and he'd reach up to scratch at it. But there was nothing to scratch. He'd taken to scratching at the scar since, but it never relieved the itch.

"I made a salve this morning. Maybe it will help," Tanessa said, placing her mug on a side table and retrieving a clay jar from the kitchen. She opened the jar and held it out toward Smarlo. The orc mage scooped a small bit onto his finger and rubbed it onto his ear. The salve had a flowery scent to it.

Smarlo's fingers slowed, as he looked up to find tears rolling down Tanessa's cheeks. He stood from his chair. "Tanessa," he whispered. "I'm so sorry. You know, I have to go. I have to sail to Kelvur and help them battle this new threat. If the wretchling army were to come across the sea ...," He let the implications linger in the room. "I'll bring Karnak back. I promise."

The lovely orc woman snorted as she wiped the tears from her face. "You're not the first one to tell me that."

Smarlo winced. He knew Merrick had told Tanessa the same thing. Likely, the huntsman meant it then just as much as he did.

Suddenly, Smarlo stepped closer to her and wrapped her in a hug. Tanessa didn't protest but melted into the embrace. Her shoulders bounced as several sobs escaped her. "None of this is how it's supposed to be," she cried softly.

"I know," Smarlo replied, shaking his head. "That's why we're going. We're going to make this right."

He rested his chin on the top of her head, holding her until her crying slowed. Eventually, she looked up at him and gently pushed herself away. Smarlo grabbed their mugs and brought them to the kitchen. They tidied in silence, and before the orc mage left, he asked if Tanessa would like him to take care of the smoldering embers in the fireplace. The orc woman told him she would take care of it, and he bid her goodnight.

As he walked away from the gar's house on the edge of the city, he glanced back at the soft, warm light emanating from the window of the house. The paddock in which it sat was bathed in the starkly different light of the moon.

The long walk back to the mage library of Calrok took him down several different streets in the city. He didn't mind the distance, especially if the night was of a comfortable temperature like that one. Those walks always gave him time to process his discussions with Tanessa and the trials that stood on the near horizon.

How many times had he walked that path in the past several months, hearing the low chimes of ships' bells as they bobbed quietly near the docks? He sniffed a deep breath, taking in the scent of the sea salt in the air.

The only thing he didn't like about the walks was how eerily empty the city seemed when night fell. The emptiness was even more palpable when he arrived back at his quarters at the library. When Master Tan-Kro was killed, Smarlo was the only mage left at the library. The orc assumed he would have to start training another in the arcane ways when he returned from Kelvur. Maybe then, the mage library would feel alive again.

He crested a small hill street and took his last look at the sprawling city below him. As large as the city was, he felt no less alone.

CHAPTER FOUR

WORDS OF WARNING

G arron bolted upright in his bed. He wiped at the matted hair stuck to his sweaty forehead. His hand ran across the stubble on his chin, which prickled lightly against his palm. The sunlight snuck through the large curtains that led to the balcony of his room. Even after sleeping in his old room for months, he still didn't quite feel right. It was the same room he'd slept in while his father was still king of Whitestone, but he was far from the same young man who'd rested there then.

He hefted himself into a sitting position on the bedside and let his feet land on the cool white stone floor. The action grounded him in the present. Birds sang their songs outside, and Garron thought he heard the distinct song of the meadowlark. Spring was upon them, and the plans for the Griffin Guard to send more aid across the Gant Sea to Kelvur were in full swing.

Come ... a whisper on the wind said.

Garron shuddered. He shook his head vigorously, and his gaze fell upon the open book on his desk in the room's corner. He padded toward the desk, running his fingers along the tapestry that covered one of the stone walls. The piece had been one of his favorites since he was a child. It depicted an intricately woven portrayal of Gildrake's meeting with an ancient wizard. The wizard held out a hand in a blessing over one of the heroes of the Second Great Black War. Gildrake held high the wizard's gift—the sword, *Wintertide.* The long thin, slightly curved sword gleamed with magical beams of light.

An uncomfortable twitch rolled over Garron as his fingers fell away from the tapestry, as though he were being dragged away from the only comfort he knew. He approached the desk hesitantly. The sunlight's beams landed on the open book. Garron grabbed the corner of the desk, as if it would save him from falling into the book's open pages.

His eyes fell upon *The Lost Notes on Nari* by Kel Joran. That book was a copy of Joran's notes about the mission he and his crew embarked on in the Nari Desert in search of great treasures and a wealth of historical knowledge. The original copy of his notes was found when a rescue team had searched some of the treacherous desert for the explorer's company. The only trace they ever found was his journal.

Even more curious than their disappearance were the several pages of transcription in the Nari language that Kel Joran included in his journal. None had been able to read or write that tongue in centuries. The explorer's notes were incomplete, since the desert had destroyed plenty of pages.

The peculiarity that captivated Garron was his mind made sense of the curious letters of the Nari transcription. In truth, he could not say that he understood them, for much of it was poetic in nature and seemed to speak of an enchanted time and place that was hard to comprehend. However, he could read it.

He'd started reading the book months ago, when he was still in the Whitestone dungeons for his crimes against his people. Since then, the bewildering words of the Nari had rarely left his thoughts. He pondered them regularly, sometimes missing the words of others while he was in conversation.

How many times had Ellaria asked him if he was even listening to her? Garron always felt bad when it happened with the red-haired guardian. She had been so kind to him and had taken such good care of him while she was tending his broken mind after the dark sorcerer from Kelvur had cursed him.

The book brightened, and a page fluttered as a light breeze billowed the curtains open even more. His eyes landed on a specific line.

"There has been and always will be a first. Is it the nature of the second to usurp the first? Could it not be that the second could complement or bless the first? The desert lily produces the seed that flies away on the winds. When the seed grows, it brings glory to the first by spreading the beauty among more oases."

Garron shook his head as he read. Whatever Nari philosopher had written the inscription tugged at the heart of deep thoughts. He wrote of peace and tranquility, qualities Garron sorely lacked. The author wrote of things as they should be and pondered at why they were not that way.

The author also wrote fascinating pages about something called the garden of the First Tree of Tarrine—the Nari Tree, according to Kel Joran's notations. Garron wished Kel Joran's notes were complete. He wished he could get his hands on the original journal to see what he could glean with his magical ability to read the language—though that artifact was somewhere in the small library of Last Town in the south.

As he pondered the writings, Garron felt an increasing pull on his heart to explore the Nari Desert himself. *What's out there? What peace can be found? What power might the Nari Tree hold?*

Could it fix him?

A knock on his chamber door jarred him from his ruminations. He slammed the book shut as though he were caught in some vile act.

"Come in," he said, shifting his stance and brushing at his tangled brown hair.

The door hinges creaked open, and the familiar bald head of a deep gnome poked in. The gnome's wide eyes searched the man as he stepped inside. *"Good morning,"* the gnome signed tentatively with his hands. *"Are you alright?"*

"Good morning, Ezel," Garron signed back—another side effect of the sorcerer's warping of the man's mind. Not only had he been able to read the words of the Nari language, he'd also been able to understand and reciprocate the sign language of his mute gnomish friend. How many other languages could he understand? He would have to ask Argus Azulekor, a dwarf mage from Galium, for some recommended reading in dwarfish or elvish.

"Are you having nightmares still?" Ezel asked. To Garron, the deep gnome, half the man's height, seemed far greater than his diminutive stature.

"I'm fine," Garron signed back quickly. *"It's nothing really."*

"If it gets too bad," Ezel replied, his eyes narrowing with concern, *"you know I'll bunk with you. It seemed to help when we were in Calrok."*

Garron appreciated the offer. In truth, Ezel's presence when they were in the orc city had offered much peace for him at night. Perhaps, if the nightmares continued, he'd take the deep gnome up on his offer. But the voice ...

"I appreciate it, and if it gets bad, I will ask."

Ezel didn't answer at first; he only stared at the man as though to stress the point that Garron had better do so. Finally, the gnome's bald head wrinkled, making his tattooed runes morph into funny shapes, as a grin spread across his face.

"We should be getting to breakfast," he signed. *"King Pernden is back from Kane Harbor. I'm sure he'll appreciate some friendly ears."*

"I'll be right behind you," Garron signed, then indicated his disheveled appearance.

Ezel whirled and slipped out of the room as the door closed. Garron let out a heavy sigh, looking at the closed copy of *The Lost Notes on Nari.* He traced his fingers along the leather-bound edge of the book and pulled himself away. He didn't want to be late for breakfast. Everyone tiptoed around him already. He didn't need any strange behavior adding to their worry over him.

Pernden pushed away his plate, his waffle half-eaten and blueberries rolling around in chaotic choreography. He placed both palms to his forehead and ran his fingers through his long blond hair. He sat in the king's chair at the head of the table in his private dining room, surrounded by those he considered friends. Everyone sat quietly, waiting for Pernden to speak. He hated the awkward tension he felt every time someone was stuck between approaching him as friend or king.

Thankfully, his cousin Garron was there and broke the silence.

"Are preparations for the voyage to Kelvur not progressing as you hoped?" Garron asked.

The preparations were going fine for the most part. Minor details and last-minute issues popped up, normal for such a journey. Though in truth, the journey was unlike any Tarrine had undertaken. The avalanche of tasks that came as a result of planning such an excursion was overwhelming.

Pernden shook his head. "No. The preparations are going as well as expected ...," he paused, "for the most part."

"Is there something Ezel and I can do to help?" Garron asked.

"Anything I could do at the Grand Corral?" Ellaria added hopefully.

"No," Pernden said, waving away their worries.

Ellaria had resumed her training at the Grand Corral with the rest of the Griffin Guard. She'd been training with the 3rd Squadron, as Nera and the Talon Squadron were still in Kelvur. As much as Ellaria had proven herself at the Battle of Galium and then again at the Battle of Calrok, she had no experience leading other warriors, nor did she have a rank to make many offers. Most of Pernden's discussions had been with High Commander Mattness over their plans to send another two squadrons to Kelvur, neither of which were Ellaria's.

"I've just got so many meetings I must attend before I go." Pernden shrugged. He was glad he could speak openly with them. It was a welcomed relief. "I have to meet with High Commander Mattness again to finalize our plans for the Guard units going across the sea."

Pernden paused, not missing Ellaria's disgruntled look. He knew she wanted to go to Kelvur, but he still felt the need to keep her close to Garron. His cousin had gone through several ordeals that were beyond the king's knowledge to fix. Ellaria's magic and healing ability had brought Garron back to him—admittedly, not without some affliction.

"After that, I have to meet with Mistress Leantz, who is still unhappy with my decision to go." Pernden paused to sigh. "She is willing to sit in as Whitestone's steward again, though she has been vocal with her frustration about the situation."

"She performed the duty admirably while we were in Calrok," Garron pointed out.

"I've told her as much. She just doesn't believe I am making the right decision by traveling to Kelvur myself," the king grumbled. "I have tried to remind her that my purpose is two-fold. It will give our guardians who've been there all these months a renewed spirit. And moreover, it will help us solidify our new alliances by showing the people of Kelvur that we are in this fight together."

"With the added benefit of being reunited with Nera," Ellaria murmured.

Pernden saw Ezel flash his hands furiously, signing something to the impetuous woman. The king sat quietly as they signed several times in succession in a silent argument. He did not understand Ezel's sign language, but he often found, as Garron or Ellaria translated for him, that the little gnome had many wise things to say.

The injustice that spurred Ellaria's comment was not lost on Pernden. When they needed to send someone across the sea to save Gar Karnak and Ellaria's brother Merrick, Pernden had sent his best and persuaded her to go to Calrok to help Garron instead. As the king prepared to go to Kelvur with the reinforcements, he was maneuvering the planning in a way that she would be stuck in Whitestone—not rejoining her brother—while Pernden would be reunited with the woman he loved.

"Ellaria." Pernden spoke as evenly as he could force the words out. The woman and the gnome's signing ceased as they looked to him. "I will admit the injustice of this."

The guardian seemed taken aback at her king's words. "Then why not let me go with the 5th or 8th Squadrons?"

Her own words came out much softer than Pernden expected, as though she were holding back a wave of anger. The king stared at her for a long moment. He wasn't sure how to explain his concerns to her.

"I'm too dangerous," Garron stated. "He wants you to be close to me, just in case something happens."

Pernden inclined his head. His lack of words was response enough.

"I can't go across the sea to Kelvur; I could be a detriment," Garron continued. "Who knows what would happen if I got close to the sorcerer. Would he be able to twist my mind again? What if he made me turn on my own cousin? We still don't know the extent of what the sorcerer did to my mind."

"I would take you both if you could honestly tell me you think you're fit for it," Pernden said, trying to show optimism but not expecting a positive response.

They all watched Garron as he poked at a lone blueberry on his plate. Finally, he looked up to meet Ellaria's green eyes. His own were heartbroken, as though he were letting her down. "I can't."

And though Ellaria blinked several times, attempting to contain the welling tears, Pernden got the sense they had all expected that answer.

After another stint of silence, Pernden stood, pushing his chair backward. When the others began to stand, he waved a hand through the air and said, "No. Please. Finish your breakfast. I need to see Mistress Leantz about another issue. I'm not sure what I'm going to do with King Hugen."

"King Hugen of Tamaria?" Garron asked.

"Yes," Pernden moaned. "The 'good king'"—Ellaria scoffed at that—"has not responded to my letters. When I received no ravens back from Tamaria, I sent a courier. He returned after the long journey, not having been welcomed by King Hugen. I was hoping he would be able to help us with supplies."

"Hard to say I'm surprised," Ellaria remarked. She and Pernden's brother, Orin, had met with King Hugen before they started their journey north to get Orin home to Whitestone. She had more firsthand experience with the king of Tamaria than anyone else in the room. "The 'good king' doesn't like to do things for others that won't benefit himself."

"Even if Jaernok Tur and his army march across Tarrine, killing everyone if we fail? Seems rather clear that our victory would benefit him," Pernden said.

"I'm not so sure King Hugen has the foresight for such notions," she said, pressing her lips together.

"Whether he does or not, this war affects all of us."

"Are we still in need of the supplies?" Ezel asked. Garron relayed the question to Pernden.

"No." The king chewed on his answer and shifted. "When I didn't hear back from Tamaria, I worked more with Stalford and Lakerun. Stalford is already providing the ships, so they worked with Lakerun to bring extra supplies for the voyage. I fear we will be leaving Whitestone a little thin; we've given much to the effort. The supplies would certainly be welcomed."

"Should we call on Calrok for aid?" Garron asked.

"No. They've had a long road to recovery already. We could ask no more of them. And at any rate, Whitestone will survive as long as we win. My main concern for Tamaria is that they would not be ready should we fail. I don't know that King Hugen has taken my words of warning seriously."

"Then send me," Garron blurted.

Pernden looked at his cousin in surprise and glanced curiously to Ezel who also stared at Garron. "What?" the king asked slowly.

Garron shifted uneasily. "Send me to Tamaria. I can take Benley, and we can fly down there. King Hugen may be able to turn a courier away, but he can hardly do so to King Pernden's cousin."

Pernden's lips pursed as he considered the notion. "You're not wrong."

The little gnome signed something to Garron.

"Ezel says he'll go with me," Garron relayed. "What else was I going to do? Sit around here and pine in my loneliness."

The king twitched. He had been left behind when the others had departed on mission. He recalled how lonely the castle halls felt. He didn't wish that on his cousin.

Perhaps that could work. Ezel had lived in Tamaria. He knew the layout of the city and its people. Even if King Hugen wouldn't listen, perhaps they would be able to talk to some of the other influential people in Tamaria.

"I'll go, too," Ellaria piped. She added, "If you would allow, my King."

Her offer surprised Pernden, but as he thought about it, he liked the prospect. It would solve several problems. Garron would get to do something to make him feel useful. If they were able to break through to King Hugen, it could prove far more useful than expected. Also, Ellaria would be with Garron, making Pernden feel better about leaving his cousin behind. And then there was the added benefit of her returning to her hometown and seeing her family. The more Pernden thought about it, the better the idea sounded.

"Alright," he said, nodding approval. As he thought of his next few days in Whitestone, he added, "But stay here in Whitestone until I leave. I'd like every moment I can spare with you. I don't know how long I'll be in Kelvur."

"Of course." Garron smiled back at him and gripped his shoulder. "Let's make the most of it."

CHAPTER FIVE

SEARCH FOR AIDEN'S DELL

N era pulled another strip of meat from the smoked hare they'd caught the day before. The guardian stuffed the remaining meat into a pouch and gave some to Shadowpaw. The griffin's black feathers riffled in the wind as she stood stoically on the crumbling edge of the Palisade. Shadowpaw clicked her beak happily at the morsel and wolfed it down. Nera smiled at her, petting the silky black feathers that hued like a raven's in the morning sunlight.

"Almost done here," Shorlis said nearby.

Nera watched the chelon as he waved his magical staff, *Menthrora,* in a purposeful arc, sweeping the embers from the campfire they'd built on top of the massive wall. How good he'd gotten at using the powers his late father's staff held.

Before her arrival to Kelvur, Nera had never seen such a creature. She often found herself studying the chelon. Shorlis stood as tall as a man but looked more like a tortoise. His green spotted, bald head held piercing sea green eyes, and he covered his shell with light linen clothing. After spending months with Shorlis, Nera was glad to have met him.

The woman looked out over Kelvur's north. The Palisade had them just above the tree line, and from there, she could see how vast Duskwood was. The wild forest stretched for miles around, appearing from that vantage as a verdant sea. The wind blew the giant black braid that ran over her head like the elegant mane of a mare. She was glad she'd tightened it that morning.

As she observed the forest, she missed home. In Whitestone, the surrounding forest was peppered with enormous white rocks that jutted skyward, towering above the trees. She had always found the stark contrast of the white giants among the deep green of Whitestone Forest to be wondrous.

Every time she thought of home, she thought of Pernden. It had been several days since their last update through the magical Shells of Callencia that Lanryn the elf mage used to communicate with their allies back home. Even then, the update was more concerned with logistics and battle details. Nera would glean what she could from the information to speculate on Pernden's well-being, but she missed talking to him directly.

"It's quite a sight," Shorlis said, stepping to the edge beside her.

"It sure is," Nera agreed.

"I know you and the Griffin Guard must be used to seeing the world from high above, but I doubt I'll ever get used to this."

Nera smiled at the chelon. "To get used to sights like this, one would have to lose any sense of wonder."

"That's fair," Shorlis said. "Though, I have to admit, the way Nelan spoke about the Palisade, I expected it to be more ... like a wall." He spoke the last part almost as a question.

The guardian couldn't fault the chelon for his observation. Nelan, a dwarf general from Javelin, had spoken about the Palisade as though it were some great architectural achievement. Nera and Shorlis had found the Palisade was more of a sheer cliff running from Kelvur's western edge at the Gant Sea. They'd spotted little in the way of architecture so far.

Nera turned to Shadowpaw, placing her hands on either side of the griffin's face. Like an enormous cat, Shadowpaw received the affection and nuzzled her guardian's outstretched hands. "We'll walk along the Palisade for a while," Nera said to her. "Fly above us and be ready for anything."

Shadowpaw chittered a response and took several steps backward. She stretched her great black wings and beat several times to loosen them, then she turned and dove off the side of the cliff. Nera watched as Shadowpaw's wings caught the air. The griffin flapped several times, ascending high into the sky. The guardian noted the look of awe on the chelon's face and smirked.

"No," Nera said. "You never get used to that."

After walking for several hours along the cliff's edge, the explorers discovered the land on the south side of the Palisade began to slope away. At first, Nera thought they were continuing along the ridge. The rocky dirt under their feet slowly turned to carefully fitted stone. At one point, Shorlis gave her a curious look and crawled toward the edges on either side. They were walking on an ancient but well-constructed wall.

"When did it transition from cliff to wall?" Shorlis asked.

In truth, Nera hadn't noticed the transition, and even looking for it, she could not tell. "I don't know."

"The Palisade may be more impressive than I first thought," the chelon admitted, clicking his soft beak with his tongue. "I may owe Nelan an apology."

"We both might," Nera said.

As they walked along, they observed that a parapet slowly rose from the expertly worked stone. So smoothly did it rise, that Nera was bewildered by its craftsmanship. As the parapet appeared on the north side of the wall, they found steep stairways carved out of the south side, though there were no cities to be seen.

"What kind of force would it take to cover such a wall for defense?" Nera asked.

"I'm not certain," Shorlis said. "Aside from Nelan's tales of the Palisade, I've seen little of note on the wall in my father's library. Only that there were numerous gates blocked up over the centuries and that Aiden's Dell is located at the fissure where the wall was broken."

"And that's where we're headed. With King Pernden and the others bringing reinforcements across the sea, it's time for us to reunite the peoples of Kelvur to fight for their land," Nera said hopefully.

"If all goes well," Shorlis responded. He seemed nervous.

"That's why we're the ones on this mission," she said with reassurance. "I will represent Tarrine, and you, Kelvur. Seeing us together will certainly open the door for a conversation at the least."

The chelon opened his mouth but hesitated. He seemed to mull over her point.

"What is it?" she asked.

"It's just that ..." Shorlis took a second to formulate his words. "I'm not sure how many chelons there are in Kelvur. I read in one of the scrolls that there are many in the lands of Delreth, but the Shoals was the only colony of chelons I know about in Kelvur."

"Doesn't make you any less Kelvurian." The guardian shrugged in her light armor. Its gold glinted in artful contrast to her ebony skin.

"I don't know," the chelon said. "What if they think me some sort of monster?"

"We'll show them you're not," Nera said with a nod. She paused and winked at him. "Plus, you'll be with me."

They spent several more hours walking in near silence. While they trudged along, Nera pondered Shorlis's words. She couldn't help but wonder at his concern. What if they did think he was a monster? What if they imprisoned both of them? What if they never even got the chance to explain themselves and the situation?

A million scenarios played out through her mind. If she were honest with herself, she knew them all to be falsehoods she should dismiss. For one thing, she didn't even know what kind of peoples made up the city of Aiden's Dell. Javelin was made up of several races, including many she'd never seen before coming to Kelvur. Though they had legends of such beings as centaurs and giants, many Tarrinians thought them to be more myth than real.

Besides, the people of Aiden's Dell could very well embrace them and join the fight. It was as much a possibility as their capture or dismissal.

Nera glanced to the sky. The evening was closing in on them, and in the dusk, it was getting harder to see Shadowpaw high above. As tired as the guardian's feet were, she had made the best decision.

She could have ridden Shadowpaw, and the griffin could have carried Shorlis in her talons. The exertion would have cost the griffin much energy, and Shorlis would have been mighty uncomfortable. Extended flight under that strain was rarely, if ever, the best alternative.

Nera took a few minutes to spot Shadowpaw. When she did, she nodded quietly. The guardian thought the griffin was probably hungry, and if they didn't see any sign of the city soon, they would need to stop for dinner.

Eventually, Shorlis stopped their progress and pulled some wood from the large sack on his back to build a fire. After several attempts to light it on the windy top of the battlement, they gave up and ate some of the bread they'd brought from Dorantown. Nera fed Shadowpaw one of the salt-cured fish they had, saving the more recently smoked hare for later.

"No tea tonight," Shorlis said glumly, stuffing things back into his pack, disappointed he couldn't make his favorite evening drink.

Elerek tea was made from the coastal plant of the same name. It was a favorite among the chelons and had quickly become a staple for the residents of Dorantown through the cold winter. At first, Nera hadn't liked it. The green tea made her think of sea foam. After a few cups, gathered with others around the hearth in the evenings, Elerek tea had grown on her. It wasn't the same honey chamomile she enjoyed back at the Grand Corral in Whitestone, but it would do.

"Who knows," Nera said, "maybe we'll make it to Aiden's Dell tomorrow, and we'll be enjoying some of their tea and hospitality by evening."

"Perhaps," the chelon replied, unsatisfied.

"I'll tell you what," the guardian said, rising to her feet. "How about we let Shadowpaw fly us for a little bit while it's dark. It's still early enough. Maybe we'll be able to spot firelight from the city. If we don't see anything, we can land for the night and get some rest."

Nera gripped her spear, *Santoralier*, as she stepped close to Shadowpaw. The magical yellow glow shimmered off the griffin's black feathers in a chaotic display of reflected light. Nera mounted Shadowpaw, and the griffin took off, diving over the edge of the battlement and gaining speed as they plummeted to the ground below. She unfurled her wings, and the two soared into a glide before the griffin worked her way back up the wall. Shorlis stood near the edge, bracing himself, his staff in his hand. Shadowpaw opened her talons and scooped the chelon up from under the arms, and off they flew.

Almost immediately, they saw firelight in the distance.

"Look!" Nera shouted over the wind to Shorlis.

"I see it!" he shouted back.

They flew toward the lights. The glow of torches atop the battlement came in more regular intervals as they approached the city. Nera figured they would have run into the guards the next mid-morning, but they were tired. Also, her excitement rose with Aiden's Dell in view.

As they soared, Shadowpaw nervously raised them higher into the sky. Nera brushed her neck feathers. "Hey, girl," she cooed. "It's alright. We need to fly a little lower so I can see."

Shadowpaw angled her wings, and they descended toward the top of the Palisade.

Immediately, Shorlis started yelling something Nera couldn't hear as the wind whipped by. Loud bells rang out, and guards atop the Palisade ran around, looking like bugs scattering atop a decomposing piece of fruit.

Nera glanced to the north, knowing that to be the direction from which Jaernok Tur and his army would come.

Have they fought the sorcerer here?

She tried to inspect the fissure, the place in the wall that had been broken down centuries before. It was hard to tell in the dark if it had experienced any recent damage. The city had grown on the south side of the wall, and the enormous gate that had been constructed to fill the gap paled in comparison to the high walls of the Palisade.

Something whizzed by Nera's ear.

"Nera!" Shorlis hollered. "They're shooting at us!"

A flaming arrow curved and fell short of them while another sailed past her. "Fly! Fly!" she urged Shadowpaw. "Get us past the wall and down to the city!"

Shadowpaw screeched a blood-curdling cry, and they began to drop.

Shorlis screamed in terror beneath them.

"Shadowpaw!" Nera cried.

They careened past the guards atop the wall, forcing them to dive to all sides for fear of being ripped from the battlement.

Shadowpaw flapped wildly with her left wing while her right wing limped with pain. They tumbled well past the boundaries of the city, heading south. Through the chaos, Nera saw the edge of the forest.

Come on! Come on! she thought.

Shadowpaw lowered close to the ground, nearly crashing. She let go of Shorlis, who dropped to the field below.

Nera looked back over her shoulder to spot the chelon as Shadowpaw attempted a few painful flaps of her wings after relieving herself of his weight. The griffin screeched again as they crashed into a copse of trees at the edge of the forest. Nera rolled to her knees, trying to calm the stamping griffin. Shadowpaw scratched at the dirt and stamped about as she tried to use her sharp beak to reach the arrow lodged in her right wing.

"Shadowpaw, stop!" Nera said. "Let me get the arrow."

The griffin's feathers bristled in anguish. As Nera stood to her feet, she raised her hands, trying to calm the anxious griffin.

Suddenly, she heard shouts and running in the distance. *Shorlis!*

"Shadowpaw, go! Run through the woods. I'll find you. I have to go back for Shorlis."

The griffin shook and clicked her tongue at the woman as though she would go with her.

"No," Nera said quickly. "You're already injured. Run ahead. I'll find you. I promise."

Shadowpaw didn't waste any more time and hurried off into the shadowy forest.

Nera paused for a long while, angling her head to hear which direction the shouts came from. Shorlis was somewhere in the field. She had to get to him.

Long grass tapped against her leg, an agonizing reminder that she was taking too long to weigh her actions. She raised her spear, left the forest's cover, and ran into the open field.

CHAPTER SIX

THE DRAGON DILEMMA

Ralowyn ran out from Dorantown's gathering building, raising her magical staff above her head. The battered state of their returning warriors worried her. She passed several Javelin warriors and the few guardians that had been stationed at the barricade, looking past them for any danger that followed.

When she came to the back of the bedraggled formation, she found Karnak and Coal. Her eyes scanned each of them quickly, ensuring they weren't gravely wounded like some of the others she'd passed. The Staff of Anvelorian hummed with magic energy, lavender ribbons of light flitting around the weapon and its bearer as she kept a wary eye on the road beyond.

"What happened out there?" the elf mage asked. "Are the wretchlings back?"

"Aye," Coal grumbled. "And they've got a dragon."

"A dragon ..." Ralowyn breathed, hardly believing the dwarf's report.

"We need to gather the council," Karnak said. "Lanryn was right. The wretchlings are on the move again."

Ralowyn nodded her understanding and rushed off. She checked several of the injured soldiers being carried or limping along with the help of their comrades.

The elf remembered when the wicked sorcerer, Jaernok Tur, brought his new army of wretchlings out of the Crags and swarmed them at Ventohl. She shivered. The monsters often haunted her dreams.

She ran past the meeting hall. It used to be the operations center for the Glinso Mining Camp when Jaernok Tur's geldrins ran the slave-worked mine. Since Shorlis and the other miners revolted and took the town, they'd renamed it Dorantown. The building had become where the leaders of the various groups met to discuss important matters.

Ralowyn turned down an alley between two wooden structures. The morning sun had not quite burned up the dew, and the warm light reflected brightly off the millions of drops of water that clung to every surface. She sprinted past the stables shouting, "Jensen! Tam! Get to the meeting hall. The barricaders are back!"

The two guardians, each preparing their griffins for a morning flight, strained their necks to see the elf as she ran by. Jensen, Talon Squadron's second in command, quickly relayed instructions to the other guardians and led his griffin back into the stable.

Ralowyn raced to the docks. Her elven eyes caught a glimpse of the glimmering sea before her. The waters were dotted with small fishing vessels out for the morning catch. How far the residents of Dorantown had come during the winter months. Orin and Tenzo discussed something with the dockmaster. The guardian and the large chelon spoke with fervor, Tenzo using his hands as he talked.

"Orin. Tenzo," Ralowyn said, interrupting them as politely as she could while expressing urgency in her tone.

"How many can the *Sellena* hold?" Tenzo asked the dockmaster.

"I don't know," the minotaur said. "You'll have to ask Captain Tin. All I know is that we've been able to build four, and Tharn says he's got three more almost ready."

Orin shook his head. The man turned to meet Ralowyn's gaze, seemingly done with the conversation for the moment. "Good morning," he greeted her. His brow creased when he saw her concerned face, and he asked, "What's going on?"

Ralowyn gave him a quick nod to return his greeting but dove into the heart of the matter. "The barricaders are back. We need to gather at the meeting hall."

"They're back already? What happened?" Orin asked, his expression deepening with concern.

"The wretchlings," she said plainly.

The statement captured Tenzo's attention. The muscular chelon turned to listen as well.

"Are they here?" Orin prompted, his eyes searching quickly around Ralowyn.

"No," she replied. "Karnak and Coal will explain everything. We need to get back to the meeting hall. Will you get Captain Tin?"

"Of course," Orin said and spun quickly toward the docks.

"Did they say anything?" Tenzo asked as he matched the elf's step, heading back to the meeting hall.

"There was not much time for words in the moment. I ran to retrieve everyone."

"Did the wretchlings attack the barricade? Was anyone injured?"

Ralowyn sighed and pulled a few wild strands of silvery hair behind her pointed ear. She knew nothing more than the chelon did—almost nothing more. "The barricaders appear as though they were in a skirmish."

Tenzo didn't respond, lost in his own thoughts. His pace quickened, and suddenly Ralowyn was attempting to keep pace with the chelon.

Once all leaders had gathered at the meeting hall, Karnak and Coal relayed what happened at the barricade. Most listened with intrigue. Coal was a natural storyteller with a flair for tales, but Karnak added details he thought important—specifically, his encounter with the varlek. That was their first experience with one of Jaernok Tur's wretchling leaders. The interaction was unnerving.

When they got to the part about the dragon, the silent listening ended.

"Where in Finlestia did they get a dragon?" Jensen asked. The guardian straightened. His features were hard-edged, and his frustration was evident. "How could they hide a dragon from our spies?"

Lanryn, a thin, wiry elf mage from Loralith and the spymaster for their army, spoke. "Our spies have been watching Ventohl. It is entirely possible the dragon came from the Fell Keep in the Crags."

"It wasn't a very large dragon," Karnak said, remembering his interactions with the young dragon Jaernok Tur had gifted the orcs' previous king in Drelek. "It can't be very old. They were probably rearing it through the winter."

"What if that's why they didn't attack during the winter?" Orin asked. The gravity of his words hung in the air, thick like choking smoke. "What if it had nothing to do with the harsh snows? What if, all this time, they were preparing? They dealt us a heavy blow in Ventohl when the wretchlings swarmed the city and we had to retreat; I don't know a single one of us that wasn't terrified by that force."

A growl emanated from the other side of the room. A tall barbarian woman with stout muscles grimaced as the others looked toward her. Vorenna clanged her iron fist on the table, picking at the wrappings that strapped it to her arm. The Javelin leader had lost her hand during the swarm of Ventohl, though the loss did not seem to dampen her resolve. "Is the baby dragon small enough for Dak to wrestle it to the ground?"

Karnak wasn't sure he understood the question. "We haven't had giants in Tarrine in a very long time. But I don't know that I've ever heard of a giant wrestling a dragon."

Vorenna merely growled in response.

Coal, sitting next to the large barbarian woman, touched her arm and asked, "Is that a thing a giant can do?"

The hardened warrior softened toward the dwarf. "How do you kill dragons in Tarrine, Master Coal?"

Karnak thought he saw a flush on the little patch of cheek on the dwarf's face that wasn't covered in black beard.

"Well," Coal cleared his throat, "we have other winged beasts we ride into battle against dragons."

"So, the Talon Squadron can kill the beast," Vorenna said, getting excited.

"Well," Coal hemmed again, "last time we fought a dragon in Tarrine, it took powerful magic to kill it."

"That's beside the point," Karnak interrupted. "If they're coming here—which seems the most likely course—we need to have an evacuation plan."

"You want to evacuate the whole town?" Tenzo asked incredulously. "Where will we go? What of the elderly or the children? What about—"

"That's why we're having this meeting," Karnak growled.

The room fell silent, and no one spoke for a long time. Several people adjusted in their seats as they processed the information.

Jensen stood, straightening his armor. "The fact is, we cannot defend Dorantown against a dragon attack—maybe against ground forces among the trenches, but not against an airborne dragon. The Talon Squadron is down a few guardians and several griffins since we arrived in Kelvur. Even at full strength, we'd be hard-pressed to ward off a dragon, let alone kill it."

"What of our reinforcements from Tarrine?" Tenzo asked.

Lanryn sat forward, leaning on the table. "They are preparing to leave, but if the varlek and the dragon showed themselves yesterday, it's unlikely our allies will arrive in time."

"What about Nera and Shorlis?" Tam asked. It was the first time the young guardian spoke. He was often invited to meetings after he played a pivotal role in their mission to Kelvur and aided the Talon Squadron's captain, Nera. It seemed Jensen had taken a liking to the young guardian as well, for even in Nera's absence, the man brought Tam along.

"They left before we knew of the dragon," Karnak said. "Even if they make it to Aiden's Dell, they will likely need time to convince the city to join our cause. And we have no way to communicate with them or to know how their mission is going."

Several people grumbled in distress. Nothing seemed to be a viable option but evacuating their town. Though it had only been theirs for a number of months—since they'd removed their geldrin overlords—the people had built Dorantown into a home. None of them were particularly fond of the idea of abandoning it.

"Karnak," Orin said over the mumbling.

The orc gar looked to the man. Karnak would take any good suggestion to help them survive the oncoming attack. Orin fidgeted uncomfortably, as though he wanted to say something the orc gar wouldn't like. "What is it?" Karnak asked in an encouraging tone.

"I know your wyvern was killed by a harpoon launcher," Orin said slowly.

Karnak's heart dropped. *Ker.* He'd lost his wyvern in an attack on the ship that brought the orc to Kelvur. A four-armed bow had hurled a harpoon right into her belly, killing her instantly. Karnak had thought about her many times over the months since. He missed his faithful friend.

Orin continued. "We've been able to build more of the launchers. Tharn, the blacksmith, was the one who built them for the *Harbinger* originally, under servitude to the geldrins. He's built several for the *Sellena*." Orin paused, clearly trying to be delicate with his question. "Do you think the harpoons would be able to kill a dragon?"

Karnak squinted and stretched his back. It was a good question. Wyverns were smaller than dragons, but it was possible that a well-placed harpoon could do similar damage to a young dragon. "Maybe," the orc said tentatively. "But the dragon would have to fly within range. It could burn the *Sellena* to cinders by the time it got close enough."

"The launchers are on wheels," Orin said.

"Yes!" Coal blurted, getting excited at the prospect. "Bring them onto the main road and launch from land."

"That's what I was thinking," Orin said.

"Lanryn and I can cover the launchers," Ralowyn put in. Lanryn nodded his agreement. "We can make sure they get their shots off."

Tenzo seemed to be getting excited about the plan, too, and suggested, "We can take the families south. We'll use the mines."

"The trenches won't give you much cover from above," Karnak said, tilting his head to the side.

"Enough to get us far south of the town, then we can cut into Duskwood for more cover."

"Alright," Karnak agreed, liking that everyone was taking part in brainstorming a plan. "Our ground troops can use the same trenches to cover our retreat if we are unable to down the varlek's dragon."

"And we can evacuate most of the docks to the *Sellena*," Orin suggested, looking to Captain Tin. The old captain nodded his approval, so Orin continued. "If things don't look like they're going well, we can sail south along the Sheer Coast. There's a city called Glain's Shoulder on the old maps. Perhaps we can find aid there."

"You'll want to be prepared with supplies for that journey," Karnak said.

"We'll get it done," Captain Tin assured the orc, in his gravelly voice.

Karnak turned in his seat, the gar in him roaring to action as he took the lead and issued instructions. "Lanryn, reach out to our allies in Tarrine. Let them know what we're up against."

"Will do," Lanryn said, taking the Shell of Callencia out of his pocket.

"Let them know, also," the orc gar continued, "that we'll contact them immediately if the dragon comes and we need to retreat. They may want to adjust their plans. If the dragon comes here, perhaps they can sneak into Ventohl while Jaernok Tur's army is busy with us."

Several excited nods and murmured agreements rolled around the room.

"What if they run into a monolith dragon?" Tam asked.

A tense silence swept over them. There was a real possibility that their allies could face that danger.

Karnak grimaced. They needed to keep the forward momentum of the meeting. "Then they will have a much greater force with which to face it. When I fought the assassin, Hazkul Bern, in Ventohl, he mentioned that Jaernok Tur might be in league with a monolith dragon. From what the wizard told you and the others, monolith dragons can breed lesser dragons. The varlek's dragon seems to prove the assassin's claim." Karnak paused and turned to Lanryn. "We'll need to make sure our allies know that. We can't send them in there blindly."

"What do we really know about monolith dragons?" Lanryn asked.

"Only stories from an old wizard," Tam said honestly.

"Stories that Tam will gladly recount for you to relay back home," Karnak said, taking control of the meeting again. When the elf and the young guardian nodded their assents, Karnak wrapped up the meeting. "We don't know how much time we have. The morning is early. Let's use all the light we have. Every time they've attacked us, it's been dark."

Karnak stood, looming above the others. He took a moment to lock eyes with every person in the room before he said, "Prepare as though tonight Dorantown burns."

Ralowyn sped up to match Karnak's stride. The orc moved with determination toward the wooden building where healers tended the wounded.

"Karnak, wait," she said.

The orc's gait slowed, and Ralowyn caught up to him.

"What about Merrick?" she asked quickly.

"What about him?" Karnak asked, not sure what she meant.

"He took Kippin out to hunt. They've been gone a few days."

Karnak stopped. "How long did he say he would be gone?"

"Maybe five days. Maybe a week."

The big orc cursed under his breath, and Ralowyn couldn't read his frustrated face. Without another word, Karnak resumed his walk as Coal overtook them.

"He's been doing that a lot lately." The dwarf groaned as he started after the orc as well.

"What will we do if the dragon comes and Merrick hasn't come back?" Ralowyn continued her inquiry.

"I don't know," Karnak said.

"Where is he, lass?" Coal asked.

"In Duskwood with Kippin, teaching him to hunt," she said quickly.

"Boehlen's Beard," the dwarf grumbled. "We can't just leave them out there. They don't know the wretchlings are back."

"What do you expect me to do?" Karnak seethed as he turned on them. "We have a dragon coming to kill us all. The only thing I can do is prepare for that. If Merrick isn't here when it comes, he may be the luckiest of us all."

"And when we retreat and leave this place?" Ralowyn asked. Her glassy green eyes brimmed with tears, lavender flecks of light threatening to erupt into purple flame.

Karnak let out a deep sigh. The big orc rolled his head, stretching his neck. He raised his hands and tightened the black knot of hair on the back of his head as he stretched his shoulders. Finally, he spoke.

"Ralowyn, listen," he began, softening his tone. "I love Merrick like a brother. And Kippin—he reminds me of Gernot.

He makes me miss home. But right now, I can do nothing for them. Right now, we have to prepare an entire town full of people for battle."

"And I am willing to help in any way I can," the elf said. "I only want to know we have thought of my family as well." Her chin quivered slightly, but she extended it, holding back her tears.

"Merrick has been through some horrible things," Karnak continued. "I don't know a more capable man than him."

"Aye," Coal agreed. "He's surprised me many times."

"Me too," the orc gar said.

Ralowyn blinked, composing herself. Merrick had surprised all of them. He was more than capable of taking care of himself and Kippin. She wanted them to be near, and it was hard for her to come to terms with the fact that they could possibly be safer away from the impending battle—even if she weren't there to protect them.

The elf shook herself and asked, "What can I do to help?"

Karnak let out a quick, relieved sigh and walked toward the healing building. "We need to get everyone fighting ready. Can you help me?"

"I'll do whatever I can," she assured him.

Karnak's stride paused again. "And if we do have to retreat, I promise you, we'll find them."

"He might find us first," Coal said with a chuckle.

Karnak smirked and dipped his head to the side. "He's the best tracker I've ever met. You're probably right."

Coal stepped next to Ralowyn, his thick dwarven hand gripping her slender fingers and squeezing slightly. The dwarf gave her an encouraging wink, and on they walked.

As they neared the building with all the wounded, Ralowyn took one last look over the town. The leaders were already at work, setting preparations into motion. People of all types jogged about, hurrying to their assigned tasks. Whatever they were off to do, something inside the elf sensed it might not be enough.

CHAPTER SEVEN

HOME

The opening of the library door ushered in a particularly cruel breeze that swirled the pages of the tome Smarlo was studying.

Come on! Smarlo thought as he hunched over his notes and the book, trying to pin everything down with his arms. He heard booted footsteps crossing the library as he recovered the parchments that had escaped his grasp and floated to the floor.

Deklahn rounded the corner to Smarlo's private office: the one designated for Calrok's master mage. Even after months of use, Smarlo still felt as though he were using Master Tan-Kro's office instead of his own. Master Tan-Kro had died in the deep mines, even before the battle, and Smarlo, whether he liked it or not, was Calrok's new master mage.

"Good morning, Smarlo," Deklahn greeted him with a kind smile. He noticed Smarlo gathering the scattered notes. The tall, slender orc mage picked one up from next to his foot. "I apologize for bringing a breeze," he added with a chuckle.

"It happens sometimes when I have this window open," Smarlo shrugged toward a window in the office. He set the stack on his desk, resolving to reorganize the notes later when he didn't have company. "How was the trip?"

"Uneventful," Deklahn said, mulling over the page of notes he held. His face scrunched with curiosity. "What were you reading?"

"I've been working my way through the black tome that Master Tan-Kro forbade me to read before."

"What's the book's name?" Deklahn asked, taking a seat in one of the high-back chairs—the one Smarlo used to sit in when he enjoyed conversation with the old master.

Smarlo decided he didn't want to sit, so he ruffled the pages of the tome to show Deklahn. "That's just one of the curiosities I've found while reading this. It has no name, no author attribution. But the penmanship changes in waves as you read on. I think it's a collection of dangerous knowledge that the Master Mages of Calrok have been compiling for generations."

"Fascinating," Deklahn said. "Have you learned anything of particular interest?"

"Lots," Smarlo said, flipping through some pages. "I can't read it all because some of the entries are written in different languages. I'm guessing they're transcriptions of some ancient writings. Some of them are annotated though. For example, do you remember the story of the monolith dragons that Lanryn relayed to us from the wizard, Enkeli?"

"Yes. The one about how the Maker created the monolith dragons to watch over the world, but then they tried to recreate it in their own image?"

"Right, but some of them tried to take it too far while others tried to stop it."

"Right," Deklahn said, nodding. "Wasn't it twelve of them?"

"Yes," Smarlo affirmed. "Eight of them decided to combine their magics and create some new power for them to wield. The other four took a branch from the First Tree to stop them, and the twelve nearly destroyed themselves."

"I remember Lanryn also said the sorcerer Jaernok Tur might be in league with a monolith dragon. Does the book speak of them? Have they done something similar before? Or maybe it mentions a way to defeat one?"

"Well," Smarlo hemmed. "This whole section about the monolith dragons—which the master who wrote it called 'colossal dragons'—is written in an ancient language I don't know. His notes are in orcish, even if his dialect is crude. Later masters wrote their notes in the common tongue."

"And they wrote about the monolith dragons?" Deklahn asked, trying to get back to the point.

"Oh, no. Sorry," Smarlo apologized. "But this master suggested there is a monolith dragon in Tarrine. Or at least there *was* one during his time. I've still not quite figured out the timeline for the book. It will take considerable effort to cross-reference some of the histories to see where important concepts and events match up. Things they were worried about in the histories could give me clues to figure out when each of the different masters may have written in this book."

Deklahn inclined his head thoughtfully. "Why would that be a dangerous secret?"

"There is inherent danger in the massive creatures, I'm sure. But I was also thinking about the magic of the monolith dragons. It's an ancient magic—one from which we are far removed by the ages. Tampering with unknown things can be a dangerous endeavor. Makes me think that may be what Jaernok Tur got into."

Smarlo watched Deklahn, hoping to read the orc's thoughts. The king's adviser didn't speak for a moment as he processed the information. Then, he asked, "Does it say where the monolith dragon was—where he built his lair? Perhaps the Chartok Tundra?"

"No. It doesn't say," Smarlo said with a hint of disappointment. His face shifted as he said, "But there are a lot of entries about strangeties in the Chartok Tundra. There was a particularly large grouping of passages from one master. But again, I haven't been able to cross-reference them with the histories to figure out who or when it was."

Deklahn laughed. "I'm sure you'll figure it out." He eyed Smarlo for a long while, smiling at his old friend. "You should probably bind yourself a leather notebook for your trip to Kelvur. You may be able to add some rather dangerous secrets to that book yourself."

"I already have," Smarlo said, tapping a smaller book nearby.

"Of course." Deklahn chuckled and nodded to him. "I'd expect nothing less from you, my friend. *Master Smarlo's Book of Dangerous Secrets* has a nice ring to it, I think."

Smarlo flushed. "Well, it's not *my* book of dangerous secrets."

"As you've described it to me, it belongs to the Master Mage of Calrok, and that makes it yours."

Smarlo twitched. While Deklahn was technically correct, Smarlo still wasn't completely keen on the situation. Though, as he thought about it, the benefits of being the Master Mage of Calrok included the opportunity for him to travel to new lands. He'd dreamed of crossing the sea to explore Kelvur since he was a young apprentice. Their recent motivation for going to Kelvur wasn't exactly exploration, but nonetheless, the notion excited him.

"Actually," he said, changing the subject, "I've seen notes on other lands of Finlestia—lands beyond Tarrine and Kelvur. No specific details, but it would make sense. If there were twelve monolith dragons that were charged with caring for all the lands, could we posit that there are at least ten other lands of Finlestia that we know nothing about? Perhaps even more!"

"That seems a fair assumption," Deklahn agreed with pursed lips.

"And what if they're all connected via the Underrock?"

Deklahn's face fell. "Then we could face far more threats to our home than we ever thought possible."

Smarlo sobered quickly. He'd gotten caught up in discovery and speculations. For a moment, he was simply having fun with an old friend.

The Underrock, an underworld of its own, crisscrossed in magnificent caverns and tunnels far below the surface. They weren't the same tunnels that orcs and goblins used for their mines in the Drelek Mountains. They were deeper and much more treacherous, filled with monsters, known and unknown.

They'd also recently discovered that the Underrock contained a vast network of tunnels and caverns that reached all the way across the sea. Jaernok Tur had sent an army of ghouls and death wings through those tunnels using a magic beacon activated by dark tongue. None knew just how far they reached.

"How many more of the dark tongue beacons have we found?" Smarlo asked.

Deklahn sighed. Apparently, he had also been enjoying their speculative conversation and was hesitant to leave it. "We found six total before I left Ruk to come here. We found them near mining operations."

"That would make sense. The operations are where we dig the deepest."

"True," Deklahn said. "We've been instructing everyone to post guards at the dark tongue sites. If they're anything like the one here in Calrok, they have to be activated on site. That means if Jaernok Tur manages to sneak any of his minions into Tarrine again, we'll catch them in the act, and at the very least, we'll know he's coming."

"Good," Smarlo said. He'd always trusted Deklahn, and the two had been friends for years. Both of them were similar in age and had traveled around Drelek with their respective Master Mages. The mage community of Drelek wasn't large, and they all knew of each other. Deklahn and Smarlo had gotten to spend much time together over the years. "You'll do great here," Smarlo added.

"I have no doubt that you've set me up for success," Deklahn said. "But if you don't mind, don't beleaguer your return. I do have my own home I'd like to get back to. Though I'll take care of yours like it were my own."

"Much appreciated," Smarlo thanked him. "I have a few last-minute things to wrap up before we set sail for Kane Harbor tomorrow. Let me know if you need anything before we do."

"I will," Deklahn said. "And Smarlo. Be safe, my friend."

"Will do," Smarlo replied. He placed a finger to his brow and gave Deklahn a slight bow of respect and gratitude.

The *Spinefish Tavern* burst at the seams that evening. Every member of the Scar Squadron was enjoying one last round of the owner's famous glorb wine before they set sail. They had no idea how long their mission would have them away from home, so the orcs of Calrok planned to take advantage of the night.

Smarlo waded through the crowded tavern, getting hugs and slaps on the back as he did. Those patrons that weren't part of the Scar Squadron bought rounds for those that were. Tark bumped into Smarlo, and he blinked his eyes blearily.

"Master Smarlo!" the younger orc shouted with glee. "You made it!"

"I did," Smarlo said, chuckling.

"Can we get a round for our Master Mage?" Tark shouted over the cacophony as he unsteadily sloshed his goblet of glorb wine.

Someone from the crowd shouted, "This one's on me!" The crowded tavern erupted with cheers and clinking goblets.

"I'm going to beat you in our next race," Tark said with a hiccup, "when we get back home. Sarntik will be so much faster!"

Smarlo patted the young orc on the shoulder and said, "I bet you will."

The mage slipped past the younger orc, looking for a quieter spot near the tavern bar. Orcs and goblins laughed and joked, many savoring their last night in town. Smarlo was glad to see that even Lehra and Jeh were engaged in the merriment. They sat at a table with several orcs from Scar Squadron.

When Smarlo finally reached the end of the bar, he propped an elbow on it to reserve his space and turned to look over the tavern. He smiled as he watched members of the Scar Squadron enjoying themselves. Across the room he spotted Deklahn laughing with Jeslora, the captain of the city watch.

That's good, he thought. *They'll be working together a lot. It'll be good for them to have a solid rapport.* Smarlo liked Jeslora too. He'd enjoyed working closely with her over the past few months. *I'll have to make sure to say goodbye to her.*

"Master Smarlo," Lehra said as she stepped next him.

"Lehra, I'm glad to see you here. I wasn't sure if you and Jeh would join the festivities."

"Why's that?" Lehra asked, shooting him an accusing look. "I don't seem like the type who likes to have fun? I mean, Jeh, I get."

Smarlo laughed. "That's not what I meant."

An orc woman behind the bar tapped on Smarlo's shoulder, handing him a goblet of glorb wine. "Didn't want you to miss out on the round bought just for you, Master Smarlo," she said with a wink. She turned to Lehra. "Another ale for you, Lehra?"

"Sure, Karilna. Thank you."

"Wow, Karilna knows your name. Maybe you *are* more fun than I gave you credit for," Smarlo teased, grinning into his goblet.

Lehra punched his shoulder, making him spill a little of his drink. "I am fun," she said with emphasis.

"I know," Smarlo said. "You just work so hard with Galbrish all the time. It's nice to see you relax, too."

"That's funny, coming from the orc mage who's always locked away in his study," she poked back, as Karilna handed the human woman a mug.

"I have a lot to catch up on," Smarlo said.

"You and me both," she responded, raising her mug.

"In truth, you and Jeh have impressed me. I'm not sure what I expected when we made the decision to bring guardians into the Scar Squadron. Mind you, I was hopeful. I guess I didn't expect you to be as good as you are."

Lehra nodded, her honey brown hair falling in front of her face. She drew the long strands behind her ear. As Smarlo observed her for a quiet moment, he saw the rose in her cheek. He wasn't sure he'd noticed before, but she was a lovely human woman. He was surprised at her quaint beauty.

"You've surprised me, too, you know," she said, not looking away from her mug. "I was heartbroken and angry when I lost Sandbeak. He'd been with me since I was young, and I just wanted revenge. I knew I couldn't get another griffin. So, I figured if I could join the Scar Squadron ... at least I'd have a chance to strike back at that wicked sorcerer."

"I understand that feeling," Smarlo said solemnly. "And you'll get a chance."

"Yeah," she said quietly. "But I found something I didn't expect. I've been training with a wyvern—a burly, sometimes stubborn, wyvern." She chuckled. "And he loves me. I know he's not Sandbeak, but Galbrish loves me that same way. I didn't expect that."

"People often underestimate wyverns."

"It's not just Galbrish," she said, embarrassment deepening the rose in her cheeks. "I underestimated orcs, too. Our squadron mates have embraced us as their own and made us feel more at home than I ever thought I could feel living among orcs. We're not so different after all."

"I learned that same thing when Merrick and Ralowyn came to stay with Karnak. You come to believe things about people groups that are unfair and often untrue. When you finally give them a chance to surprise you, more often than not, they do just that."

"Maybe we all need to give people more credit," she said.

"Agreed," Smarlo said, raising his goblet.

Lehra clinked her mug to it. She took a long swig and turned a raised eyebrow on the orc mage. "And some people need to give themselves more credit."

Smarlo paused, then looked up from his drink. The woman was already returning to her table. She turned over her shoulder and shot him a wry wink.

When Smarlo realized he was staring, a smile spread across his face.

"She's an attractive 'uman," a voice said next to him.

"She is ..." Smarlo started to say but turned quickly to the goblin standing next to him. "Reglese!"

The goblin, much shorter and leaner than the orc mage, laughed and pressed an elbow into Smarlo's ribs. "My, 'ow things 'ave changed since I've been gone!"

"In so many ways!" Smarlo said. "When did you get back? What are you doing here?"

The goblin smiled a pointy grin and said, "Come to the back. I 'ave a special bottle back there. I'll tell you of my enterprises, and you can tell me everything I've missed."

Catching up with Reglese was not something Smarlo had expected, but he welcomed the reunion. They sat in the back office, a quiet, cozy room with inventory parchments and business miscellany stacked about. One wall displayed bottled glorb wine with wax seals on them, each hailing from a special batch—at least they were special to Reglese.

The small goblin poured Smarlo and himself another goblet full. "So, you and the Scar Squadron leave tomorrow."

"Yes," Smarlo said, letting the sweet aroma of the glorb wine fill his nostrils. It was already making his belly warm.

"I seem to recall a time when we were younger, and a certain orc mage sat at my bar telling me of all the great mysteries to discover out beyond the sea. 'Ave those dreamy eyes faded?"

Smarlo smiled at the reminiscent phantom of his younger self. He'd always thought he'd go to Kelvur someday, but he never expected it would be in the capacity they planned to do so the next day. He had always assumed it would be under the premise of learning new magecraft.

"No," Smarlo replied slowly. Part of him was excited to go. Part of him thought that if everything went accordingly, maybe he could travel some of Kelvur and get to know the ways of the people that wanted nothing to do with the wicked sorcerer Jaernok Tur. That would only happen if they could finally put an end to him, once and for all.

"But …" Reglese said, taking another sip from his goblet.

"But, there is a lot to be done before I could possibly think of adventuring in Kelvur," the orc mage said frankly.

"True," the goblin agreed. "If you can make it past the danger, though, there can be great personal reward. I 'ave seen it myself."

Smarlo nodded. He remembered the day Gar Karnak brought Reglese to the Scar Squadron amphitheater on the Scar Cliffs. The goblin had been shaken by the gar's request for him to go to Ruk as a spy.

Eventually, it was the potential for something greater that spurred him into agreement. Reglese opened another tavern in Ruk, letting one of his assistants take care of the *Spinefish Tavern* in Calrok. In the end, Reglese had served his city faithfully during an orc rebellion and successfully opened a new tavern location.

"The new tavern in Borok 'as been going strong for months now, and when I 'eard you all were leaving, I figured I'd better come 'ome for a visit before moving on to Dak-Tahn," the goblin said.

"How long do you plan on being here?"

Reglese's pointed face grew into a smirk. "Well, I figured, with all you leaving, Calrok would be a little short on folks to 'elp out in times of need."

"After the battle that took place here, you may find yourself surprised," Smarlo said.

"Maybe," the goblin admitted, nodding at his goblet. "As much as I 'ave enjoyed traveling to other cities and entrepreneuring, Calrok is my 'ome, and I want to 'elp if I can."

"I appreciate that," Smarlo said, raising his goblet. "Deklahn will need all the help he can get."

"Besides, if you all defeat the sorcerer, Dak-Tahn will still be there, ready and waiting for a new tavern," Reglese added, not wanting to sound too beneficent.

"True enough," Smarlo replied with a chuckle.

The friends shared conversation and laughter, comforts Smarlo had missed. He'd spent too much time worrying. He was grateful for the moment, but eventually, he had to leave.

"It's not so late. 'Ave another cup with me," Reglese implored.

"No," Smarlo said, apologetically waving his hand. "I have one more thing I need to do tonight before the hour grows too late."

"Alright," Reglese submitted. "I suppose I should talk to Deklahn anyway. Let 'im know I'm 'ere for 'im and all."

"Good idea," Smarlo said. "I'm sure he'll appreciate you doing so."

The orc mage turned to leave as Reglese stood to look for a specific bottle of glorb wine. Before Smarlo exited, he turned back and asked, "Reglese, can I ask you a personal favor?"

"Anything." The goblin looked up from the bottle in surprise.

"Will you look after Tanessa and Gernot while I'm gone?"

Reglese stared at him, bewildered, as though he were trying to piece together some sort of puzzle. "The gar's family?"

Smarlo shifted awkwardly. "Yes. I've been looking after them while Gar Karnak has been away, and now I'm leaving, too. I just don't want them to be all alone. I'm planning on bringing Karnak back as soon as we've defeated the sorcerer. But I can't say when that will be."

Reglese eyed him curiously for only a second, but it felt like an eternity. "I'll look out for them. But if I remember the gar's wife, she is a fierce orc woman. Kind of like one I knew in Ruk," he said, his eyes glazing with a fond memory.

"She is," Smarlo agreed. "But they've been through a lot. So, if you'd please?"

"Say no more." The goblin raised a comforting hand. "I will check in on them. You worry about what you need to worry about over there, and I'll 'elp out 'ere 'owever I can."

"Thank you, my friend," Smarlo said with a grateful nod. Though he was sure that neither of them believed his next words, he said them anyway. "I'll see you soon."

The goblin nodded. "And then we'll 'ave to open another one of these bottles. I 'ave one somewhere around 'ere that I mixed with 'uckleberry. It's a real treat."

Smarlo agreed. He left the back office and waded through the crowded tavern. Several orcs patted him on the back as he went, but he didn't tarry. He exited the boisterous building into the starkly quiet night.

The flickering of firelight cast out of the modest home on the edge of the sloped paddock. The sight tied Smarlo's heart into knots. It would have been much easier if Tanessa had already gone to bed and he was too late to say goodbye. He considered for a moment that maybe she was asleep already and had let the fire burn in the fireplace, but he knew he was grasping at any notion that might save him an uncomfortable goodbye.

As he stood at the door, he heard nothing inside the cozy home. He became self-conscious about his ear and scratched at the scarred ridge. He took a deep breath, resolving himself to get it over with, and knocked quietly. Just in case she were asleep—though he knew she wouldn't be.

The door opened slowly, and Tanessa's lovely orc face appeared. She looked as though she'd been crying, her eyes puffy and glossed. She punched him in the chest and said, "Waited so long, I was starting to think you wouldn't come to say goodbye."

"I'm sorry," Smarlo apologized, rubbing at the spot she'd punched. "I got held up at the *Spinefish Tavern*. I—"

"Well, you're here now, and I'm pretty sure your tea is cold."

Smarlo looked past her into the living area. The two tall-backed chairs were in their usual spots next to the hearth, and two tea mugs sat on the small table between them. Smarlo smiled. "I'm sorry. How about I pour us some more?"

They sat in silence for a long time, watching the low crackling fire in the hearth, sipping at Tanessa's favorite red rooibos tea. They enjoyed each other's silent companionship—neither wanting to say something in emotional haste and ruin the moment.

After a long while, Smarlo finally spoke, deciding on a less direct topic than his imminent departure. "Reglese is back in town."

"Reglese?" Tanessa repeated in surprise. "When did he get back?"

"Only yesterday," Smarlo explained. "I was surprised to see him myself."

"I'll have to stop by the *Spinefish Tavern* to see him. I haven't seen him since he left for Ruk."

"Well, hopefully you'll see lots more of him. Says he's in town for a while to help where he can. He's going to be helping Deklahn with whatever he needs."

"Well, I'll be asking Deklahn for updates regarding the Kelvur operations since he has one of the shells, too. So, I'm sure I'll get to see Reglese then."

"That and ..." Smarlo said, then regretted opening his mouth.

"That and what?" Tanessa asked, eyeing him.

"I asked Reglese to look out for you and Gernot after I leave."

Tanessa's face turned cold. "You didn't have to do that."

"I know. I just—"

"Our care is not your responsibility." The orc woman stood and turned away from Smarlo. His heart dropped. He didn't mean to overstep.

"Tanessa, I'm sorry," Smarlo said, also standing. "Karnak is my best friend, and I wanted to look out for you and Gernot since he was gone."

"And now you're leaving," Tanessa said, turning on him.

Smarlo opened his mouth to speak, but he wasn't sure what he could say to erase the hurt on her face. It pierced him.

Tanessa picked up her mug, sloshing the little bit of tea that was left into the fireplace. She walked into the kitchen, leaving Smarlo to stew.

After a moment, the orc mage followed her and said, "Tanessa." She half-turned toward him, not showing her face. He assumed she was trying to hide her tears. "Over the last several months, you and Gernot have shown me so much love. Our evenings by the hearth have meant the world to me. I started out coming here for Karnak. As we grew closer, I was coming for you, so you weren't here alone. And then eventually, I was coming here for my own interests. You've become more a friend to me than anyone."

Tanessa faced him.

"I want you to be safe and looked after because I care for you," he continued. "I'm going to do everything I can to get Karnak back home to you as fast as possible. But, I feel terrible, knowing I have to leave you alone to accomplish that."

Smarlo scratched at his half-ear scar. *Why is this thing so annoying?* he thought, his mind trying to distract him from the pain he experienced elsewhere.

Tanessa slapped at Smarlo's hand. "Stop scratching. You're only going to make it worse."

She retrieved the clay jar of salve and rubbed some between her fingers. She carefully spread it on the scarred section of Smarlo's ear. The orc mage smiled sheepishly. She gave him a half-smile back. She replaced the lid on the jar and handed it to him. "You better take this. Or by the time you get back, you'll have scratched off what's left of that ear."

"Thank you," Smarlo said.

"You better use it."

"I will," he said, putting his hands up in surrender.

"You're a better orc than you give yourself credit for," she said, looking him directly in the eyes. Smarlo was struck by how similar her words were to those of Lehra. If too many people told him that, he might start believing it. "As much as I want you to get my husband back to me, I also want you to make it home safely. I know a little orcling who would be terribly upset if you didn't."

Smarlo smiled and looked down the hallway toward Gernot's room. He imagined the little orcling sleeping with his hind end straight up in the air, snoring away. Smarlo didn't know how Gernot could sleep like that, but he thought it was adorable.

"I promise," Smarlo said.

"Good," Tanessa said, stepping close to him and wrapping him in a hug. "Because his mother would be just as upset." Her words grew quiet. "Be safe out there."

"I will," he said, hugging her back.

They stood for a moment, thinking if there was anything left unsaid. Tanessa was a strong orc woman, and she and Gernot would be fine. It had been difficult for Smarlo to admit that his actions had been more for his own peace of mind, but he was glad he'd told her.

Eventually, Tanessa grabbed at his shoulders and pushed him to arm's length. "You better get going," she said. "You're going to need all the rest you can get tonight. You've got a long journey ahead."

"Thank you, Tanessa," he said as he turned to leave.

She walked him to the door. As he walked down the short path to the road, Tanessa called after him, "Smarlo."

"Yes?" he said as he spun back.

She placed a hand to her heart and said with a grateful nod, "Thank you."

Smarlo nodded to her, knowing no words were necessary. He stepped along the road, looking over the city of Calrok. His home looked rather beautiful that night under the cool light of the moon. It struck him then that he didn't know when he'd see his city again.

CHAPTER EIGHT

THE MIRROR

When the door to the king's planning room in Whitestone Castle banged open, Pernden, Mistress Leantz, and Master Feink looked up from the table in the center of the chamber to see an elder dwarf, wheezing from exhaustion. His blue robes were rumpled as though he'd been running through the castle's long hallways. The hood of his cloak was thrown back, exposing the white hair on the top of his head. His long white beard swept the floor as he doubled over to catch his breath. Pernden laid the parchment he'd been inspecting on the table and rushed to the dwarf.

"Master Argus, are you alright?" the king asked.

"I'm sorry for the intrusion, my King," Argus Azulekor said quickly. He stopped short, eyeing the other two in the room. "I have something very important to discuss with you."

"Alright," Pernden said, patting the dwarf on the shoulder. "We were just finishing up."

Master Feink, a rotund balding man, grimaced. He gathered the parchments he'd brought with him to apprise the king and Mistress Leantz of the city's merchants' affairs. Master Feink was a talkative man, and he would likely have preferred another hour with the king, but when Pernden gave him a sideways look to indicate he was excused, the round man waddled out of the room.

Argus nodded to Mistress Leantz. "Mistress," he said.

"Master Argus," she greeted him back. "Quite the entrance."

The dwarf mage shuffled uncomfortably, straightening his blue robes. The stars stitched into his robes seemed to twinkle as he ruffled the fabric. "I apologize for my abrupt and unannounced entrance, Mistress."

"Nonsense," Pernden said, shooting a glance to Mistress Leantz. "I think we were both ready to move on from the merchants update."

"What is it you have for us?" Mistress Leantz asked.

Pernden silently nodded in approval. Mistress Leantz was the keeper of the Library of Whitestone and one of the wisest people Pernden knew. She was also one of his most trusted advisers, and her kindness and empathy with him had made her his instant choice for Steward of Whitestone when he needed to fly to Calrok to support their allies. With him leaving for Kelvur, she was stepping back into her role as steward with a marvelous grace.

"It's the Alkhoren Mirror, my King," the mage said.

Panic flooded Pernden, and he gripped the hilt of his sword, *Wintertide*, ready to draw. "What's happened?"

Jaernok Tur had used the Alkhoren Mirror to bring orcs and goblins into Whitestone. The sorcerer also used the mirror to escape to Ruk where he used its sister mirror to escape to Kelvur. They didn't know how many Alkhoren Mirrors existed, nor did they know how to use them. So, they'd locked the mirrors in rooms under guard in Whitestone and Ruk. Argus was the only one Pernden had given express permission to enter the room. He expected that if anyone could learn something of the mirrors, it would be the old mage.

"I was studying the mirror. You know, of course, I don't know the language of the runes on the frame. I was thinking I need to ask Garron if he can read them."

"Argus," Pernden stopped him, "what happened?"

"Right," he said, brushing his white beard quickly with his hands. "I thought I saw someone."

"What do you mean, 'saw someone?'" the king pried.

"Just that," the mage replied. "I thought I saw someone in the mirror."

"Was it activated? Did they try to come through?"

"No," Argus said. "It was like a phantom. I couldn't really see them. I turned around, thinking them in the room behind me, but there was nothing."

Pernden looked warily at Mistress Leantz. The elder woman pursed her lips in thought, tapping a finger on her chin.

"We need to bring Garron and Ezel to the mirror room," Argus pleaded. "Maybe they can see something I was unable to."

"They're preparing to leave for Tamaria," Pernden said.

"Well, I suggest we get them before they do. Even if it's only to confirm that I've been working too hard and I'm losing my mind, seeing things that aren't there."

Pernden huffed, amused at the dwarf's blatant statement. "Alright. Mistress, would you mind finding the others and meeting us in the mirror room?"

"Of course, my King," Mistress Leantz said with a slight bow of her head.

"Alright, Argus," Pernden turned back to the dwarf. "Lead the way. Show me this phantom."

Garron patted Benley on the side of the neck. The pegasus bobbed his head several times, appreciating the extra attention. Garron tossed the brush to the side, having finished his work. He wanted Benley to be well prepared for the journey, not certain how long they'd be gone. Spoiling him a little wouldn't hurt. Garron slipped an apple from his cloak, and Benley stamped and bobbed happily, his great wings skittering.

"Here you go," Garron said with a smile, raising the apple to the happy pegasus.

Ezel rounded the corner into the stable, carrying his small pack. *Is Benley ready to go?* he signed, grinning at the scene.

"Almost," Garron said aloud. "I wanted to give him a good brushing before we left."

Garron stepped back to examine the pegasus. Benley was white with brown spots. His horselike body was strong and sturdy. His great white wings furled tight to his sides as he chomped on the apple.

Next, Garron ensured their packs were tied tightly. He didn't anticipate any aerial acrobatics from the pegasus, but if one of their packs fell from the sky, they'd be hard-pressed to retrieve it unharmed.

Garron turned to grab the harness for his reins and stopped at the sight of Ezel, sitting atop a stall railing, watching him.

What? Garron signed, since his hands were free.

You volunteered to go to Tamaria rather quickly, Ezel signed back.

It made the most sense for me to go, Garron reasoned, walking past to collect Benley's tack.

79

"And that's all it was?"

Garron didn't answer the little gnome right away. Ezel's big eyes watched him unnervingly. How could the man tell his gnomish friend that he'd been dreaming in the Nari language? How could he tell him that he was hearing a voice? The last time he heard voices, it was the wicked tongue of Jaernok Tur.

The new voice was different, though. It called to him. It didn't manipulate him. It implored him—like the speaker needed him. As strange as it was to hear, the voice did not instill fear like the sorcerer's had; instead, it comforted.

Ezel waved at Garron to get the man's attention again. *"You know I'll have your back no matter what,"* he signed with a flourish of his hands.

"I know," Garron said, his hands full of Benley's tack.

"What's going on?"

Garron finished what he was doing and faced his friend. *"I want to go to the Nari desert after we're done in Tamaria."*

"The Nari Desert?" Ezel signed back, his bald head scrunching with his face. *"Why?"*

Garron hesitated. As much as he worried about what Ezel might think, he also didn't want to make the trek alone. It would be unfair for him to withhold information that could potentially endanger his gnomish friend. He pressed out a long breath and signed, *"I've been dreaming in Nari. I don't know how or why, but something is calling me to the desert. And ..."* He paused. *"For some reason, I think it's important."*

Ezel's eyes narrowed but didn't shift from Garron's face. The man squirmed under the watchful gaze. Suddenly, the deep gnome nodded slightly. *"Alright."*

"Alright?"

"Alright. We'll go to the Nari Desert after Tamaria," Ezel signed his assurance.

"Just like that?" Garron signed in confusion.

"What else will we do? Come back to Whitestone and twiddle our thumbs? If you think this is important, then we'll go."

"I do," Garron signed. *"I'm not sure how or why yet. But I think we have to go."*

Ezel smirked and gave a sideways shrug. *"You have been connected to everything that's happened. Our friends are going across the sea to join our other friends in the battle against a wicked sorcerer. If there is some way we can help them—some reason why going to the Nari Desert will help them—then I say we have to try."*

"I don't know how it could help, but—"

Suddenly, Mistress Leantz turned into the stable. "Master Garron," she said. "I'm here to summon you to the mirror room. King Pernden and Master Argus are waiting for you there."

"The mirror room?" Garron asked, his brows furrowing worriedly. He looked to Ezel, but the gnome shrugged his shoulders, knowing nothing about the summons. "Let's go," Garron said, lifting Ezel from the railing and setting him down on the ground.

Mistress Leantz surprised them with her haste, and they hurried after her.

When Garron and Ezel entered the mirror room, they found Pernden and Argus slowly circling the Alkhoren Mirror, inspecting its intricacies. Garron thought the scene rather odd.

The mirror stood in the center of a large room, one of the many guest rooms in Whitestone Castle that had been emptied during Jaernok Tur's occupation of the castle. The room was filled with bunks when the Griffin Guard recaptured it. Instead of returning it to a guest room once more, they decided to house the dangerous mirror there. It was a large room for the single artifact, and their footsteps echoed off the naked stone floor.

"Ah, Garron and Ezel," Argus said, beckoning them to join him beside the mirror.

"What's going on?" Garron asked.

"Master Argus," Pernden said his name with slight amusement, "believes he may have seen someone in the mirror."

"What?" Garron asked, looking to the mirror.

The light from the window glinted off the ornate frame, and Garron saw only his reflection. The mirror was tall enough for an orc to walk through, something Garron had witnessed. Being that close to the mirror again set a pit in his stomach.

"What did you see?" Ezel signed.

"Yes," Garron said. "Did you see the sorcerer?" He could not bring himself to say Jaernok Tur's name.

"No," Argus said.

Before the mage could explain, Ezel signed, *"Orcs? Goblins? Geldrins?"* Garron related the thoughts.

"No. Nothing like that," Argus explained. "It was almost like a phantom, a ghost. Or like a reflection on the water. Something you can't quite make out."

"I don't understand," Garron said bluntly. "Did you see it, too?" he asked Pernden.

"I've seen nothing," Pernden admitted.

Garron eyed the dwarf mage.

"I'm not crazy—well, not entirely." Argus chuckled. "I really did see something. Unfortunately, I can't read the runes around the mirror. I was hoping you could take a look."

A heat rose on one side of Garron's body as a shiver ran through him. Since his manipulation at the hand of Jaernok Tur, the man had been able to read and understand all sorts of languages he didn't know beforehand. Garron was afraid of trifling with the language of any magical artifacts. Smarlo had told him that words and magic are delicately linked in an eternal dance.

Ezel patted Garron on the forearm. The man looked down to his gnomish friend. *"Can you read it?"* Ezel flourished with his hands.

Garron released a long, heavy sigh and took a few steps toward the mirror. The runes seemed to be just that, markings for imbuing magic. As he looked longer, the markings began to make sense to him—not that they said anything in particular—but as though they were leading him to something.

The others watched as Garron drew nearer to the mirror. He stepped next to it, inspecting the runes as they led his eyes to a particular rune near the corner of the mirror's frame. He reached out to touch it.

"Wait!" Pernden said.

Garron turned over his shoulder, not looking directly at his cousin. "What?"

"Are we sure this is safe?" Pernden asked.

No one answered.

Garron turned back to the Alkhoren Mirror. A runic marking called to him, as though it would be the one that explained everything they needed to know about the mirror. He didn't know why he felt that way about the marking. It was smaller than the others, almost like a side note. He pressed his finger upon it, feeling its small grooves.

"This one," Garron said.

Ezel stepped forward. Several runic tattoos on the little bald gnome erupted into azure light. His eyes blazed with blue fire. The little gnome reached toward the rune that Garron had indicated, and only a moment later, golden letters, not matching the runes, appeared one by one, snaking around the frame. The letters seemed to be made of pure light and hovered a couple of inches away from the frame.

"What is this?" Argus whispered more to himself than anyone else.

As the ancient letters appeared, Garron did not recognize them. But slowly, as the letters formed into words, he was somehow able to read them.

"It's a ... a poem?" Garron said, not entirely convinced.

"A poem?" Pernden asked curiously.

As the golden letters completed their travel around the frame of the mirror, Garron was almost certain of it.

He read the words to the others.

Designed to dig deep and greatly explore
The depths and wonders of this world.
So, on with the help of the Melior,
The hem of Rikad can unfurl.
Blood cannot continue to work its art
If desp'rate loneliness shall be
The preeminent captor of the heart.
Thus for the need to hear and see
And most importantly — be.

"Boehlen's Beard," Argus muttered. Ezel looked at the dwarf, shocked by the mage's reaction. "What else does it say, lad?"

"That's it. The rest is a list of names, I think," Garron said, his eyes not leaving the golden words that floated just off the mirror's frame. "It's the only part that doesn't really make sense."

"What are the names?" Pernden asked, standing right next to Garron, transfixed by the magic.

"I do not recognize them," Garron said, but he listed them anyway. "Lando, Glain, Kaliman, Gali, Nantis, Marwen, Dentin, Solev, and Janbil."

"Boehlen's Beard," Argus said again.

"What is it?" Ezel asked the mage, and Garron translated.

"This is ancient magic," the old dwarf explained, hardly able to believe what he was saying. "These are the nine sons of Rikad. They were the dwarves that scattered to the outer reaches of Finlestia. The nine sons are the forefathers for every dwarf in Finlestia."

"So, this is dwarven magic?" Pernden asked.

"No," Argus said, shaking his head. "This is something older. But it seems like it was made for Rikad and his sons. When the dwarven forefathers scattered, maybe this was a way for them to stay connected."

"You mean for Rikad and his sons to see each other," Ezel signed, catching on to the mage's thought. Garron translated as he processed the thought himself.

"Yes. And hear and be, like the poem says. Perhaps they were able to use it to communicate, but like Jaernok Tur did, maybe they also used it to visit one another."

"What's the Melior?" Garron asked, stuck on that part of the poem.

The group fell silent, waiting for the dwarf mage to answer. The old dwarf brushed at his white beard thoughtfully. As if suddenly realizing everyone was waiting for him to answer the question, he started. "I have no idea, lad."

"My question is, if the mirrors are ancient artifacts of the first dwarves, then why would the sorcerer have one in Kelvur?" Garron asked.

"Why do we have one?" Pernden put in. "The Talon Squadron and I found this one in a destroyed wisdom tower in the Gant Sea Narrows. Maybe he found one in Kelvur too."

"We have two in Tarrine," Ezel pointed out. *"One in Ruk and one here."*

"True," Garron said pensively.

"Ancient artifacts are ancient because they outlive generations," Argus said. "We do not know the history of the Alkhoren Mirrors. They have likely switched hands and positions many times over the ages. It is bewildering that the records of such unique pieces would be so limited."

"Perhaps your ancestors were wiser than us," Garron murmured. Everyone turned to look at him. "We've seen the power and danger of these mirrors firsthand."

"It is sad that something created with loving intention can be twisted for malice," Ezel signed.

"Truly," Garron signed back, not taking his eyes away from the mirror.

"Maybe there is something more?" Pernden suggested, waving his hand in an arc and indicating the frame. "Maybe there is another rune that has more poetry?"

Garron scrunched his face and scratched at the stubble on his chin. "No. That marking was different from the rest. Almost like a painter's mark at the bottom of their painting."

"Wait!" Argus started. "Did you see that?"

"See what?" Pernden asked, looking at the mirror, trying to decipher what the dwarf mage saw.

"A phantom," Ezel signed.

Garron was struck by a clearer image. Though it seemed far off as if he were looking through warped glass. He saw a man—or what looked like a man with blue tinted skin.

The hue was that of the sky when it was paler in the sun's peak. His hair was white, but he looked not much older than Garron himself. The man appeared surprised by Garron staring straight at him. The blue-skinned man raised a hand slowly and confidently, and the vision vanished.

Garron tried to see more through the mirror, but all he saw was himself. His gaze lingered on the man he'd become. He realized he hadn't spent much time looking in mirrors of late. His brown hair dropped to just above his shoulder, not entirely tidy.

The scowl on his face made him wonder if his reflection was as underwhelmed by him as he was of it. *Am I always scowling like that at people?*

"Garron!" Ezel signed wildly in the reflection.

"What?" Garron snapped out of his trance. "Sorry, what?"

"Did you see the phantom?"

"I … I don't know." He hesitated, regathering his wits. When Garron told them of the blue-skinned man, everyone was disconcerted.

"You think he saw you too?" Argus asked.

"He looked directly at me," Garron affirmed.

Argus grumbled something to himself.

"The poem said, 'Hear, see, and be.' We have no idea how many mirrors are out there. What if Jaernok Tur could see through this mirror? What if someone even worse could?"

The implication of Argus's words hung heavy in the room. The dwarf broke the silence again. "I would guess there are nine. Or ten. Or at least there were." When no one responded, he explained his theory. "Rikad's sons were nine, and if the mirrors were created so they could commune with one another from great distances, it's possible they each were given one. And if Rikad himself had one, that would make ten."

"We know where three of them are. Well, we know where two of them are and know the sorcerer has one somewhere in Kelvur," Ezel signed.

"Correct," Garron said.

Ezel fiddled with the wooden token tied around his neck. It was a habit he'd gotten into since the wizard trinket had protected him from an arrow and saved his life at the Battle of Galium. Garron knew the gnome did it whenever he was nervous or thinking.

"We should cover the mirror again," Garron said to Pernden. "Keep this room guarded and let no one in until you return."

Pernden nodded thoughtfully.

"I have to agree," Argus said with a hint of sadness. "As much as I'd like to continue studying this, it would be unwise to do so until we have Jaernok Tur's mirror in our possession."

"Agreed," Pernden said. "We do not have time to solve every mystery right now. We can reconvene on this after the sorcerer is defeated."

They wrapped the Alkhoren Mirror back in the canvas that had covered it before. They tied ropes with tight knots around it to ensure the canvas wouldn't fall of its own accord. As they left the room, Garron took one last glance back at the covered mirror and wondered, *Who was that?*

CHAPTER NINE

DRAGON OVER DORANTOWN

K arnak cursed under his breath. He watched as Tam flew his griffin in low and fast, hurtling toward Dorantown. The young griffin landed smoothly and clicked with excited energy.

"They're coming!" Tam heaved. "The dragon is coming. I didn't see any wretchlings on the road, but you know they're out there."

Karnak turned and shouted, "Make ready!"

Soldiers of Javelin and guardians of the Griffin Guard set into motion, all running to their designated tasks.

Karnak hurried to Tenzo. The muscular chelon was only a few inches shorter than the big orc and carried himself well. "Remember," Karnak said, "head south and cut into Duskwood. Keep heading south until you reach the Palisade and follow that all the way to Aiden's Dell."

"Right," Tenzo nodded. There was no argument in his determined look. "Then if you defeat the dragon here, you'll send the guardians to find us and bring us home. And if you don't..."

"If we don't, hopefully we'll be right behind you," Karnak said reassuringly.

"And the guardians will retreat to the *Sellena*." Tenzo finished reiterating the plan.

"Correct. It would be far too easy for the varlek to find you if you have griffins flying about," the orc said. "Now, get going. They need you."

Karnak patted the chelon's strong shoulder. He liked Tenzo, even if he annoyed the orc gar sometimes. The chelon had been one of the more vocal leaders, and sometimes Karnak wished he would be quiet. But Tenzo wanted to help his people any way he could, and Karnak appreciated that fervor.

He was sorry to send the strong chelon to the forest. Karnak would rather keep everyone he could to defend Dorantown, but their chances of defeating the dragon were slim, and he couldn't send all the elderly and younglings into Duskwood Forest without any protection.

As Karnak watched the young chelon saunter away, Tenzo halted suddenly and turned back toward the orc gar. "Karnak," he called back, "don't die, alright? I kind of like you."

The chelon smirked and ran off.

I kind of like you, too, Karnak thought with a grin.

Karnak found Tam and his griffin, still near the barricade they'd hastily constructed on the main road into town. The guardian was speaking to Ralowyn, Lanryn, and the archers set to launch the harpoons from the four-armed bow contraptions.

"Tam!" Karnak barked. "Get to the docks and get them underway!"

"Yes, sir!" Tam said. He quickly turned his griffin, and the two leaped into the air to fly off.

"He was relaying what he saw of the dragon," Ralowyn said, twisting the Staff of Anvelorian in her hand.

"A dragon is a dragon," Karnak said shortly.

"I would have said the same until I learned of monolith dragons," Lanryn stated.

Karnak grunted. He looked over the barricade they'd constructed out of wagons and mining carts. It wasn't much, but hopefully it would help keep the wretchlings from running directly into the launchers.

Javelin warriors formed lines on either side of the barricade to protect from flanking, while Ralowyn and Lanryn set themselves behind the launchers, prepared to loose their arcane arts on their attackers.

They only had four launchers, and setting the harpoon was difficult work. They wouldn't get many chances.

Karnak grimaced.

He heard the final remnants of townsfolk heading into the mining trenches on their way out of Dorantown. They moved as quietly as they could, so Karnak lost their footsteps shortly. The only noises left were the landing guardians as their griffins flew into place behind buildings.

The hope was they'd be able to surprise the dragon and confuse it by flying into the air in no semblance of organization. It was a long shot, but over the three days and two agonizing nights since their meeting, many plans and ideas had been thought up to give them some sort of edge in the fight.

Jensen and his griffin landed silently nearby, behind a building to Karnak's left. The orc gar nodded to the guardian. Jensen returned the gesture and patted his griffin's neck feathers.

Karnak looked out over the darkening, silent road. The sun was nearly gone. Night was upon them.

"Here we go," Lanryn said to Ralowyn.

She looked at her long-time friend for a moment. The elves had known each other for more than two hundred years. It was strange to think how far they'd come from the wisdom tower at Loralith. All those years of study and training under Master Tenlien had been good, but in many regards by comparison, most of those years seemed entirely uneventful to Ralowyn.

Her life had completely changed when Merrick came running through Elderwood Forest while she was on her walk. Since then, her life had been nothing but adventurous.

Lanryn must have been thinking something similar, for he said, "How strange that we find ourselves a world away from Loralith, preparing for battle like the old stories."

Ralowyn laughed silently. "How strange indeed."

Lanryn pulled from his pocket the Shell of Callencia. He whispered something in old dwarfish to activate its magic. A glowing orb of light flickered into existence, floating a few inches above the abalone shell. Radiant light reflections bounced off the shell and onto Lanryn's face and cloak.

"Smarlo," he said to the shell.

"I'm here," Smarlo replied, the light orb bouncing with the distant words.

"It's begun. The dragon comes."

There was a long pause before the orb bounced again. *"I wish you great safety, my friend. Keep us apprised of your situation. I've already discussed it with Argus, who assured me he would pass it along to King Pernden. I am not yet sure whether we will still sail to Dorantown or shift our destination."*

"I'll reach out again as soon as I can," Lanryn said. "Until then, full sails, my friend."

The light flickered erratically before disappearing, covering the shell's beauty with darkness. Lanryn pocketed the shell and readied his wand.

"They still do not know which way they will go?" Ralowyn asked quietly.

"No," Lanryn said. "It takes time to relay the information. But also, they are all traveling to Kane Harbor. It is difficult for them to make those kinds of decisions before they arrive and can discuss the matter."

Ralowyn bobbed her head thoughtfully. Before her run-in with Merrick, she'd spent the majority of her 240 years of life in the wisdom tower where she'd had little need to organize groups of people. There were other students, of course, and Master Tenlien often had them train together. But nothing like what their allies were attempting, nor what she and the rest of Dorantown had put together for this battle.

Organizing themselves for the coming attack had taken distinct planning and bold execution. Ralowyn was glad Karnak was there. She greatly admired his ability to lead and organize the groups to work in unison.

As they stood in silence, the night grew long. Every moment that passed, the tension weighed heavier, dripping with thickness. Javelin warriors twitched and rolled out their shoulders and calves, loosening their tense muscles. Tightness could mean death when the battle started.

But start it did not.

For several hours, they waited quietly, though their insides were raucous with nerves.

Lanryn broke the silence. "Wait!" he half-whispered, half-called. He twisted slightly, elevating his pointed ear as though he were trying to hear something.

Ralowyn did the same, but she heard nothing. She knew Tam would not have flown back to Dorantown without having seen the dragon. Certainly, it was coming. *But did it change*

93

course? she wondered. *Did they change their minds? Did they get distracted by something else?*

The thought of avoiding a battle was preferable to facing off against a wretchling army and their dragon-riding varlek. But somehow, that seemed unlikely.

Her doubts proved correct.

"Wretchlings!" a javelin warrior on the southeast side of the road hollered.

The call was echoed as wretchlings poured from the woods, cackling with malevolent delight. The horrible creatures ran, some ambling more than outright running, to meet the defenders of Dorantown. The piercing sound of metal clashing rang out through the night as the wretchlings hit the Javelin warriors like a wave crashing against the rocks.

Painful screams and smoke erupted from the mayhem.

"I've got them," Lanryn said to Ralowyn, running off to help the others.

Ralowyn stayed next to the launchers. Her task was to protect them at all costs, so they could take the shots on the dragon when it arrived.

Where is that dragon?

For a moment, she thought her question was about to be answered as the trees of the forest on the northwest side of the road cracked and swayed. *Did they land the great beast in the woods for a sneak attack?*

From the woods sprang a wretchling giant, more than twenty feet tall. His skullish face and dark—almost translucent—skin made him appear like an enormous shadow monster. Smaller wretchlings skittered past his legs as he reared back and released a horrible roar.

The appearance of the monster confirmed Ralowyn and Lanryn's suspicion that Jaernok Tur used dark magic to alter his army. When they'd first seen the sorcerer and his army of wretchlings at Ventohl, they were caught off guard by his new stony skin, but there was no denying it was him. The sorcerer carried his staff, and while the shadowy wisps that trailed him contained flecks of orange mixed with the black, it was clearly Jaernok Tur. How he had turned into that creature, they did not know.

They did piece together the fact that his geldrin army was full of creatures of different species remade into the stony brutes. Seeing the giant wretchling, Ralowyn assumed it was the next stage in the transformation of the sorcerer's geldrins. She wondered if the geldrins had retained too much of their individuality for the sorcerer's liking and that's why he transformed them into the raging wretchlings.

Thundering footsteps rushed up behind her. She turned for a split second to ensure it was what she thought, and saw Dak, Dorantown's lone giant, as he sprinted past her.

The giant wretchling stood its ground, readying for the oncoming giant. Dak lunged forward, his fist outstretched, and blasted the wretchling in the face. The enormous creature tumbled over, cracking and snapping tall trees as its falling mass slammed into them.

A short burst of cheers rose from the Javelin warriors on that side before the smaller wretchlings viciously crashed into them.

Ralowyn conjured several lavender fireballs and lobbed them into the gaggle of wretchlings, chomping at the bit, waiting for their turn to engage the Javelin warriors.

Suddenly, Karnak blistered past her to join the fight.

The large orc barreled over a scrawny wretchling that waggled its head as it raised its jagged dagger. Karnak roared as he heaved his axe around and slammed it down, finishing the wretchling in a disgusting cloud of smoke.

"Forward! Forward!" he yelled to the Javelin warriors around him.

They had to reach Dak, he knew. The giant would need all the help he could get. Several of the smaller wretchlings had turned on the giant and were clambering on his legs to bring him down.

A blast of lavender fire exploded into a group of wretchlings before him, and Karnak didn't bother to look back. He would thank Ralowyn for that one later. He ran along, chopping down wretchlings as he went, a stream of Javelin warriors following in his smoky wake, finishing off whatever creatures managed to avoid the fearsome orc's deadly axe.

Karnak slowed his approach as he watched the massive wretchling heave itself to its feet. Several broken trees and other debris had punctured him, for smoke poured out of odd places.

Dak kicked a handful of the smaller wretchlings, sending them flying into the Javelin warriors. As the wretchling giant rose, the smaller ones were more inclined to fight against Javelin again. Dak and the wretchling giant collided in a great struggle, each trying to bring their weapon down on the other.

Karnak thought the massive wretchling's weapon to be no more a large hunk of sharp metal—as if a blacksmith had intended to create a massive sword but quit halfway through the process.

The orc slashed through another wretchling as he lurched ahead into an all-out sprint. He ran, hacking down a wretchling on one side with his double-bladed axe and punching out at another on the opposite side. Though his axe did not compare to the might of his former weapon, Dalkeri, Karnak's skill in battle was not diminished. The hordes of wretchlings that Jaernok Tur had at his disposal were staggering to the orc.

By the time Karnak got close to the giants, they were locked together, almost immobile. They struggled, each tense with brute strength. Karnak wasn't sure whose strength would give way first, but he didn't intend to let the contest play out evenly.

The orc gar heaved back his axe and brought it around with a heavy swing like he was chopping at a great tree trunk. The axe tore through the back of the wretchling giant's leg, smoke billowing out. Karnak coughed as the massive wretchling fell to one knee with a horrific roar.

Dak pressed harder, recognizing the advantage quickly. Karnak moved out of the smoke and brought his axe into another swing, biting into the back of the massive creature's other leg. That did the trick. The pain was so severe that the big wretchling loosened its grip on Dak.

The giant lifted his enormous club, which Karnak had always thought more of a tree trunk, and slammed it down on the monster's head. Smoke erupted from the fallen creature bathing the whole area in putrid clouds.

Karnak and Dak stepped out of the smoke and nodded to each other, both of them looking exhausted from their efforts.

Suddenly, a great roar filled the night. Karnak and Dak turned their faces skyward.

The dragon!

Ralowyn lifted the Staff of Anvelorian, readying herself for the dragon's approach. She glanced over at Jensen. The guardian's griffin slowly creeped up the side of the building, its talons piercing the wood with ease. As Ralowyn turned back toward the sky, the dragon appeared to be swooping directly for the launchers.

For a second, she wondered why the varlek would lead his dragon directly at them. She realized that seeing the battle from the sky, with the way their forces defended the position, likely made it appear a prime target.

This might just work, she thought.

As the dragon glided, its leathery wings outstretched and whipping, the launch team nervously braced themselves. The dragon soared low over the roadway, hurtling with terrifying speed toward them. The dragon's maw opened, and a roaring firelight burned within.

"Ready!" Ralowyn called to the launch team. "I will shield you!" she reassured them.

As the dragon spouted its flame, covering the road and scorching its own wretchlings, three out of the four launchers released their harpoons. Two of the projectiles missed entirely, and one of them glanced off the dragon's hardened scaly head. The fourth member of the launch team dove to the ground, too terrified by the oncoming dragon and hoping beyond hope to avoid its fires.

The magical barrier Ralowyn erected withstood the flames, but holding the conjuration required great effort. The dragon flew just overhead, halting its fiery breath as griffins took to the sky all around it. The surprised beast flapped its wings wildly, kicking off the road in the center of the town and flying higher into the sky.

Jensen and the Talon Squadron chased after the great monster, hurtling spears and shooting arrows. Ralowyn didn't assume they would be able to down the dragon. What chance did they have?

Suddenly, a wretchling exploded into a smoking heap next to her.

"They're making their way through now, lass," Coal grunted as he raised his hammer again. "We've got to sound the retreat."

"We did not even strike the dragon," she said mournfully.

"Well, we can't hit it from here," he said, clearly upset as well. "We've missed our chance."

Ralowyn turned and saw that the launch team had abandoned the launchers to fight the raging wretchlings. The fourth launcher still stood ready.

"If I can get the dragon to come near, can you hit it with the last harpoon?" she asked quickly.

Coal hesitated as he looked at the wretchling forces engaging their own all around. His shoulders fell, and his gaze dropped as he shook his head. "We don't have much time," he growled, hurrying over to the launcher. "You better get it over here quick."

Ralowyn took the Staff of Anvelorian in both hands before her. She tapped the bottom of the staff twice on the ground, forcing the purple light that emanated from it to burst into greater magnitude. She opened herself up to the power of the staff, reaching from her heart, through her arms, into her hands, and finally, connecting with the staff's pinnacle. The Staff of Anvelorian *verved* with energy, sending pulses of light into the night sky.

Come, she thought. *Come here,* she willed.

As if the dragon heard her, the great beast swiveled in the air and dove toward them.

"Ralowyn," Coal said nervously behind her.

Yes. Come to me, she willed, her gaze not leaving the dragon's. It was as though there was nothing else happening around them. It was only the dragon and her, their eyes locked in communion.

The varlek atop the dragon fought with the beast, trying to get the creature to obey its commands. The dragon roiled awkwardly as a horse twitches to rid itself of a fly. As the creature neared, Coal loosed the last harpoon. It hurtled through the air.

Suddenly, Ralowyn cut off their connection, shifting into a defensive posture and conjuring a bubble of protection around Coal and herself.

The dragon shook out its daze, but the harpoon struck its wing, just under the shoulder. The creature attempted to flap a few times but couldn't regain control of its flight.

"Oh, no," Coal murmured behind Ralowyn as the dragon plummeted toward them.

The monster crashed down on top of the fighting forces. It lashed its wicked tale and spouted flames in every direction.

One of its great wings beat on the magical barrier that protected Ralowyn and Coal. The elf and the dwarf watched as the barrier sputtered with lavender light, taking blow after blow from the massive wing.

The dragon rose to all fours, spewing flames at the griffins that dove in after it. They couldn't approach it like that. Buildings all around erupted like kindling as dragon fire consumed everything nearby.

"We have to get out of here!" Coal yelled, his volume amplified under the protective dome. "We're going to be crushed."

Ralowyn knew he was right. She couldn't hold the barrier forever, and their best chance to get away from the young dragon was to escape while it was distracted with the guardians.

"On three," she said, nodding anxiously to the dwarf. Her silver hair was matted to her face from the sweat of her efforts.

"Alright," Coal said, gripping his war hammer tightly.

"One."

She waited as the dragon shifted to spout flames in another direction.

"Two! Three!" she shouted in rapid succession, recognizing their chance.

The dragon's leathery wing dropped on them heavily, pressing them to the ground as they ran. The wing raised. The power with which it did lifted the elf and the dwarf off the ground for a split moment before dropping them again. They stumbled to their feet and fled again. The devastation of the dragon's crash was evident. All around them were smoking heaps and the remains of their own fallen.

They ducked quickly as the dragon's tail lashed above them. Ralowyn narrowly escaped a spike to the crown of her head. Coal grabbed Ralowyn, helping her up from her knees.

"Run!" he shouted, knowing the dragon could not hear them over its own commotion.

As they made it to a burning building and rounded the corner—or what was left of the corner—Ralowyn turned to look at the dragon. The varlek was nowhere to be seen. It must have been thrown from the dragon in the crash.

"Retreat!" a lumbering voice called.

Ralowyn watched as Dak the giant dove on top of the young dragon.

Coal grabbed her hand, and they ran.

Karnak struck another wretchling that ran to the aid of the dragon. The orc gar hollered at Dak, but the giant couldn't hear him.

Is he actually wrestling a dragon? Karnak thought in shock.

The orc roared, "Retreat!" as he cut down another wretchling that thought it might sneak up on an already engaged Javelin warrior. The young woman finished the wretchling she'd been fighting and turned to the gar. Her eyes were wide, and a great sorrow mixed with rage twitched at the corners of her nose and mouth.

"We need to retreat," Karnak said to the few warriors around.

The wretchlings swarmed the dragon and the giant. Dak beat at the great beast with his flaming club.

A pang of regret hit Karnak. The club was a skillfully carved piece, detailing scenes of the giant's homeland and people. Whenever they had spoken of Dak's past, the giant got a dreamy look in his eye, explaining that the Eastern Knolls had once been a marvelous place, before the Crags erupted. The regret of losing such a wonderful cultural piece, however, was quickly replaced by a greater loss.

"Retreat!" Dak hollered as the dragon bit his shoulder. "Get out of here!"

Karnak started forward but realized he would be able to do nothing to aid the giant. Wretchlings surrounded him and drew twisted bows, loosing arrows at the griffins that flitted above. Karnak tried to wave them off, not wanting to lose more guardians.

Jensen must have seen the orc gar, because he signaled to the other guardians. The griffins adjusted their flight paths, heading toward the Gant Sea.

When Karnak turned back, he saw Dak, still beating on the dragon, only much slower. Dozens of arrows stuck out of the giant's back. The dragon bit hard on Dak's side, and the giant cried out.

No ...

Karnak caught sight of the varlek. The wretched creature stood near the epic brawl, not watching the two behemoths tussle. Instead, he stared at Karnak with that wicked grin scrawled across his horrible face. A rage boiled within the orc, causing his chin to quiver and his tusks to shake.

"Gar Karnak, we have to go," the Javelin woman implored.

Karnak snapped to, his sense of duty to protect the others overwhelming the passionate anger that flared within. He scanned the scene. They were cut off from the retreat of the others. There was no way they'd be able to make it to the mining trenches.

"Get to the docks," he said quickly.

The group ran as fast as they could, slashing at wretchlings that crossed their paths. Unfortunately, they garnered the attention of more wretchlings that soon gave chase. A centaur clopped along in front of them, swinging his great sword left and right, lopping off wretchling heads, turning them into toppling fountains of smoke.

A dwarven warrior from Javelin ran next to Karnak until he took a jagged spear to the back and crumpled to the ground. The young woman with them cried out and paused for a moment before Karnak picked her up and threw her over his great green shoulder. She didn't fight him and sobbed softly as he ran.

As they turned onto the docks, Karnak tripped over a pile of ropes. They crashed onto the hard wooden boards, and he yelled to her as he hurriedly pushed himself up, "Run!"

She clambered to her feet and ran. The centaur and several other warriors leaped off the end of the dock, a desperate last attempt to escape their attackers. An arrow whizzed by Karnak's head, and a second later, another one planted itself into an upright post next to him with a hard *thwack!*

Karnak's legs pumped faster as he ran to the end of the dock. Without slowing down, he barreled to the end and leapt.

CHAPTER TEN

CRIMSON SHADOWS

Nera stumbled over the uneven ground between the forest and Aiden's Dell. Her hands landed in the cool dirt, and the long grass prickled at her face as she hunched over in the darkness. She breathed and surveyed the scene.

The forest where Shadowpaw ran for cover was behind her. The sky twinkled with starlight before the moonrise, and the massive form of the Palisade cut the sky with a dark and rigid silhouette. She could still see the glinting torches on top of the wall and in the city of Aiden's Dell. The longer she knelt, the more torches gathered at the city's southern end. Someone was coming to find them. With the shoot first, ask questions later mentality they'd already witnessed, Nera didn't want to be found.

"Shorlis!" she hissed, trying to call loudly enough for the chelon to hear her, but quietly enough to go unnoticed by the gathering hunting party.

When the chelon didn't answer, Nera began beating herself up. She felt foolish. Why hadn't they just waited until morning when the guards would have been able to see them clearly? If Aiden's Dell had faced off against Jaernok Tur's army as well, the guards would certainly be more alert at night.

Nera hurried along, more careful with her footing. Every few feet she whisper-shouted, "Shorlis!"

The hunting party was on the move. Suddenly, she heard a shuffling to her left. Nera squatted to the ground, squinting into the darkness. She saw only a large rock and some long grass waving around it. A large bush blew quietly, its leaves not yet having grown back after the harsh winter.

When nothing moved or caught her attention, she called again, "Shorlis!"

The large rock moved, startling her half to death. Shorlis's head popped up on one side, and the rock shifted upward. "Nera?" the chelon asked, curiously, fixing his linen cloak back over himself.

"Your shell ..." she said dumbfounded. "I thought you were a rock."

Shorlis gave her a weak smile. "I thought it would be a good way to hide in the dark. They're gathering a hunting party over—" Shorlis didn't finish the thought.

"They're already on their way," Nera said quickly. "We have to get to the forest. Maybe we can hide there. I told Shadowpaw to find a hiding spot and we'd catch up to her."

"Is she alright?" Shorlis asked as they set off toward the forest, hunched over to avoid being spotted.

"She took an arrow to the wing. I'll have to get a better look at it in the daylight tomorrow."

"If we can evade the guards of Aiden's Dell," Shorlis mumbled.

The voices of the hunting party grew louder as the guardian and the chelon crossed into the forest. They hurried along, climbing quietly over fallen trees and overgrown underbrush. They picked their way through, following the easiest paths, but it struck Nera as odd that the forest would be so overgrown in a place where she assumed at least the hunters from Aiden's Dell would frequent. *Wouldn't they?* Then again, she'd never been to that forest, and they could have well-trodden paths elsewhere.

She scanned around them, looking for any spot she might remember. The dark night and her lack of familiarity with the place lent her no aid.

They heard shouts near the forest's edge. Nera grabbed Shorlis and ducked behind a massive fallen tree. The footsteps drew closer, and Nera discerned the voices of two men. She could see the torchlight flickering between the trees, but to her surprise it drew no closer to them.

What are they waiting for? she wondered.

"Well, go on then," one of the men said. His voice cracked, and Nera thought he sounded young.

"I'm not going in there," the other man said. He didn't sound much older than the first.

"You think the creatures went in there?" the younger asked.

"No one is foolish enough to go into the Forest of Wirra. I don't care how scary they are," the older said. "You think a shadow beast is scarier than a forest hag?"

"You think it really was a shadow beast? I've never seen them fly before."

"Of course it was," the older man scolded the younger. "What else could it have been? It was like a flying shadow."

"Well, they've only ever attacked in packs. Never seen one alone."

"Posh," the older man said. "Captain said, shoot if anything moves, and I'm not going to get caught off guard."

The torchlight flickered between the trees as the holder lifted it high and moved it side to side. "I can't see anything," the younger man said.

"Nah. If no one else finds the creatures, I'm thinking we'll have to search the forest tomorrow in the daylight. No way in Malkra anyone's going into the forest at night."

As the men's footsteps moved away from the forest, Nera looked to Shorlis, who'd also been listening in silence. The chelon bore a grave visage.

They spoke no words, but Nera knew they shared the same thought: *What dangers lie in wait in this forest at night?*

As the night drew on, several other pairs of hunters moved by the edge of the forest. Nera was caught between her desperation to find Shadowpaw, worried the griffin may be in grave danger, and her need to protect Shorlis and herself from capture—or whatever dangers the hunters feared from the forest.

When the rotation of searchers slowed and no more came near the forest's edge, Nera urged Shorlis to follow her closely. They wandered quietly along the forest's edge, hoping to find where she and Shadowpaw had crashed earlier that night. If she could find that spot, at least they'd have a place to begin their search. Once they were farther into the deep forest, they'd feel more comfortable calling out for the griffin.

A while after their pursuers had given up for the evening, Shorlis held *Menthrora* in front of him and whispered under his breath. A red light shone from the staff's pinnacle and illuminated the forest around them in an eerie crimson glow. With his light, they made short work of finding all the broken branches and stamped ground where Nera and Shadowpaw had crashed.

"Great work," Nera whispered.

"Thank you," Shorlis said, "though it was one of the first things Ralowyn taught me. I think it's a rather rudimentary trick."

"Do not put yourself down, my friend. Sometimes the things we think are mundane about ourselves are actually the most marvelous to others. And you are marvelous."

Shorlis took the compliment in stride, stepping through the trees, and followed the rather obvious tracks of Shadowpaw. They wandered through the dark, the red glow bathing the world around them with dancing crimson shadows.

Every once in a while, they'd hear the loud cracking of a broken stick and pause. Shorlis would extinguish the light as they crouched to listen and watch, surprised that the red light didn't diminish their night vision. When nothing would appear, Nera took many chances to quietly call out for Shadowpaw. Many times there was no response.

After a long while of searching, Shadowpaw's tracks seemed to have disappeared. Nera doubted the griffin would have taken to the sky with the arrow in her wing. She may have been able to waft herself into the trees, though, so Nera had Shorlis raise the staff and illuminate the canopy above. Perhaps they could find broken branches that snapped under the weight of the griffin. After another long while with no sign, they needed to come up with a new plan.

Shorlis brought the staff down with a long sigh. "We may need to start again in the morning, when we can see better."

"I think you're right," Nera said, but her words were slow. Her heart beat faster in her chest, and for some reason, the world seemed to slow around her. The trees swayed quietly, but something was not quite right. She felt as though someone was watching them. "Shorlis," she managed to say, "what is that?"

Shorlis turned and illuminated the remains of a broken tree that stood the height of a man. "What do you mean?" the chelon asked, a twinge of nervousness in his voice.

Nera breathed heavily for a moment, squinting through the dark. "Nothing," she said quickly. "I just had this strange feeling like someone was watching us."

A shiver shook Shorlis' shoulders as he slowly spun to illuminate the areas all around them. "I don't see anyone."

"It was probably just my mind playing tricks on me," Nera reassured him, though she sounded more like she was trying to reassure herself. "There was a large tree back there that we could climb for some rest. I'm not sure I want to sleep on the ground in this forest."

"Agreed," Shorlis said.

The guardian and the chelon positioned themselves in a large tree, each taking a wide branch to prop themselves up for some rest. It was much needed. They'd pushed themselves past their normal stopping point that evening and, in doing so, had run into a heap of trouble. Their nerves were on edge, and wandering through the forest following difficult tracks in the dark required much focus and effort. They were exhausted.

Nera watched as Shorlis illuminated the area below them with the red light.

"Just wanted to take one last look," the chelon said.

He scanned around, and as he moved the light toward the tree, Nera's eyes were already drooping. She could hardly keep them open. Her head felt heavy, too, as she began to nod.

Her eyes drifted to another broken tree the size of a man. She wondered what had happened to the trees. Perhaps they were struck by lightning. Or perhaps they were broken by some large monster that roamed the forest. As she peeked through the last crease of her closing eyelids, she thought the tree had soft glowing eyes.

Nera snapped her eyes open with great effort but saw nothing but the broken tree. She shook her head slowly before succumbing to sleep.

CHAPTER ELEVEN

ASHES

Merrick watched Kippin for a few minutes. The halfling lay cuddled in his blanket, his mouth wide open, snoring softly. The early morning sun shone through the tree branches and cast golden light on his peace-filled face.

"Hey, Kippin," Merrick said quietly as he shook the halfling's shoulder. "Hey, little man, it's time to get up. I want to show you something."

Kippin sat up, his head lolling as he wiped at the drool on his cheek. He stood up quickly, and Merrick held his hands out in case he needed to catch the little fellow. Kippin teetered for a second and opened his bleary eyes wide. He pushed some of his wild curls out of his face and smiled. "Good morning," he said.

Merrick couldn't help but smile back. "Good morning," the huntsman returned the greeting. "You ready to learn some more about falconry?"

That woke the halfling up quickly. He snapped to, gathering his blanket and stuffing it in his pack. "Will I get to fly him today?"

"No," Merrick said with a chuckle. "First, we have to get him used to being around us. If we tried to fly him today, he would fly off and never come back."

A sad look swept over the halfling's face. "I don't want that."

"No. We don't want that," Merrick said with a grin. "In order to get him used to us, we need to make him a few things."

"Like what?" Kippin asked, as he started to pull at the bottom of the cloak that covered the caged bird.

"Not yet," Merrick corrected gently. "Let's keep him covered for a little bit this morning. We want him to be calm."

The halfling let the edge of the cloak fall again, disappointed he couldn't sneak a peek at the bird underneath. He moseyed over to Merrick and sat close to the huntsman, who pulled his arrow quiver close and cut a small square from the top edge with his dagger. Kippin watched him curiously.

"One of the most important pieces of equipment we need for training a falcon is a hood."

"So it can ride on my head?" Kippin asked nervously.

"No." Merrick laughed. "Not for you. For him."

The huntsman worked the leather with his hands, softening and molding it. He cut a few other shapes into the square's sides and began to puncture tiny holes around the edges.

"What are you doing?" Kippin asked.

"We're going to use string to sew this together here," the huntsman said, bending the leather in two places to make what looked like a bowl. "It won't be the fanciest hood, but it'll have to do until we get back to Dorantown. There, we can use leather-working tools to make him one that fits just right."

"Why does he need a hood?" the halfling asked, leaning closer on his knees.

Merrick halted his work and forced Kippin to scoot back slightly while the huntsman was still using his knife. "Falcons have very keen eyes. They rely on them heavily. But because of that, falcons can get really nervous when there are lots of new things in sight. With the hood, we'll be able to cover his eyes and slowly reveal things to him. What a falcon can't see, he won't be scared of. We'll be able to get him used to us quicker this way."

"Just like the cloak over the cage?"

"Right," Merrick said. "The cloak on the cage keeps him calm because he can't see anything outside the cage. When we take it off, we make him a bit nervous. We just have to train him to know that we're friendly."

"I'm going to be his best friend," Kippin said resolutely.

"I know you will. *He* just doesn't know it yet. So, we have to teach him."

Once Merrick finished sewing the piece of leather into a makeshift hood, he handed it to Kippin to examine. The halfling gawked at it in wonder as though the makeshift hood was the most fascinating of enchanted relics.

"Let's see if our traps caught us any more rabbits," the huntsman said. "I'll carry the cage for now, and you can gather our game."

They checked the traps they'd set and were excited to find two more hares caught in their snares. Merrick was alright with them already being dead. He explained to Kippin that they had needed one alive for the falcon trap to work. They'd been very lucky.

Even though they were almost out of the bread they'd brought from Dorantown and only had two more apples, Merrick decided it would be good to stay another day, just in case they could catch a few more hares. Additionally, it would give them more time with the falcon before bringing him into town.

A short time later, Merrick allowed Kippin to uncover the cage. The falcon inside was a beautiful grey with black spots. He was larger than Rora had been when Merrick had first caught her, though not by much. When they first drew away the cloak, the falcon glanced around nervously, clicking its talons on the sticks that made up the bottom of the cage.

Kippin examined the bird with his mouth agape.

What wonder you still have, Merrick thought as he watched the halfling. Though in truth, the bird was a stunning creature.

"Do you want to feed him?" Merrick asked.

"Yes!" Kippin half-squealed.

"Settle," Merrick said, smiling from ear to ear. "We don't want to scare him."

Merrick handed Kippin a piece of rabbit meat. The halfling slowly reached toward the cage, but when the falcon snipped at the meat, Kippin tossed it in and pulled back his hand.

"It's alright," Merrick said. "For now, we need to feed him like this. Make sure he will take the meat. We still need to make you some sort of glove or bracer and then a short talon leash. We'll want to tie his ankle before we let him out of the cage."

Kippin scrunched his features and nodded as though everything Merrick said made the most sense in the world.

They covered the falcon again but periodically revealed themselves to him, giving him a piece of meat every time. They did that for the rest of the day while Merrick worked a leash out of the extra bowstring he had. He showed Kippin how to tie a slip loop on one end. That evening the huntsman wrapped his hands with cloth until he could barely maneuver his fingers.

"You're going to need to give him some meat so he's busy with that. I'll loop the leash around his talon, and we'll tie him to the cage bars for now. Then we'll be able to try and feed him inside the cage," Merrick explained.

The falcon was surprisingly amicable about the whole ordeal, and Merrick was able to loop and tighten the leash around its talon. He tied the other end to a cage bar as the falcon picked at the rabbit meat.

"I think he's already getting used to us," Merrick said, shooting Kippin a wink and a smile. "We'll keep him caged, but we can try and feed him through an open cage tomorrow. We'll have to wrap your hands, like mine, just in case."

The halfling nodded vigorously, thinking the huntsman the bravest man in Finlestia for the stunt with the leash.

As they lay next to the fire that evening, Kippin turned to Merrick and whispered, "Will we go home tomorrow? I want to show Ralowyn my new falcon." As he spoke, he picked at the wrappings on his hand. He'd been wrapping, unwrapping, and rewrapping them all evening.

"We'll check our snares first thing, and then we can head back to Dorantown," Merrick said gently. "We didn't catch much this time, but with your new falcon, we'll be able to catch a lot more on future hunts."

Kippin grinned. Merrick knew it was because he called the bird the halfling's falcon.

"I've been thinking we should name him," the little halfling said as he cuddled under his blanket.

"That would be a good idea," Merrick said. "What should we call him?"

"Davir," the halfling said without hesitation.

"Davir, huh?" Merrick asked. "Why Davir?"

The halfling paused to think about his answer. "Well, I don't know."

"Did you hear it somewhere?"

"Ralowyn says it to me," Kippin explained.

"Oh?" Merrick raised his brows, though he didn't lift his head.

"When she says it to me, it makes me feel good. She strokes my hair and says, *'Davir lolel non.'* I don't know what it means, but I know it's nice," Kippin said airily and then yawned.

"Sounds elvish to me," Merrick said quietly.

"Well, your falcon's name was elvish, and I thought mine could be, too."

Merrick pressed his lips together. The moment was so sweet he wished he could capture it in a jar. The bridge of his nose tingled as a wave of emotion hit him.

"I think Davir is a wonderful name," the huntsman said, attempting to keep his voice even.

They said no more, and the halfling fell asleep soon after. Merrick smiled as sleep enveloped him with the sound of Kippin's quiet snores.

Kippin leaped at the sight of another hare caught in their trap. The halfling wanted to untie that one himself, proclaiming it a great rabbit to use for feeding Davir. Merrick laughed at his excitement. It was hard not to. Kippin's pure joy was contagious. The excitement faded, however, as they found no more rabbits in the rest of their snares.

The sooner we can train Davir, the better, Merrick thought sullenly.

It had been a difficult winter, and Merrick had taken Kippin on numerous days-long hunts that rendered little game. They never came home empty-handed, but Duskwood was a new place for him, and with the harsh snows and shifting snowbanks, it had been difficult for the huntsman to get his bearings. Finding the regular game trails during the warmer seasons would have been easier, but he hadn't been allotted that luxury.

He worried the wretchlings would return as the season warmed. He still saw the smoky creatures and their candlelight eyes in his dreams.

Several of the council members in Dorantown theorized the harsh winter had halted the vile monsters from marching on Dorantown. Merrick wasn't entirely sure. *Would cold really affect them?* If that were the case, they'd likely return sometime during the spring, and he might not be able to get the lay of the land at all during the warmer months.

Merrick and Kippin spent the day walking west toward Dorantown—toward home. It was strange to think of the place as such. He'd enjoyed his time in Calrok greatly, and the orc city had felt similar in a lot of ways. Perhaps Merrick didn't need a place to be his home. Perhaps home was the people who gathered around the fire with him and loved him.

As Kippin teetered, balancing along a fallen log, the huntsman watched him. The halfling had lost his father when Javelin took Ventohl—for the short period they held the city. His father was a brave halfling, a skilled leather worker, who'd felt the call to action when Vorenna had called upon Javelin to "finish the fight" at Ventohl.

Sadly, many had died rallying to that cry. When they took the city from the assassins and geldrins that held it, many thought it was the beginning of the end for Jaernok Tur. But the wicked sorcerer had cooked up secret plans they could not have anticipated.

As the little halfling jumped off the end of the log, he turned to Merrick and asked, "Can I carry Davir's cage now?"

"Sure," Merrick said. "But first, why don't we take a break and let him see us for a little while?"

They carefully removed the cloak that covered the cage. Davir skittered at them but twitched his head excitedly as Kippin produced a piece of meat from the pouch Merrick handed him. The halfling slowly brought the meat toward the cage, and Davir roiled his grey feathers, stepping tentatively with his talons.

"Easy now," Merrick said to the halfling. "When you get close, drop it into the cage."

Kippin did so, and the falcon pounced on the meat with urgency. The halfling giggled. "He must be hungry."

"I think so," the huntsman agreed. He looked at the wrappings on Kippin's arm, as the little halfling scratched at them with his other hand. "Later, I'll rewrap your arm, and we can try to feed him through an opening."

The halfling's eyes went wide. Merrick grinned at him. He loved how full of expression his face was.

As they continued, the huntsman watched the halfling carry the cage with great care. It was odd to Merrick how much joy he felt just having Kippin along. He wondered if his father, Grell, felt the same way taking Merrick or his brothers along on hunts when they were young. There was nothing quite like being out in the wilderness, especially with someone he loved.

They walked for most of the day. They had gone farther into Duskwood's vastness to hunt. Every once in a while, they stopped to reveal Davir and feed him pieces of meat. The falcon appeared less nervous each time.

As they drew closer to home, the winds picked up, swaying the trees and sending them into a cascading melody of swishing and crackling branches. White flakes began falling from the sky, swirling in the wild winds.

"It's snowing again!" Kippin called over the wind.

"I see that ..." Merrick responded curiously. It didn't feel cold enough for another snow. They'd had a good dusting a few days earlier, but the weather had warmed since then. The smell of smoke wafted by him in waves with the changing wind. He lifted his hand to catch some of the flakes. As they landed, he found they didn't have the biting chill of ice.

"Kippin," he said hurriedly. "Stay close to me. This isn't snow. It's ash."

The huntsman posted Kippin near a tree they'd marked months ago, knowing he'd be able to find his way back to the halfling there. Merrick stalked near the edge of Duskwood, taking in the scene.

Dorantown was burned.

A wrenching in his gut nearly made the huntsman vomit, but he breathed through the distraction.

Ralowyn, he thought with terror. *Where are you?*

He scanned the area, seeing nothing but charred buildings, some of which still spewed white smoke. The ashes whipped up in great white tornadoes before scattering in the higher winds and falling like snow. Merrick continued to move along the forest's edge, attempting to see everything he could before leaving the safety of the trees.

The huntsman watched a long time, using the patience he'd developed over years of waiting on game. A tear streaked down his cheek at the prospect of Ralowyn being injured or killed. *And Karnak! Or Coal!* Merrick thought with revulsion. *Maker, please ...*

After watching the ashen town for a long while, Merrick stepped out of the woods quietly. He hurried to a half-burned wall where he could hide and survey more of Dorantown's inner streets. He didn't see anyone. Good or bad. Neighbors or wretchlings.

He placed a hand on the wall, leaning around it to get a good look at the main street through town. As he did, the light pressure made the charred wall give way. It creaked loudly and crashed to the ground, sending up swirling ash all around him.

Merrick stood there, dumbstruck and exposed.

When no one acknowledged his presence, he walked toward the center of town. Smoldering shells of buildings looked like the eerie charred carcasses of large beasts.

What could have done this? Merrick wondered.

He meandered to the edge of town where the road came in, assuming that if Jaernok Tur had sent his army, the huntsman would find tracks. And did he ever. There were thousands of tracks from men, elves, dwarfs, chelons, centaurs ... and wretchlings.

Merrick's heart squeezed within him. He could feel his pulse in his neck as a wave of anguish washed over him. As he continued to survey the scene, he found an area with some broken launchers and harpoons.

They must have known the wretchlings were coming, Merrick surmised, a glimmer of hope returning to him. *Perhaps they were able to retreat to the ships.*

Merrick turned toward the harbor. The docks seemed to be in relatively good shape, but he wasn't sure he'd be able to tell if the ships had gotten away. If they were also burned, they likely would have sunk to the bottom of the harbor.

He looped around what looked like makeshift barriers—or what was left of them—and found where most of the skirmish had happened. As he stepped into the ash that had gathered along the road, smears of red appeared under his boots.

The huntsman spent a long time wandering about, inspecting the tracks. The fact that he found no bodies didn't surprise him. If the wretchlings had won the battle, they probably took the dead for feeding. The thought sickened him.

He stopped dead when he found large footprints that appeared to belong to a great clawed beast.

Dragon. If Jaernok Tur has another dragon ...

Merrick's steps quickened, but he didn't stop searching for signs of his friends. When he found a significant amount of tracks headed toward the mining trenches, he followed them with haste.

Pieces of armor, helmets, lost weapons, and other miscellany lined the trenches. Wretchlings cared little for items and trinkets. The horrible creatures were ravenous. Blood stains covered the trench walls, making the dirt there darker.

Something glinted from the side wall, as Merrick kicked through the thick ash that collected in the trench's bottom. He drew nearer to inspect it and found an abalone shell half-buried in the dirt wall, a bloody handprint smeared from it to the ground. Merrick grabbed the shell and knelt, pushing the ash away. Something skittered across the ground with the sound of wood rolling on gravel. He managed to find it with his fingers and lifted a wooden wand in his hand. *Lanryn ...*

Merrick continued to search the trenches for another few hours. The sun was beginning to set, and he'd seen no sign of Ralowyn or her staff, nor had he seen anything from Karnak or Coal. He dared to believe they may have escaped the attack.

The wretchling footprints seemed to double-back to the road. They likely assumed no one would return to the charred town and retreated to Ventohl for future orders from their master.

As Merrick walked into the forest, he leaned on a tree and retched. Tears streamed from his face as he took a moment to process everything he'd seen. The horrors he'd seen would haunt him for the rest of his life. He refused to subject Kippin to them.

The huntsman had no idea where any of his friends were, but judging by the tracks, whoever had survived retreated to the south. He debated for a long while what his and the halfling's next move should be. If he and Kippin were caught by wretchlings all alone, the huntsman would hardly be able to protect them. They had to get somewhere with other people.

He remembered Tam showing him a map the young guardian was copying that said there was a city toward the center of the Palisade. If they headed southeast through Duskwood, perhaps they could make it.

When he found the marked tree, Kippin was nowhere to be seen.

"Kippin!" Merrick let out a hushed holler as panic set in.

"Up here," the little halfling said from a branch above the man's head.

"You scared me half to death," Merrick said. "Climb down here now!" Kippin did so and was surprised at the tight hug that Merrick wrapped him in. "Don't you ever do that again. You hear me? I thought you were gone. I thought they took you, too."

Kippin's eyes glossed with big tears. "Ralowyn?" he croaked.

"I don't know," Merrick said, not letting the halfling loose. "Everyone's gone. Dorantown is burned."

"No ..." The little halfling collapsed into a sob.

"It's alright. It's alright." Merrick comforted him but didn't believe the words himself.

"What will we do?" Kippin asked.

Merrick pulled the halfling away to look him in the eyes. "We're going to be strong. We're going to figure this out. I remember Tam showing me a map. If we head through the forest, it may protect us from view. We need to get to the city on the wall."

Kippin's chin quivered, and Merrick wiped the tears away from his little face.

"We're going to be strong," Merrick said again. "We'll find our way. If our people somehow escaped, they'll be headed to the city as well. Maybe we can even beat them there and welcome them when they arrive."

"Do you think Ralowyn will be there?" Kippin asked.

The huntsman didn't bother to hide the tears that fell from his eyes. "I hope so," he said. "She's going to be so proud to see that you've become a little falconer."

CHAPTER TWELVE

EMBARK

The sunlight warmed Pernden's face, and he breathed deeply, smelling the salt in the air of the seaside town of Kane Harbor. The people had come a long way over the winter, and the combined efforts of man, orc, and elf proved to be a beautiful cooperation. The buildings were elegantly designed by the elves, while the harbor docks were well developed by the growing number of orcs and men who frequented them.

"Quite the little city ye're building here, yer Lordship," a voice called from nearby. "Soon enough, it'll be as big as Crossdin in the east."

Pernden turned to greet the dwarf. "Lotmeag Kandersaw," he said with a grin, "foredwarf of the garvawk warriors of Galium. How were your travels, my friend?"

Lotmeag shuffled up to the king and extended a thick dwarven hand. "It was alright. Got in late last night. Wasn't sure the new inn was going to let us stay."

"You have trouble with the innkeeper?" Pernden asked, concerned. He watched the dwarf pull out a pipe and scratch at his thick brown beard with it.

"Nah," he said, amused. "He was alright. Young lad taking the night shift. Nary a hair on his chin. Seemed surprised to see a bunch of dwarves show up in the middle of the night."

Lotmeag chuckled as he prepped his pipe.

"So, no real troubles then?"

"Nah," Lotmeag said. "Though yer Lordship should consider more stables. All of them were taken up by yer griffins. Luckily, we were able to set the garvawks to stone in the field over yonder for the night."

Pernden peered over to where the dwarf pointed. A good twelve garvawks sat statuesque in the field. Pernden remembered when he'd first seen the garvawks, the panther-like creatures with great bat-like wings. They were marvelous and terrifying beasts. He was fascinated by the dwarves' process to turn the garvawks to stone and tame them with magic. Two dwarven warriors stood nearby, chatting.

"We had to set guards through the night, but I told them they'd be able to rest on the ship when we leave," the dwarf said frankly as he puffed his pipe. "Nigh bit more grumbling than they should give, but I'm still whipping them back into shape."

Pernden nodded, understanding the dwarf's situation. Lotmeag had become the foredwarf of the garvawk warriors when the previous foredwarf and Lotmeag's mentor, Bendur Clagstack, died at the Battle of Galium. Pernden had also taken over as Whitestone's king after that battle.

"It would be nice to see some dwarves from Galium here," Pernden said as they looked over the docks.

"I'm standing right next to ye," Lotmeag mused.

"I know, I meant—"

"I know what ye meant," Lotmeag said. "There's been a lot of rebuilding to do in Galium. The winter wasn't easy. The mountains dropped many snowstorms on us this year. And though I don't tend to dabble in the politics, I have had regular meetings with King Thygram Markensteel. He wants to send dwarves for this settlement; we just have to fix up some things at home first. The garvawk warriors being here should definitely settle the issue for ye. We wouldn't be here if the king didn't want to be part of this."

Pernden nodded and said, "I'm grateful you are here. We'll need all the help we can get across the sea."

"Aye," Lotmeag said contemplatively. "And where are the elves anyway?"

"They should be arriving today."

"And the orcs?" Lotmeag said, his tone slightly different.

"Also, today. We have much to discuss. Smarlo suggested that the leaders of each group travel the Gant Sea on the *Harbinger*. Says it will make a good flagship."

As Pernden remembered the ship, he didn't disagree. Stalford had sent two of their largest fishing vessels for them to use as transport, the ship owners being more confident after hearing that the *Sellena* made the voyage.

The Riders of Loralith and the garvawk warriors would be on one ship and the Griffin Guard on another in an attempt to keep the griffins separate from the other mounts. The pegasi of the elves and garvawks of the dwarves would be fine, as the dwarves would turn their garvawks to stone belowdecks. The only ship large enough for the wyverns was the *Harbinger*, and it was best for them to be separated from the others anyway.

Pernden turned to Lotmeag, long strands of the king's blond hair whipping in front of his face. He brushed it away as he watched the foredwarf chew on his pipe. "Are you worried?" he asked.

"Aye," Lotmeag said quietly. "Seems a great way to get all the leaders in one place. Not that I'm saying our allies would betray us. But if they had a mind to do so, seems the best way to do it."

The king's teeth ground slightly. He couldn't blame the dwarf. They'd all spent generations fighting against the orcs. Pernden's involvement in fighting alongside the orcs in the battle of Calrok and his working with them in the endeavor to build the burgeoning town of Kane Harbor had given him much confidence in their allies.

"I assure you," he said to Lotmeag. "If I believed any ill will from them, I would not allow you to endanger your people for this voyage any more than I'd endanger my own. I have spent much time with the orcs over the last months, and I can tell you I have witnessed many things to give me assurance of their honor and loyalty."

"Aye," Lotmeag said again. He looked up to the young king and squinted at the bright sky. "I trust ye. If ye're anything like yer brother, Orin, I'll fly anywhere with ye."

Pernden patted a hand on the dwarf's armored shoulder. "Thank you."

Some hours later, the Riders of Loralith arrived. Pernden and Lotmeag greeted Commander Fario, lead elf of the squadron sent from Elderwood Forest. The elf was tall and seemed more muscular than most of his elven brethren. The feature that Pernden liked most about him was his thick black mustache. Rarely did one see an elf with facial hair. That, combined with Commander Fario's already stern—compared to other elves—face, he seemed a force to be reckoned with ... a true warrior.

"Glad to see you and your squad mates made it to Kane Harbor," Pernden said to the commander.

"Hm," Commander Fario responded with an affirmative grunt.

Pernden and Lotmeag shared smirks. The king recalled his previous encounters with the elf commander. Fario wasn't an elf to mince or idly toss words. He was highly tactical and analytical with a great sense of purpose.

He and his riders had saved Pernden and the Talon Squadron. While Whitestone was under Jaernok Tur's control, an orc wyvern squadron flew to reinforce it. The Talon Squadron had executed a daring ambush on them. Although the new allies celebrated the victory later, the elf commander never let his guard down. All of his questions and conversation pieces tended toward their eventual attack on Whitestone and how they'd get it back. Even after they'd taken the city back, his words were few.

"Your pegasi squadron will be on the *Lentoria*, over there." Pernden pointed to one of the Stalford ships. "The Griffin Guard's 5th and 8th squadrons are currently loading up on the *Wenli*."

"Aye," said Lotmeag. "And we've already got the garvawks loaded and set to stone in the *Lentoria's* underbelly. So, ye should have no problems loading yer feather horses."

"Hm," Commander Fario said again. He spun away, grabbing the attention of one of his lieutenants. He gave the elf quick and direct instructions to load up the squadron.

"Oh, and we'll be on the *Harbinger* when it arrives," Pernden said quickly.

Commander Fario revolved on his heels to look back at the king. Pernden pressed together a smile and raised an eyebrow. The stern-looking elf narrowed his eyes and pushed a sigh out through his nose, before swiveling back to his lieutenant for another word.

"He seems as excited by the prospect as I was," Lotmeag said.

"Great," Pernden whispered back.

The Riders of Loralith took to the air. Their gleaming white pegasi and the riders' golden armor created a brilliant flurry through the sky. The elves flew their steeds in impeccable formation, keeping them tighter than any Pernden had seen by the other races. Not all of the pegasi were perfectly white. In fact, many of them had varying or complementary shades of brown and grey patches and spots. In their rapid flight, it was hardly noticeable.

Shortly afterward, the *Harbinger* sailed into Kane Harbor. Sailors from the other two ships lined the decks for a view of the massive vessel as it approached. Dockworkers and other folks also gathered to watch the ship come in.

The *Harbinger* was larger than any ship built in Tarrine. Its intricate pulley system hoisted painted sails over the entirety of the vessel to cloak it. Though the painted sails themselves did a number to trick the eye, they were also imbued with magic to give the ship unprecedented stealth.

"Whoa," Lotmeag said. "Have ye ever seen the like?"

"Hm," Commander Fario said. Pernden was pretty sure that was his way of expressing awe.

Pernden, however, was not so enamored with the ship. The last time he'd seen it sail into port was during the Battle of Calrok. The ship had been cloaked and rammed into the docks before opening the storage hatch and releasing a swarm of death wings. Not to mention the geldrins that tumbled over the sides, ready to ransack the orc city, and Jolan the traitor.

No. The ship had lost its luster the moment Pernden saw it the first time.

An orc stepped next to the king and said, "Isn't she beautiful?"

Pernden recognized the voice immediately. "Porg!"

"King Pernden," he said cheerily, placing a finger to his brow and giving a slight bow.

The man had hardly gotten to see the orc in the past several months, with his kingly duties and Porg's responsibilities in Kane Harbor. The orc had come from Calrok with their representatives for the new settlement, and the two had struck up a quick friendship. In fact, it was their friendship that made most of the dealings with the representatives bearable.

"How are you, my friend?" Pernden asked, grabbing the orc's forearm in greeting. "Come to see us off?"

"Not quite," he said, his tusks parting his lips into a wide toothy grin. "I'm going with you."

"What?" the king asked in shock. Admittedly, he liked the idea of spending more time with the orc.

"We still have a lot of work to do here in Kane Harbor, but with all the good work we *have* done, Master Jalko suggested I go with you across the sea. Said we could lend aid to those in Dorantown who are trying to do something similar there."

Pernden's face fell. "Well, actually, there may be a change in plans."

"Change in plans?" Lotmeag started nearby. Commander Fario turned toward the king as well.

"Yes," Pernden sighed. "I was waiting for the *Harbinger* to get here. That way, we could all discuss it together. You're welcome to join us, Porg. It may change your course as it does our own."

Smarlo found that the *Harbinger's* awe-inspiring exterior was matched in equal measure by a utilitarian interior. A couple of windows were swiveled open in the cabin that was otherwise a large wooden box. The room was not uncomfortable. It was large, with plenty of windows letting in great amounts of light, but the area contained little in the way of furnishings—something Smarlo had asked Captain Bilktor to address. The old fishing captain sent one of his crew into Kane Harbor while they were docked to gather more supplies. Particularly, Smarlo wanted a tea kettle.

The orc mage started scratching at his ear, then stepped away from the large table in the center of the cabin. Parchments and makeshift maps covered the table. A few months back, he and Lanryn had spent days relaying map information to a mapmaker from Borok. The mapmaker did everything he could with the information Lanryn passed from Tam. It wasn't the most effective way, and the map likely had great discrepancies, but it was the best they had.

Smarlo walked to a ledge built into the wall of the cabin, grabbing the clay jar of salve and scooping a little on his finger. The smell of wildflower brought him back to Calrok as he rubbed it on his scarred ear.

After replacing the jar, Smarlo looked out one of the windows. The sun was high, and he heard nautical bells and the sound of workers hurrying along the docks. That was his first time seeing Kane Harbor, a venture that had happened almost entirely under his time as the interim gar of Calrok. The growing town looked good to him. Many of the buildings were of obvious elven design, but their sleek exteriors didn't model the typical opulence found in elven cities. Instead, the buildings complemented the bay and the other structures and systems being constructed. It truly was a mixed-race city, an exciting prospect for more such endeavors in the future.

"Right this way," Captain Bilktor said in his hoarse voice.

The cabin door swung open, and the captain ushered several people into the room.

"King Pernden," Smarlo acknowledged the king first.

"Smarlo," the man replied, a slightly disappointed look on his face.

The orc mage quickly took stock of the others. Lotmeag, foredwarf of the garvawk warriors from Galium, crossed his arms in front of his barrel chest.

He doesn't look happy, Smarlo thought.

Then there was Commander Fario. The stern elf looked even less pleased.

The good king must have mentioned we may have to shift plans.

There was another orc, shorter than Smarlo but stockier than the thin mage.

"And who might you be?" Smarlo asked.

"Ah, I'm Porg, Master Smarlo," the orc said awkwardly. "I was sent here to Kane Harbor with Master Jalko."

"Oh, right," Smarlo said, searching his memory. He'd never met Porg, but he remembered the orc's name from correspondences with Jalko. Suddenly, the orc mage realized he had no idea why Porg was here. "And what can I do for you, Porg?"

Captain Bilktor chuckled.

"Ah, well ..." Porg stammered. "Master Jalko intended to send me along so I might aid the folks in Dorantown. Seems like they are trying to build the same thing we've been building here. I know I'll be able to share what we've learned in Kane Harbor."

"I see," Smarlo said, mulling it over. Jalko had performed his duties admirably and seeing the port town for the first time did ignite something within him. He trusted Jalko's judgment.

"I won't get in the way none. I'm only here to serve," Porg added nervously.

"I can vouch for Porg's character," Pernden said, slapping a hand on the orc's shoulder. "Though I've already told him he may not actually be needed."

"Right," Smarlo said. "Well, let us discuss the matter."

They drew close to the table in the center of the cabin, and Smarlo explained what they'd learned over the Shells of Callencia. He described the plan that their allies made in Dorantown to ready themselves for the attack of a dragon. Lotmeag growled at the mention of the beast, having lost many of his friends in the fight against the dragon that came to Galium.

"The last we heard from Lanryn," Smarlo continued, "the wretchling army and their new dragon were descending on Dorantown."

"Have we heard anything since the battle?" Pernden asked.

"Lanryn mentioned that he'd keep us updated if they had to retreat ..." Smarlo hemmed.

"But?"

"We haven't heard from him since before the battle. I fear for the condition of our allies."

"They planned to evacuate everyone, if need be. Many of them may have escaped," Pernden pressed.

"There is no way to know without communication from Lanryn," Smarlo countered.

"So, our friends are dead. The mission's off?" Lotmeag interjected.

"Not necessarily," Pernden argued. "They could be alive. They had several plans of escape. It's possible many survived, even if Lanryn didn't."

A quiet fell over the cabin. Waves lapped against the anchored ship, the only noise.

"When we discussed it with them," Smarlo cut the silence, "it was suggested that we attempt to flank the enemy by sailing north and attacking Ventohl directly."

"Ye mean where the nasty sorcerer and all his baddies are holed up?" Lotmeag grunted incredulously.

"Hm," Commander Fario said. Those gathered turned to the elf, watching him intently as he leaned over the large map that contained Tarrine on the left side and Kelvur on the right. He traced a long finger along the coastline from Dorantown to Ventohl. "I am no sailor," he said, looking to Captain Bilktor. "Would it be out of the question to sail past Dorantown? We don't have to get too close to the coast. As soon as we see land, we could send a scouting party from one of the squadrons. Perhaps we can reestablish contact with our allies if they are still there."

"It's possible." Bilktor nodded.

"And what if we're spotted?" Pernden asked. "We may lose the element of surprise that we would gain by heading straight to the north."

"That's why we send a small scouting party from a distance. We do it from the *Harbinger* since we can cloak it," Smarlo said.

"Hm," Fario agreed.

"This can work," Smarlo said excitedly.

"And what if our friends aren't there?" Lotmeag asked.

The room fell silent once more, each leader pondering the possibility.

"Then we head to Ventohl. We bring a storm down on Jaernok Tur and his minions, the likes of which he's never seen. We end him so he can no longer harm our home and the ones we love," Smarlo said through clenched teeth.

The others glanced around at one another. Smarlo wondered for a moment if he'd let the rage inside him show too much.

Pernden leaned over the map and knocked on the spot where Ventohl was positioned and said, "Let's end this, once and for all."

The others nodded their agreement. They spent another hour deliberating the finer details before exiting to the main deck to watch as their ships embarked on the foreboding voyage.

Smarlo didn't leave the cabin for a long while, pouring over his *Book of Dangerous Secrets.* The orc mage was surprised when Lotmeag reentered the cabin several hours later. The dwarf banged the door open with his hip and steadied two mugs in his hands. He kicked back at the door, swinging it closed with his foot.

"Foredwarf Lotmeag," Smarlo said.

"No need for the formalities," Lotmeag laughed. "How can ye even see in here? Ye got no lanterns to burn?"

Smarlo realized how dark it had gotten. His orc eyes, acute in the darkness, hadn't noticed the shift. "Sorry," the mage said, hurrying to a lantern on a small side table between two chairs. He lit the lantern, and the room burst to life. Strange shadows cast from knots and knobbles on the wood surfaces.

"Only teasing," the dwarf said with a wink. Smarlo then remembered how well dwarves also saw in the dark. Lotmeag walked over and plopped himself into one of the chairs. "Ah, that's better," he said, lifting one of the mugs to Smarlo.

The orc mage took it tentatively and sat in the other chair. "What is—" he began to ask but stopped. He lifted the mug to his face and breathed in the steam. The red tea smelled similar to the tea he and Tanessa enjoyed in the evenings, but there was something else in the tea. He sniffed at it suspiciously.

"Yuck," the dwarf said next to him. "I think this one is yers." Lotmeag set the mug on the table between them and pushed it toward Smarlo. The orc mage looked at it, motionless, while the dwarf waved a thick hand toward the mug in his own grasp. When Smarlo didn't immediately hand it over, Lotmeag smirked, pulled out a skin flask from under his cloak, and asked, "Oh, ye like yers with a little nip in it, too, then? I can just add some to this one as well."

"No," Smarlo said, quickly handing the mug to the dwarf.

"Oh, well. Suit yerself," Lotmeag said, taking the mug and breathing it in. He took a good swig and smiled. "Ah, that's better now. Was looking for a little bite from the galley, and Cook said if I brought ye yer favorite tea, he'd send me with some blueberry scones. Oh, yeah," he said, suddenly reaching into a pocket. "Brought you one, too."

Lotmeag pulled two crumbling scones out of his pocket and made to pass one over to Smarlo.

"No, thank you," the orc mage declined, lifting a hand to wave it off.

"Suit yerself," Lotmeag said, tucking one back into his pocket. He patted it and said, "I'll save that one for later."

Smarlo watched the dwarf, sipping and eating merrily. Neither of them said a word for a long while. Smarlo eventually drank his own tea, relishing its flavor and reminiscing of home. In a strange way, he was glad for the quiet company. After a while, curiosity overtook him.

"Is there something I can help you with?" he asked the dwarf. "Or did you just come to enjoy some evening tea with me."

"Aye," Lotmeag answered, setting his empty mug down on the table between them. "That, and I thought we could get to know each other."

"Oh?" One of Smarlo's eyebrows perked up.

"Way I see it, ye and the good king have worked together before. I've worked with dwarf mages before; they're mighty helpful on *glendon* teams when we hunt for new garvawks. Need them to put the rune on the beasts' shoulders after turning them to stone. Only way to bond a garvawk with a dwarf."

"Fascinating," Smarlo said. He was intrigued by the process and hoped to have Lotmeag explain it to him further. Maybe it was something worthy of inclusion in his *Dangerous Book of Secrets.*

"Aye, it is," he agreed. "But I've never worked with an orc mage. Barely ever worked with an orc."

"Oh, I see," Smarlo said, softening. "You're worried about me."

"Not necessarily," Lotmeag said, judging now to be the "later" he'd meant to eat his other scone, and pulled it from his pocket once more. "Just like to know who I'm working with," he said through a bite.

"I can assure you, I have no ill intention for anyone except the sorcerer of Kelvur."

"That was plain," Lotmeag said brashly.

Smarlo's face scrunched. "I didn't mean to let my anger get the better of me earlier."

"Don't worry about it. I'm a dwarf. We're about as passionate as they come. I actually kind of liked yer outburst. Told me ye got some fire in ye."

Smarlo snorted a chuckle. "I've got lots of fire for him."

"Good," Lotmeag said. "I think we might need it."

CHAPTER THIRTEEN

BACK TO TAMARIA

Ellaria's mother, Marie, turned and bumped into Ezel, as she swung a plate of flapjacks toward the table. The house of Grell bustled with excitement. All of Ellaria's younger brothers were eager to meet another member of the fabled Griffin Guard—one that wasn't her, anyway.

Garron happily answered all their questions. Some of them were even about Ellaria. The former king expressed how great she was doing in training and made sure her brothers knew she was quite the heroine.

Ellaria watched him interacting with her brothers, and if Garron was seeing it right, her cheeks rosed with color. It was hard to tell as she wore her wild red hair down. He stole glances at her while he told them stories of her heroics. There were lots of "Oohs" and "Ahhs" and a few gasps from Marie. Ellaria's father laughed as though he expected nothing less from his only daughter.

Garron, Ellaria, and Ezel had been lucky. Grell and the boys had just gotten home from a hunt two days prior. Marie whipped up a feast of a breakfast for them with eggs and bacon and flapjacks covered with oozing honey.

A meal fit for a king, Garron thought but quickly rejected the notion. He was no king; he was a failed king. Boisterous laughter and more prodding from the boys pulled Garron from the moment of self-loathing that had snuck up on him.

Eventually, Grell sent the boys outside for chores and turned a graver tone toward the others. They'd arrived late the previous evening and had been travel weary, so they hadn't gotten to discuss everything on Grell's mind.

"What about Merrick?" he asked in his deep, gravelly voice.

"Da, I told you in me letters that Merrick is across the sea in Kelvur."

"Aye, I know that," he said sullenly. "I just mean, is me boy okay?"

Garron leaned forward after emptying his cup of water. The fluid did little to help his dry throat in the moment. "My cousin is sailing across the Gant Sea himself, as we speak," he emphasized. "The winter was harsh in Kelvur."

"Winter was harsh here," Grell said.

Garron nodded and continued. "We've got two Griffin Guard squadrons, a wyvern squadron from Calrok, a garvawk squad from Galium, and the Riders of Loralith all going to reinforce our people there and fight the wicked sorcerer."

"Aye." Grell smirked and looked to Ellaria. "The sorcerer Merrick shot with an arrow, yes?"

"Aye," Ellaria affirmed. "But Da, he's got a whole army out there."

"That's why we have to talk to King Hugen," Garron explained. "King Pernden hasn't gotten any responses from him, and Tamaria needs to know of the danger. If the sorcerer's new army somehow makes it to Tarrine like they did before, everyone will be at risk."

"Aye," Ellaria said. "And speaking of that, we need to get going to the Flag Keep."

They all stood from their seats, Garron thanking Marie for the excellent breakfast and translating Ezel's thanks, even though the man was sure she understood. Grell walked them out the door, moseying to find the boys, who were off playing around instead of doing their chores.

"Probably sword fighting," Ellaria whispered to Garron with a smirk. "You got them all riled up this morning."

Garron smiled. How many times had he and his brothers and cousins shirked their chores to gallivant around Whitestone on "daring quests?" When they eventually went to train at the Grand Corral with the Griffin Guard, they felt right at home with the wooden training swords.

The sun was bright in the early spring morning, and Tamaria was abuzz with noise. Garron had rarely heard a city so loud. Whitestone only ever got that loud on special occasions like festivals. Even then, the noise paled in comparison to the massive plains city.

"Over here," Ellaria said, grabbing Ezel's hand and wrapping her arm around Garron's.

She pulled them into a market square, one of Tamaria's many, and walked straight toward a stall with an elderly woman selling bread.

"Ella, deary! Look at ye in yer fancy armor," the woman said excitedly. Her eyes lit up behind the wrinkles on her kindly face. "Who do you have here, then?"

"Gabby!" Ellaria almost sang. "This is Garron, and this is Ezel."

"Oh my," Gabby said, looking up to the taller man. "Ella dear," she said, putting a hand to the side of her face and leaning closer. "This is a new one, eh?"

Ellaria laughed. "This is Orin's cousin."

"Pleased to meet you, Miss Gabby," Garron said with a slight bow.

"Another charmer," Gabby said with a blushing grin. "Where do ye keep findin' these handsome 'uns again?"

"Not sure why I keep having to save these Whitestone boys." Ellaria smirked at Garron.

They had a quick chat with Gabby before she sent them away with some "rolls for the road."

When they arrived at Reimald Square, Tamaria's main square in front of the Flag Keep, Garron's mouth dropped open. There were merchant stalls lining the entire perimeter of the square, aside from a single tavern in one corner called *The Flagkeep Tavern.*

Ezel signed to Ellaria that they should take Garron over to the tavern after they met with King Hugen. *"That's where we met,"* Ezel signed to the man.

Ellaria laughed, obviously remembering something funny. "Oh yes, my favorite place."

The Flag Keep was aptly named. It looked like the castle had a multi-colored fur coat as flags of every shape, size, and color waved in the wind. As he stared, Garron wasn't sure how they'd managed to mount all of the flags. There were hundreds.

"Come on," Ellaria said.

As they walked up the steps to the keep, Garron saw an elf knight with dark black hair speaking to one of the guards. The elf looked put out even though his armor gleamed brighter than any Garron had ever seen.

"Ah, perfect," Ellaria said, hurrying ahead of them.

Garron and Ezel glanced at each other and shrugged before stepping quickly after her.

The guard tensed, which forced the elf knight to turn around. A look of surprise crossed his face, and he hurriedly stood straighter. "Miss Ellaria," he said greeting her, still stunned. "It's been some time."

"Kaelor," she said, "we need to speak to King Hugen. Where is the lard of the keep?"

The knight grimaced at the name calling.

Garron looked to Ezel in shock. The gnome signed to him, scrunching his face, *"He's not a very good king ... "*

"King Hugen," the elf knight said, emphasizing the proper way to address the king, even though it appeared to pain him, "is inside the keep somewhere. If you'd like an audience with him—"

"Kaelor." Ellaria cut him off. Her face went deadpan, and she stared at him for a long moment.

The elf knight cleared his throat and turned to the guard. He pointed at the emblem on Ellaria's armor, a blue shield emblazoned with a silver griffin flanked by white wings. "The Griffin Guard has urgent business with the king. Please excuse us."

Kaelor led them into the keep, navigating the halls with ease.

"Maybe I should do the talking," Garron whispered to Ellaria as they followed the elf.

Ezel signed his agreement.

"That would probably be wise," Kaelor said, his pointed ears having heard their hushed conversation.

Ellaria rolled her eyes.

They walked through the king's trophy room. The walls were adorned with weapons and shields, some of Griffin Guard origin and some of orc. Garron slowed to look.

"Rayin's sword was right there," Ellaria said to him, pointing at a decorative sword that Garron assumed the king got from a merchant who had lied about its great battle history. He doubted the sword had ever been sharpened for battle.

One piece stole Garron's attention over the rest. It was a layered armor chest piece. The armor was dented and dinged and discolored in a section. The crest of Whitestone was scratched and tattered.

How many Guardians have worn that crest to their doom? he wondered. *How many of them died because the sorcerer got inside my head?*

Ezel's little hand gripped Garron's wrist and pulled the man along.

Kaelor eventually drew them into a dining hall. A long table spanned the length of the room. Plates and goblets and utensils lined the table before each seat. Several glass vases dotted the center, equidistant from each other. Each of them blossomed with vibrant flowers.

Garron imagined the flowers were brought in from somewhere south where spring came early. It seemed a gratuitous expense to him, but that's how the entire castle felt. Tapestries hung on every wall, and flags dangled from the ceiling from one end of the hall to the other.

"Please, have a seat," Kaelor said.

They did.

"Where is the king?" Ezel signed.

The elf stared for a moment.

"Oh, sorry," Garron said quickly. "He asked where King Hugen is."

"I ..." Kaelor paused and sighed. "I am not entirely sure. But if I can leave you for a moment, I will find him as quickly as possible."

"That would be wonderful. Thank you," Garron said.

"And what may I tell him your visit is in reference to?"

"Well," Garron hemmed. "My cousin, King Pernden, has sent correspondence to King Hugen through pigeon and raven, and he even sent a courier but has yet to receive word back."

Kaelor squirmed uncomfortably under his pristine armor. "Mmm," he let out a soft groan. "This is about the mission to Kelvur."

"Yes," Garron said, surprised the elf knew about it. "So, the king has gotten the letters?"

"I ..." The elf knight paused again, forming his words. "I will find the king as quickly as I can and bring him to you here. I'll start in the kitchen. Perhaps Neli has some pastries she can bring to you."

"Thank you, but we've been well fed this morning," Garron said. Ezel signed something to the man, and he added, "Actually, pastries would be wonderful as well."

Kaelor gave a slight bow and hurried off, leaving them alone at the long table.

"What is wrong with you two?" Garron asked, his eyebrows stitching together.

"You never say no to pastries from a king's kitchen," Ezel signed with a shrug.

"And you?" Garron said, turning on Ellaria.

"What? You said to let you do the talking," she chimed, crossing her arms in front of her.

"Really?"

"Not all of us have lived with good kings," she spat.

Her words pricked at him like a barb to the ribs. Garron's cheek twitched several times. Then he said, "Well, at least he never betrayed his people."

Ellaria sat up, her face shifting into a pained expression. "I didn't mean to—"

"No, it's fine," Garron said, standing and pacing.

"There are lots of ways to betray your people," Ellaria said quietly. "I mean, do you see this place?"

"His actions haven't gotten people killed."

"What about his inaction?" Ellaria countered.

Garron didn't know what to say. He knew he was fighting a losing argument. For whatever reason, Ellaria would not let him stew in his self-loathing. Neither would Ezel. He supposed that's what made them good friends, but he couldn't fight the nagging voice of doubt in his head.

While they waited, Neli brought them tea and apple muffins. They were perfectly baked, soft and sweet with a sugar and cinnamon crunch on top. Ezel ate four.

"There's something wrong," Ellaria said after another thirty minutes.

"What do you mean?" Ezel asked.

"Kaelor," the woman said, sweeping her red hair out of her face and fiddling with the green stone tied around her neck. "He didn't seem like himself."

"Did you know him well?"

"No," Ellaria admitted. "He's King Hugen's aide. I didn't have a habit of spending my time with the king while I was still living here. But even so ..." She trailed off for a minute. "Kaelor usually runs this place. He's the only one who ever gets anything done when it comes to kingly duties. Everyone knows it. I just don't know what's taking him so long."

Ellaria stood, beginning her own pacing.

Ezel nervously twirled the wooden token hanging from his neck. The etching of a massive tree with seven runes encircling it flitted back and forth. For a second, Garron thought he saw something else on the token, but Ezel's fiddling made it impossible to tell.

"You two need to settle down," Garron said. "Don't work yourselves up. I'm sure Kaelor will be back with the king soon."

I hope.

When the king's aide rounded the corner into the dining hall, Garron patted Ezel's little shoulder to wake him. The gnome had slipped into a deep sleep, his body likely overstuffed with apple muffins.

"I-I'm sorry," Kaelor said, shaking his head in defeat. "You'll have to leave now."

"What?" Garron asked.

"What do you mean leave?" Ellaria crooned. "We've been waiting here for hours."

She wasn't wrong. Garron had noticed a distinct change in the room's lighting. The windows weren't bright like they were when the trio arrived. Not to mention, several servants entered the dining hall and strode past the elf to light lanterns hanging from hooks along the walls.

"The king refuses to see you," Kaelor said.

Garron watched the elf closely; it seemed like he was wrestling with something. "Can we set an appointment for tomorrow?"

"What?" Ellaria blurted.

Garron stayed her with an outstretched hand.

"I fear that would be in vain," the elf said. "The king insisted that he has no interest in speaking with you—with any of you."

"Where is that lard?" Ellaria growled as she hustled out of the room.

"Miss Ellaria!" Kaelor called as he chased after her.

Garron and Ezel joined the pursuit.

"Miss Ellaria," Kaelor hollered as Ellaria bobbed this way and that, checking rooms throughout the hallways. "The king has requested you leave."

The group passed several guards who were descending a flight of steps. The guards hesitated a moment as Garron shrugged his apologies. Soon, they were following along.

Ellaria burst into a room and said, "There you are, you tub of butter."

A pitiful wail sounded.

As Garron and Ezel entered the room on the heels of the king's aide, they found Ellaria swiping a plate of food from another ornate table and the king holding a fork and knife in his chubby hands, quivering.

"You won't see us?" Ellaria asked furiously. "You remember when Orin took up your stupid crusade for you? Do you remember that?"

"Kaelor?" King Hugen bumbled. "Do something! Your king is in danger."

To Garron's surprise, the elf knight stood off to the corner and said, "I perceive no danger. The Griffin Guard has always been a friend to Tamaria, and her sword is sheathed."

A wicked grin scrawled across Ellaria's face. "No one to save you now," she said. "Have you gotten King Pernden's letters?"

The guards came up the hallway slowly, eyeing Garron and Ezel who stood in the doorway. Garron gestured to them to hold for a moment. They listened and stood by. Garron figured the guards had seen the king's aide with them when they'd passed by.

"What letters?" King Hugen asked, jelly falling from the corner of his mouth onto his fine tunic.

"You know what letters. The ones about the mission to Kelvur. Kaelor knows what I'm talking about. I highly doubt such a devoted king's aide like himself would keep secrets from you." Ellaria gripped the table and leaned in, menacingly.

"Oh, yes," King Hugen said quickly. He waved a sausage-like finger in the air as though remembering. "I do recall those letters. What of them?"

"What of them? What of them?" Ellaria was working herself into a frenzy.

Garron stepped into the room. "King Hugen," he said, trying to keep his voice level. "My cousin, King Pernden, has sent you numerous letters about the threat from Kelvur. Numerous letters about Whitestone needing aid and supplies during this mission. Not to mention warning of what the sorcerer's army could do if he crosses the sea to Tarrine again. Why have you not responded?"

"Why?" King Hugen said, throwing his fork to the floor with his dinner, clearly disappointed about not getting to finish it. "Why, you say?" He looked to Kaelor. Garron assumed the man looked to the elf to answer a lot of difficult questions for him. When the elf knight said nothing, King Hugen asked, "What would you have me do?"

"A response to start," Ellaria growled.

"A response? And what do I say to news of our imminent demise?" the king said, his large belly knocking the table as he stood.

"It's a warning, not a threat," Garron said. "The threat is across the sea for now. We just want to make sure the people of Tamaria are aware."

"Yes, let's send the people of Tamaria into chaos with wild rumors and hearsay."

"Hearsay?" Ellaria balked.

"Yes! Do you see any 'wretchlings' running around the plains?"

"No, but that's not the—"

"Right!" King Hugen raised a hand to stop Garron from speaking. As he did, the fat on his enormous arm jiggled. "Do you know what it takes to keep a city this large from devolving into chaos and disorder? No, of course not. You guardians, always thinking you're better than the rest of us. Always thinking about glory. I work tirelessly to ensure my people and my city remain in order."

Kaelor grunted next to Garron. The man looked at the elf and thought that statement might have jabbed the king's aide a little.

"But if you don't warn the people or the city guard, how can you prepare?" Garron asked. "We had to get the extra supplies we needed from Stalford and Dahrenport. Stalford even sent ships."

"Well, maybe they're foolish enough to follow your wild crusade for glory, but I am not. And if the threat is real, won't my people need all the supplies for ourselves? Hmmm?"

Garron's fists tightened in front of him. "If you can't defend the city, supplies won't matter," he said through gritted teeth. "The people need to know what's out there."

"The people don't *need* to know anything. I'm their king, I know what's best for them."

"Ha!" Ellaria laughed outright. "You've never known what's best for others—only what's best for you and your belly," she said, stepping forward and jabbing his belly with an outstretched finger.

King Hugen waddled backward to get away from her and fell on his hind end. He let out another wail.

"Come on, now," Ellaria growled at him and stepped closer to heave him up.

Just then the guards poked their heads in the doorway.

"Is everything alright in here?" a young guard asked.

"Oh, Trevor!" the king squealed. "Seize them! They've attacked your king!"

The guard hopped to and said, "It's Travish, my King." Even with the correction, several other guards swarmed into the room, cramping the place.

King Hugen burbled a wretched cry, rocking himself on the floor. "They attacked me!"

"We did no such thing!" Ellaria tried to yell over the king's cries.

The guards drew their swords in the tight quarters, intensifying the situation. Several runes on Ezel's arms and his eyes erupted with magical blue light.

"Wait!" Kaelor called. "Stand down."

The guards looked around nervously, and even King Hugen shut his trap and listened. The blue faery fire flickered from Ezel, bathing the room in a strange hue.

No one moved.

"I will see them to the dungeons," Kaelor said. Ellaria's face scrunched in confusion, but Garron shook his head slowly at her. "I do not think they want a fight. I am sure they are willing to be taken peacefully."

"Like Malkra," one of the guards said. "They attacked our king!"

"I believe all this to be a mere misunderstanding," Kaelor said assertively.

A few of the guards hesitated, their swords lowering slowly.

"That's it," Kaelor continued. "I'll take them to the dungeons myself."

"We'll escort you," Travish said dutifully.

The elf knight let out a short sigh and pressed his lips together into a thin smile. "Thank you, young Travish."

Kaelor looked directly into Garron's eyes as they exited the room. The elf said nothing, but as he stared at the man, Garron heard, *Trust.*

Garron attempted to catch Ellaria's and Ezel's gazes to convey the same word. They seemed to get the message as they followed him, silently escorted to the Flag Keep's dungeons.

CHAPTER FOURTEEN

THE TREK

When the last of the retreated warriors caught up with the evacuees from Dorantown, a solemn silence fell over the tired people. They had run for two nights and a day. Beyond being exhausted, they were swept with grief. Ralowyn, herself, was worked up. She hadn't seen Lanryn or Karnak, and she feared the worst for both of them.

Coal was comforting a young woman and her daughter, having seen her husband fall in the battle himself. Quiet sobs could be heard like boiling water, rolling up all around. The people were scattered over a swathe of Duskwood. The mountains to their west stretched high above them, sloping easily into the forest, but none of the refugees marveled at their beauty that day. Instead, the rocky faces of the mountains loomed high above as cold and indifferent observers of their mourning.

Ralowyn stepped next to Coal and pulled him to the side.

"We have to get these people moving," she said quietly.

"They've been running for days," the dwarf said, his tone begging mercy. "They're scared and tired."

"They will be dead if the wretchlings catch up to us," Ralowyn said plainly.

Coal looked from side to side and grabbed her by the arm, pulling her farther into a copse of trees. "Quiet now," he whispered. "Aye. We have to move them, but they can't go on forever. They need a little rest."

Ralowyn pursed her lips and looked around. Knots of people from Dorantown were huddled together, many crying or holding loved ones in terrified embraces. She sighed and pushed her silvery mess of hair out of her face. She saw Tenzo speaking with Vorenna and hurried to them, Coal on her heels.

"We need to get people moving," Tenzo was saying. "We have to get to Aiden's Dell as fast as possible. If the wretchlings attack us in the forest, we may not survive."

"Have we ever seen the wretchlings attack during the day?" Vorenna asked calmly.

"No, but that's—"

"Why is that, do you think?" the barbarian woman continued. She had that curious look in her eyes that Ralowyn had seen before. Vorenna was a calculating and cunning warrior, even if she was a bit brash. She was always trying to understand their opponents.

"Maybe the sun damages them," Coal proffered, hopefully.

"What does it matter?" Ralowyn asked, trying to keep her voice even.

"It matters," Vorenna said, flexing her muscular arms as she crossed them, "because, even if we don't know why, we can at least give the people some rest during the daylight."

When Ralowyn and Tenzo only stared bemusedly at her, Coal jumped in. "Let them rest for a few hours, and we'll move after that. We only caught up to them last night, and we haven't heard wretchlings on our tails since the first night. It's possible they stopped chasing us and went back to Dorantown."

Ralowyn rolled her neck, trying to work out a crick in her shoulder. She wasn't even sure how she'd hurt it. "Three hours, and then we move." The authority in her voice surprised the others, but no one argued.

The elf woman walked toward the north where she found a tree leaning on another for desperate support. She smoothly loped up the fallen tree, finding a perch on which to sit and observe. She did everything she could to filter out the sound of the people in their disparaged states. Ralowyn closed her eyes and focused on her breath and expanding her focus from there. The muffled cries faded away, and she could hear the forest. Duskwood groaned with the sound of creaking timbers. The swaying of the large trees put pressure on their trunks. A painful shiver ran up her spine.

Master Tenlien in Loralith had always called Ralowyn's empathy with nature a gift. But when she was young, it always seemed a curse. The gift made the world around her unbearably loud and painful. She could feel the rocks crashing upon one another as they rolled down hills. She could feel the waters of a creek slowly pulling stones apart. She could feel the tired effort of ancient trees, doing everything they could to keep standing. It had been horrible.

Over time, however, she learned to listen differently.

"Too often people hear what they come to expect rather than what there is to be heard. You must open your ears and your heart to what you never thought possible," Master Tenlien had told her.

It wasn't easy figuring out how to attune her senses to the world around her, but in time, she did. Instead of only hearing the pain and discomfort, she heard the joy and pleasure. She heard the tree's great purpose in loosing its seed to the ground, proud of its accomplishment and grateful to its friend the soil for its aid. She heard the waters bubbling with laughter as the creeks cascaded down ravines. She heard the leaves dance in merriment with their friend the breeze, creating an orchestral ballad together. The world was wild, but it was also beautiful.

While the world held a great many beauties, worry still existed.

She opened her eyes suddenly, staring into the distance. She could not hear them nor see them, but she wished more than anything that Merrick and Kippin would walk into view.

Where are you two? she wondered. And she let several tears escape her eyes from high in the tree where no one would see.

Moving that many people through thick woods was a daunting task. They trekked slower than Ralowyn liked, but she knew they couldn't be pushed faster. They'd traveled two more days, and night was falling upon them again. The initial shock seemed to be wearing off; people were jumping in to help wherever they could. In an unexpected way, people fell into a routine, readying camp for their rests. Javelin had lived a nomadic lifestyle for years and was quick to show the others how.

Evenings darkened quickly in the forest, the reason—Ralowyn suspected—for its name. Duskwood was largely overgrown in the area near the mountains, but the game trails they ran across were formed by large beasts that roamed the slopes and valleys.

That evening they found a large cliff, which Vorenna explained was part of the Palisade. Even though the sheer face of the cliff halted their march southward, it seemed to shift the mood of camp, as if the cliff were a sign. They hadn't seen or heard any wretchlings chasing them, something every one of them was grateful for. Since they'd found the Palisade, as long as they stayed in the cover of the forest and kept the wall in sight, their hopes of reaching Aiden's Dell were higher. Better yet, Shorlis and Nera were likely already there and preparing the way for them.

Ralowyn hadn't slept in days, and the fatigue was wearing her down. The elf had opted to stay on watch each night, knowing her elven body could handle more nights without sleep than most. After days with no sign of pursuers, she finally felt as though someone else could take a shift. She sidled up to Coal and sat on a log next to the dwarf, who handed her rabbit meat he'd pulled off the spit.

"Here," he said. "You need to eat something."

"Thank you," she said, taking it without argument.

She slowly pulled the meat apart and ate it while Coal pulled more for himself before passing the spit to Tenzo.

"You going to get some rest tonight?" the dwarf asked her quietly. "Plenty of others on watch this eve."

"Yes." Ralowyn nodded to him. She ate quickly and made herself comfortable nearby. The warm glow of the fire beyond her eyelids flickered light into her mind as she drifted off to sleep.

She dreamed of Merrick and Kippin. It was a warm summer day. The grasshoppers were chirping, and butterflies flitted from flower to flower in the meadow. She did not know the place with her eyes, but her heart knew it to be home. Kippin ran along the path to greet her, his arms wide and ready to wrap her in his tightest hug. Merrick walked behind him, a quiet, contented smile on his face. The huntsman looked at Ralowyn as though she were the only one he'd ever loved. And somehow, she knew it to be so.

The scene was the dream of all dreams—the one that welled within her as her deepest hope. The one she was too afraid to admit to anyone else, for fear it would never come true. The one she'd desperately fight for.

Even the thought of losing such a gift immediately shifted the dream. Dark clouds began to cross the sky. Kippin, gripping her cloak, worriedly hid himself in the folds. She hugged him close, uttering her comforting words, *"Davir lolel non."* Brave little one.

Merrick had not quite reached them. He pulled out his bow. *Where did that come from? He wasn't wearing it a moment ago.*

"Run," he shouted.

Darkness closed in from all around them. Where could they run? Deep guttural growls accentuated by hungry yips echoed from every direction. Merrick loosed arrow after arrow, but the darkness pressed in.

A shape suddenly formed from the darkness. A wolf of pure shadow leaped upon Merrick's back. Ralowyn wanted to run to him. She wanted to lift the Staff of Anvelorian and rip the wolf into a million pieces. For some reason, she could not.

She heard the howls of the other wolves as Kippin, somehow out of arm's reach, was pounced upon by another of the shadowy beasts.

"No!" she screamed. She felt a heavy weight upon her back, as though it were pinning her in place.

Another wolf walked toward her with a vicious glint in its orange, fiery eyes. The beast snarled, revealing teeth of fire inside its maw. Its shadowy form tensed in preparation.

She wanted to scream. She wanted to cry. She wanted to destroy the wolf.

Suddenly, it leaped.

Ralowyn woke to Coal shaking both of her shoulders. "Wake up! Wake up, lass!" the dwarf was saying.

She immediately recognized the sensation of the lavender magic flowing through her. Ralowyn felt energy surge from the top of her head, tingling through every limb and down into the staff she gripped tightly in her hand. Had she grabbed it in her sleep?

"Are you alright?" Coal asked, breathing heavily. "You scared me there for a minute."

"I ..." she started to say, but she wasn't really sure what he meant.

"You were having some kind of nightmare," he finished the thought for her. The dwarf tugged at the braid in his black beard, eyeing her with concern. "What was that all about?" he asked, nodding to the extinguishing magic from the Staff of Anvelorian.

Ralowyn shook her head. "My dreams are always more vivid when I have not slept in a while."

"I can see that," Coal said sympathetically. "Was it wretchlings?"

"Wolves," she said quietly.

"Wolves?"

"Attacking Merrick and Kippin."

"Oh," Coal said, seeming to understand. "You do know Merrick has killed wolves before?"

"I do."

"And you know he loves that little halfling more than life itself. He'll protect him from anything that comes their way."

"I know," she whispered.

"Well then, see? There's nothing to worry about," he said. Though something in his voice betrayed his confidence and a worried far-off look crossed his face. "Just a bad dream."

Ralowyn gave him a weak smile. She couldn't bring herself to tell him that she wasn't worried about wolves specifically, but rather, losing her future with them.

And that's when she sensed them.

A shrill scream erupted from the edge of the camp.

"Boehlen's Beard," Coal said, grabbing his war hammer and hurrying toward the cry that shattered the night.

Ralowyn passed him, swiftly navigating the tree roots and underbrush. She slid to a halt as she came into a small opening between the trees. A little girl sobbed in her mother's arms.

They were surrounded by wolves.

Chapter Fifteen

Glain's Shoulder

T he ringing of the bell on deck woke Orin in his swaying hammock. He slowly opened his eyes. The knotted wood above him was easy to see. Light poured in from the stairs to the main deck and the few windows on that deck. Orin studied the knots. For some reason, his awakening reminded him of the day he'd woken up in Ellaria's home. There he'd been greeted with fresh tea and Ellaria's kindness. Here he was greeted with the soft—and not so soft—snoring of his crewmates. And yet, somehow, he found a sense of contentment in his surroundings.

Orin made his way to the top deck. The bell toll hadn't been a warning ring, but rather, a signal that they were approaching their destination. Over the months he'd been sailing with the *Sellena*, he'd learned to distinguish the different bell rings. He'd taken a few night shifts at the helm since their departure from Dorantown, opportunities for which he was grateful since he loved to steer the ship.

Though he was tired from those shifts, he didn't want to miss the sight as they arrived at Glain's Shoulder. He'd only seen the dots on the maps, and when wretchlings weren't a pressing concern during the winter, he'd often wondered what it would be like to sail into the other cities of Kelvur.

As he emerged from the belowdecks, he was greeted by a sullen Karnak.

"Good morning." Orin nodded to the orc.

The orc gar grunted.

Orin stepped away, knowing Karnak had been angry since the attack on Dorantown. They all had, though Orin found solace in steering the *Sellena*. While he was still bitterly upset, he was able to work out some of his emotions, finding an odd peace at the helm under the stars.

He moved to the port railing and gawked at the sheer cliffs rising out of the sea. He looked left to right, following the coastline, not finding where there might be a beach or a relief where the city would be.

Orin glanced to the sky. Several griffin riders soared high above. He assumed they were scouting the area in search of Glain's Shoulder, but he wasn't sure what they were going to find. That is, until a strange scar revealed itself on the cliffside as they continued to move slowly south. He hadn't seen it before, but it appeared to be an angular staircase meandering up the sheer face of the cliff.

As his gaze followed the staircase, he realized there were windows cut away, high in the cliffs. From a larger window, a griffin rider emerged and dropped. The griffin's wings opened wide and beat furiously to keep it high above them. He turned to ask Karnak what the Griffin Guard had found but realized Jensen was standing there, staring as well. And to Orin's surprise, so were most of the Talon Squadron members.

The griffin riders flying above them weren't their own.

A deep resonant growl bubbled within Karnak. He'd found it increasingly difficult to tamp down the rage that always burbled just beneath his surface. His upper lip twitched as the ship's boat bounced dangerously in the crashing waves. Cold mist sprayed him, and water droplets clung to the hairs on his muscular green arms as one of the sailors paddled them toward the cliffs.

He felt remorseful for his constant grumpiness with the crew of the *Sellena*, but inside him a tempest raged. Karnak wanted nothing more than to defeat Jaernok Tur and end the threat for good. He'd convinced himself that staying and fighting was the best choice for his family. After all, if the sorcerer were able to get even stronger and bring his wretchling army to Tarrine, they wouldn't stand a chance. But lately, Karnak felt as though they weren't making any progress toward that goal.

Since Jaernok Tur emerged from the Crags with the wretchlings, it seemed that he and the rest of the warriors in Kelvur had only lost ground—first Ventohl, then Dorantown.

If he were really honest, on top of the rage and disappointment in him, was a sprinkle of jealousy. As much as he loved Merrick and Ralowyn, it was hard for him to witness their budding love for each other and the way they'd adopted Kippin as their own. He liked the little halfling, but even though Kippin was several years older, he reminded Karnak of his own son, Gernot.

Karnak had been gone so long. He wondered how big Gernot had gotten. How much had he missed? Would Gernot understand why his father was away, why he couldn't be there with him? Karnak growled at the thought. With all the defeat they'd sustained, he wondered if his reasoning for being in Kelvur was even valid anymore.

Though he'd gotten secondhand information from Lanryn about his family, Karnak wondered how Tanessa was doing.

Tanessa, he thought. *I'm so sorry.* It broke his heart how many times he'd sent that thought across the sea to his lovely wife.

He hated how jealous he was of Merrick. For a second, he wondered if that hatred of his own emotions had amplified the storm within him. Too many thoughts nagged at him.

Maybe if I had been more focused during the winter, we wouldn't have lost Dorantown, he thought. *Maybe we could have killed the dragon.*

Karnak recognized the false self-doubt for what it was. They didn't even know about the dragon until a couple of days before the attack. Still, the doubts jabbed at him.

"You alright?" Orin asked, placing a hand on the orc's thick shoulder.

Karnak realized he was gripping his axe a little too tightly, and he loosened his tense muscles.

"You going to be sick?" Jensen asked.

"I'm fine," Karnak said.

"If you are going to be sick," Captain Tinothe said, "I'd appreciate if you did it outside the boat." He paused with a chuckle and pointed a thumb back to the sailor who was rowing the boat. "Or at least Lonny would. It's him who has to sit down here with it."

"I'm fine," Karnak assured them all, pushing down the boiling rage within. "Really."

As they paddled closer to the cliffs, Jensen tightened his grip on the boat's edge. "Are you sure we won't be smashed on those rocks?" he asked nervously.

"Might be. Might not," Captain Tin said.

Jensen's eyes widened, and he looked to Orin.

The other man laughed and explained, "Tam said he could see calm waters and a small dock next to the bottom of the stairs.

The way the cliffs jut into the water creates a small area that seems safe. Probably why they built that stairway there."

"Aye," Captain Tin affirmed.

The explanation and affirmation seemed to do little to comfort the guardian, but Jensen didn't say anything else.

Karnak watched as their little boat bobbed on another wave and glided into smoother waters. It was a strange sensation, as if they'd passed through some magical barrier. Lonny rowed them between the tall cliffs, skillfully maneuvering their boat next to a dock made of stone. Karnak marveled at the engineering, thinking it must have been carved straight from the cliffs. He wondered how useful it would be during high tides. Then again, they hadn't seen any other vessels on the water. Perhaps it was rarely used.

As they stepped off the boat and onto the stone dock, Karnak's gaze wandered upward. The stairs jutted at strange angles, disappearing behind turns and reappearing around bends higher up. From the bottom, the staircase looked ominous.

Tapping, like the sound of hurried footsteps, echoed above them. The pattering echoes bounced off the walls of the cliffs on either side of them, obviously amplified by the shape. Karnak suddenly realized the waves behind them were quiet.

Magic, he thought, glancing around for traps.

The sound of the steps seemed to be getting closer, so Karnak gripped his axe in both hands, unsure what to expect. He was glad to see that Jensen held his spear warily, and the others also rested their hands on the hilts of their swords. He felt better knowing he wasn't unduly anxious.

A young orc woman rounded the last bit of stairs and stopped. They all stood there, staring at one another in confusion. She was a pretty orc, and the corners of her mouth stretched into a wide grin.

"So, it's true then!" she said triumphantly. "The scouts said there was an orc aboard. Where have you been?"

Something pricked at Karnak's heart. It wasn't a painful prick, more like bursting a bubble. He started to laugh at the sudden realization that he hadn't seen another orc in months—not since he was taken from Calrok by Hazkul Bern and the Sons of Silence. He couldn't explain why he was laughing, but the sight of the young orc and the absurdity of her question had him in stitches.

It wasn't long before Orin and the others started laughing as well. Though the young orc woman didn't seem to get it, the pure and deep laughter rolled over her and instigated her own giggles.

"Where have *you* been?" Karnak asked, wiping tears out of his eyes.

"Come. Come," she said. "My father wishes to speak with you."

They learned that the young orc woman's name was Lenza. She led them up the stairs and through a maze of tunnels that eventually looped back to the staircase. That explained why they couldn't see all the stairs from below. Orin found it a fascinating piece of architectural genius that he had rarely seen.

"Have you ever seen anything like this?" he asked Karnak.

The orc gar smirked. Orin was glad for his reaction. He hadn't seen anything but a grimace on Karnak's face since

Dorantown. "Goblins," Karnak said. "Say what you want about them, but they're fantastic engineers."

"You think goblins engineered this place?"

"Not goblins." Lenza cut into the conversation.

"No?" Karnak asked. "Only engineers I've seen capable of such a thing are goblins." He paused. "Though what I saw of Galium was rather impressive. Dwarves?"

"Dwarves," she affirmed. "Glain's Shoulder was discovered by some of the first dwarves in Kelvur. At first it was just a series of caves and tunnels that opened to the cliffs. They dot the entire Sheer Coast. Farther south, the griffins use the caves for nests and breeding."

"Really?" Orin asked, curious. He couldn't think of any place in Tarrine where griffins were still wild. The Griffin Guard had gotten all their griffins long ago from the dwarves in the hills of Garome during the Second Great Black War.

"Yes," Lenza said with a smile. "Even around the next bend to the south, you would have seen dozens of them on the cliffs."

"I should like to see that if we can," Orin said, sincerely excited.

"Perhaps, after we meet with my father, I can take you down that way."

They rounded another of the myriad stairways, which drew them into a corridor that looked distinctly different from the others. High windows let light fill the hall, and the wall stones were meticulously worked and polished. Orin assumed they must have moved above ground level. He caught a glance of Jensen and Karnak, both awestruck by the beauty of the hall's craftsmanship. Captain Tin puffed away on his pipe, humming softly. His great mustache occasionally popped with his eyebrows as he spotted something of interest.

Orin was more intrigued by the immense tapestries that lined the hall. They depicted scenes much like the ones back home in Whitestone. He didn't recognize any of the events. Back home he knew them all. He could point to any of them and tell the tale of some great warrior of the past. The images before him were completely foreign to him.

He stopped to examine one. It had a large tree woven into the fabric. The tree was beautiful, adorned with flowery blue leaves hanging from drooping branches. Light rays were woven in intricate swirls around it. A single silhouetted figure stood before the tree with a staff in his hand.

"Orin," Karnak called back to him.

The guardian shook his head and hurried to catch up to the group before they exited through another door at the end. They twisted and turned through hallways in a dizzying fashion. Orin had long lost track of their turns and expected he would not be able to lead them back through. He hoped one of the others had a better memory of the route.

They walked along an open hallway, and as Orin peered over the railing, he realized they were several floors up from the ground. The wet grass below shimmered like emeralds with the ever-present mist clouds soaking the blades to a shine. He felt as though they were even higher than they were as wisps of cloud swished by and he glimpsed the sea far below. He wondered where the *Sellena* was. They hadn't been able to see the castle from below, so he doubted they would be able to spot the ship from there.

When they finally arrived at their destination, Orin breathed deeply, inhaling the aroma. Before them sat a table, big enough for twelve, covered in food. Several servants hurriedly placed more platters on the table as an orc stepped forward to greet them.

"Hello," the orc said. He was shorter than Karnak by nearly a whole head and was probably half the large orc gar's weight. "I'm Yenklin."

Orin watched as Karnak placed a large finger to his brow and gave the greeter a slight bow.

"Oh, please," Yenklin said, waving his hands in front of himself. "No need for any of that. It's been some time since we've seen an orc from outside Glain's Shoulder. As you might suspect, we are mighty curious as to why you are here."

He turned with his arm out, indicating the others that were gathered. Orin was stunned to see two men, an elf, a dwarven woman, and a minotaur. They stood anxiously by, waiting for something.

"Well," Orin said with a slight chuckle, "do we have a tale for you."

They ate heartily, their hosts prodding them with questions about Tarrine. Yenklin continued to steer them back to the topic of Jaernok Tur's army in the north, which Karnak appreciated. When the main course was done, the servants brought out a rich brown drink that steamed with an intoxicating aroma.

"What is this?" Jensen asked in surprise.

"Coffee," Lenza said with a snort. She'd picked a seat right next to the handsome guardian, and she seemed to be enjoying his excitement and surprise at all their delectable cuisine. "You don't have coffee in Tarrine?"

"Not in Whitestone," the guardian said. Jensen took another sip, and his eyes lit up again. "This is good. Do you have this in Drelek, Gar Karnak?"

"No," Karnak replied.

"They have it in the southern isles," Captain Tin said. "Know of a dwarven bean brewer on Aleron that makes a killing on the stuff. Might be a good retirement gig," the captain said, sipping his drink, which seemed to perk him up.

"You'll never retire," Orin said to the older man. "You've got the sea in your bones."

"Might be. Might not," the old sea captain said, pulling his pipe from his coat. "Seems you might have the sea in your own bones."

"Might be," Orin said, amused.

"And what are these called again?" Jensen asked, grabbing his fourth helping of a square-shaped treat from a platter.

"Raspberry crumble," Lenza was all too happy to tell him.

"Raspberry crumble," Jensen barely managed to mumble through his bite.

Karnak turned back to Yenklin, who seemed to be pondering something deeply troubling.

Yenklin noticed the orc gar's stare and shifted. "If Jaernok Tur's army is as dangerous as you say—"

"It is; I assure you," Karnak said, setting his mug of coffee on the stone table.

Yenklin nodded. "Then he's a threat to all of Kelvur, not just the north."

"And Tarrine as well."

Yenklin turned to the dwarven woman next to him. She was elderly, and her face wrinkled at him as though she were trying to hear what he was saying. "We'll need to outfit them with more griffins," he said to her.

"Unfortunately, I don't think we have the time it takes to bond a rider and a griffin," Orin said.

"I'm sure they know that. They do ride griffins, too," Jensen pointed out softly.

Orin bobbed his head to the side with an agreeable shrug.

"What do you mean, bond?" the dwarven woman asked.

"It takes years for riders and griffins to train together," Orin explained. "We start training riders at eleven years old and don't pair them with a griffin until they're sixteen. And we pair them with young griffins so the bond will take."

"You do not use magic to speak the words to the beasts?" she asked curiously.

Karnak leaned forward, suddenly very interested in what the elder dwarf had to say. He was no expert in the training practices of the Griffin Guard, but it was a well-known fact that if a griffin lost its rider or a rider lost their griffin, they'd become essentially useless to the Guard, unable to be paired again. Or at least, that's how Karnak understood it.

"We know of no magic to do this," Orin said plainly.

"Do you?" Jensen asked, suddenly less interested in the food before him and more intrigued by the conversation. "I have several guardians who have lost their griffins and have been reassigned to the ground forces. If you could show us such a thing to get them back in the fight ..."

"You mean, you can use magic to pair the beasts with a rider?" Karnak asked the woman to clarify. "Is this something any race can learn to do."

Her wrinkled lips pursed into a slight smile. "Anyone can ride," she said. "Not all can do the magic."

"Dwarven magic," Yenklin cut in.

"Is this something an orc mage could learn?" Karnak asked, thinking of Smarlo. Then he thought of Ralowyn. "Or an elf mage?"

The elderly dwarven woman placed a bony finger to her lips and thought for a moment. "I can teach," she said with a shrug.

"We have several dwarves who know the talent," Yenklin said. "It's always been the dwarves to do it. I guess, I never thought about it much."

The possibilities ran through Karnak's mind—endless possibilities.

"How long does the magic take?" Jenson asked.

"Not long," the dwarven woman said.

"Can you imagine how that would change the way we train?" Jensen mused, hardly able to believe it.

Karnak looked to Orin. The young man sat there with a ponderous look on his face. "Orin?" the orc gar asked.

"What?" he asked, as though the orc had snapped him out of some sort of trance.

"Are you alright?" Karnak asked him.

"I ... yes," he said shortly. "I just never thought I'd get the chance to fly on griffin-back again."

Karnak nodded. In truth, he understood the feeling. Losing Ker had been one of the most painful moments of his life. Still, he felt her loss. A realization struck him. "Wait," he said to the dwarven woman. "Did you say anyone could ride? Even orcs?"

The dwarven woman's wrinkled cheeks reshaped around a thin smile.

CHAPTER SIXTEEN

STRANGE TIMES

Davir flapped his wings as Kippin stepped down from a log. Over the past few days of traipsing through Duskwood, Merrick and the little falconer had been slowly revealing themselves to the grey falcon, getting the bird used to their presence.

The day before was the first time they'd taken Davir out of the cage—leashed, of course. Merrick had shown Kippin how to hold the falcon on his arm, and since then, they'd been taking Davir out of the cage for brief stints on one of their arms. Kippin took a majority of the shifts with the bird, but every once in a while, the little halfling's arm would get exhausted. Davir was going to be a big falcon for the halfling, but neither of them were fully grown, and Kippin's arm would strengthen with time.

While working with a bird again brought some sense of joy to the huntsman, it was hard to feel anything but worry over Ralowyn. Merrick found himself praying to the Maker over her, a habit he did not have previously. When he wasn't thinking of the elf mage, he was thinking of Coal and Karnak or Tanessa.

What must the people back in Tarrine be going through? Merrick thought as he thumbed the Shell of Callencia in his pocket. They hadn't had an update on the happenings in Kelvur since Lanryn fell. What must their allies think?

He retrieved the shell from a deep pocket and held it in his hand, inspecting it for the thousandth time. It seemed such an insignificant trinket, and yet, he knew it was imbued with fantastic magic. He cursed himself again for having no idea how to make it work. Merrick had tried everything he could think of. He tapped it with Lanryn's wand—even balancing it on the tip of the wand. He'd uttered every elvish and dwarvish word he knew, which were few—another shortcoming he cursed himself for. He'd even gotten frustrated and thrown it.

Of course, he immediately regretted his action and ran to find the tool, cleaning the dirt from it and inspecting it for damage. Luckily, it hadn't broken.

Merrick and Kippin had fallen into a good routine over the past few days. Each day, they'd get up and check the snares they'd set the night before. Unfortunately, they'd only caught one more hare since they started on their journey. Merrick was an expert field dresser, though, and rationed portions for each of them from their previous catches. Their bread and apples from Dorantown were long gone.

They spent most of the days trudging along through the dense forest, Merrick always on the lookout for scat or tracks. Much of the time they walked in silence, but if Merrick found something of note, he'd stop their progress to teach Kippin. The halfling himself was a rather adept forager. The day before, he had found them some edible mushrooms—something Merrick would have passed by, unsure of Kelvur's varieties.

"Can we stop?" Kippin asked.

The little halfling had been hustling along, requiring a few steps to every one of the taller huntsman's.

"Sure," Merrick said with compassion. "Why don't we get Davir back in the cage for a little while?"

They did so, offering the bird a bite of rabbit as a reward for good behavior.

"How much farther to the wall city?" the halfling asked, drawing a long swig from his water skin.

"I'm not sure. I've never been there. I suppose when we see a wall, we'll be getting close."

"Then we follow the wall," Kippin repeated the directions Merrick had explained to him numerous times.

"Right," the huntsman affirmed. He'd discussed the plan with the halfling over and over again, making sure that if they were separated for any reason, the halfling knew what to do.

"Why can't we just ride Valurwind again?" the halfling asked.

Merrick sighed. He'd considered the question numerous times himself. The astral falcon certainly could have gotten them to Aiden's Dell faster, but the idea posed several problems. "Because, if we take to the sky, we're much easier for a dragon to spot. Did I tell you about the time Rora was chased by a young dragon?"

"No," Kippin said as he blinked excitedly.

"I'll tell you about it sometime. Let's just say, it was not good. Plus, if we're in the sky, we won't be able to see our friends' tracks if we come across them."

"But couldn't we see them better from high up?"

"No," the huntsman said solemnly. "Most likely, we wouldn't see them through the canopy. And," Merrick elongated the word to emphasize his final point, "it would be rather difficult for us to take Davir along."

Kippin grabbed at the cage. "I don't want to leave Davir!"

"No," Merrick said with a smirk. "Neither do I."

After a long silence between them, the little halfling's stomach growled.

"Is there any more bread?" he asked.

Merrick shook his head with an apologetic grin. Kippin knew the answer to that question, but he still brought it up. They'd finished the bread two days earlier, and the poor halfling's insatiable appetite kept him longing for it.

"I bet the wall city will have mountains of bread. All kinds!" Merrick said enthusiastically. "Warm and delicious. The kind that pulls apart and tastes so good. And I bet they'll have butter. Warm butter, melting inside our bread."

Kippin moaned and laughed. "Stop!"

Merrick ruffled the halfling's curly hair.

"Come on," the huntsman said. "I bet we can get a couple more miles in before we make camp."

Kippin gripped at his hairy toes and nodded his agreement.

They walked another couple of hours before they set up snares and found a place to set a small campfire. They'd lit one every night after the first night, Merrick thinking them far enough away from potential wretchlings but also wanting to protect them from forest beasts. Who knew what might see them as a tasty midnight snack in Duskwood?

That evening, they didn't do much talking. Kippin held Davir as they ate around the campfire—another thing the falcon would have to get used to in order to become a good hunting bird. Eventually, they returned him to his cage and set up their bedrolls for the evening.

While the fire crackled quietly, they closed their eyes and attempted sleep. The sound of quiet sobs from under Kippin's blanket broke Merrick's heart. He wanted to comfort the halfling, tell him everything was going to be alright, but the huntsman wasn't sure himself. Frankly, he'd let plenty of his tears dampen his own bed roll the past few nights, but he was all out of tears.

All he had was a resoluteness steeped in one truth: if Ralowyn was still out there, he would find her. But they had to reach the wall city first.

"Well, what do we have here?" a voice said through the darkness.

Merrick awoke from his light sleep, bewildered at how he hadn't heard anyone approaching. The forest was dark, and the faint orange glow of the dwindling embers of their fire did little to illuminate their surroundings.

"Who goes there?" Merrick asked, sitting up slowly.

"Easy there, friend," the voice said. "I'd rather we didn't have to shoot you and the kid."

"What's going on?" Kippin asked with a yawn and a big stretch as he sat up from his own bedroll.

"Kippin, stop," Merrick said quickly.

"What?" he asked and turned toward Merrick.

"We have ... visitors." The huntsman chose the word, hoping to keep the situation calm.

"Well, isn't that hospitable," the voice said again.

Merrick was more awake and caught what direction the voice came from. Of course, the man to whom the voice belonged was well hidden in the shadows.

"Is there something you need?" Merrick asked, trying to keep his voice even. He slowly worked his fingers over his bow, lying next to his bedroll.

"There are plenty of needs that go unmet in Duskwood," the man said.

The huntsman slowly began to draw an arrow from his quiver.

"Like he said ..." a woman's voice came from nearby. The sounds of leathers stretching and a tightening bow caught Merrick's attention. "We'd prefer not to shoot you and the kid. If it's all the same to you."

Merrick froze. He didn't know what to do. He and Kippin were sitting ducks.

"I think that would be preferable for everyone," Merrick agreed.

"What's it you got in the box under that cloak?" the man's voice asked.

"No!" Kippin cried.

"Kippin! Don't!" Merrick hollered.

The halfling threw himself onto the cloak-covered cage. "I won't let you hurt him."

"I wasn't planning on hurting anyone," the man said. "But who is 'him?'"

"Davir never did anything wrong to nobody!" Kippin said, his voice shaky as he started to cry.

"And who's Davir? You don't have a shadow beast in there do you, boy?"

"What?" Kippin asked.

Merrick's mind raced. *Shadow beast? Does he mean a wretchling?*

"It's a falcon," Merrick blurted. "Go ahead, Kippin. Show him."

"No," the halfling yelled. "You can't hurt him."

Suddenly, a man stepped out of the shadows. He was dressed in a cloak that hid his face and blended in with the night. His bow was lowered, but an arrow was drawn halfway.

"Ven ..." the woman's voice called uncomfortably.

"It's alright," the man said, slowly walking toward the halfling and the cage. The man's voice softened. "If it's really a falcon you've got in there, I don't mean to hurt him."

Kippin hesitated, looking over his shoulder to Merrick. The huntsman couldn't seem to catch his breath, his heart pounding in his chest. He nodded slowly to the halfling, careful not to make any sudden moves that would end up getting himself stuck with an arrow.

The halfling grabbed at the cloak.

"Easy now," the man said, readying his bow.

Merrick wanted to rip the man's arms off and stick him with his own arrow for even pointing it in the direction of the halfling. Though he doubted he'd make it two steps before an arrow downed him. He hated how helpless he felt. All he wanted in the whole world was to protect his little boy.

Kippin pulled the cloak slowly, revealing Davir inside. The falcon chittered and cocked its head several times, clearly confused at the scene.

The man stopped moving and stood straighter, lowering his bow. "Well, isn't he a handsome bird."

"He's mine!" Kippin barked and dove over the cage once more. "I caught him. And he's my best friend. And I won't let you take him."

The man laughed softly, and the woman behind Merrick said, "He's sure a little dragon spit, isn't he?"

She also laughed, and several other chuckles rippled on the outskirts of their little camp.

"Sorry to scare you like that," the woman said. She appeared from behind Merrick, stepping off to the side where he could see her. She also donned a hooded cloak, but she pulled the hood back to show her face. The elven woman gave Merrick a shrug and an apologetic grin and said, "Strange times."

CHAPTER SEVENTEEN

THE FOREST OF WIRRA

Verdant shadows cast by the sun glowing through the leafy canopy during the day replaced the crimson shadows cast by *Menthrora* at night. The Forest of Wirra was an overgrown, tangled mess.

Nera and the chelon traversed the woods slowly, following what they believed to be Shadowpaw's tracks. Occasionally, they'd lose sight of the tracks, and the pair would split up, searching the nearby area in hopes that Shadowpaw had merely jumped and fluttered for a moment before landing again.

There were plenty of tracks to see, however, as the wild forest was well populated by creatures. Unfortunately, that fact made their task all the more difficult. They had no way of knowing if broken tree branches or well-worn game trails led to the lost griffin or not.

The only distinguishable markers they had were the occasional raven-black feathers and talon prints followed closely by large cat-like prints. Nera had seen neither of those markers in several hours. She was pretty sure they'd lost Shadowpaw's trail altogether.

"Nera." Shorlis beckoned to her.

"Yes?" She hurried over, hopeful he'd found something.

"What do you make of this?"

The chelon held his magical staff in front of him. The hardened wood glowed from every grain with a pulse, as though a heart of light beat within it.

Nera shook her head. "I don't understand. What am I looking at? Are you preparing a spell to help us find Shadowpaw?"

She gritted her teeth. Nera had enjoyed getting to know Shorlis better over the winter, but she regretted not spending more time with him while he was training and learning from Ralowyn and Lanryn.

Maybe I would know more about this magic, she bemused.

Something else had always been more pressing. As the commanding guardian in Kelvur, Nera always had something requiring her attention. She wondered about Pernden, not for the first time. He certainly would understand the weightiness of leadership.

In a strange way, even in their dire circumstance, Nera felt a great relief being in the forest with none but Shorlis. The weight and responsibilities she'd managed through the harsh winter were nowhere in sight, and they'd converted to one singular task: find Shadowpaw. There was a simplicity to the immediate challenge.

"No," Shorlis said. "I'm not doing anything. *Menthrora* just started to ... do this."

He held the staff before her. Its normal spiraling grains were beautiful, but she had never seen them glow the way they were. It was a faint glow but noticeable upon inspection.

"Can you feel it?" she asked, again wishing she knew more about the magic. She would have to remedy that when they were back in Dorantown.

I'll make some time with Ralowyn. Maybe she can teach me more about Santoralier, *too,* she thought, rolling the golden spear in her hand. The yellow stone at the center of the spear glinted as a sunbeam snuck through the tree canopy.

"Yes. It's vibrating in soft pulses with the light."

"*Santoralier's* not doing anything weird," she offered. Though she wasn't sure the observation was worth much.

"It feels like *Menthrora* is pulling, almost like it wants us to go that way." He raised the staff and angled the strange swirling top that held the red stone.

"Could it be trying to lead us to Shadowpaw?" Nera asked, suddenly excited.

"I don't know," Shorlis hemmed. "Could be. I don't know what else it would be trying to lead us to." He paused and scratched his spotted bald head. His face scrunched into an apologetic look. "We haven't seen a good sign of her in a few hours ..."

Nera sighed over the lingering concern. He was right, of course. At that point, they were grasping at wisps. Maybe *Menthrora* could help them find Shadowpaw. The guardian stretched her back and twisted from side to side, glancing around the forest in all directions. Frankly, *Menthrora* might be their best hope.

As she turned, she could have sworn she saw a strange-looking man out of the corner of her eye. She gripped her spear in a ready position in front of her as she spun in that direction.

"What is it?" Shorlis asked, readying his own stance and looking around.

"I thought I saw someone," Nera said.

"Where?"

"Just there," she said, nodding in the direction, but she saw nothing, save for the broken remains of a tree.

Am I losing my mind in this forest?

Shorlis waded through the underbrush, slowly approaching the area she'd indicated. *Menthrora's* pinnacle blazed with red faery fire. "There's nothing here," the chelon said, turning his burning red eyes on her. "You sure someone was here?"

"I'm not sure of anything," Nera said softly.

Shorlis eyed her with worry. "Perhaps we should take a break—eat something—before we continue onward."

Great, Nera thought, under his scrutinous gaze. *He thinks I'm losing my mind as well.* But she said, "Perhaps you're right."

Nera followed Shorlis in near silence. They'd been following the pull on *Menthrora* for hours. The chelon meandered slowly.

"The pull is faint," he'd explained. "If I try to focus on it too hard, I lose it."

Nera didn't like the feeling of being held captive to the artifact's whim. What choice did she have? After following the staff for hours, occasionally stopping for Shorlis to refocus—or as he called it, "Let go,"—she began to wonder if they were following the staff to nowhere.

The forest was growing dark as evening approached. Suddenly, Shorlis whipped *Menthrora* to the side, hurtling a fireball toward a bush, which erupted into flame. Nera rolled to the side and was up in a fighting stance, quicker than a great cat.

Shorlis began to laugh. It was a chuckle at first, but soon enough he was laughing heartily.

Nera's heart was pounding in her chest. "What? What is it?" she asked, completely confused.

"Only dinner," the chelon said, swirling the staff in the air and containing the fire.

"Dinner?"

"Boar."

The guardian crept toward the fire. The bush had been reduced to sparks, but where the bush had been lay the searing body of a boar.

"Why didn't you say something," Nera growled. "I thought we were being attacked."

Shorlis laughed even harder. "I didn't want to scare the boar."

"But scaring me into a heart attack ... that's alright?"

The chelon couldn't contain his mirth. He wiped tears from his eyes, and chuckles rolled from him. His turtle face looked so funny to Nera in that moment, that, despite herself, she laughed, too.

"I'm sorry. I'm so sorry," Shorlis said, barely able to catch his breath.

When he drew near to the smoldering boar, Nera punched him in the shoulder.

He took it in stride, not losing his wide grin.

They ate to their filling points, sitting around the actual fire they constructed and basking in its warmth.

"You know, eventually, we're going to have to go back to Aiden's Dell," Nera said in all seriousness.

"True," Shorlis agreed. His wide sea green eyes flickered with the reflection of the campfire. "But we need to find Shadowpaw."

"Oh, I won't leave Shadowpaw out here," Nera said plainly.

"I know."

"But," she continued with some hesitation, "we've been wandering the forest all day. It seems to me we've come no closer to finding her. As far as I can tell, the staff has only guided us deeper into the forest."

"For what, I cannot say," Shorlis said softly. "I know it draws us to something, but I know not what."

"We still have a mission, though," Nera said.

"True, but what if the staff leads us to another way to complete our mission?"

"What do you mean?"

"I mean ..." The chelon hesitated. "What if *Menthrora* knows what we need better than we do?"

"How would it know that?"

"I don't know," Shorlis said quietly.

Nera sighed and leaned back. She froze, seeing what appeared to be a pair of eyes in the darkness. The guardian slowly grabbed her spear. The electrical arcs of energy bounced off *Santoralier* and immediately worked their way up her arm to alight her eyes with a golden glow.

Shorlis noticed her shift and swiped *Menthrora* in the direction of her gaze, lobbing a magic missile. It clattered into a tree with a loud bang and bright red light. They leaped to their feet and ran in the direction of the eyes. There was nothing to be found.

"He was here," Nera said. "Sure as I am now, he was here."

"I believe you," Shorlis said, wafting *Menthrora* to put out the fire behind them. "The question is, where is he now?"

The forest was once again bathed in a crimson glow as the pair followed *Menthrora* onward. There was no discussion about rest; they had neither the nerve nor the inclination for such a thing. They were completely on edge. Whoever was watching them in the forest had expedited their need to find Shadowpaw and leave. Still, the only clue they had on where to go was the prompting of the chelon's magic staff.

Nera followed, close on his heels, her own ability to see in the dark far less than that of the chelon's magically enhanced vision. Unfortunately, he hadn't yet learned how to share that magic—an ability he swore he'd ask Ralowyn about when they returned to Dorantown. Clearly, they both needed lessons with the elf mage.

The guardian grabbed the chelon and pulled him toward a tree. Shorlis let the light of *Menthrora* go out.

"What is it?" he whispered.

She shushed him, angling her head as though it would help her hear something. *What is that?* she thought, then mentally shushed herself.

A distant humming navigated the light breeze through the trees. It came in and out of her hearing as the leaves added their song to the wind. Shorlis turned to her and nodded, indicating he heard it as well.

They inched along, doing their best to step through the forest's duff noiselessly. They moved painstakingly slowly. Nera could feel her pulse in her throat. She did not know what type of creature they approached. Remembering the fear in the voices of the men from Aiden's Dell, she was terrified by the unknown watcher. As she crept along, her skin crawled. She wondered if he was watching her even then.

What if the watcher is in league with the hummer?

Shorlis held out a hand to her as they came to a thick knot of trees. He waved his hands, telling her to stay there while he took a look.

How far they'd come. Nera remembered when they'd first met and she had been protective over him. His reciprocity in that moment was endearing. And, if she were honest with herself, Nera wasn't entirely sure she wasn't losing her mind in the woods. She decided to let the burgeoning mage work his magic while she held back.

Shortly after the chelon disappeared around the trees, the humming stopped. Nera thought her heart might stop, too. She squinted and leaned sideways, as though the act would help her hear what was happening. She heard a distinct clicking like that of a temperamental griffin.

Shadowpaw!

Nera navigated around the trees and saw a small hut with what looked to be a lean-to stable nearby. Perhaps it wasn't an actual stable, but there was Shadowpaw, tied to a post. A small fire burned in front of the hut, but no one was in sight. Nera hurried along the tree line, keeping herself hunched to hide behind the underbrush. She did her best to keep quiet but found herself rushing toward her griffin.

When she approached Shadowpaw, Nera clicked at the griffin from the brush. Shadowpaw looked directly at the bush where the guardian hid.

Yes. Come on, girl. I'm right here.

Shadowpaw chittered the recognizing noise she made whenever Nera arrived.

Yes.

A great clattering rang out from the hut.

Shorlis?

She watched the hut for a long while but saw no movement. Nera realized that may be her only chance to free Shadowpaw and get her away from the hut.

The guardian hurried to the griffin, Shadowpaw clicking happily at her. She shushed the griffin. *Why must I shush everyone?* Shadowpaw stamped at the ground merrily.

"Let's get you into the woods," Nera whispered into the feathers on the side of the griffin's head. Instead, Shadowpaw loped toward the fire, while Nera grabbed at her in horror. A pile of biscuits filled a platter, clearly just baked in the cast iron pot that lay cooling next to it. The aroma struck Nera. They smelled sweet, a nice accent to the scent of the campfire.

"Shadowpaw!" she whispered.

The griffin leaned down and took one of the biscuits in her beak. She threw her head back and downed the thing.

"Shadowpaw!" Nera whispered more fervently.

The griffin ignored her and downed another.

"You may have one too, if you like," a slow steady voice said behind her. The voice was deep and flared with the hint of an accent she'd never heard before.

Nera whirled on the voice, bringing *Santoralier* to bear. Electrical arcs of magic jumped from the spear, landing on the ground nearby.

"I was hoping to have one myself as well," the man said, seemingly unworried by her powerful weapon.

The man that stood before her was not like any she'd ever seen before. He stood taller than most men she knew, and his chiseled face and toned arms made him appear like the statues of heroes of old. Stranger still, his eyes glowed a pale yellow, like the eyes she'd seen in the forest.

"You've been watching us!" she accused. "Tell me why."

"Your griffin was hurt," he said in a smooth tone.

Nera's eyebrows furrowed, and she shook her head. "That doesn't answer my question."

"As you say," he agreed with a nod. "There are many dangers in the Forest of Wirra. Few venture so deep into its embrace."

"What?"

"Perhaps I can explain over some biscuits before there are none left for us?" he suggested, holding an arm out toward Shadowpaw who was in the act of downing another one.

"Shadowpaw! Stop," Nera said to the griffin. Her mind was reeling, confused by Shadowpaw's obvious lack of concern. "Where is Shorlis?"

"You mean the chelon?"

"Yes, I mean the chelon," Nera said, her anger rising. She took a menacing step forward, but the man stayed as cool as ever.

He raised his hand toward the hut without a word, but Nera didn't look. She wasn't going to take her eyes off the man and lose him again.

"What did you do to him?"

"I have done nothing to him. Though, it sounded like he knocked over my pans."

"Nera?" Shorlis said from behind her.

She couldn't help but turn and look. Shorlis stood just outside the door of the hut. He appeared fine, but his gaze was held past her. She whirled back to the man and found him walking toward the fire.

In the light, she saw that he had furled wings protruding from his shoulders. They were stark white with feathers. He patted Shadowpaw on the face, an act that would have gotten many a sharp beak bite. He spoke quietly to her, and the griffin backed away. The man—or not man—stooped and lifted what was left of the platter of biscuits.

"Please," he said, "there is still enough for all of us."

Nera and Shorlis shared a glance as Shadowpaw bounded back to the lean-to and made herself comfortable.

Santoralier lowered in the guardian's hands out of pure confusion. Nera took hesitant steps toward the biscuit bearer.

As she did, she noticed his skin was of an odd color. His skin appeared to have a blue hue.

CHAPTER EIGHTEEN

THE HARBINGER

Pernden's long blond hair whipped in the sea breeze. The sails high above cracked and *thwapped* loudly, a noise he hadn't expected before setting sail.

They'd enjoyed fair winds and run into little issue crossing the sea. The three ships maintained a fine balance amongst them. The *Harbinger* could make great speed on the open sea. The orc captain, Bilktor, made several adjustments along the way so they didn't leave the *Lentoria* and the *Wenli* behind. They were fine vessels in their own rights—some of the finest ever produced in Stalford. But the *Harbinger* was in another class altogether.

Pernden watched the griffin riders off the starboard side. They were taking turns giving the griffins exercise—a tip they'd learned from the *Sellena's* voyage across the Gant Sea.

How he wished they had an update from the Talon Squadron in Kelvur. At that point, they expected the worst. Lanryn would have made contact if he were able. The king tried to remind himself that even if Lanryn was dead or captured, it didn't mean everyone in Dorantown shared the same fate.

Nera, he thought. *Be alright. Whatever's happened. Just ... be alright.*

He inhaled deeply through his nose, breathing in the spray from the ship's bow. The salty smell did little to affect him, but he'd gotten reports from the *Wenli* that several of the guardians from the 5th and 8th Squadrons were "green around the gills." A phrase that the orcs seemed to find very humorous.

Pernden suspected that Commander Fario found the phrase less humorous. The mustached elf had visited the railing numerous times since leaving Kane Harbor. Commander Fario stoically stepped next to the king.

"Commander," Pernden said.

"Hm," Fario grunted his greeting.

"Feeling slightly better today?"

"Hm."

Pernden smirked and turned back toward the view. The great sea's waves rolled, and the *Wenli* sliced through them, keeping pace with the slowed *Harbinger*. Pernden stepped back from the railing and asked, "How are the Riders of Loralith holding up?"

Commander Fario hesitated for a moment before he followed Pernden across the main deck to the port side. "The riders are tough."

Pernden smirked again. That didn't answer his question, but in an odd way, the elf commander's consistent and short responses were comforting to the king. At the very least, they were reliable.

"How is everyone getting along?" Pernden asked. With men, dwarves, and elves all stuck on the *Lentoria* together, he worried that the Loralith elves might have some complaints. There were men that lived in Galium and dwarves that lived in Whitestone, so he wasn't so worried about them. Loralith, however, had few residents of non-elvish heritage.

"Hm," the commander said.

Pernden was getting pretty good at translating Fario's grunts, and he gathered that the elves were fine. They'd probably voiced some minor complaints to the Commander when a rider flew his pegasus over to the *Harbinger* to report. But the elves would stuff them down deep and complain quietly in an effort to keep the peace. Pernden appreciated the effort, knowing it wasn't easy for them.

He watched as several pegasi riders flew maneuvers high above the *Lentoria*. They moved beautifully through the air. Pernden saw dwarves and men on the ship's main deck watching the spectacle themselves.

The other ships would have exercise time for their mounts for another hour or so, and then the *Harbinger* would open up the storage bay and the great wyverns of the Scar Squadron would get their turn. The system had worked for all the days they'd been at sea and there was no sense in changing it. From their estimations and the information they had from the *Sellena's* journey, they guessed they would make landfall in another day or so.

Pernden caught Lehra at the bow of the ship out of the corner of his eye. "Excuse me," he said to Commander Fario.

"Hm," the elf said with a twitch of his big mustache.

Pernden wondered if the elf was waiting for the king to leave so he could vomit over the railing.

"Quite the sight," the king said, walking up next to the woman.

"You see the pattern they fly?" Lehra asked him.

Pernden looked out to the pegasi-riding elves. They flew in a unique formation, zig-zagging between each other.

"Some sort of drill," Pernden remarked.

"Yes," she said. "I'm wondering if we can attempt it. The Scar Squadron, that is." She added the last bit quickly, realizing she may not have been clear.

Pernden chuckled. "I assumed."

"It would be difficult," she continued. "The wyverns don't like flying too close to each other."

"Right," he said, pondering what she'd told him over the past few days. He'd enjoyed the opportunity to speak with her and Jeh of their experiences with the Scar Squadron. The king had been pleasantly surprised at how highly the two spoke of it. To him, it sounded as though they felt as much a part of the squadron as any orc—a good sign for their continuing alliance. "How are the wyverns handling the sailing, by the way?"

"Galbrish doesn't care for being stuck belowdecks. Then again, he's a rather large wyvern. Smart to have the ships rotate the exercise schedule. He's been a bit agitated, and I wouldn't want him to get aggressive with any of the griffins or pegasi."

"No," Pernden agreed. "That would not be helpful."

"Good tip from the crew of the *Sellena*, though."

"Hm," Pernden replied. Maybe Fario was rubbing off on him, but the king was not entirely present for the conversation. The mention of the *Sellena* made his mind shift toward Nera again.

It had been so long since he'd seen her. How he missed her. It wrenched him that she might be out there, scared and alone, not knowing what happened in Dorantown. He imagined she had to know by then. In his heart, he hoped she'd returned from the wall city and maybe they were able to help Dorantown fight off the dragon. Who knew? Without updates from Lanryn, they'd been in the dark.

Even though that concern nagged at him, he could hardly complain about their voyage across the sea. Where the *Sellena* had met storms and sea serpents, the *Harbinger* and the others had met fair winds and smooth sailing. He hoped that luck would continue. Maybe they'd find Nera and the others in Dorantown, waiting to receive them.

"My King?" Lehra said next to him.

"Sorry. What's that?" he asked, not sure what she'd said.

"I asked if you're doing alright. I know you and Captain Nera are close."

"I'm fine," he lied. He hated himself for it, but sometimes it was his responsibility to lie about his own misgivings to keep those under him confident and ready for action. He pressed his lips together in a thin smile. "We'll see what tomorrow brings."

Smarlo winced as the cabin door swung open and banged against the wall. *Lotmeag certainly has a way with entrances,* he mused. The orc mage closed his *Book of Dangerous Secrets.* He rolled his eyes at the fact that he'd come to refer to it in that manner. *Thank you, Deklahn, for that gem.*

"You've not pulled yer nose out of that book since we set sail," the dwarf said, swinging a tray onto the table. He handed one of the mugs of tea to Smarlo and added, "Where'd ye get this cook of yers? I'm not sure what this is, but I like it. Thinking it's something I could bring home to Galium when we're all done out here."

Smarlo snorted and gratefully took a plate from the tray. On it was a cooked yellow half-circle. "We call it an omelet," Smarlo said.

"Is that orcish?"

"As far as I know," Smarlo said with a shrug.

"I like how he puts all the stuff inside the egg. Like this green stuff," Lotmeag said, picking at it with his fork.

"That's spinach."

"Oh," the dwarf said, chewing his bite thoughtfully. "Didn't know I liked spinach."

Smarlo shook his head in amusement. He and Lotmeag had struck up a surprising friendship on the voyage. It didn't hurt that the dwarf brought him food and tea from down below. More than that, Smarlo actually found himself enjoying the dwarf's presence. His entrances could use a little work, but his friendly demeanor and thoughtfulness went a long way toward endearing the dwarf to the orc.

"Find anything useful?" Lotmeag asked through another bite, pointing his fork toward the tome.

"No," Smarlo sighed. He took a sip from his tea and slid the tome between them. He opened it to the page he'd been pondering. An inscription in a language unknown to him scrawled across the page.

While Smarlo couldn't read the words, he was trying to gather what he could from the accompanying illustrations. Whichever Master Mage had written the surrounding pages had also been a good illustrator—his ink drawings were quite beautiful. On that page, were waves and a sea serpent that matched the description Smarlo had gotten from Lanryn when the elf described the *Sellena's* encounter.

Smarlo hoped the page described the Gant Sea. Perhaps the old master that wrote the pages had ventured to Kelvur, but Smarlo found nothing in the writing to indicate that. Some of the notes on the edges were written in orcish—another master trying to decipher the old script.

"Pretty pictures," Lotmeag said.

"They really are," Smarlo agreed. "I was hoping these pages had something to do with Kelvur, but I don't know the language."

"Don't recognize it myself. Looks old," the dwarf said.

"It is. And then there's this page," Smarlo said, turning the ancient tinted pages until he found the one he was looking for.

"This one speaks about what the author called colossal dragons, which I think is what he translated from the original word instead of monolith dragons."

"Ah," Lotmeag said with a nod. "Does it tell ye how to kill one?"

"Well, not that I can tell." Smarlo deflated.

"Pity. Would have been a mighty good piece of information if the sorcerer is in league with one. And what about this book ye've been scribbling in?" Lotmeag asked as he grabbed the smaller leather-bound book from the table.

Smarlo snatched it away and said, "It's nothing."

"Nothing?" The dwarf said, eyeing him. "I thought us to be better friends than that."

The orc mage sighed. His eyes flicked between the dwarf and the notebook in his hands. After a long stare from Lotmeag, Smarlo relented. "It's just some notes I've been taking. Some things about the journey. Some things that shouldn't be forgotten. The thing we're doing is an historical event. It should be chronicled."

Lotmeag pursed his lips and scratched at his big brown beard. "I suppose that makes sense. And ye fancy yerself the writer to author the thing?"

"I ..." Smarlo wasn't sure how to answer the dwarf. He believed someone should chronicle the events, but maybe he wasn't the best one for the task. Maybe there was someone who could marry words with skillful illustrations like those in his *Book of Dangerous Secrets.*

"I think ye are," said the dwarf at length, taking a big swig of his own tea. "Who better?"

Smarlo still didn't know what to say. Lotmeag's kind words had shocked him into silence. Perhaps the dwarf was an even better friend than Smarlo believed.

"Thank you," the orc mage said finally.

"Aye," the dwarf said and turned an upraised eyebrow toward the orc. "Did ye get the part about my glorious beard just right? When they make paintings about the heroes of the *Harbinger*, I want them to capture it properly!"

Smarlo laughed and assured him that he'd describe the foredwarf's beard in all its splendor.

Heroes of the Harbinger, he thought. *Not a bad title.*

When the bells rang the next day, dozens of crew and riders made their way to the main deck to get their first glimpse of the land beyond the sea.

As planned, the *Harbinger* broke off from the other ships, leaving them far from shore. Captain Bilktor issued commands to the crew, and Pernden watched the efficient orcs work the pulleys and lines to cover the ship in the painted blue sails. As they went up, the king was fascinated by the way they shimmered.

"Rather impressive magic," Smarlo said next to the man.

"Rather," Pernden said, nodding his agreement as he looked at the intricate sail and rope work above him. "Brilliant craftsmanship. It must have taken a lot to plan out that mess of lines without getting things tangled."

"Agreed."

Pernden looked to the bow of the ship, surprised at how well they could still see the fore area.

"How many wyverns are we sending?" Pernden asked.

"Just two," Smarlo said.

"Good. Send too many, and they'll know we have an army coming."

"Right," the orc mage agreed. "But we want to make sure they can search the area quickly. Figured two sets of eyes are better than one."

"Makes sense to me," Pernden said.

Porg stepped up next to Pernden's other side and asked, "What do you think we're going to find out there?"

The question stung Pernden like a thorn, and for some reason he didn't want to answer. Perhaps he was afraid of the answer. Thankfully, Smarlo responded to the orc craftsman's inquiry.

"Hopefully, we'll find our friends."

Porg nodded silently, gripping the railing and leaning to see between two of the stealth sails.

Captain Bilktor hollered more commands from the sterncastle, and the orcs busily ran to the proper lines, pulling rope and drawing the wind sails in tight. The *Harbinger* noticeably slowed, and several sailors worked the storage bay doors, sliding them open. Others ushered curious onlookers, trying to spot their first glance of Kelvur, out of the way.

Two wyverns crawled out of the bowels of the ship like spiders from a hole. When Pernden first saw the creatures clambering out of the hold, he thought the sight creepy and ominous. Having seen it many more times on the voyage, he was more accustomed to the startling way the wyverns moved. An orc rider sat atop each, and the wyverns ambled over to the railings on the starboard and port sides. They kept low on their two legs and the claws on their wings to stay under the vast network of ropes and pulleys.

Pernden watched as Smarlo placed a finger to his brow and bowed to one of the riders. Belguv returned the gesture, and the two wyverns leaped from the edge of the ship, beating their wings hard to gain altitude. The king tapped his fingers nervously on the wooden railing as the pair of wyvern riders flew toward Kelvur.

Porg placed his large hand on Pernden's shoulder. "I'm sure she's alright," he said calmly. "I remember her to be a fierce woman. Would give even the toughest orc woman a run for her worth."

Pernden gave the orc a weak smile. "I'm sure you're right," he said, though inside, he was sick with dread.

Belguv and Tark were gone for what seemed like hours. Smarlo rubbed at his temples and his strained eyes. He'd hardly looked away from the land in the distance. He could see the wyverns floating and dipping and diving to the ground. If they had found enemies, the riders would have flown back immediately. The fact that they hadn't was good news. Their delayed return was the unnerving part. Smarlo assumed if they'd found their allies, the pair would have hurried back and given them the all clear.

"Did you give them a set time to be back for reporting?" Lehra asked, suddenly appearing next to the orc mage.

"I didn't," Smarlo replied with regret. He scratched at his half-ear.

"You shouldn't scratch," Lehra said, not even looking at the orc.

Smarlo stopped and eyed her. The woman's honey brown hair was done in a braid, the tip of which flopped in the wind.

She was shorter than he and had the lean build of a trained warrior.

Who is this woman? Smarlo wondered. He had come to know her well over the winter months, but recently there was something … else between them. Something unspoken.

"I have some salve," he said stupidly.

"You should probably use it," she said with a smile, turning her large nut-brown eyes on him.

He stared at her, feeling as though he'd forgotten how to say anything intelligent.

"I can grab it for you, if you'd like," she said awkwardly under his gaze. "Where did you leave it?"

"I … no," he said quickly.

She eyed him, her eyebrows high on her lovely face.

"I mean, it's fine," he stammered. "I can put it on later. I'm just nervous about what's going on out there." He waved toward Kelvur, hoping to shift her gaze onto anywhere but him.

"I know what you mean," she said, leaning onto the railing and peering over the water. "I'm not worried about the battle. I'm just worried about some of my friends. I mean, I knew many of the Talon Squadron well. I can't imagine what King Pernden is going through."

"My best friend is out there," Smarlo said quietly. Then he thought of Tanessa back in Calrok. "Well, one of my best friends."

"Gar Karnak, right? The others have mentioned how close you two are."

"We grew up together," Smarlo said with a nod. "It was always the two of us getting into trouble. Karnak was the son of Gar Plak, and I was the weird orc boy training with the Master Mage."

"Your parents left you?" Lehra asked, turning to him and placing a soft hand on top of his, resting on the railing.

The soft white skin of her hand was stark in contrast to the green of his own. A warmth crept up through his body from his legs.

"Well," Smarlo hemmed, trying not to say something dumb. "I was chosen at a young age. Master Tan-Kro told me my parents brought me to the mage library because I was showing odd behaviors, and he recognized it as a propensity toward magic."

"That must have been hard."

"Not really," the orc mage said. "Master Tan-Kro took great care of me, and Karnak never treated me any differently. He was just ... my friend."

"And you've been a great friend to him. The others told me how much you've done to care for his family while he's been away."

Smarlo paused at her words. In truth, he felt as though he'd gotten as much—if not more—out of his nightly visits with them than they did. Perhaps he was learning that he needed more than just books. Maybe he needed a family of his own someday. His eyes fell on the woman holding his hand.

He pulled his hand away awkwardly. He immediately regretted it, wishing for her touch again. *You fool,* he chastised himself. *How can you think of such a thing at a time like this?*

"I'm sorry," Lehra said. "I didn't mean to ..."

He really felt like a fool.

"No," he said, starting to scratch at the scar on his ear again. "You didn't ... I mean, I was ..."

"They're coming back!" someone yelled from high in the fighting top.

Smarlo whirled to see Belguv and Tark flying back toward the *Harbinger*. Lehra gave him a nervous glance, and Smarlo steeled himself for whatever news they bore.

CHAPTER NINETEEN

ESCAPE TO LAST LAKE

A deep resonant sigh escaped Garron as he leaned against the stone wall of their cell. The stay in the dungeons of Tamaria was not quite as nice as his stint in those of Whitestone. In fairness, there was a distinct circumstance of nepotism while he was imprisoned in Whitestone. No such luxuries existed here.

"What are we still doing here?" Ellaria asked bluntly.

They'd been in the musty cell for two nights and days. Garron couldn't blame her for her frustration. The situation grated on him as well.

"We have to trust Kaelor," he said with another sigh.

"And why's that?" Ellaria barked. "We've been in here for two nights already, and he hasn't come back. I don't know about you, but I don't plan on spending another night in this squalor. Me parents are probably worried sick over us."

"We have to trust Kaelor," Garron repeated.

Ellaria huffed a growl and threw her hands in the air. Water dripped slowly from the corner of the cell, and the dark was nearly complete with the torches yet to be lit for the evening. The small window outside their cell glowed with the last light of day, only a deep navy blue left in the sky.

Ezel's eyes and hands glowed blue so the others could see them while he signed, *"Why* do *we have to trust the elf?"*

Garron hesitated. When Kaelor escorted them to the dungeons, Garron had seen in the elf's eyes that he was going to do what he could to help them. But the voice ... the voice said, "Trust." How could he explain that to them without them thinking him a lunatic?

"Ellaria and I could break us out of here," Ezel signed, a blue fireball forming in his little gnomish hand.

"Easily," Ellaria said, her own eyes lighting with emerald power.

"Wait," Garron said.

"What are we waiting for?" Ellaria growled again, extinguishing the lights in her eyes.

"Just give him one more night," Garron said quickly.

"What aren't you telling us?" Ellaria's face scrunched with disappointment.

"I ..." he hemmed.

"Garron," Ezel signed, *"you know we've always got your back. What is it?"*

In that moment, the man had a choice. He believed the deep gnome meant what he said, but Garron couldn't understand why. He'd betrayed his own people, the ones he'd bled with for years. Why did they think he wouldn't do the same to them? How could they put so much trust in him? Would they if he told them he was hearing a voice again?

"I've been ... dreaming in Nari," Garron said. "We have to go to the desert."

"What?" Ellaria was about done with the conversation and almost to her breaking point.

"I already told Ezel, but I've been dreaming in Nari."

"What does that even mean? Can you dream in another language?" she asked the second question to Ezel.

The deep gnome shrugged and signed, *"I'm not entirely sure, but he could be. I dream in a few different languages, but they're languages I learned in due course."*

"I am," Garron said aloud.

Ezel raised his hands before himself in apology. *"All I'm saying is that I don't know how."*

"We need to go to the Nari Desert," Garron said with more conviction.

"What?" Ellaria threw her hands in the air again. "What are you even talking about?"

"There's something out there. It's calling to me. I think it's important."

"And you knew about this?" Ellaria turned on Ezel.

"I said we'd go to the Nari Desert after we finished here in Tamaria," he signed quickly.

"Oh, right. Perfectly logical. Come down to Tamaria. Speak to the lard of the keep. Maybe make a day trip down to the Nari Desert. And neither of you knotheads thought to tell me? I hate to be the one to point out the obvious, but we're not going to make it to the Nari Desert anytime soon while we're stuck in this dungeon." She paused and turned back to Garron. "And what do you mean, 'it's calling' you?"

Ezel also seemed curious about the notion, and the gnome inclined his head and eyed the man.

"I—"

"Supper time," the jailer said, clanging a tin cup against its matching plate as he came into the hallway. His grey hair fell to his shoulders, and his fat cheeks creased into a broad smile. The jailer clearly enjoyed his leisurely assignment. "Got fresh bread for you. Special request from the king's aide, himself. I took the liberty of ... taste testing it ... and the ... the ... the ..." The guard made a funny face. His words slurred, "Whay in finlesian ..."

The large man swayed before he slammed to the floor, the plate and cup clattering away. Garron and the others stared in horror, not understanding what just happened.

Suddenly, a cloaked figure slipped into the hallway, stepping around the jailer's great girth and plucking the keys from his belt.

"Hurry," the figure said. "He made more noise than I was hoping."

Garron leaped to his feet and met the others as the cell door squealed open. The jailer hadn't gotten to light the torches yet, a task he normally did after passing out dinner. Ezel lit up his hands to see the cloaked man and discovered the king's aide.

"I apologize it took me so long," Kaelor said, nodding to them with a sorrowful look on his face. "We must hurry."

"Eh, Lorenso! You alright in there?" a voice called from the next corridor.

Kaelor ushered them to a shadowy alcove nearby and quickly removed his hood, just as another guard came into the hallway.

Garron and the others watched in silence as the young guard said, "Oh no! What happened to Lorenso?"

"Travish!" Kaelor said. Garron thought the elf sounded surprised to see the young man. Kaelor straightened himself and asked, "What are you doing down here?"

"Oh, well," the young man twitched with embarrassment, "I got reassigned down here. Captain said it was because King Hugen didn't want any of your known friends to be on watchtower duty anymore on account of you being relieved of duty and all."

"Travish," Kaelor said, his tone softer. "I'm so sorry. I never expected him to take it out on you."

"Ah, it's nothing. I 'spect Lorenso will see how hard I work and I'll get moved to day shift in no time. Speakin' of, is he alright?"

Kaelor leaned down and patted the jailer on his round back. "I think he had a little too much to drink," the elf said, tipping his hand like a bottle toward his lips.

"I heard he's bad about that," Travish said solemnly. Then he looked back to Kaelor with a curious look on his face. "Wait. What are *you* doing down here?"

Kaelor stood rigid again to face the young man.

Travish's eyes moved toward the empty cell before widening. "And where are the prisoners?" he exclaimed.

"I'm sorry, Travish," Kaelor said, pulling his sword from its sheath.

Travish did the same, but the young guard hesitated. Kaelor slapped the sword right out of the young man's hand and brought the pommel of his own down on Travish's head, knocking him unconscious.

"Sorry, Travish," Kaelor said again as he checked the next corridor. He called back to the others, "Come on!"

They ran through the underbelly of the Flag Keep, the former king's aide leading them with ease. They heard several guards down a side passage and backtracked to a different corridor. To Garron, they all looked the same—a dingy maze of stone walls.

"This way," Kaelor whispered to them.

They hurried up a set of stairs that brought them to the ground level. Kaelor led them through several more elegantly designed and decorated rooms. Ellaria grabbed one of the flags from the wall and tucked it into her leather belt. Ezel gave her a look.

"What?" she said with a grin. "He'll be looking for that one for weeks."

Garron shook his head. He was glad to see her spirits were back up but didn't think they had time for such antics.

Suddenly, an alarm sounded and was echoed by several other horn blows around the keep. Garron knew they no longer had time for any kind of antics.

"Hurry!" Kaelor shouted. "They know you're gone now!"

They rushed through another room and out to a side corridor that opened up to the night. It was dark, but the garden was lit by the moonlight, painting it in a silver glow. Kaelor led them through a number of twists and turns around brilliantly arranged flower boxes and sculpted bushes, before bringing them to an area with tall trees.

"Silverwing!" Ellaria said excitedly.

The griffin stood anxiously beside Benley, the pegasus, who was tied to a tree.

"How in Finlestia did you get him to come with you?" she asked.

"I didn't," Kaelor said quickly. "He wanted nothing to do with me. I only brought the pegasus. The griffin must have come to find him."

"Oh, you silly boy," Ellaria said, ruffling the griffin's face feathers.

"You have to go now," Kaelor said, the sound of voices growing closer.

"Come with us," Garron said fervently, untying Benley. "They're going to know it was you who freed us. You'll rot for it."

"I can't go to Whitestone," the elf said quickly.

"We're not going to Whitestone."

Kaelor looked to Ellaria and Ezel, surprised by the man's words.

"We're going to the Nari Desert," the woman said with a sigh.

"The Nari Desert?"

"Hop on," Garron said, quickly mounting the pegasus. "Ezel can ride with Ellaria."

Kaelor hesitated for only a moment longer, and guards came into view down one of the paths.

"There they are!" one of them shouted.

"Come on!" Garron beckoned and helped the elf up behind him.

Silverwing took off immediately, while Garron kicked Benley into a gallop straight at the running guards. The pegasus opened his wings and flapped them, his legs running through the air as they left the ground. A couple of the guards took swinging swipes at Benley's hooves, but most of them dove to the ground to avoid getting kicked.

"Haha!" Kaelor laughed aloud. "I wasn't sure we were going to make it!" he shouted over the wind in his pointed ears.

They flew higher into the night sky, catching up with Silverwing and the others. The griffin and the pegasus flew calmly near each other, beating their wings in smooth rhythm to keep themselves high in the moon's glow.

"So, south then?" Ellaria shouted over to them.

"Follow the river to Last Lake," Kaelor said to Garron.

"Last Lake?" the man asked.

"Yes," the elf continued. "You'll need some supplies before going into the desert, and I've got a place we can stay for the night."

Garron relayed the message to Ellaria and Ezel, and they soared through the night, following the silvery snake of the Palori River far below.

When they landed in Last Lake, the night was late and the moon was high. Kaelor directed them into a paddock on the edge of town that was fenced for horses. Garron didn't see any horses but assumed that Kaelor knew the owners. They dismounted Benley, and Kaelor led the group to the stables. The elf didn't hesitate and seemed to know exactly where everything was. He'd obviously been there before.

The stables were clean, and judging by the fact that there were no horses or hay, Garron assumed they hadn't been used in some time.

"We'll get some apples for Benley from the house," Kaelor said, fondly petting the pegasus on the neck. He eyed Silverwing as Ellaria brought the griffin into the stable.

"Silverwing would prefer some meat if you have some," Garron said.

Kaelor clicked his tongue and said, "We'll have to see what she has."

"She?" Garron asked.

"My mother," the elf replied as he strode out into the unkempt field.

As Garron stepped through the long grass sprouting between old crusted stalks, he guessed no one had worked the field since it last had livestock. He wondered about Kaelor's mother. He'd not seen many elderly elves in his life, though he wasn't sure if he'd be able to tell. Elves did have a tendency to live for a couple thousand years and always had a youthful look to them. At least, that had always been his experience with the fair folk.

He followed Kaelor at a bit of a distance until Ellaria and Ezel caught up with him.

"So, who are we visiting in the wee hours of the night?" Ellaria asked quietly.

"Kaelor's mother," Garron replied.

Ellaria stopped, mock shock on her face. "I should like to meet this woman," she said and hurried past the man.

Ezel shrugged and followed along.

They quietly entered the house, Kaelor holding up a finger to his mouth, insisting on their silence. He waved a hand over a living area with a lounger and a chair as though the others should make themselves comfortable there. The elf crept away through the dark house and returned moments later with some knit blankets and pillows.

"You all can sleep here tonight," he whispered. "I'll see you in the morning, and we'll get some supplies for your journey."

"What about your mother?" Garron asked. "We won't frighten her?"

Kaelor huffed a chuckle. "If you do, I promise you'll be the more frightened."

The elf spun and strode back into the dark hallway. His menacing words lingered with Garron as the man drifted off. How could an elderly elven woman be more frightening than a bunch of strangers sleeping in her house?

Garron's nose breathed in the delicious scent of sizzling bacon and eggs. The morning light warmed his face, and his eyelids were a bright pinky orange. He smiled at the crackling sound of the bacon in the pan and opened his eyes.

Two enormous eyes stared back at him, only inches from his face.

"Ah!" Garron cried out.

"You say he's the son of King Farrin?" an elderly dwarven woman asked incredulously. She was round with a grey mop of hair on her head. She wore great round spectacles that magnified her eyes, making her look insect-like. "I don't see it."

Garron clutched at his chest, trying to slow his heart. Ezel sat at a table nearby, laughing through his mouthful of bacon.

"You don't see much at all nowadays, Mother," Kaelor said from the kitchen.

The dwarven woman climbed onto the sofa to eye Garron again. She grabbed the man by the front of his shirt and pulled him closer. She licked her hands and brushed at his shoulder-length brown hair, pushing it behind his ears. Finally, she slapped her thick dwarven hands on his cheeks and pulled him close.

"There it is," she said, calling over to Kaelor. "I see it now. Spittin' image. Just like your father, deary."

Garron blinked a few times, still not sure he was awake. Then he asked, "You knew my father?"

"No." She waved the notion away as though it were the silliest question she'd ever heard. "Yer father never came to Last Lake. I met one of your great, great, great—" She paused. "Well, I don't remember how many greats. But one of your great grandfathers, Laigon, and I never forget a face, mind you. I met him the same time I met Kaelor's father," she said, her face wrinkling into a grin, "and his lovely mother."

"I thought you were his mother," Garron said, though as the words slipped out, he wished he could take them back. Maybe his brain was still asleep. *How could a dwarf be an elf's mother?*

"Ha!" the old dwarf barked a laugh. "That I am. That I am."

Garron was dumbstruck. He felt as though he'd really lost his mind.

"King Garro—sorry." Kaelor cleared his throat. "Garron, please meet my mother, Inga. She's the one who raised me when my parents left for the Nari Desert on an expedition. The same one that brought your ancestor King Laigon to Last Lake. Apparently, there was much pomp and dazzle. The whole city of Last Lake was abuzz."

"Aye, that it was," Inga said with starry eyes. "I remember the envoy. I was a young dwarf then—only ninety-two." She primmed the mop of white hair on her head.

"How long ago was that?" Garron asked. He'd been taught to know his family line, but keeping track of years was hard for him as a child. He remembered King Laigon from the list but couldn't remember when his ancestor had lived.

"Two hundred thirty-eight years," she said.

"So, you're ..." Garron struggled to do the math in his head.

"Three hundred thirty this summer!" she said with enthusiasm. "And don't look a day over two hundred fifty."

Garron wasn't sure he agreed, but her gusto made him smile.

"You hungry?" Kaelor asked, dishing some bacon onto a plate.

"Yes. Thank you."

Inga let Garron up and scuttled around the couch to the table. Garron stood and stretched, feeling several relieving pops in his back. He twisted his trunk a few times to warm up his muscles. As he did, he noticed the three sets of armor along the wall.

Kaelor's armor was pristine. It shone in the morning light, each piece set in order and standing ready. Everything was placed with such care. Garron thought if he took a ruler to the gear, he'd find it all to be perfectly and symmetrically placed. By comparison, his and Ellaria's looked like heaps of metal.

Ellaria's bore the crest of Whitestone as all guardian armor did. He remembered her telling him that it felt cumbersome at first. She had been so used to wearing light leather armor. She'd eventually adjusted to the layered metal armor that all guardians wore. The armor was well-designed for flying and fighting on griffin-back.

His own was much like hers, but it lacked the customary crest. His almost looked plain. The darker metal seemed sad somehow, as if it were missing something.

Suddenly, the front door swung open. Ellaria strode through the doorway. Her wild red hair cascaded over her shoulder and burned bright in the morning light. For the second time that morning, Garron's heart almost stopped.

Her emerald eyes fell on him. "Well, look who's up and at 'em this morning," she teased.

Garron chuckled. "Good morning."

"Good morning," she said with a smirk. "I let Benley out of the stable. Thought he might like to graze some of the field you got there, Inga."

"Thank you, deary. He can have the whole field if he likes. The long grass attracts nibblers. Come have some bacon. My boy is quite the chef!" she exclaimed.

"It is just bacon, Mother," Kaelor said. Garron thought it humorous how the regal elf flushed under his mother's doting.

"Well, you'll have to find a new job after that sloth of a no good, big breeches, knothead, bull nosed, bumble-brained—"

"Alright." Kaelor waved a fork in the air. "We get it. He is the worst king."

"He never appreciated ye for all yer hard work."

"No. He didn't," Kaelor shrugged. "But his father was a good king, and I had hoped Hugen would eventually follow in his footsteps."

"Fat chance of that," Inga grumbled, stuffing a bite of eggs in her mouth.

Garron joined them at the table. He took a bite of the eggs and found them to be overcooked, and the bacon was a little crunchier than he thought it should be. He didn't say anything, of course. He merely ate it, knowing he'd need the energy. At the same time, he didn't think Kaelor's future rested in the restaurant business.

"You could always come with us," Garron suggested. "I'm not sure what we're heading into, but I, for one, wouldn't mind the extra help."

"And where is it ye all are headed?" Inga asked.

The question struck Garron as odd. *Have none of you told her our plans?* he thought, glancing around to the others.

The look on Kaelor's face and the slight shake of his head answered that question.

"Well?" Inga said, tapping her fork lightly on her plate.

"I ..." Garron tried to come up with something—anything—but he couldn't seem to lie to the little old dwarf. "The Nari Desert."

"No way my boy is going to that place," she said quickly.

Kaelor put his face in his hand and ran his fingers through his black hair.

"Nothing but death and dehydration out there," Inga continued.

"People have been going out to the desert for hundreds of years, Mother," Kaelor said, rolling his eyes.

"Hunting narilope on the edge of the desert is one thing. Is that the plan?" Garron's hesitation was all she needed to continue her chastisement. "No, of course not. You're going out there to find the great hidden treasures Kaelor's parents went to find." She sniffed, and her chin began to quiver. "Nothing but death out there."

"What treasure?" Garron asked, suddenly very curious about the expedition. "What did they think was out there?"

"Bah!" she said, waving a hand high. "Kel Joran was a fool ... a handsome fool—where Kaelor gets some of his looks and his black hair. Oh, but his mother was a right beauty. Her hair was silver like the moonlight. Most beautiful elf I ever saw. I remember when she and I met."

"Wait," Garron stopped her. "Kel Joran was Kaelor's father?"

"Aye, that he was. The envoy was in town, preparing for their journey into the Nari Desert. It was a big to-do. King Solorin of Loralith and King Laigon of Whitestone were both here. Said the envoy would be searching for an ancient magic—one that could change the course of history. It was all so dangerous and exciting. But not for her. Aelwyth was so worried. She'd left her daughter in Loralith already, and she was trying to ween her baby boy so she didn't have to bring him to the desert. She was afraid they may never come home."

"That must have been terrible for her," Ellaria said sadly.

"Aye. I asked her, why did she have to go. Said she had a way about feeling things. Magic type things. Things normal folk can't sense. The expedition needed her abilities to find what they were seeking. It was dreadful. I told her I could take the child. I could keep Kaelor safe. Herol—Maker, rest him—and I had goats then, and the babe would do fine on goat's milk. I remember, her tears glistened like starlight." Inga choked on the last few words, the memory working her up.

"Mother," Kaelor said softly. He stood and walked around the table to embrace her. "It's alright."

"No, it's not. What kind of dwarf would I be if I let Aelwyth's son go into that desert after she left him in my care to protect him from that very fate?"

The elf sighed and gave Garron an apologetic glance.

"I'm sorry," Garron said to Inga. "I didn't mean to upset you."

"No harm, young man. No harm." Inga sniffed, wiping away her tears.

"Perhaps we should go," Garron continued. "Maybe you can point us in the direction of the market where we can get supplies?"

"Nonsense," Inga said. "Finish breakfast, and we'll all go. My boy hasn't taken me to the market in a long time. I should greatly like Malinda to see how strong he is now. Always said he was too skinny. Old bat has worse eyes than me."

Garron met Ezel's gaze across the table. The little gnome's large eyes narrowed in thought. Garron wasn't exactly excited about what Inga had shared either. What were they getting themselves into?

Did the envoy have flying beasts? He didn't recall that from *The Lost Notes on Nari.* Perhaps he and his companions had an advantage on Kel Joran's expedition. Frankly, he couldn't recall any mention in any book of a group flying over the great desert. Unfortunately, his lack of recollection about any note on such a detail did little to comfort him.

CHAPTER TWENTY

REFUGEES

Ralowyn couldn't meet Coal's gaze as they walked through the woods, following the great wall of the Palisade. The dwarf had been watching her closely ever since the night the wolves attacked. She couldn't blame him. She was probably more worried about herself than he was. They'd spoken little of the incident, but she couldn't stop replaying it in her head. Something about that night stuck with her like a burr in her cloak.

When Ralowyn saw the wolves surrounding the little girl and her mother, the elf had lost it. She reached into the power of the Staff of Anvelorian and, without hesitation, ripped one of the wolves to shreds.

The scene was horrifying. The wolf squelched as it went from a living creature to a mist that fertilized the forest floor. The other wolves bounced back in shock at the loss of their brother and high-tailed it out of there, whimpering as they fled.

Ralowyn's heart was broken. Silently, she debated for two days if that was who she was. She knew it wasn't. She'd gotten herself and others out of plenty of dangerous circumstances with wild animals. She could have used her empathic abilities to calm the wolves and send them on their way, but in the moment, she'd been overcome by emotion.

It was that blasted dream.

It had gotten under her skin, and she was afraid. Afraid of losing Kippin. Afraid of losing Merrick. Afraid of losing their future together. But Merrick and Kippin had been nowhere near the situation. While a woman and her daughter had been in danger, she could have resolved their situation differently. Now, she was afraid of what she would become.

Ralowyn's shoulders slumped, and she let out a heavy sigh, shaking her head.

"You alright?" Coal asked. "That was a big sigh."

"I am fine," she said, regretting the loud exhale.

"You've been awfully quiet the last couple days," he prodded gently.

Ralowyn smirked at him. "I was quiet in Elderwood Forest for forty years."

"Aye," he said with a grin. "Suppose you got plenty of practice to go longer than a couple days."

She raised an eyebrow and gave him a sideways nod in response.

The dwarf laughed. "Fine. Fine," he said. "But you were also alone then. Now, you're not."

Ralowyn sighed again and eyed the dwarf. Coal was careful not to look at her directly as he walked along. His short stature was not indicative of his big heart. The elf shook her head again, amused, knowing he was doing his best to open the door for her to speak.

Coal shrugged, still not looking at her, and said, "The wolves really seemed to rattle you. Seems to me you could use a kind ear."

Knowing he wouldn't let her stew on it forever, she relented. "The dream scared me."

"Aye, it was a mighty frightful one. I could see that with the way you were kicking."

"And it was not just the wolves."

"No?" the dwarf asked, chancing a glance at her.

"No." She hesitated. "It was Merrick and Kippin. It was our life. I saw a future for us, something I have dreamt of for months now. And it was dashed away."

Coal pulled at the braid in his beard as he took in her honesty. "You know, when I sold the *Lady Leila* ... She was my boat. She was a beauty. Ezel and I paddled her up and down the Palori River delivering goods and toting good folk. Anyway, when I sold her, I thought it was the end of a dream. Funny enough, dreams can change."

"Not this dream," Ralowyn said quietly.

"No," Coal agreed. "See, my dream was of a kind of life, filled with friends and folk who love me. Turns out, it was never about the boat at all. Seems to me, most of us hope and dream for the same things. Mind you, it varies, but we all want to be loved."

Ralowyn nodded along.

"Worrying about losing something like that is a battle we all face," he continued. "We can't give in to worry. Otherwise, we live in fear. We can't do that, because that's not living at all."

"Fear is what made me do that ... to that poor wolf," Ralowyn said. Her nose prickled, and her eyes welled with tears.

"I know it, lass," Coal said, gripping her slender hand in his own. "Fear has a nasty habit of tricking us into doing the wrong thing when, if we were patient, we often would have found there was nothing to fear in the first place."

He stroked his beard, nodding his head at the notion, obviously thinking himself rather wise in that moment.

Ralowyn squeezed the dwarf's hand as she blinked away the tears. "Thank you," she said quietly.

"Aye," Coal said. "Any time."

Ralowyn took his words as a promise. She knew he meant them. He would be there for her, if ever she needed his help. She'd seen his devotion and loyalty toward Orin and Ezel and Merrick, even crossing the Gant Sea to find the huntsman. Coal was a good friend to have. He loved his friends fiercely and strove to always be there for them.

Dear, sweet Coal, she thought. As they walked on in silence, her mood far better, she wondered whether the dwarf knew how much his friends loved him back. She hoped to one day show him.

"Halt!" a man's voice cried out as the refugees of Dorantown neared the end of Duskwood.

"What is this?" Coal grumbled, pushing through the gaggle of people.

Ralowyn followed him closely. Tenzo and Vorenna joined them as they moved to the forest's edge.

"I said, halt!" the voice shouted again. "That, or we rain arrows down upon you."

"So, shall we discuss whatever this is from the shadow of the forest?" Coal yelled out, more perturbed than Ralowyn would have liked.

"Are you the leader of your people?"

Coal glanced back to the others. He shrugged and nodded as he hollered back, "Aye!"

"You may step out into the light," the voice called. "Slowly!"

"Can I bring my partners? We like to discuss grave matters together."

There was a short pause, before the man yelled back, "You may bring one other!"

Coal turned back to Ralowyn. "Alright," he said quietly. "I'll go out there with Vorenna. We'll see what this is all about. You and Tenzo stay hidden, in case things go bad. You'll need to lead the people to safety."

"I am going with you," Ralowyn said swiftly. Coal opened his mouth to argue, but she cut him off. "I am the only one who can wield magic here. I am the only one who could protect you from a volley of arrows."

Coal glanced to Vorenna. The barbarian woman nodded, unable to argue with the elf's logic. "She's right."

"Fine," Coal grumbled and whirled on his heels. "Alright! We're coming out."

As they exited the forest, the landscape opened to fields with scattered rock formations. They were nothing compared to the giant monoliths in Whitestone, but they looked to be made of the same stone from which the Palisade was built. Ralowyn soon saw why.

In the distance, she saw a great fissure in the wall where a massive chunk had been broken from it. Were all those great stones shattered pieces of the wall? The large gap was filled with a great gate, but there was a much smaller wooden wall built on the north side of the Palisade in which rested buildings and what appeared to be farmland.

That must be Aiden's Dell, she thought. They were almost there. They'd almost made it. Their goal was in sight ... as long as they could deal with whatever stood before them.

There were several hooded figures, each wearing dark green cloaks that would certainly make them difficult to see in the forest at night. Most of them stood atop the stones that pocked the area, but Ralowyn sensed there were more nearby she couldn't see.

Two of the hooded figures—the ones not aiming their bows directly at Coal and Ralowyn—whispered quickly between themselves.

"What brings you here?" the man asked.

"We're refugees from Dorantown," Coal said.

"Dorantown?" the man said aloud. He turned and whispered again.

Ralowyn winced. *If they don't know about Dorantown, what happened to Nera and Shorlis?*

"From what do you flee?" the man asked.

"Wretchlings and a dragon," the dwarf replied bluntly. "The creatures attacked us. There was a varlek riding the dragon that burned our home."

More whispering.

Ralowyn began to get nervous. They hadn't inquired further about Dorantown. Perhaps Nera and Shorlis had made it to Aiden's Dell after all. She took a risk and spoke, "We're friends of Nera and Shorlis."

The two hooded figures stopped whispering and stared at her.

Ralowyn gripped the Staff of Anvelorian in her hands.

"Easy, lass," Coal whispered out of the side of his mouth.

"We know no Nera or Shorlis," the man said finally.

At that, Coal gave Ralowyn a worried glance.

"Perhaps you have friends by another name?" the other hooded whisperer asked. That one was a woman. An elf, if Ralowyn guessed correctly.

"Another name?" Coal grumbled and looked up to the elf.

"I do not understand," Ralowyn said.

"Captain Nera of the Talon Squadron and Shorlis ... of the Shoals?" Coal shouted, but his lack of confidence in the adjusted answer was evident.

The two figures turned and whispered. Finally, the man turned to a short and stout hooded figure. Ralowyn guessed that one to be a dwarf. The man said, "Bring them."

Coal gripped his war hammer in both hands. His feet twisted in the grass, as he readied himself. "I'm not thinking we'll be going anywhere with you without the guarantee that our people will be safe."

"Not you," the man said, shooing the hooded dwarf to hurry him.

The dwarf ran off and disappeared behind another large stone.

Everyone stood quietly in a silent showdown. Several of the archers rolled their tense shoulders and muscles, but Ralowyn and Coal were always under the aim of numerous readied bows. Finally, the dwarf came running back around the stone, followed by a child.

"Ralowyn!" Kippin yelled.

"Kippin!" she cried. She didn't care how many bows were aimed at her. She left the Staff of Anvelorian standing upright of its own volition and sprinted across the grass. The hooded dwarf didn't hamper the little halfling as he ran to greet her. She heard the hooded man command his group to lower their weapons as she dove to her knees and scooped the halfling into her arms.

Tears streamed down her face, and she kissed the top of his head, over and over again, breathing in his mess of curls.

"I was so worried about you," Kippin sobbed into her chest.

Ralowyn laughed, despite herself. "I was so worried about you, *davir lolel non.* I was so afraid."

They cried together as she rocked him back and forth, when suddenly, Merrick's arms wrapped around them both. The huntsman's face was dripping with his own tears as he kissed hers off her face.

"Ralowyn," he whispered to her. "Thank the Maker."

Coal sidled up next to them and patted the huntsman on the shoulder. "By my beard," he said with a twinkle in his eye.

Merrick loosed one arm and pulled Coal into the hug.

"See," the dwarf said with a wink to Ralowyn. "Nothing to worry about."

CHAPTER TWENTY-ONE

ASSASSIN IN THE ALEHOUSE

O rin followed a dwarf named Dimble step for step down a thin corridor. Karnak was guided by another dwarf, and they'd parted ways down separate tunnels earlier. The guardian found it fascinating how the griffins' nests were wedged into great holes in the sides of the cliffs. He asked Dimble if the griffins got aggressive with them for walking the tunnels behind their nests. The dwarf shook his head and said, "We just don't want to jump out and surprise them."

Jensen plodded along behind them, too curious to let the opportunity to witness such a thing pass him by. The fact that the dwarves of Glain's Shoulder used magic to bond a griffin and a rider was something entirely unheard of for them. If they could learn that magic, too, it would change the way they trained guardians for the future.

Orin wondered if the dwarves of the hills of Garome knew that magic all those years ago. If they did, why hadn't they passed it on to the men when they gifted them the griffins for the war effort?

They passed another opening to their right where a baby griffin napped quietly in a massive nest.

"We leave this one and his mother. She is a good breeder. This is her fifth cub," Dimble explained.

"Really?" Orin responded curiously.

He knelt next to the baby griffin and stroked its fluffy head feathers. It slowly rose, stretching its wings and arching its back like a cat.

"Did you ever think we'd see wild griffins?" Jensen asked quietly. "Let alone a nest?"

"They look much like the nests at the Roost in Whitestone," Orin said.

"Sure," Jensen agreed, but he waved his hands past the nest out toward the open sky and the sea far below. "Not the same view, though."

"True enough."

Orin scratched at the griffin cub's hind end, its tail stretching high, clearly enjoying the affection.

"Come," Dimble said. "There are more down this way. We will find a suitable griffin to show you the ways."

They followed Dimble, who scurried along the tunnels, clearly having traversed them many times. They passed several more nests before Dimble stopped next to one.

"This one," he said quietly. "When the sun is high, she will come for shade."

"Will she come back if she senses us? Certainly, she'll smell us," Orin reasoned.

"She will come," Dimble said, waving it off. When the guardians didn't appear confident, he added, "They are used to us in their tunnels. They know we mean them no harm."

They didn't wait long before griffins were heard entering the other pockets that dotted the cliffs. When the griffin whose nest they stood behind didn't show up right away, Orin grew more skeptical, though he recognized he knew little about wild griffins.

Griffins in Whitestone were bred and hatched at the Roost. Then they were reared for a year before being paired with a young guardian in training. The trainees were taught proper care and started developing companionship with their griffins until the day their griffins were large enough to ride. It was a long process, and nowhere in it did guardians learn anything of wild griffins. Everything was so closely regimented and contained.

Suddenly, the *whomp-whomp* of beating wings echoed in the entrance of the nest. A moment later, a griffin landed on the edge, clawing at the stone gracefully, bringing itself into the alcove. The griffin was clearly a female, her grey and brown spotted feathers not as vibrant as those of her male counterparts. Aside from that, she was slighter than the larger males.

Her eyes were piercingly blue; something Orin had never seen in a griffin. She cooed and clicked at them, her head bouncing this way and that as she surveyed the scene. Even if she wasn't frightened by them, the uninvited surprise guests in her den certainly intrigued her.

"Cross your hands over your heart and downcast your eyes," Dimble instructed, doing the same.

Orin did as instructed and followed the dwarf as they drew near to the griffin. She stamped at the nest, kicking branches and sticks as she did. Dimble held out a hand before himself, palm up. Orin could hear the dwarf mumbling some words the guardian did not understand. He ventured a glance toward the dwarf and watched as the griffin placed her beak into his palm.

"Come closer," Dimble whispered to Orin.

The guardian didn't hesitate. Keeping his eyes downcast with a slight bow and his hands over his racing heart, he slowly approached. A moment before, a million thoughts whirled through his mind. They all melted away. Nothing remained in that moment but him, Dimble, and the griffin. The dwarf calmly ushered the griffin's face toward Orin's, placing them forehead to forehead.

"*Lentelin gor amonwai,*" he said. Orin felt the griffin's head feathers against the flesh of his head. He heard her calm breath. After a long moment, Dimble said, "Raise your hands and greet her."

Orin opened his eyes and ran his hands over the head and neck feathers of the griffin. Even though outside observers might not think her to be a particularly fine griffin, in that moment, Orin thought there none more beautiful than she.

Dimble invited Jensen to bring the saddle harness over and join them. They readied the griffin smoothly, surprised at how easily she took the saddle for the first time. Orin slipped over her back and into the saddle like he'd done a million times before. It was a strange feeling as the griffin adjusted to carry his added weight. He hadn't been on griffin-back in so long—and hadn't expected to ever be again. A grin covered his face.

"Take her easy," Jensen said, seeing the man's shifted attitude. "We don't know how well this magic works. You wouldn't want her to buck you off into the sea."

Orin pulled on the harness slightly, and the griffin backed up slowly.

"The bond is good," Dimble said, a bit of offense in his voice.

Orin tilted his head to the side and said, "You heard the dwarf."

"Orin," Jensen growled cautiously.

Suddenly, the griffin flapped her great wings and launched them out of the opening.

When his dwarven guide placed the large griffin's forehead against his own, Karnak couldn't help himself. A wave of emotion crashed over him. The dwarven guide had picked a large male griffin for the big orc, thinking it wise to give him a sturdy steed. The griffin was a regal specimen, his head feathers white like a bald eagle and his wing feathers brown like his cat-like hind end. The griffin nuzzled at him as Karnak brushed his neck feathers gently.

"Hey there," the orc whispered. "What do you think about trying to fly with me?"

Though Karnak knew the dwarf had used magic to bond them, the griffin's immediate acceptance of him pricked at something inside the orc. He missed Ker, but the griffin already pulled at his heart.

His dwarven guide helped him saddle the griffin, a process Karnak found altogether interesting. The rig was similar to saddles for wyverns, but different as well. The larger wyverns carried wider saddles, while the one they placed upon the griffin was slight.

As Karnak climbed onto the griffin's back, he adjusted his position several times before finding the most comfortable way to sit.

His guide wafted his hands at them, shooing them onward.

Karnak hesitated, but the griffin turned toward the open portal. Karnak inhaled a nervous breath before the griffin tilted out the hole and dropped from the cliff.

The sun was high, and after being in the tunnels for a couple hours, its warmth touched Karnak's green skin with revitalizing life. Their plummet to the crashing waves below was short-lived as the griffin's brown wings shot wide and sent them into a glide.

His griffin flicked its talons at the top of a rolling wave before it beat its wings and climbed through the sky. Karnak nudged the beast, and it turned without hesitation. They easily navigated the sky, finding Orin flying toward the *Sellena*. Other guardians of the Talon Squadron looked on in shock at first but soon hooted and clapped their excitement at the sight.

Karnak was surprised at how easily the griffin listened and changed course. He'd always found them formidable foes, quicker and more agile than the larger wyverns. Not to mention, wyverns could be stubborn sometimes and didn't always listen as well as one would hope. The big orc wondered if the griffin was so well behaved because of the magic bonding, or if that was a common trait for the creatures.

They flew through the sky, Karnak trying some of the acrobatic aerial moves he'd done on Ker's back hundreds of times in the past. When the griffin proved adept at the maneuvers, Karnak spurred him on to moves he'd never tried with Ker.

"Nice flying!" Orin called over to him.

The two flew to the top of the cliffs, landing on the grassy pinnacle.

Karnak laughed, unsure what to say.

"Well done," Orin said, his own griffin clawing at the grass happily. "How does it feel?"

"It's ... different," Karnak replied, stroking the griffin's feathers. "He's much smaller than Ker was."

"And much larger than this lovely girl," Orin said, patting his own. "He reminds me of my griffin—the one I lost in the skirmish outside Tamaria."

"I'm sorry," Karnak said. He knew how it felt to lose such a close companion.

"No, no," Orin said. "There's been plenty to keep my mind busy since then. Truthfully, I never thought I'd ride a griffin again." He paused, lingering on some internal wrestle. Shortly, the man decided to share. "Admittedly, I was getting used to the idea of being a sailor."

"There may yet be time for that, too," Karnak said. "But for now, we need every griffin rider we can get. The sea will still be there waiting when we defeat Jaernok Tur."

Orin smiled at him. "I like that optimism."

Karnak chuckled. "You don't think this changes the landscape?"

"Oh, I definitely do," the guardian agreed. "With Glain's Shoulder behind us and their griffin riders, we can fly to Aiden's Dell and mount a combined force against the sorcerer and end this once and for all."

"And I'm the optimist," Karnak retorted with a wry grin.

Orin laughed back. "Come. Why don't you show me what your wyvern training has taught you about flying?"

The guardian's griffin flapped her wings several times before launching them from the cliffside. Karnak's face split into a wicked grin. *Let's see what you've got.*

Lenza led them through the tunnel and out into the open air. They crossed a large square where most merchants had closed their stalls for the evening. With the help of the dwarves of Glain's Shoulder, Karnak, Orin, and Jensen united the guardians who'd lost their griffins with new steeds. It was impressive to watch. Karnak had been stunned at how easily his griffin synchronized with him.

"Hurry now," Lenza called back to Karnak and Orin. She held a tight grip on Jensen's arm. He wasn't likely to fall behind. "There is an elf at the alehouse who's been making a drink from our apple stores. It's called cider."

"Cider?" Karnak asked, moving the foreign word around in his mouth.

"Yes," she said excitedly. "It's been all the rage in Glain's Shoulder recently. It's delicious. I think you'll like it, Jensen."

The guardian peered back toward Orin. He wore a smile on his face, but Karnak could tell the man wasn't entirely comfortable with all the affection he was receiving from the young orc woman. He seemed to be fine with her doting when they were trying the different treats of Glain's Shoulder around the table earlier, but he was rather distracted by trying all the new foods then. Karnak snorted a chuckle.

Karnak observed the quiet night and the dazzling stars. He thought how nice it would be to sit on the porch and look out over the city of Calrok. He missed home. He missed Tanessa and Gernot. He missed sitting on the porch and laughing with Merrick. Where was the huntsman anyway? The orc hoped the man was alright.

As much as he missed all those things he loved, their group had made major strides toward finishing the war. The day had been busy and full of work, but the addition of new griffins and their new allies had revitalized them more than he'd expected. While he would not be opposed to collapsing into a soft bed, there was much to celebrate. As the leader of the boisterous Scar Squadron for years, he'd learned that celebrating was a vital part of boosting unit morale.

While they neared the alehouse, the music and raucous merriment seeped out of the old wooden building. A weathered sign next to the door read, "High Winds Alehouse." A second sign, newer and hastily nailed underneath, boasted, "Try Our New Cider. It'll Blow You Away."

Clever, Karnak thought.

The *High Winds Alehouse* bustled with folks from all over Glain's Shoulder. Lenza explained it wasn't the only tavern in the city, but it was where Yenklin was to meet them. Karnak didn't immediately see the orc leader. All of the tables were crowded, and many had folks standing around them.

"Come," Lenza called over the noise. "Father knows the owner and has a special table in the corner."

They weaved through the crowd. A tavern maiden squeezed by Karnak, lifting several mugs high to keep them from spilling. The big orc had to press between multiple crowded tables. He bumped into a minotaur, one of the few people in the tavern bigger than him, and quickly apologized.

"Nonsense," the minotaur said, shaking his furry face and his horns. "I do it all the time. Just watch out for the little ones," he added with a sheepish laugh.

They finally navigated to the table where Yenklin sat alone, nursing a mug. The empty seats around the table were a refreshing sight. Karnak didn't feel so cramped anymore and gladly took a seat.

"I took the liberty of ordering a round of cider for everyone," Yenklin said. "I was glad to hear your guardians were able to pair with the griffins in fine order."

"Thank you," Jensen said, his eyes widening after his first sip. "Cider?"

Lenza nodded at him enthusiastically.

"I like it," he proclaimed, taking another swig.

Karnak sniffed at the drink. It smelled nothing like glorb wine, and he couldn't quite place it. As he sipped, he found it to be fruity and enjoyable.

"It's good, eh?" Yenklin watched him as he drank.

"It's nice," Karnak agreed.

"Delvin, the owner, is rather fond of it. Says it's been big for business. Seems everyone likes trying it. Can't say I blame them. His ale was always good, but it's nothing compared to this."

Suddenly, a round dwarf with a thick yellow beard, wearing a large apron and a towel over his shoulder, appeared next to Yenklin. "You got words to say about me ale?" The dwarf eyed the orc.

"No," Yenklin said with a laugh. "My friend, I was just explaining to Karnak how your new cider has been good for business."

"Aye, that it has," Delvin agreed. "That elf has been the best thing to happen to the *High Winds* in ... well, ever. Folks can't get enough of the stuff."

"So, it's an elven recipe then?" Jensen asked as he set his finished mug on the table.

"Aye," the dwarf continued, jutting his thick thumb over his shoulder toward the back of the tavern. "Halber brought it from ... well, wherever he's from."

"Yes, and quite the conversationalist," Yenklin said. "I've talked to him a number of times. Says he's from Lod originally."

"I don't know about that," Delvin said with a shrug. "I just know he's a mighty fine brewer, and the people are taking to his cider."

"Delvin is quite the conversationalist, too," Yenklin said to Karnak with a smirk.

The dwarf inhaled deeply and rolled his eyes before he scurried off to the bar again.

"Thank you for your hospitality," Karnak said. "It has been more than we expected. It's been a welcome change to our difficult last few weeks. As much fun as we've had, I hoped to get some rest before we leave tomorrow."

"Tomorrow?" Lenza perked up. "I was hoping you would stay a little while." Her words were said for all to hear but seemed directed at Jensen.

"Well," the guardian said, his cheeks flushing. "We need to get to Aiden's Dell and find the rest of our people. Only then can we mount a counterstrike against Jaernok Tur and his wretchling armies."

"It will take us a couple days to muster our own riders. Most of them have other trades that they engage in daily," Yenklin said with some apology in his tone.

"I see," Karnak said, tilting his chin up and wriggling his tusks from side to side.

Suddenly, he did see. The elf that Delvin had hired nudged his way through the door behind the bar. He carried a tray filled with freshly cleaned mugs and slid them atop a counter. He was a pale elf with long black hair. He laughed as he said something to Delvin. The dwarf pointed to Yenklin's table, and when the elf turned to find the orc, his face shifted from excitement to utter shock as his eyes locked onto Karnak's.

Hazkul Bern!

Karnak bolted from his chair, knocking the table and spilling his own mug. "You!" he roared. His outburst was drowned in the cacophony of noises in the loud tavern. No one except his own table seemed to notice.

"Karnak?" Orin said, standing. The guardian's head swiveled as he tried to figure out what had caused the orc to start.

The orc brushed past his friend and bumped several patrons as he hurried toward the bar. He ran into another large minotaur and nearly toppled over. The big minotaur grabbed the orc, keeping him upright. "Sorry about that," the minotaur said. "Almost knocked you clean off your feet."

Karnak pushed away from him and scanned the bar.

No. Where did you go?

He hurried and burst through the door from which he'd seen Hazkul Bern appear, looking this way and that, hoping to spot the elven assassin. "Hazkul Bern," he said menacingly. "Show yourself."

The back area of the tavern was starkly contrasted from the front. The back room housed huge drums and pipes for brewing ale. It was dark; only a couple of candles flickered in the corner near a washing basin.

"What are the chances," Hazkul's voice said from the darkness.

Karnak spun but saw nothing. He stepped slowly around the great drums, looking carefully. A glint of silver to his left caught his eye. Karnak picked up the cooking knife—the only weapon he had.

"A rather strange fate to run into each other here. Wouldn't you agree?" the elf asked.

"Show yourself, and I'll show you what fate I have in mind," the orc spat.

"That might be the longest sentence you've ever said to me," Hazkul mused.

A clattering and cheering from the other room startled Karnak. He moved slower through the dark room.

"I take it you've survived the wrath of the sorcerer?" the elf asked.

Something in his tone stopped Karnak. It didn't sound like the elf assassin he'd encountered in the past. It sounded curious. It sounded ... scared?

"Barely," Karnak answered with a growl. "His wretchlings swarmed us at Dorantown. And a dragon burned the city to the ground."

"I see." The elf's words were quiet. As if he were trying to force something away, he asked, "And Ventohl?"

"Overrun. We lost the city shortly after we took it." Karnak paused. His eyes had adjusted to the dark quickly, but he still could not spot the assassin. *Keep him talking,* Karnak thought. *He does so like to talk.* "We weren't expecting Jaernok Tur to lead an army of wretchlings out of the Crags."

"I suppose not," Hazkul said shortly.

"You don't seem as talkative as I remember," Karnak said, quickly poking his head around a corner.

The elf laughed. "I'm not having to carry our conversation this time. Previously, you proved to be a rather dull conversationalist. I'll grant you that the circumstances may have hindered your mood. But it seems you're in a much better mood now."

"Come out, and I'll show you what kind of mood I'm in."

"There's the mighty orc warrior I know. Always so aggressive," Hazkul said clicking his tongue. "Did your father not give you enough presents when you were a little orcling?"

Karnak growled.

"Speaking of presents," Hazkul continued. "There's a room upstairs. It's where I've been staying. Good ole Delvin has been kind enough to let me stay there since I've been in town. Admittedly, he's getting a little pushy about my father's cider recipe. Rather rude, considering all the coin I've made him. Wouldn't you agree?"

Karnak whirled around another large drum. Nothing.

"There you go, forcing me to carry the conversation again. I'm really not so prone to the monologuing as they say. Perhaps I find myself in too many talks with stoic folks like yourself." Hazkul chuckled at the thought. "Anyway, I do have a present

239

for you in my room. I'd love to give it to you myself, but I think I'll be going now."

"Wait!" Karnak said, sounding more desperate than he meant to.

"Oh, Karnak. I didn't know you cared."

"I don't," he said grumpily, angry at himself for the slip.

"Oh, but I think you do." Hazkul chuckled for a moment but soon fell silent. There was a long quiet between them; Karnak no longer searched but stood in the middle of the dark room, listening. Then Hazkul asked, "So, you and your friends haven't managed to kill him then? Jaernok Tur ..."

The soft tone in which the question was asked struck Karnak as odd. He had been surprised before to find out the assassin had never been manipulated under any of the sorcerer's spells like so many others. Hazkul Bern had fallen in league with the sorcerer to save his own skin, and allegedly, the skin of his group of assassins, the Sons of Silence. Karnak knew the elf had no love for Jaernok Tur, but his question seemed ... off.

"No," Karnak said. "We haven't seen him since Ventohl." Another long silence followed, and Karnak wondered if the assassin had slipped away. "Hazkul?"

There was another pause, and then, "Go home, Karnak." The elf's words weren't harsh or filled with vitriol. They seemed resolved—almost worried. "I've seen the monolith dragon. Jaernok Tur truly is in league with Kilretheon the Red. His might ..." Hazkul's words fell short. "Go home to your wife and your little tyke. Bring them my regards ... and my apologies."

Now, Karnak was altogether confused. "Hazkul, I—"

"There's nothing left to be said, my friend."

"I'm not your friend."

Hazkul stifled a humored chortle. "Perhaps, in a different time, we could have been. I would have liked that chance."

Karnak couldn't say he shared the sentiment.

"But as it is, we need to get as far away as we can," the elf continued. "The ruin that Kilretheon will leave in his wake will shake all of Finlestia. Go home to your family. Spend what time you have left with them. I'm going home as well."

"To Ventohl?" Karnak asked incredulously.

Hazkul barked a laugh before he simply replied, "No."

"You know I can't let you leave," the orc said firmly. When the elf didn't answer for a long while, Karnak said, "Hazkul?"

When he received no answer again, he knew the assassin was gone. The big orc banged his fist against one of the large drums, over and over again, venting his frustration.

He said nothing to Orin, who stepped through the door to the back room of the *High Winds Alehouse*, watching the orc and as he worked through his anger. Karnak marched past the guardian, straight to Delvin behind the bar, and asked, "Where did the elf sleep?"

"Where *did* he sleep?" the dwarf asked, his face contorting. "What's happened to him? Ye know, I still don't know his cider recipe. If something nefarious has come to him, I deserve some kind of compensation. I—"

"His room," Karnak growled, looming over the dwarf.

Orin stepped closer, but Delvin quickly conceded, throwing his hands in front of himself in surrender. "Up the stairs over yonder," he said, pointing to a staircase in the corner.

Karnak brutishly pushed his way through the crowd, caring little for finesse that time. He was in a foul mood, indeed. He doubted he'd find something in Hazkul's quarters that would cheer him up either.

Orin followed close behind as they ascended the stairs. "Karnak, what's going on?"

"Hazkul Bern was here."

"The elven assassin that kidnapped you and Merrick?" Orin was so taken aback his steps stuttered.

"Yes."

"Did you kill him?" the man asked. "What happened?"

"He got away," Karnak growled. "Again."

"So, we'll search his room for clues," Orin said. "Maybe we can find something that will give us some hint of where he's going."

"He is long gone," Karnak said with certainty. He remembered scouring the castle at Ventohl after the assassin had escaped his grasp. He never saw hide nor hair of the elf. If anything, Hazkul Bern was quite adept at disappearing. "But there's something I need to check."

Karnak walked toward the first door, not debating whether it was the right one or not. There were only two others. The way the hallway was built, one appeared to be a broom closet and the other at the end of the hall was likely Delvin's. Karnak's big orc fingers slipped around the doorknob.

"Wait," Orin said. "What if he's laid a trap for you?"

"Then it's good you're with me," the orc said, the scowl never leaving his face.

Karnak saw the guardian tense out of the corner of his eye as the orc slowly turned the knob and opened the creaking door.

CHAPTER TWENTY-TWO

FIRST TREE OF KELVUR

Nera and Shorlis took turns on watch through the night. Momoah, their host, had been cordial throughout the evening, and Nera had to admit his biscuits were good. They reminded her of Enly's famous biscuits, which made her miss the castle cook and, more so, home.

She'd spent much of the night—awake or asleep—dreaming about Whitestone. She dreamt about Pernden and what their life would be like once all the troubles were over: leading the people of Whitestone into a new age of peace. Beating him in their sparring matches at the Grand Corral.

Oh, how she missed him.

The sunlight crept between the tree trunks, bathing the scene in its golden light. Shorlis stirred next to her. She was worried about the chelon. He'd spent most of the night rolling in his own dreams or sitting up next to her.

It was not as though Momoah had given them any reason to distrust him. In fact, he had been rather forthright with answering their questions, even if he answered them strangely. He'd explained that he was a melior, a keeper of the tree. But the pair was downtrodden and conceived all sorts of possible tricks he could use against them.

Shorlis snorted awake as the hut door swung closed. Momoah had offered them his hut for the evening, but they'd politely refused, opting to sleep out by the fire.

In the morning light, Nera saw Momoah's blue skin ripple over his muscles as he stretched his white wings wide. The melior's wings matched his hair, an off tint of white. Shorlis recognized some of Momoah's stretches and sidled over to join him.

Nera hoisted herself from her seat on a log and made her way to the lean-to, greeting Shadowpaw and taking the opportunity in the morning light to inspect the griffin's wing. Shadowpaw clicked and nipped as Nera prodded at the injured wing. The arrow had been removed, and some sort of patch and ointment covered the wound.

"You should leave the patch for today," Momoah said in his smooth, even tone. He did not look at her but continued his stretching. "The ointment will help her heal quickly, but it requires some patience."

"You took the arrow out and dressed this yourself?" Nera asked.

"As you say," Momoah replied, not opening his eyes as he twisted into a new pose.

Nera watched Momoah and Shorlis for a moment. Shorlis seemed pleased to find someone else with whom to do his morning stretches. The chelon followed the melior's lead, appearing to recognize most of the poses. Suddenly, the melior twisted in tight, wrapping his wings in a strained spiral. Shorlis paused, not really sure what stretch the melior had fashioned, and shortly gave Momoah a nod of appreciation.

"Thank you for allowing me to join you," the chelon said before turning to retrieve *Menthrora*.

Momoah nodded back to the chelon but turned and gave Nera a wry grin and a wink over his wing. Clearly, the melior was teasing the chelon with the final stretch. "I can show you some, too," the melior said to the guardian. "I can teach you to breathe."

Nera cocked an eyebrow at him. *Teach me to breathe? If I didn't know how to do that, I wouldn't be standing here,* she thought. She patted Shadowpaw's neck to ground herself. "I'm fine, thank you. We'll be going soon anyway. I thank you for what you've done for Shadowpaw."

"She will not be flying today," Momoah said, untwisting his body and finding a straight stance as though there was a line from his heels to the top of his head.

"Nera," Shorlis called, sounding confused.

She hurried to him. The chelon gawked at the magical staff in his green hands. The grains of the staff continued to light with the pulsing glow.

"Do you still feel the tug?" she asked. "Does it lead us out of the forest?"

"I don't know," Shorlis shrugged. "I mean ... I can sense the pull. It's stronger, actually. But I can't say if it will lead us out of the forest."

"The tree calls," Momoah said. He stood next to the fire, having just placed another log into it. His other hand held a cast iron pan.

"What tree calls?" Nera asked.

Momoah bent over the fire and placed a few pieces of boar meat into the pan. Shortly, they started to sizzle, filling the air with an intoxicating scent. "The staff tree," he said, pointing at *Menthrora.*

Shorlis raised the staff, not understanding the melior. "You mean the tree from which the staff was made?"

"As you say," the melior replied, happily cooking them some breakfast. "You must answer its call."

"Are you saying that the tree from which this staff was made is in this forest?"

"As you say."

Nera rolled her eyes and cut into the conversation. "What does that matter? We have a mission to complete. We need to get to Aiden's Dell and set up an alliance with them before Jaernok Tur brings his wretchling army south."

"You do not fly today," the melior said evenly.

"Is the tree close?" the chelon asked.

"Shorlis," Nera said, hoping to stop that line of thinking before the chelon got too excited.

"What if it makes *Menthrora* stronger?" he asked. "Wouldn't that be worth finding the tree?"

"I can lead you to the tree," Momoah said.

"You know where *Menthrora's* staff tree is?" Shorlis asked.

"As you say," the melior replied. "Though, we should have some breakfast first."

Nera wanted to disagree. She wanted to push back to Aiden's Dell. She knew if they used the sun, they could determine north and head in that direction. They'd eventually find the Palisade.

Finding the tree was also a tempting prospect. Nera knew Shadowpaw needed to recover. And what if the tree could make *Menthrora* stronger? Imbuing the artifact with even more power to fight against the sorcerer certainly wasn't a bad thing.

"How far is it?" Nera asked.

"It is not far," Momoah said with a smile and a nod. "But breakfast first."

After several hours of marching, Nera was regretting their decision to follow the melior deeper into the Forest of Wirra. They trudged onward via no discernible road or trail. Momoah walked with an even pace that frustrated the guardian. She wondered if the melior ever had any sense of urgency. If so, she had yet to see it. The pace made her angry, even though she knew they wouldn't have been traveling with Shadowpaw that day anyway. Regardless, it made her feel like she could be doing something more—something that could possibly work toward their mission of bringing the peoples of Kelvur together to aid them in the north.

She glanced at Shorlis who stared at the glowing grains on his magical staff as they continued to pulse with light. If Nera didn't know any better, *Menthrora* did seem to be glowing slightly brighter as they walked.

Occasionally, Shorlis would give a small start and excitedly hurry to Momoah's side to tell the melior that the staff was doing something strange. She was glad to see that Shorlis liked the melior. Maybe she was just in a bad mood.

She kept thinking back to the night they flew over Aiden's Dell. *If we had just waited until daylight, maybe we wouldn't even be here.*

Eventually, they found themselves walking on a well-worn trail, and Nera wondered how it had appeared. The trees in that part of the forest were immense, growing high above them, stretching up into the sky. Nera had seen large trees in Whitestone Forest. The ones in the Forest of Wirra, though, were so wide at the base, she thought someone could build a house into them.

"Momoah," she said. "What kind of trees are these? I have never seen their equal."

Shorlis pulled up short. He hadn't noticed the massive giants while staring at *Menthrora* but gaped with awe when he looked up. "Woah!" he said. "They're huge!"

Momoah smiled and said, "We call them reds."

As Nera walked up to one of the reds, she could see why. The tree's thick bark was of a reddish hue. "They're beautiful," she said. As she stood next to the great tree, it appeared even larger. She scanned the tree, her eyes following the trunk straight up into the sky until she nearly fell as she leaned backward to take it all in. "I've never seen a tree this large."

"These are not even the big ones," Momoah said with an amused grin.

"There are bigger ones?" Shorlis asked in surprise.

"As you say," the melior replied and continued walking.

The other two fell in step, Nera finding herself a tad more enthusiastic about the walk. Though she still felt the need to do something, she was also intrigued by what else they might see in the strange forest.

"*Menthrora* doesn't come from one of these trees. Does it?" Shorlis asked.

"No," the melior replied.

The chelon's face scrunched slightly as if he were disappointed in the answer. "I suppose the staff would have more of a red tint to the wood if it came from one of these giants."

"As you say. But ..." Momoah looked Shorlis over. "You may find that your staff tree is more than you expect."

This seemed to put a pep in the chelon's step, but they still plodded along at the melior's unhurried pace.

Nera gawked as the sunlight bent into immense angular shadows around the enormous trees. Momoah had been right. Even the largest of the reds they'd passed earlier paled in comparison to the enormity of the ones they strode past then. And to her surprise, she saw a door cut into one of them.

"Shorlis," she said, hardly believing her eyes.

The chelon looked up as Nera hurried over to the tree with the door. Just before she entered, a chiseled face exited the threshold. Nera skidded on the duff, nearly running into the melior. His blue face contorted with confusion.

"Good season," Momoah called.

The other melior stood in his doorway, dumbfounded.

"Good season," he managed to say. "What is ..."

"Nera, we must continue to the tree," Momoah said.

Finally, some urgency, she thought, thankful to get out of the awkward scenario.

She hurried over to Momoah, determined not to get too far away from the melior.

"Do people run into other people's homes a lot in your cultures?" Momoah asked.

Nera flushed with embarrassment. "I ... we ..." Suddenly, she didn't know what to say as she realized Shorlis had done the same thing, running into Momoah's hut only the night before.

A smirk crossed Momoah's face.

Nera turned over her shoulder. The other melior still stood outside his door, watching them walk away. He looked no less confused.

As they continued, they passed more great trees with doors cut into them. Nera was fascinated. She would love to see the inside of one of the tree homes. There were numerous huts scattered between the large trees as well. They saw more activity as they pressed onward as well. Melior of all ages stopped to stare at them.

Several melior children excitedly ran up to them.

"Master Anthanar, you've returned!" one of them hollered. Several of the others gasped and whispered excitedly.

Shorlis stopped. Nera closed the gap between them.

"I am not Master Anthanar," the chelon said softly. "I am his son, Shorlis."

"Master Shorlis," several of them whispered to each other.

A tear streaked down the chelon's face. "My father was here?"

"As you say," Momoah said with a gentle nod.

"Where are we?" Nera asked.

"Come," Momoah said. "Children, Master Shorlis and his friend seek the First Tree."

"The First Tree!" several of them exclaimed. "We will show you."

Children grabbed their hands, pulling them along. Nera shot a glance over her shoulder. Momoah followed them at his regular pace, a wide smile splitting his blue face.

They hurried along, the melior children excited to show them "the First Tree." The children sang a song in another language as they ran and skipped. Nera did not recognize the tongue in which they sang. It sounded old—ancient even.

The ground beneath their feet grew harder, and it didn't take long for Nera to realize they were hurrying along a massive root that climbed out of the ground. She followed it with her gaze before her eyes widened at the sheer mass of tree before them. The root climbed into an immense trunk dotted with windows and balconies. To their left and right, she could see other melior making their way along more roots extending from the great tree, like sloping hills lead to a mountain.

"What in Finlestia?" she whispered.

The tree's great canopy reached out wide above them, meeting the canopies of the reds all around. Melior flitted from branches, carrying on with their daily tasks. Many of them slowed to nod at Shorlis and Nera. Most of them chuckled at the sight of the children dragging the pair along.

"Come! Come!" The children urged them onward.

The root road led to a great archway proceeding into the tree. Nera was drawn to it by wonder. She had never seen anything so magnificent.

Shorlis tapped *Menthrora* on the root as he climbed over a great knot. The staff burst to life, swirling red magic beaming from every grain. The children laughed and cheered, thrilled by the display. The chelon turned to Nera, a look of surprise and joy written across his face. She shrugged at him and shook her head, hardly able to believe what they were witnessing.

The children had stopped pulling them along. They crowded around, watching the chelon in anticipation. Shorlis grinned and tapped the staff against the root again. Sparks and ribbons of red light exploded from the staff in a whimsical flurry. The children erupted in elation. Nera and Shorlis began to laugh as the adorable melior children begged him to do it again.

A moment later, Nera realized Momoah had caught up to them and was quietly watching them interact with the children. He nodded to the guardian with a warm smile. She nodded back, trying to hide her own grin with a smirk. As Shorlis tapped *Menthrora* again and the children cheered, Nera couldn't help but laugh.

Many melior had gathered round while Shorlis entertained the children, but Genuoh, the leader of the people, invited the pair into the First Tree of Kelvur. Nera couldn't say which was more spectacular, the outside of the gargantuan tree or the intricate interior.

The First Tree of Kelvur had crisscrossing stairways and balconies and rooms and great halls and parapets. It was an engineering and architectural marvel, the likes of which Nera had never seen.

"The Tree gives us what is necessary. In the earliest days, our people carved and built. But those days are no more. The Tree has grown on, and we have learned to guide and shape it," Genuoh explained.

A lovely melior woman walked next to him. Her facial features were softer than the man's, but her toned arms were clear indicators that the female melior were strong as well.

Nera also noticed the sentries they'd passed upon entering the great tree. They wore light armor that looked as though it were made from some sort of resin. The guardian was curious about that but followed the leader of the melior, saving her questions for later.

"This tree is unlike anything I've ever seen," Nera said, not for the first time.

"It is an ancient tree. It was the first of all the trees in Kelvur," Genuoh said with the same even tone as Momoah.

"Thus, the First Tree of Kelvur," Shorlis reasoned.

"As you say," Genuoh affirmed with a nod. "It has been the melior's responsibility to watch over every first tree since the beginning."

"Almost the beginning," the female melior corrected him.

"As you say, my love," Genuoh replied. "Toniia is correct. The melior were created to keep the trees when the monolith dragons failed."

"Yes. Enkeli the wizard told us of the monolith dragons and how they were supposed to be the watchers and protectors over all creation, but they tried to create a new power to reshape it instead," Nera put in.

"Master Enkeli is a melior friend," Genuoh said, grinning, "though it has been many seasons since he visited."

"Enkeli and my father were both here?" Shorlis asked.

"As you say. How did you think Master Anthanar acquired *Menthrora*?"

"I guess I didn't," the chelon said quietly.

They climbed a set of stairs leading to a long hallway with openings on the side to various rooms.

"Only the sovran wizard of each land is granted a staff from the First Trees."

"What is a sovran wizard?" Nera asked.

Genuoh looked to Momoah in confusion. "Why, Master Shorlis is the sovran wizard of Kelvur. He carries *Menthrora*."

The chelon turned to Nera. Clearly, he was at a loss as much as she was.

Momoah's head dipped to the side toward the melior leader before he turned to Shorlis and explained. "Every land of Finlestia has a sovran wizard, a wizard who leads and teaches all the other wizards. They are the ones that meet at Candara. Though I do not know much of wizard meetings. Enkeli is the sovran wizard of Tarrine. You did not know this?"

"No," Nera said quickly. "We haven't known wizards in Tarrine in many an age."

"As you say," Genuoh agreed. "Enkeli and Anthanar were not training new wizards for fear of them learning the powers of the monolith stones."

Nera's head swam, and judging by the look on Shorlis's face, the chelon wasn't understanding much better. "What are the monolith stones?" she asked, not sure she could handle any more new information.

Genuoh looked at her incredulously. "They are the magic stones the monolith dragons forged to give them power to reshape the world."

Shorlis looked at *Menthrora*, eyeing the swirling wood that cradled the red stone. "Is this one of the monolith stones?" he asked, his breathing becoming more labored.

"As you say," Genuoh replied, concern etching his face. "You carry the red. Master Anthanar and Master Enkeli brought *Menthrora* back to us so we could embed the stone. They believed that only staffs from the First Trees could contain the power of the monolith stones. You did not know this?"

"No," Shorlis said, shaking his head.

"You carry the red," Genuoh said again, as though all of that should have been obvious to them. "Jaernok Tur carries the black."

"What?" Nera started. "You know of the sorcerer?"

"We see many things," Genuoh said.

They rounded a corner into a room where intricate arches formed windows that allowed for the sun's light to illuminate the area. Light glinted off a reflective surface, and Nera grabbed at Shorlis to protect him. The chelon looked at her strangely, confused by her sudden worry. A young melior male turned to see who had entered the room.

"Good season," he said, greeting them and turning back to a mirror.

"Where did you get that?" she asked.

"Dwarf friends gifted the mirror to us long ago," Genuoh said. "The watcher sees many things through it."

"Is that what you told me about before?" Shorlis asked, raising his staff in readiness.

"It's an Alkhoren Mirror," Nera said with a growl.

"As you say," Genuoh said. "Let me show you what we can see."

CHAPTER TWENTY-THREE

NO MORE UNCERTAINTY

S marlo pounded the table in the middle of the cabin. He let loose all the pent-up emotions he'd been holding back as was required for an orc of his station. He'd been so close to reconnecting with Karnak, only to find no sign of his gar at Dorantown. He gripped the table and leaned, letting his weight settle while he felt the *Harbinger* move underneath him with the rolling waves.

One of the Riders of Loralith had developed the skill of tracking after many decades in the dangerous and wild Elderwood Forest of Tarrine. He'd been called upon to examine the scene at Dorantown before anyone else set foot in the charred place. His report was both disturbing and encouraging, though it came with little in the way of sure answers.

The crew of the *Harbinger* knew the city had been attacked and a great battle had raged before it was burned to the ground. Enormous claw marks, dug into the ground, were further evidence of a dragon's involvement. Then there were the footprints of what seemed to be an exodus from the town through the mining trenches.

Their best guess was that Lanryn had not survived the encounter, otherwise they would have heard from him. There was no telling who had survived, as the tracks were overlapping and chaotic, indicating that many had fled the town during the devastation.

Smarlo ground his teeth together, baring his small tusks. None of the information they'd gathered told him whether Karnak was dead or alive. He felt like they'd come all that way and still learned nothing. The orc mage growled at the tome on the table, swiping at it and sending the book flying to the floor and sliding near the door. He'd still found nothing in the *Book of Dangerous Secrets* to help him and the others.

Just another one of my many shortcomings on this entire endeavor, he criticized himself.

Suddenly, the door to the cabin flung open and crashed against the wall. Smarlo didn't have to look up from the messy table to know Lotmeag had entered. The orc snarled unexpectedly.

"So," the dwarf said cautiously. He picked up the book sprawled near his feet. "The author didn't wrap up the mysteries? I do hate when they do that. Though, I'm a sucker for a good cliffhanger."

Smarlo looked to the dwarf stoically.

"Aye. Not in the mood for a joke." Lotmeag aimlessly thumbed through the tome. "You know, you can't learn everything from books. Sometimes, you have to live and learn."

"What if none of them are alive?" Smarlo spat. "What if none of them made it? What if the wretchlings chased them down and slaughtered each and every one of them?"

Lotmeag pursed his lips and nodded, understanding what was wrong with the orc mage. "You know, I lost a lot of good friends when the dragon came to Galium. Did you know the garvawk warriors lost half our number that night? All those dwarves and garvawks, dead. And only one of the dwarves survived his fall. I lost my mentor and leader—Bendur Clagstack, be rested.

"When the battle was over, I was devastated. I didn't know what I was going to do with myself. But King Thygram assigned me as the new foredwarf of the garvawk warriors. I'll never forget his speech at the victory feast. Do ye remember it?"

Smarlo sighed mournfully, a tear escaping his eye. "I do."

"So, ye remember he spoke of a future hope. A hope for friendship and something greater. A hope that never ceases. A hope that when one of us loses it, another of us can take it up to carry the others. We can lose a lot of things, my friend, but hope must not be one of them."

"I'm sorry," Smarlo said, his nose twitching as he fought back more tears.

"Aye. I know. And I forgive ye," Lotmeag said with a grin and a slight shrug. "Friends are the ones ye should be able to express yer worries to."

Smarlo nodded gratefully to the dwarf. He watched Lotmeag for a moment, the dwarf flipping through the pages of the tome. The orc mage thought it strangely humorous that he'd come to such friendship with the garvawk warrior. At first, their regular visits and discussions over tea were a brash and stark contrast to those he'd enjoyed with Tanessa. But quickly, they'd become full of laughter and fellowship, joys Smarlo cherished.

Watching the dwarf, Smarlo realized Lotmeag had become mesmerized by something in the book. "What did you find there?" the orc asked, without expectation.

"This," Lotmeag said, stumbling over his words. "This here is written in old dwarvish. My Da used to make me and my sister study it when we were half pints. He only had two books, but he made us read them over and over to practice."

"What?" Smarlo hurried to the dwarf's side, peering over his shoulder. How could he be so foolish? Just because he didn't recognize all the languages in the tome didn't mean others wouldn't. "What does it say?"

"Well," Lotmeag hemmed as he traced the lines with his thick dwarven finger. "This part talks of the mighty dragons. Says something about how the Maker turned toward other creations after the monolith dragons betrayed their duty ... Says they destroyed themselves ... no, wait ... Says they created their own destruction? I don't understand that part."

Smarlo quickly ushered Lotmeag to the table, grabbing his own notebook and scribbling. "Read it for me, word for word."

"Aye," Lotmeag said, the dwarf's excitement growing with the orc's. "I'll start back here."

The dwarven warrior read the inscription as the orc mage hurriedly wrote out the translation.

"I'm so sorry," Porg said to Pernden. "I know how worried you are, but she's still out there. I know it."

The king chewed on the inside of his mouth. He wouldn't believe Nera was lost until he saw it with his own eyes. He fought the pit in his stomach that tried to convince him otherwise. He reached out and grasped Porg's forearm. "Thank you."

"Of course." Porg's countenance shifted. "I'm just sorry I couldn't be more help on this journey. I was really hoping I could help build up the town. I'm sad to see it in ruins."

"There are a lot of things to be sad about here. We can't let sorrow overwhelm us," Pernden said. "Every breath we take in this world is a reminder that there is more for us here. We will not be drowned by woes."

"Are you trying to convince me or yourself?" Porg asked quietly, staring out toward the shore.

"Both," Pernden said, matching the orc's soft timbre.

"King Pernden."

The king turned to face the mustached elf commander of the Loralith Riders.

"Commander Fario," he acknowledged.

"I wonder if we should not discuss the possibility of a scouting party. We could send a small unit to follow the trail of the evacuees and see what became of them."

"I appreciate the thought," Pernden said, knowing that the elf commander could plainly see how their discoveries at Dorantown were weighing on the humans, dwarves, and orcs. "I fear it would make little difference. Our best hope is that they made it to the wall city."

"Aiden's Dell," Porg put in. He'd studied their makeshift map numerous times over the trip.

"Right," Pernden continued. "Hopefully, they've found refuge there. The best way we can help them now is to flank the enemy with our forces. We already know Jaernok Tur's sending his armies to attack other cities. If we can catch him unaware ..."

"Hm," Fario grunted.

Pernden tensed. That grunt seemed unsure. "What is it?" the king asked.

"I doubt we will catch the sorcerer unguarded," the elf commander said.

"Unguarded and unaware are two entirely different things," Pernden replied. "I have no misconceptions that we will take Jaernok Tur without a fight."

"Hm."

Good, Pernden thought. That one sounded like a satisfied affirmative.

"So, we sail north along the coast to Ventohl and flank the sorcerer while his dragon rider isn't home," Porg said with a glint in his eye.

"Yes, and we cut off the head of the serpent," Pernden agreed.

"Hm," Fario agreed.

"The last of the griffins are landing on the *Lentoria*, and then we'll be underway," Pernden said.

"I'll talk to Captain Bilktor," Porg said. He dipped his head to the side with a grin and added, "Perhaps he can make use of me as we continue onward."

They walked toward the aft cabin under the sterncastle.

"We should discuss strategy with Smarlo and Lotmeag. Also, gather the captains of the squadrons," Pernden added.

"I can do that," Porg put in. "I'll let Captain Bilktor know to signal the other ships."

"Thank you, my friend," Pernden said. Porg placed a thick orc finger to his brow and gave the man a bow before hustling up the sterncastle steps. The king turned toward Commander Fario, the elf matching him step for step. "We're going to need—"

Suddenly, the cabin door slammed open before them. Smarlo emerged from the threshold, with a slight wince at how aggressively he'd opened the door. Pernden and Fario stared at him, stunned.

"Sorry," he said quickly. Lotmeag chuckled behind the orc mage. Smarlo straightened and said no less fervently, "I think we may have found a way to kill the monolith dragon."

Little time was wasted getting the ships underway. They sailed north around the coast of Kelvur, following it toward Ventohl. Smarlo appreciated the maps they'd found in one of the few buildings that hadn't been completely reduced to ash by the docks of Dorantown. The new map's lines were no more masterfully marked than the ones they had made, but their accuracy was far superior.

Fair winds filled their sails, and Captain Bilktor called out regular adjustments to the crew of the *Harbinger* so they didn't leave the other ships in their wake. A difficult tension laced everyone on board. The building anticipation of battle and the patience to arrive as a fully outfitted army were at odds with one another.

The map flitted in the breeze, pinned to the railing by one of Smarlo's hands. He'd brought it outside, wanting to see it under the bright moonlight rather than the warm candlelight inside the cabin. They'd discussed their plans at length. Hours had passed before any of the leaders left the cramped cabin. Eventually, they all knew their plans were as strong as they could make them without seeing Ventohl in person.

Most people had gone to their beds or hammocks to rack out for the night, though Smarlo wondered if any of them would actually sleep. He'd found many sleepless nights since he'd become the leader of his people.

The sails stayed taut, rippling only slightly as the helmsman steered clear of any rocks in the treacherous waters along the coast. Smarlo inhaled the night, smelling the sea. It was odd to him how the place smelled so similar to home. For a moment, he thought of Tanessa and Gernot. He wondered if they were sleeping, having settled in for the night some hours before, or if the sun had even set in Calrok yet. Smarlo scratched at his ear scar, wishing he'd grabbed the salve from the cabin.

"You know, you shouldn't scratch at it," a voice said from behind him. He turned to see Lehra. Her honey brown hair wore a different hue in the moonlight. She strode next to him and held out the small jar of salve Tanessa had made for him. She smirked and said, "But what do I know?"

"Thank you," Smarlo said, embarrassed.

"I went to find you in the cabin but found a snoring dwarf heaped over a book."

Smarlo grinned. Since their discovery of the old dwarvish, Lotmeag had been particularly interested in helping Smarlo scour the rest of his *Book of Dangerous Secrets*. Frankly, Smarlo was glad for the help. They'd spent much of the rest of that day discussing plans with the others, but Lotmeag went back to the book as soon as the last leader had turned in for the evening. The dwarf was more tired than he let on and soon fell asleep reading. The sight amused the orc mage, and Smarlo wondered how many times he'd fallen asleep reading himself.

Too many to count, he mused.

Shortly after Lotmeag started snoring, Smarlo had stepped out of the cabin and into the night, looking for some fresh air and moonlight.

"Let me help you," Lehra said quietly, scooping a small amount of salve. She rubbed the contents between two of her fingers before reaching for Smarlo's mangled ear. She smeared the salve onto Smarlo's ear, massaging it into the scarred tissue.

"Thank you," Smarlo said, turning to her. "But why are you up? Tomorrow is a big day. Captain Bilktor guesses we should arrive in Ventohl by tomorrow evening."

"I couldn't sleep," Lehra said. "Why are you up?"

"The same reason."

"I had a feeling," she said with a smirk as she capped the jar again. "It was the gar's wife who gave this to you?"

"Tanessa. Yes," he said.

"She is a good friend, then."

"One of my best."

"Do you have room for more?"

The question stung Smarlo. "Of course," he said quickly, drawing closer to Lehra. For some reason, he felt a deep desire to never hurt her and to do anything to rid her of pain.

"And what about *more*?" she asked, her brown eyes wide as she met his gaze.

"More ..." Smarlo whispered. He'd grown fond of Lehra, but had she grown so fond of him? As he stood there facing her, sea spray splashed up into a mist off the *Harbinger's* bow, glittering in the moonlight.

Lehra stepped closer to Smarlo—something he'd not thought possible—and placed a hand on his chest.

"I know it seems foolishness," Lehra whispered. "But after I lost my griffin in the Battle of Calrok, I thought my life was over. I thought everything I worked and trained for all those years was wasted. Those days were the worst of my life. I was aimless. I hated not knowing what I would do. Then, the Scar Squadron took Jeh and me in. You've treated us like one of your own."

"You are one of us," Smarlo said comfortingly, not realizing how his hand had slipped behind her back. The blood in his veins ran like hot lava, warming his muscles.

"I know," she said. The thankful smile she wore glowed radiantly. "But I learned that the enemy we face is beyond dangerous. Any battle could be our last. I learned that I despise the feeling of uncertainty. And sure, it would be foolishness to start something in the midst of battle, but I don't want to die with uncertainty. I want to—"

Smarlo didn't know what came over him, but with his other hand, he grabbed Lehra's chin and drew her face to his. To his surprise, Lehra melted into the kiss and squeezed him closer rather than pulling away. His lips slowly pulled back, sticking slightly to hers before releasing with a little pop.

"I'm sorry," Smarlo whispered. But Lehra didn't seem upset. Her top teeth bit at her lower lip in a strange grin.

"I'll take that as a promise that we can at least consider *more* if we make it through this."

"*When* we make it through this," Smarlo assured her.

She smiled at him, gripping the arm that held her close to him. "How are you so sure?"

Smarlo realized then that Belguv had told the Scar Squadron to prepare themselves, discussing only their role in the battle to come in order to keep them focused. He had likely not mentioned anything about their discovery.

Lehra's eyes narrowed at him curiously as he grinned wanly, but Smarlo hugged her close. He would explain it to her, but he wanted that moment to last as long as possible. Then he whispered, "I believe we may have one of the few weapons in Finlestia that can kill a monolith dragon."

Chapter Twenty-Four

The Nari Desert

A n emerald light glinted far to Garron's left. *Ellaria's stone,* he thought. Sand whipped in their faces, even as they flew high above the dunes below. Little flecks of blue sparks danced around in front of them as Ezel attempted to cast a magical barrier before them. The barrier caught many of the granules but not all. Garron's cheeks above the stubble on his face felt as though they'd been rubbed raw.

In the distance, a great sandstorm raged across the Nari desert. The winds were gaining speed the closer the trio flew toward the storm, so they'd decided to fly with a little more distance between them to avoid any accidents. Ellaria was obviously trying to tap into the magic of the stone tied around her neck but had far less experience in the magical arts than Ezel. She and Silverwing looked uncomfortable, to say the least.

"Perhaps we should land and find some shelter," Garron called over his shoulder to Ezel.

The deep gnome tapped Garron's shoulder, leaning over to shake his head. He signed with one hand, *"What shelter?"* and wafted his hand out wide.

Ezel was right, of course. Since they'd left Kaelor at the old abandoned wisdom tower on the edge of the Nari Desert, they'd seen no sign of anything but rolling sand dunes. At first the spectacle was awe-inspiring—wonderful curving formations with golden waves of sand. But after seeing nothing else for hours until they spotted the storm, Garron was starting to think Kaelor had the right idea.

Inga had proudly shown off her big strong elven son to Malinda in the market. The other dwarven woman looked just as old as Inga and likely didn't have much better vision than Kaelor's bespectacled mother. Malinda seemed very curious about how long Kaelor would be in town and wondered if he would be able to spare some time to help her, since he was so big and strong. Apparently, Malinda had lost something recently and suspected foul play. Garron wasn't entirely sure she hadn't just misplaced it, but Kaelor seemed eager enough to help her when he could. Garron had asked again whether the elf would rather join them, but Kaelor had politely declined.

"My mother is old," he'd said. "I've spent many years in service to the crown of Tamaria. I think it may be time to help my mother." He paused and laughed before adding, "And apparently Malinda."

"Thank you. Truly. For everything," Garron said, grasping the elf's forearm. "I will send you some coin from Whitestone when we get back, for everything you've sacrificed for us."

"No need," Kaelor said, placing a fist to his chest and giving Garron a slight bow. "It was an honor to serve a king worthy of service again."

"I am no king," Garron said quietly.

"I know," Kaelor said softly, though he did not seem willing to take back his words. "Anyway, I'll find some work in Last Lake. It's a growing city. Plenty to do."

"Maybe not a chef though, eh?" Garron said with a wry smile.

Kaelor laughed. "I don't know why she likes everything overcooked."

"Thanks again, my friend," Garron said.

Ellaria had wrapped the elf in a hug. "I might be more inclined to see you again now that it means I won't have to see that good for nothing ..." Her words trailed off. "Well, anyway. Thank you."

"You are very welcome," he said.

Kaelor and Ezel shared a nod before the trio had mounted up and flown directly south into the Nari Desert.

As sand blasted his face, Garron was regretting their departure. Benley snorted uncomfortably, not liking the sand any more than the rest of them.

Ellaria flew as close as she dared and hollered, "Garron! What are we doing? We won't be able to fly through that storm."

Garron looked ahead. The storm was enormous. Sand sprayed and flew from the ground. He had hoped the sandstorm would move to the east or the west so they could continue their flight southward. He wasn't entirely sure where they were headed, but he hoped that if they could make it to the center of the desert, maybe he'd hear the call. The storm seemed to be swirling in on itself, extending for miles around.

"Maybe the storm will wane!" he called back.

"We've been flying toward it for hours, and it doesn't seem any less angry," Ellaria groaned. "Do you think we can fly over it?"

"No," Garron said. He remembered flying through a thunderstorm that had come off the sea years earlier. His unit had flown higher to get above the storm, but the air shifted in the middle of the storm, dragging them into its spiraling torrent. He didn't want to think what that would mean in a storm of sand. They could be torn to pieces.

What are we going to do? he wondered.

Suddenly, he heard the voice.

Come, it beckoned.

268

"Where? In the storm?" Garron called out.

Ezel tapped Garron's shoulder, not understanding what the man was saying.

Garron waved him off, extending his chin and closing his eyes to concentrate.

Come, was all the voice said.

Without further communication, Garron knew. Into the storm they must go.

"Ellaria?" he called hesitantly.

The woman looked at him intensely as she and Silverwing bobbed in the wild winds. She shook her head at him slowly, figuring out what he meant to do. "You're going to lead us to our deaths!"

"I know you have no reason to trust me. I'm not sure I even trust myself. But I know it inside, unlike anything else I've ever known."

Ellaria grimaced and took a quick glance at the storm ahead. Though he couldn't hear it, Garron could tell by the look on her face that she growled at him. The woman leaned in closer to Silverwing, her blazing red hair trailing behind her like a flame. Silverwing began to descend, flapping his wings harder into the storm's fury.

Ezel didn't bother tapping Garron that time. His little gnomish hands gripped the man's armor. The deep gnome secured himself on the back of the pegasus without a sign.

Garron nodded his head and heeled Benley in the flanks. Though the pegasus didn't seem entirely thrilled about the idea of flying further into the storm, he flapped his wings and hurried his pace.

They rode into the whipping winds, buffeted by sand that felt like shards of glass scraping across their exposed skin. Ezel pushed Garron's hood over the man's head, and Garron secured it before the gnome pulled his own hood down over his face. He extended a tattooed hand out toward Ellaria. The runes flickered to life with blue flame.

Ellaria held one arm out at an angle, trying to protect her face from the wicked lashing of the sand. Blue sparks erupted in front of her, another barrier from the deep gnome.

Unfortunately, the sand blasting became even more intense for the pegasus and his riders. Benley whinnied with frustration. As they rode further into the storm, the sand darkened the world around them.

Where are you? Garron thought. *Are you calling us to our deaths? Will you let us be torn to shreds?*

Suddenly, a light burst through the gloom. At first, it was a pinprick, like the tiniest hole through a linen sheet. But the light grew brighter and wider. Soon the sand separated, the tumult of the storm opening into a tunnel before them. The invisible barrier of the tunnel staved off the storm as sand blew and exploded around it like smoke.

Benley slowed his flapping as the tunnel grew outward, wide enough for him to fly comfortably. Ellaria burst through the side of the tunnel as it extended to her as well.

She shook the sand from her hair as Silverwing settled into a comfortable glide.

"What in Finlestia?" Garron said in wonder. He was so struck by the scene, he hardly noticed the sand burn on his face.

Ezel tapped him on the shoulder and pointed ahead through the protective tunnel. The light was bright in that direction, and Garron could see only the silhouette of what appeared to be a man.

"Enkeli," Ellaria said aloud, turning to Garron and Ezel with a relieved smile.

"The wizard?" Garron asked.

Ezel only patted the man's shoulder and waved him onward.

They flew through the protective tunnel, sand whipping and dispersing all around them, leaving them untouched. Garron remembered Ellaria telling him about something like that when she was out on the Tandal Sea with his cousin Orin. Was Garron about to meet the wizard Enkeli? Or was the magic before them only similar to the wizard's?

As they flew nearer, the light from the opening faded to reveal a glorious sight. An enormous tree climbed into the sky far above a great city covered in smaller trees. Huts and natural-looking buildings sprawled throughout. The sun shone brightly, sending brilliant reflections off the leaves of the massive tree in the center of the area. People appeared to be flying all about the great tree, but Garron's mind couldn't make sense of it.

Benley flew through the entrance, leaving a wall of sand behind them. Garron gaped at the swirling wall of sand that extended for what seemed like miles in a circle around the city, not destroying the place where they found themselves but protecting it.

A figure with blue skin and great white wings flew up to greet them. Her face was beautifully angled, and her arms toned. She flashed him a smile, almost as white as her hair.

"Good season," she said to him and the others.

Ezel stared and breathed heavily over the man's shoulder.

"Thank you," Garron said, breathlessly.

"It was not me," she said with a slight bow, "I will take you to Master Enkeli momentarily."

Garron looked over at Ellaria, who stared back excitedly. The man heard nothing but grand things when the others had spoken of the wizard, and he would get to meet Enkeli himself.

Is he the one who's been calling to me? he wondered. Suddenly, he was very nervous to meet the wizard. He was frustrated and confused. *If it was the wizard calling to me this whole time, why didn't he come to speak to me in person?* It certainly would have been a lot easier to explain to his friends.

"Let us get you some water first," the blue woman said, "and some food for your mounts."

Garron heeled Benley onward after the woman as he felt Ezel's breathy chuckle on the back of his neck. The man had no idea what he had expected to find in the Nari Desert, but if someone had given him a thousand guesses, he would not have guessed what he saw before them.

As they landed gingerly—for Benley was still hesitant after flying through the storm—Ezel slipped from his perch and ran headlong into a tall figure draped in burgundy robes. The little gnome seemed all the smaller hugging the tall wizard, whose laugh made his long beard bob and sweep the top of Ezel's bald head. Ellaria didn't waste time either, punching Garron's arm playfully as she ran to greet the wizard.

Garron, however, dismounted and strode slowly, watching the scene unfold. He was struck by the fact that one of the blue-skinned beings was able to approach Silverwing without receiving a swift talon slash.

Silverwing had already proven to be an anomaly by bonding with Ellaria after his original rider died. Perhaps the griffin was more amenable to strangers than others. Garron wasn't convinced that was the answer. Silverwing hadn't seemed willing to go with Kaelor back in Tamaria when he was trying to gather the mounts for their escape. No, it was something else—something about this place.

Though a storm brewed and swirled all around, the sun beamed down, lighting their surroundings magnificently. No winds tormented them there. The turmoil seemed to be cast out, while inside remained only peace.

A blue-skinned figure petted Benley on the snout and offered the pegasus an apple. Benley chomped it and snorted a short whine to let the being know he was not pleased about the ride through the storm, but he would take the apple as a start to amends.

"Rano will care for his sand burns," said the blue woman who had greeted them in the sky.

Garron hesitated but gave Benley another pat before walking away. The affectionate slap produced a cloud of dust, and Garron suddenly realized how brown the pegasus was. He looked at his own arms and found them to be covered in sand as well. Glancing over to Ezel and Ellaria, they looked like dust shadows next to the vibrant cloak of the wizard.

"Come," the woman said next to him.

"What did you just say?" he asked.

"Come," she repeated. "Master Enkeli is excited to see you."

"Were you the one calling me?" Garron asked but felt stupid as soon as the words came out. Her voice sounded nothing like the voice he'd heard calling to him across the world.

She smiled. "No. I am Lotnoa. I do not have the magic you speak of. We are melior. Our magic is little compared to others."

"But I saw one of your people through the mirror, didn't I?" Garron prodded.

At that she paused. A curious look swept across her face. "I should speak to Kanku about this."

"Is Kanku your leader?"

"As you say," she responded with a nod. "But first, let us convene with Master Enkeli."

As they approached, Ellaria talking the wizard's ear off and Ezel signing along the whole way, Enkeli gently placed his hands on their shoulders to stay them. They each fell silent and followed his gaze. Garron stopped short, the wizard's ancient eyes piercing him as though Enkeli could see everything inside him. All the things Garron had done. All the things Garron had broken. All the things broken within him.

A tear streaked down Garron's face, but he had not the strength to wipe it away.

"Come," Enkeli said, beckoning the man closer.

The word rang out in Garron's mind, as he compared it to the voice he'd heard for the past few months. They didn't match, but was that some trick of the magic the wizard would have used to reach out to him across the vast distance?

"You have come so far," the wizard said.

For some reason, in his heart, Garron suspected the wizard didn't speak of distance. It felt to him as though Enkeli spoke of the great internal war Garron had waged ever since his Griffin Guard squadron was killed so long ago. It was then that he was captured by Jaernok Tur and manipulated and twisted. Ever since, Garron had been waging a war within himself.

"You are tired," Enkeli continued. A compassionate smile spread across his wrinkled face.

Tears streamed from Garron's eyes at that. *I am tired*, he thought.

So tired, he could hardly move. He had hardly slept for months until Ellaria and Ezel helped him with their presence at night. Suddenly, he found them helping him again. They flanked him on either side, holding each of his hands and gently ushering him toward the wizard.

Garron examined the wizard through his tears. Enkeli's burgundy cloak was accented with gold stitching. It matched the ribbon Ellaria had shown him one time in the dungeons of Whitestone—the same stretch of fabric that had been tied to Silverwing when the griffin had saved her and Ezel during the Battle of Galium.

Next to the wizard stood his staff, held upright by its own power. Strangely, the staff wood seemed to match that of the enormous tree in the center of the desert city.

Enkeli cupped Garron's neck and shoulder comfortingly. "You're safe here," the wizard said.

Garron melted into the wizard's embrace and wept.

Shortly after their arrival, Enkeli ushered them through the city and up the roots of the giant tree.

"This is the First Tree of Tarrine," he said with reverence. "The same tree from which my staff was borne."

"This place is wonderful," Ellaria said, gawking all around.

Garron couldn't help but agree. Melior flitted with their great wings from ledge to branch, going about their daily business. The homes they'd passed were built from the trees that filled the area. Sparkling pools of fresh water dotted the landscape, a paradise compared to the desert that surrounded them. Garron had no idea where the pools came from, but he remembered reading something in Kel Joran's notes that the only place to find water in the Nari Desert was below ground. He guessed the great pools must be from some of those underground springs.

"Is the storm a protective barrier, like the mist we encountered on the faery island?" Ezel signed.

"Very good," Enkeli responded as a master mage would to his students.

"A clever bit of magic that," Ellaria said, staring out at the swirling clouds of sand.

"We never would have known this whole city was here," Garron agreed. "Does it dissipate when you leave the city?"

"Oh, no," Enkeli laughed. "That enchantment was placed by another."

"Another wizard? In Tarrine?" Garron asked.

"He is no wizard, but his magic is mighty. Let us meet with Kanku, and we can explain everything."

They followed the wizard up the roots of the tree. Garron had never seen something so massive. The tree felt to him as large as a mountain. Entering the tree, they found it to be both hollowed and alive, a beautiful balance between use and preservation. The group walked up several spiraling stairs that were carved directly from the tree but sprouted leaves and flowers and mushrooms as the steps brimmed with life.

Kanku, the melior leader, greeted them pleasantly and led them to a beautiful terrace off the back of the great tree. In that direction, a wide pool of water, like a great lake, stretched out for several miles. It glistened in the sunlight, and Garron wondered how the sunlight came through the storm so brilliantly. When they were flying toward it, the storm seemed unrelenting, and they could see nothing through it. The great illusion bewildered him.

Garron tugged slightly at Enkeli's sleeve. The wizard turned to regard him, popping a curious eyebrow.

"Master Enkeli," Garron started hesitantly. "Were you the one who called me?"

Enkeli smiled. "No, my boy. He did," the wizard said, waving a hand toward the lake below them.

Suddenly, the lake roiled and shifted as though it were alive. The water expanded and grew until it began to splash and fall away from a rising mountain—a blue-hued mountain.

Ezel tapped Garron several times, but neither of them could take their eyes away from the scene unfolding before them.

Dark blue-hued scales stretched over gargantuan muscles and bone. A great neck rolled up from the waters to reveal a massive head of horns and a jagged maw. Intense blue eyes blinked open to stare upon them.

The mountain was no mountain, but a dragon.

Garron's throat dropped into his stomach. He had fought some of Drelek's fiercest wyvern riders, but he'd never faced a creature that compared to the magnitude of the dragon before him.

The melior leader and the wizard did not seem phased by the dragon's appearance but stood in silent reverence. Ellaria and Ezel looked as terrified as Garron felt. None spoke for a long while. Pools that had gathered between ridges on his back continued to pour from the great dragon like waterfalls.

"You've come." A deep resonant voice boomed out, shaking the tree with its might.

Garron wasn't sure if the earth below him shook him to the ground or he was merely overwhelmed, but he dropped to his knees, knowing the voice intrinsically.

"It was you," Garron said, his own voice sounding like that of a mouse speaking to a lion.

"Hmmm," the dragon answered with a deep rumbling. "I am Elrenigeth the Blue."

Garron placed a fist over his chest and bowed. "I am Garron, son of Farrin the Just, former king of Whitestone."

"I know who you are," Elrenigeth said, and Garron knew it to be true. "And I know your friends. Ellaria, only daughter from the house of Grell, bearer of the emerald monolith stone. And Ezel, deep gnome of Lornteris, bearer of the blue monolith stone, my chosen."

Ellaria twiddled the emerald stone on her leather necklace with awe. As Garron looked to Ezel, the runes on the gnome's hands blazed to life with blue fire. The man stared at the gnome for a long while. He'd never seen Ezel carrying a stone of any sort, nor did he produce one from some hidden pocket.

"Long ago, I ..." Ezel paused his signing to his confused companions, trying to find the right words. *"Obtained a stone—a blue stone with great magical power."*

"Yes. You did," Elrenigeth said, his booming voice a stark contrast to Ezel's silent signing.

"When I was nearly killed by the pirate Captain Baltacor, a sea witch used her magic and the stone to save me."

"That's not exactly what happened," Enkeli said. Ezel turned to the wizard, stunned and confused. "Talrina, the sea witch, brought you to me. I was in the southern isles at the time."

"What?" Ezel signed.

"Talrina was a skilled witch, but she would not have been able to save you," Enkeli continued. "Her runic tattoo work was brilliant, but the stone needed to be crushed to powder for her to mix into the ink. Between the power of my staff, thankfully being of the First Tree of Tarrine, and Elrenigeth's blessing, I was able to transmute the stone and mix it with the ink."

Ezel inspected the runic tattoos all over his body. *"I'd always thought the witch made that happen. I knew she used the stone in the ink. She'd told Coal as much."*

"She did," the wizard said. "But nothing can destroy a monolith stone aside from the monolith dragons or a staff of a First Tree."

"Are you suggesting there are more First Trees and more monolith stones?" Garron got the nerve to ask.

"Yes," the monolith dragon rumbled. "There are First Trees in each of the twelve lands of Finlestia. And one First Tree of Finlestia. And the stones ..." Elrenigeth's words faded before he added, "The stones were our greatest mistake."

"I don't understand," Garron said.

Enkeli explained. "When the blue stone was rendered to dust and mixed with the ink to form Ezel's tattoos, Elrenigeth called me back here. We immediately went to work. I was sent to Candara, the isle of the First Tree of Finlestia to retrieve a branch. It was a treacherous journey, and I nearly perished."

"That would have been a travesty," Elrenigeth said. "For we needed the branch to create that token around your neck, Ezel."

The deep gnome thumbed the token that hung from a leather string around his neck. The hardened wood was carved with the image of a great tree and seven runic symbols from an ancient language. For the first time, Garron got a good look at it and realized they were Nari.

"Those symbols," he stammered, "they're Nari."

"Correct," Enkeli said. "When Ezel took on the blue stone and lived ..."

"It was the first time in many centuries that I found hope to correct the mistakes of my past," Elrenigeth finished the thought. The monolith dragon sounded pained as he continued. "We were foolish to think that we could recreate this world in our own image. Kilretheon convinced many of us that we could forge new powers to rewrite the world if we worked together to produce powerful magic. We were greedy. We wanted the power of the maker. Kilretheon's plan seemed sound to my foolish young mind, for we were not always so ancient. His words were convincing, so I joined him."

"You were one of the eight …" Ellaria murmured, recalling the story that had been shared through the Shells of Callencia.

"I am sad to say it is so," the monolith dragon said with a disappointed snort. "We created a stone for each of us, but the process was incomplete. Four of our siblings shattered the world with a branch from the First Tree of Finlestia. The earth erupted, tearing fire from the land. Some of my brothers and sisters died that day. Others, like myself, were injured and have remained dormant for years. Others scattered to the lands we were supposed to protect and nurture. I have been here since, waiting for the day I'd have the chance to undo my foolish actions. It is fortunate that you found my stone, Ezel."

"But why did you call me?" Garron interrupted. "Why not call Ezel?"

"I could not," Elrenigeth said. "I can only call out in Nari. It is an ancient and powerful language. And before you, Enkeli was the only one who could understand it. Or at least the only one outside this city."

"So, you called me to bring Ezel here?"

"No," Elrenigeth said. "You have brought two stones to me. You are as much a champion to me as Jaernok Tur is to Kilretheon the Red. Ezel and Ellaria, come forward."

The two glanced at Garron and then to Enkeli. The wizard nodded, assuring them it was alright. They stepped forward to the edge of the great terrace, seeming even smaller compared to the monolith dragon as they approached him.

"Ellaria, please hand your necklace to Ezel," the dragon said.

"Her brother gave that to her before he died," Ezel signed. *"You can't ask her to part from it."*

The monolith dragon made a noise that sounded like a repressed laugh, but his tone softened. "Your compassion for your friends is what makes you so well suited for the task before us. We will ask many to part with dear things before this is over, but there will be life afterward."

"It's alright," Ellaria said, untying the necklace and handing it to Ezel. "I trust you with it."

The deep gnome's eyes rimmed with tears as he accepted the stone like it was his friend's greatest treasure.

"Now, hold it against the token and raise it high," Elrenigeth instructed.

The deep gnome did so, and the monolith dragon raised an enormous claw up high from the lake, dripping and casting Ezel in its shadow. Elrenigeth lowered the claw toward the upraised token and stone and tapped them with the claw's chipped tip.

A sudden burst of magical energy exploded from the stone, sending the others to their rears and sliding backward. Enkeli held his staff before him and, with great effort, remained on his feet.

Garron rolled over, watching his friend as magical ribbons of blue and green light danced around the gnome. Just as quickly as the ribbons had burst forth, they folded in on themselves, hurtling back toward the token.

Ezel inspected his hands to find that the stone was gone but one of the runes carved into the hardened wood of the token glowed with a green light while the tree blazed blue. The deep gnome wriggled his fingers, and the usual blue magic blazed to life on his tattoo runes.

Garron ran up to him. "Ezel, are you alright?" he asked, checking the little gnome over.

"Yes," he signed. *"But the stone. It's gone!"*

"You now carry the green stone as well," Elrenigeth said plainly. "We designed the token so that you could carry all the stones. One rune for each. It is the only way. For just as much as I have come to regret my involvement in the wicked creation of the stones, Kilretheon's anger has festered into a lust for vengeance. You must gather all the stones. With them, you will end this."

The little gnome's eyes fell. Garron couldn't imagine what he must be thinking. *This is too great a burden,* the man thought.

Ezel didn't respond to the monolith dragon's words. Instead, he leaned over and picked up the leather string that had once held the green stone. He looked mournfully at it before holding it up toward Ellaria. *"I'm so sorry,"* he signed.

Ellaria took the string in her hand, and a tear fell from her emerald eye. "It's ... It's alright," she managed to say.

"Tie it around your neck again, young one," Elrenigeth instructed. "It will not have the same magic it did with the stone, but the magic has worked its way into the very fibers. You may be surprised at its usefulness. Enkeli, we will need to get them to Kelvur. He must collect the rest of the monolith stones. It is the only way to stop Kilretheon. Prepare them."

The monolith dragon stretched his wings wide, astounding them with his grandeur as they watched.

"Let us see if my old bones can do this," Elrenigeth said. "Touching the power of the stones has given me much fervor."

Where there was no wind, winds roared like a hurricane. Garron grabbed onto Ellaria and Ezel, bracing them against the great wing wash as the monolith dragon beat his mighty wings and took to the sky.

"Come," Enkeli said, as the dragon flew far enough above them that they no longer felt the effects of the great beating of his wings. "Let us get you some food and ointment for your sand burns before we depart."

Garron glanced from Ellaria to Ezel. None of them really had words to describe what they were feeling after the experience, so they followed the wizard in silence.

While they ate, Enkeli and Kanku answered as many questions as they could for the weary trio. The ointment of the melior—something they mixed together from the unique plants that grew in the shadow of the First Tree of Tarrine—worked wonders on the sand burns, soothing and healing their raw skin.

Kanku assured Garron that they had no mirror like the one he described but suggested that perhaps one of the melior tribes from another land did. As far as Kanku knew, they were dwarvish artifacts.

"What about Kel Joran's expedition?" Garron asked, drawing the book from his leather satchel. "What happened to them?"

Enkeli clicked his tongue and shook his head. "They made great strides toward their goal. In fact, they found numerous melior ruins in the desert, but there are many dangers. Great sand serpents and krellievs—nasty creatures," the wizard said with a shake. "I found their remains many years ago. I still remember the days I toiled near the ruins of Matloa, burying each of them."

"They died? All of them?" Garron pressed.

"All of them," Enkeli said sadly. "But you found what Kel Joran sought. You finished his expedition. You found the First Tree of Tarrine."

Though the wizard's words were encouraging in tone, Garron did not relish in the victory. It seemed a sad fate that Kel Joran and his wife and crew had suffered. Perhaps, at some point, he would be able to bring word back to Kaelor. Maybe they would be able to find the ruins of Matloa someday and visit the explorers' final resting place.

Enkeli explained the plan that he and the monolith dragon had come up with. After some short pleasantries and less dire conversation, he shooed them to find a bit of rest before their departure.

Garron found Benley, happily munching on some sort of grass the melior had brought the pegasus. "Hey pal," he said to the pegasus, patting his neck. One of the melior had treated Benley's sand burns as well, something for which the man was grateful. Garron pulled an apple from beneath his cloak, and Benley immediately turned his attention from the grass. The man laughed. "You're a sucker for a good apple."

Ezel stepped around a building and nodded to Garron, signing, *"Somehow, I thought you'd be here."*

"Were you looking for me?" the man signed back with a chuckle.

"Enkeli said we'll leave as soon as Elrenigeth returns."

"Yeah, where did the dragon go, anyway?" Garron asked.

"Enkeli said Elrenigeth hasn't had the strength to fly in centuries. Touching the power of the stones gave him strength. Supposed he just wanted to soar the skies again for a bit."

"You mean before the flight all the way to Kelvur?"

Ezel chuckled and shrugged. *"I suppose it's better he finds out if he's strong enough to fly before we're riding on his back. Not sure I want to be in that crash."*

"Fair enough." Garron nodded. *"I suppose you don't really need Benley and me now that you've got a monolith dragon."*

"What's that supposed to mean?" Ezel signed, stepping closer and eyeing the man.

"I was just the means to get you here, is all."

"You led us here," Ezel flipped his hands quickly. *"And I plan to follow your lead to the end of this thing."*

"I led us here because I heard a voice no one else could," Garron said aloud.

Ezel shook his head and closed the gap between them. *"We didn't have to come. We could have let you come here by yourself, but we followed you because we trust you."*

"Why?" Garron asked aloud.

"You're my friend, and it seems to me that my trust was not misplaced," the gnome signed and then motioned for Garron to look around and see where they were.

"After everything I've done ... I didn't even trust myself."

Ezel let out a silent chuckle. *"Friends are there in times when you don't trust yourself and you need someone to believe in you."* The gnome climbed atop Benley and perched himself on the pegasus's back. He crossed his legs and placed a hand on Garron's shoulder. *"I know it's hard, but someday you'll come to know this truth. You cannot define your life by your greatest mistake. Learn from it and press on to something greater."*

Garron wasn't sure how to respond.

Suddenly, Ellaria turned the corner and spotted them.

Ezel signed quickly to the man, *"If you get stuck looking at the past, you might not see the greater things that come looking for you."* The little gnome's eyebrows wriggled.

Garron pushed him, and Ezel nearly toppled over the other side of the pegasus. He wheezed little laughs and popped up to greet Ellaria.

"There you two are," she said. "They offered me a room with a big bed and furs, but I couldn't sleep."

"Missed us that much, huh?" Garron teased.

"Stuff it," Ellaria said, her cheeks flushing to the color of her wild hair. "You two know where Silverwing is?"

"Yes," Garron said. "Come on. I'll show you."

Ezel eyed the man with a smug grin on his face. Garron pushed the gnome again, and that time he fell, laughing all the way, into a high pile of the grass the melior had brought for Benley.

CHAPTER TWENTY-FIVE

UNION OF FATES

T he cool spring breeze wafted through the window of the keep. Merrick stood his ground, knowing the short blast of cold air would pass and the sun would warm his back again momentarily. He'd perched himself next to the window many times over the past few days.

There had been much discussion since their arrival in Aiden's Dell. The city itself was significantly larger than the huntsman had anticipated. When he'd first seen the great fissure in the Palisade from the north side, he hadn't been able to see the sprawling city on the southern side.

He stood in Queen Pellad's war room, while the leaders discussed Jaernok Tur's armies. The people of Aiden's Dell were well aware of the wretchlings, which they previously called shadow beasts. The Duskwood Rangers had encountered several wretchling scouting parties over the past months. The folks from Dorantown were surprised to hear that not only had they encountered the wretchlings, but they'd also had word that several villages on the northern islands in the Zors had been burned and destroyed. Apparently, Jaernok Tur was waging his war on multiple fronts.

Tempers were high with so many unanswered questions. Aiden's Dell had known almost nothing of Dorantown, in its seclusion and previous use as a slave mining camp. They had worried more over what had been happening in the northeast of Kelvur as Jaernok Tur made waves from the Crags. The refugees from Dorantown were also shocked to find out that Aiden's Dell had not seen nor heard from Nera or Shorlis. They feared the worst about their friends, wondering what fate could have befallen them.

Though Merrick had passed the Shell of Callencia to Ralowyn, they'd been unable to work its magic. The she elf mentioned numerous times over the previous few days how frustrated she was that they had not thought to train others on the use of the shell. It seemed a grave oversight with one of her oldest friends gone. Merrick knew that fact hurt her as well. On top of all those things, they still had no way of knowing what happened to those who were supposed to evacuate on the *Sellena*. The huntsman did his best to support her in the midst of the discussions and in the quiet moments they found between sessions with the queen.

"The scouting parties have been moving closer and closer to Aiden's Dell," Ven said. The domin ranger's curly black hair cascaded over the furs he wore around his burly shoulders. His black beard was flecked with white hairs, giving him a weathered appearance. When he spoke, he did so with intentionality and a determined tone. "We abandoned the Duskwood Lake Lodge as soon as their attacks became a daily occurrence. They will be here any day now."

Queen Pellad, a dwarf woman, beautifully adorned with gems and a regal dress to match, placed her head in her hands. Her brown hair, braided with intertwining stone beads, encased her, giving her the appearance of being trapped in a net.

Merrick didn't envy her position. In a sense, she was trapped. They couldn't abandon Aiden's Dell. The stories they'd told him of the Forest of Wirra to the south made the place sound more dangerous than the Wildlands of Tarrine. The road to Antalon on the coast was treacherous in the spring as the mountain snows began to melt, creating waterfalls and snow slush that could bury an army. And then there was the army of wretchlings coming from the north.

"What would you have me do, Domin Ven?" the queen asked. "I already have the city guard on constant watch. If they aren't on shift, they're resting for when the wretchling army arrives."

The domin ranger leaned forward on the table. "At least help me find a place south of the Palisade for the non-fighters from Dorantown. The Dell Lodge is large but not big enough to house them long-term. We both know, anyone north of the wall will be at the greatest risk during the attack."

"Aye, and we will keep our fighters at the lodge to help when the wretchlings show their ugly faces," Coal said, but quickly added, "Your Majesty."

"We were able to hold them off long enough for many of our people to retreat from Dorantown," Ralowyn added.

"There is no retreating from this fight, Lady Ralowyn," the queen said.

"No," Vorenna put in. The barbarian woman's muscles tensed. "But you have much greater defenses in place than we did. With our combined forces, we could make a great stand here. Javelin is tough."

Ralowyn held out a slender hand to settle Vorenna before she worked herself up again, like she had several times over the past few days. "Fate seems to have brought us into a union unlike anything seen since the days of the old heroes of Kelvur," Ralowyn said, recalling some of the tales Shorlis had shared with her. "And just like those heroes, we stand against impossible odds. But we must fight. We must fight for life. For love." She paused to glance at Merrick. "For everything good in Finlestia. The sorcerer's wretchlings are a wave of death, and I do not intend to die here. I have a vision for tomorrow and the many tomorrows to come."

Merrick smiled at her. He believed she meant what she said. He believed she would do whatever it took to see that future unfold. Best of all, he knew she meant a future with him. The huntsman suddenly felt stupid for all the times he'd wondered if he were good enough for an elf like her. They'd faced certain death multiple times, and yet, even the darkest of hours had not torn them apart. He found a simplicity to things when considered under the crystal clear light of life and death.

The huntsman walked away from the window, sat in the chair next to Ralowyn, and grabbed her slender hand, squeezing it lovingly.

He turned toward Queen Pellad and said, "The situation is not what any of us would hope for. Since I left my home in Tamaria so long ago, I have found that things rarely go as planned. The most important thing we can do is make decisions for the present and embrace the moments in which we've found ourselves."

The dwarf queen heaved a great sigh as the others watched her, awaiting her answer. Merrick eyed her sympathetically, as she seemed to calculate something he could not see. Finally, she said, "Domin Ven, we have already pulled the farmers and workers from the north side of the Palisade and brought them into homes here on the south side. I will have my staff put out a call to any home that does not host a guest. We will find the Dorantown refugees places to shelter."

"Yes, my Queen," the domin said with a grateful nod. He turned quickly to the elven ranger who had not interjected a word in all of the proceedings. "Lidrea, please return to the lodge and prepare all the non-fighters for replacement."

"Yes, Domin," she said and spun out of the room.

"Thank you, Your Majesty," Coal said. "I assure you, the rest of us will fight as though your home were our own."

"What choice do you have?" she asked solemnly.

Not a single person in the room had a response to her melancholic words. With Nera and Shorlis never having made it to Aiden's Dell and no word from those that retreated on the *Sellena,* their outlook was bleak at best.

Queen Pellad dismissed them all. "Let us reconvene tomorrow if there is time. Should any of you come up with a brilliant plan to get us out of this predicament, know that my door will remain open to you."

Merrick squeezed Ralowyn's hand tightly in his own, leading her out of the keep. They followed Ven through the busy streets of Aiden's Dell with the rest of their group. He led them through the wide makeshift gate that tethered the two sides of the fissure that scarred the Palisade. The jagged edges of the great wall loomed above them like cliff faces on either side.

"What happened here, anyway?" Coal asked the domin ranger as they walked.

"There are a number of stories," Ven answered. "Some say it was a battle between the heroes of old and the giants of the Eastern Knolls. A war waged over the slaying of a princess. Others say it was a dragon attack when the cities of the north were still in their prime. They say Grumbol the Grim decided he wanted all the riches of the northern cities and destroyed them to gather a horde for himself. They say he tried to destroy Aiden's Dell and the Palisade, but the effort to tear down the wall was too much. Dragons prefer lounging with their luxuries to working hard. Still, there are other theories."

"And which theory do you hold to?" Merrick asked.

Ven huffed and smiled. "I think there must have been some magic involved. The way the stones are scattered in the fields north of the Palisade makes me think they were thrown that way. Could giants have hurled such great chunks of stone? Perhaps. But how did they break the wall to begin with? I think there was once a great battle here, long before our time. I think the destruction was caused by a war of wizards."

"A war of wizards?" Coal asked incredulously.

"Powerful masters of the arcane arts wielding their might at each other could cause a serious mess," Ven said with a bob of his head.

"Maybe," Merrick agreed. "It would be nice to have a wizard on our side for the battle to come."

"Well, unfortunately, you will have to settle for me and the rest of the mages of Aiden's Dell for your magic wielding," Ralowyn said.

Merrick stopped her, pulling her close with his hand. "There is none I'd rather settle with."

A slight smile creased her lips, and she stared into his eyes as he brushed silvery strands of hair away from her fair face and behind her pointed ear.

Ven cleared his throat. "You know, as domin of the Duskwood Rangers, I have the authority to wed folks. We're out in Duskwood for months at a time. It's not uncommon for some to fall for each other. I could—"

"Tonight?" Ralowyn asked Merrick.

"Tonight and forever," the huntsman said.

Coal only chuckled.

Ralowyn wiped away the tear that tickled her cheek as she watched Merrick and Kippin working with his new falcon, Davir. When she told the little halfling that Davir meant "brave" in elvish, his eyes went wide and he jumped around, laughing hysterically.

"That's the perfect name for him!" he'd said. "I knew it was right! I just knew it."

The halfling had celebrated until he realized that when Ralowyn said it to him, she was calling him brave. The sentiment washed over him then, and he dissolved into joyful tears, cuddling into her. Eventually, she became the one with joyful tears streaming down her face.

Many of the lands north of the Palisade were hemmed in by a wide wooden wall that extended in a semicircle from one side of the fissure all the way around to the other. The place had been cleared of workers, leaving the whole area for Merrick and Kippin to run and play with Davir. As Ralowyn watched them laugh and work together in the golden glow of the waning sunlight, she thought it was a moment that would be etched in her memory forever.

"Tonight and forever," Merrick had said. A promise of things to come.

A prickle rolled across her nose and in between her brows. More tears would come, even though she sat there with a quiet smile.

The shuffling of long grass behind her pricked her ears, but she didn't need to turn to know those footsteps. After all, she'd run through Duskwood with the not-so-stealthy dwarf.

"Well, isn't that a sight," Coal said, sitting upon the great log next to her.

"The most beautiful I have ever seen," she said, with a slight sniff.

Coal glanced at her and chuckled. He reached an arm around the slender elf and gave her a side hug. "Aye," he said softly.

"I should probably prepare for the ceremony," she said, wiping her face with both hands. "If I don't stop this crying, my face will be streaked with tears."

Coal laughed again. "Lass, you look lovely as ever."

"Thank you."

"Aye, it's an easy thing to say. I just ..." His words trailed off as he stared down and picked at the wrappings that always covered his hands.

"What is it?" Ralowyn asked with a curious smile.

"I was just thinking. In royal dwarven weddings, the clan kings usher the brides to their new husbands," the dwarf said bashfully, though his words got quicker as if he were trying to explain himself. "It's a great honor because the clan king reveals his mark."

Coal unwound the wrappings on his hand, revealing the clan tattoo on his palm that marked him as a clan prince of Clan Carraignyk. The intricate tattoo, made with dwarven ink from the depths of Kalimandir, looked as new as the day it was inked. "And then the bride gets to hold his marked hand. And I was thinking, since Master Tenlien isn't here, that maybe I could be the one to escort you to Merrick at the ceremony."

He nervously rubbed the clan mark on his palm.

"Coal," Ralowyn said softly.

"It's alright lass. I understand. I'm not your father or anything. It was silly of me to ask. I just thought since I don't have a clan anymore, and we don't know what tomorrow will bring, maybe it would be my only chance. I just—"

Ralowyn placed a hand on the dwarf's shoulder and kissed his cheek.

The little patch of exposed skin above his great black beard rosed with color.

"Coal," she said again, "first, you are a young dwarf."

"In my seventies," he interjected.

"Young for a dwarf. You have a good 275 more years in you, I am sure."

Coal bobbed his head to the side. His hesitance was not unwarranted. As much as she liked to think of the wonderful future she had envisioned, a battle still loomed before them.

She continued, "You will have the chance to do many things you do not expect." She paused and pointed to Merrick and Kippin who were huddled together, talking about something pertaining to Davir. Then she pointed to herself. "And *we* are your clan."

A big tear escaped the dwarf's eye, disappearing into the forest of his beard. "Aye, that you are."

"It would be my honor if you would usher me to my new husband."

Merrick sat in a tall-backed chair in the corner of the great hall of the Duskwood Rangers' Dell Lodge. The structure was built from massive logs taken from Duskwood. The interior was sparsely decorated with uniquely patterned pelts and the occasional woven tapestry, clearing the way for the beauty of the knots and natural curves of the logs. The stone fireplace blazed with light, warming the lodge. Though it was large, the building had a homey feel, and Merrick took note, thinking he might like to build a cabin with such elements for him and Ralowyn and Kippin to live in someday.

The huntsman watched as a few of the rangers gathered to the side, tuning their instruments. Merrick had never taken to music. His mother, Marie, had a lovely singing voice. She used to sing him songs when he was little, but the gift hadn't passed down to the huntsman.

Ven crossed the great hall to him, holding up a coat. His eyes flicked between the coat and the huntsman as if he were sizing the man up.

"Here," the burly domin said. "Try this on."

Merrick looked skeptically at the large man but took the coat and slid his arms into it. He pulled it over his shoulders and found that it fit better than he'd anticipated. He'd never owned a coat like it. The cut was of a design more for looks than utility, something Merrick had never needed as a huntsman. The stitching was artful, and it looked as though whoever had created the piece had done so with great care.

"Wow," Merrick said. "Thank you."

"I got it from Lonny," Ven said. "He's not as big as me. Not many people are, actually." He laughed. "My wedding coat hasn't been used by another since me."

"You're married then?" Merrick asked, realizing he hadn't considered the fact.

"Was," Ven said with a sad smile. "She passed some years back."

"I'm so sorry," Merrick said. "I didn't mean to—"

"It's alright, lad," the domin said. "We had a good life together. Three grown kids. A life full of love. That there's one of my boys. He took to music like his mother." Ven pointed to a young man who fiddled with a lute and chatted casually with another ranger who tightened the skin of a drum.

"Do all the rangers have families?" Merrick asked.

"No," the domin ranger said. "Some just love to patrol the wilds by themselves. There is a certain peace to it. Hard to describe."

"I know the feeling," Merrick said.

"Right. A huntsman would know," the big man said, patting Merrick on the shoulder and falling into the chair next to him. "Do you plan to go back to ... to ..."

"Tamaria," Merrick offered.

"Right! Tamaria. I couldn't remember, sorry."

"It's alright," the huntsman offered. "I don't know, actually. I suppose it will be something Ralowyn and I have to discuss once this is all over—once Jaernok Tur is defeated. I've hardly been able to think what that might look like. Everything has changed. I tried to be the huntsman again back in Dorantown, but war followed us. I'm not entirely sure what we'll do. Plus, we have Kippin."

"Yes. I like the little one." Ven barked a hearty laugh. "Reminds me of my daughter. Tinli was a dragon spit, too. Now she's one of the best rangers we have."

"Really?" Merrick chuckled.

"Oh, yeah. Took to it like a trout to the stream. Nothing like getting a child outdoors. It's a simple life, but I think it's the best way to raise them. But that's just an old ranger talking."

Merrick smirked. "My Da said something similar to me when I was little. I didn't always like him for it, but I'm grateful now."

Another laugh rumbled out of the burly ranger. "No, I don't suppose you did. I had plenty of days my children didn't like me for it while we trudged through the deep snow in hard winters. But they all seem to love me still. Could be they got that from their mother, but I like to think it was all the time we spent together."

"I can say with certainty, that's what it was for my father and me," Merrick said. He paused for a long while, thinking about his parents. He thought about his sister, Ellaria, and how he wished they were there for that moment. He knew they might consider it impetuous, but after everything he and Ralowyn had been through and with no promise of tomorrow, he didn't want to waste any more time.

"You alright, lad?" Ven asked. The domin ranger's crow's-feet wrinkled around his soft eyes.

"Yes. I was just thinking about my family. I haven't seen them in such a long time. I miss them and wish they were here for this."

"I understand," Ven said, stroking his black and white beard thoughtfully. "Well, I know I'm not your family, but I'll be up there with you in any case. And Kippin and Coal will be here. Where is that little spit anyway?"

Merrick chuckled. "Kippin wanted to pick some flowers for Ralowyn, so Coal took him to the field."

"Very good," Ven said with an approving nod. He eyed the huntsman for a long moment, and Merrick wondered what the ranger was thinking. "I know you miss your family, and you'll probably want to go back to Tamaria, at least for a visit—introduce them to your new wife and son. When all that's done, if the wild still calls you but being a huntsman doesn't fill the hole in your chest, you could always come back here. A huntsman with your experience would make a fine ranger, I'd wager. And Ralowyn seems quite capable herself." Ven laughed again.

"Oh, she is," Merrick said with a chuckle.

"Seriously, lad," the domin ranger said, leaning toward Merrick and placing a big hand on the younger man's shoulder, "you and your family would be welcome among the Duskwood Rangers."

A sense of irresistible gratitude welled within Merrick, and all he could say was, "Thank you."

Honestly, the huntsman had no idea what he was going to do afterward. He hoped there was an afterward. He had an overwhelming urge to spend decades with Ralowyn and to see Kippin grow up. Perhaps they would have more children—give Kippin a brother or sister. Who knew what the future might hold? He intended to find out.

As evening came upon them, Ralowyn was greeted at the lodge by Lidrea, bearing an elegant green dress. It was the color of spring, embroidered with white lace.

"One of the other rangers wore it for her ceremony last summer. I'm sorry I don't have anything fancier for you," the ranger said.

"It is beautiful," Ralowyn said. "Thank you."

The ranger helped her get the artful dress on, tightening the strings in the back.

A knock sounded at the door of the cozy room. Lidrea answered the door, while Ralowyn examined the intricate lace work of the dress. She'd spent her whole life at the wisdom tower in Loralith, where they paid little attention to luxuries. Then she lived in Elderwood Forest for forty years where clothes had been practical for survival. Since then, she'd been on the move, not slowing much to think about such things.

As she performed a slow twirl in the dress to see its flow, a stunned "Wow" came from the dwarf at the door.

Coal stood between the frames, looking rather unlike himself. Someone had gotten their hands on his beard, turning his usual single braid into an intricate array of braids. Someone had also gotten a comb through his thick black hair.

"Wow, indeed," Ralowyn said with a nod and a smile.

Coal blushed and scuffed his boot against the floor. "I, uh ... well, I brought you some flowers for your hair. We usually do stone beads, but I couldn't find any, and well, you're more like a flower anyway. And—"

"They are lovely," Ralowyn said before he could get into one of his excuse ramblings. "Thank you."

"Right. Well." Coal stammered and handed the flowers to Lidrea. "I'll let you get to it, then."

"Wait," Lidrea said, stopping the dwarf mid-spin. She took one of the flowers that still had a long stem and tucked it into the chest pocket on his cloak. She straightened it so the petals were on full display. "There," she said. "Now, off you go. I'll get her all ready."

Coal nodded and hurried out of the room.

"He is sweet," Lidrea said as she separated the flowers to braid into Ralowyn's hair.

"He is," Ralowyn agreed.

"Does he have a wife?"

Ralowyn inclined her head to look at the other elf.

Lidrea gave Ralowyn's silvery hair a gentle tug to make her look away. "Only curious."

When Lidrea opened the door and led Ralowyn into the hallway, Coal jumped to his feet and stared in astonishment.

"You look ..." The dwarf's words caught in his throat. "Just beautiful," he finally managed to say.

Lidrea hurried off to the great hall, Ralowyn and Coal following at their own pace. They walked in companionable silence, neither daring to speak, for worry of more tears.

When they made it to the open doorway of the great hall, they paused. Rangers and Javelin members filled the room. The excited whispering buzz ceased as Lidrea shushed them and they recognized Ralowyn's arrival. Vorenna immediately started sobbing at the sight of the elf, the barbarian woman's big shoulders heaving with her stuttered breath. Ralowyn smiled at the woman's great capacity for emotions.

Ralowyn scanned the room and realized she heard the sound of quiet music. The rangers of Duskwood were a surprising bunch. She had not expected such a showing for an impromptu wedding. The smells of freshly baked bread and flickering candles filled the great hall. Lanterns warmed the scene with soft light. Before the hearth, stood Merrick and Kippin, both glossy-eyed.

Coal cleared his throat and unwrapped his hand, revealing the clan mark. "My lady," he said with as much etiquette as he could muster. He held out his wide dwarven palm, and Ralowyn gripped it softly.

The dwarf's body twitched as he pushed down his emotions, and he escorted her to the front of the gathering. As they neared the hearth, she turned and hugged Coal. He pulled away, wiping the tears off his face with his beard.

"Onward you go," he blubbered. "For glory and home."

"Thank you," she said with a slight bow.

Kippin stood in front of her then with the collection of flowers he'd gathered. "These are for you," he said with a sniff.

"Oh, *davir lolel non*," she whispered. She brushed the curly mop of hair out of his eyes. "Thank you."

Kippin promptly returned to Merrick's side, standing as straight as he could, as though all the world depended on his duty to do so.

When her glistening eyes met Merrick's, Ralowyn's heart pounded, and the warmth of joy flooded her body. The rest of the world melted away in that moment. There they stood—just them.

"In the wilds between Duskwood and the Eastern Knolls, every ranger carries one thing: a rope," Domin Ranger Ven announced. "A rope is necessary for survival. It can be used in countless situations to give life and hope where otherwise there might only be despair and death. While every ranger has their own expertise with different tools, none leaves the lodge or home without a rope."

He produced a rope from a small table nearby and handed it to Merrick.

"What is it that makes a rope strong? A rope is braided from more than one string. A string on its own has many great qualities. Many a ranger have used string to catch fish or tie traps. And while the string is versatile, it cannot bear the weight of a ranger hanging from a cliff. When strings are braided together, they are stronger—just like two people who come together in life."

Merrick unraveled part of the rope as Ven had instructed him. Ralowyn watched as the huntsman looped it around her forearm. He then wrapped it around his own.

"With this loop, I bind myself to you," Merrick said, "to guard your heart as if it were my own. Will you walk this path with me?"

A prickle on the bridge of her nose bolstered the tears in her eyes, several of them running over and streaking her fair cheeks. She inhaled, overcoming her wild emotions, to speak their words. "Tonight and forever."

Merrick exhaled a suppressed laugh as he grinned at her. His eyes were steady, gazing upon her with pure and intimate joy.

Domin Ven let out a chuckle of his own before composing himself and continuing. "On the eve of what could be the greatest challenge of all our lives, these two are bonded in marriage to face the danger together. May the bond make you a strong rope, capable of carrying you both through the most difficult things in this life. And when the difficult times are far away, may you tie it into a net to catch all the joys of this life!"

The rangers around the room let out a great cheer, which was quickly joined by the rest of the people gathered.

Ven laughed heartily and said, "Well, kiss her then!"

Merrick slipped his hand behind Ralowyn's back and pulled her close. She could feel his gentle breath on her lips as he whispered, "Tonight and forever."

His lips pressed against hers, a warm reminder of his love and promise.

More cheers rang out around the great hall as Ven announced, "Let's celebrate!"

The musicians began playing an upbeat folk ballad that encouraged many in the room to dance. Others went for the food—an impressive array considering the impromptu nature of the wedding. It was only when Ralowyn was congratulated by a dressed-down Queen Pellad that she realized where the feast had come from.

"My Queen," Ralowyn said with a grateful nod.

"Not tonight, my dear," she said with a wink. "Tonight is your night."

Merrick convinced Ralowyn to dance with him, though she didn't require much coaxing. Eventually, Kippin tapped in to dance with her, and the little halfling's adorable efforts melted her heart. She laughed as she spotted Vorenna attempting to tap out Lidrea for a dance with Coal.

Ralowyn couldn't remember a time when she'd been so happy and surrounded by such love and mirth. She thought of their dinners full of laughter and merriment with Karnak and Tanessa back in Calrok. For a moment, she wished they were there, too, dancing around the lodge's great hall with them. She thought of Master Tenlien back in Loralith, how he would likely be smiling at her across the room with that fatherly look in his eye. Though they weren't present for the celebration, she knew they'd be ecstatic to celebrate with them when they were together again.

Merrick tapped Kippin out again as the music slowed, whispering something in the little halfling's ear. Ralowyn watched Kippin as Merrick swept her in, holding her close as they rocked. The halfling tapped on Coal's shoulder, taking Vorenna, a move the barbarian woman couldn't get upset over. She did, however, give Lidrea a quick leer as the elf ranger swooped in to dance with the dwarf again.

Ralowyn chuckled. Merrick pulled away slightly so he could look her in the eyes. He smiled. "What is it?"

"Kippin and Coal," she said.

Merrick chuckled, too. "I saw Coal dancing with Lidrea earlier. Seemed like a sweet pairing. Thought I'd help it."

"To the chagrin of Vorenna," Ralowyn said, popping an amused eyebrow.

Merrick shrugged innocently.

The party continued for a long while. Rangers and Javelin warriors enjoyed the break from their looming peril, until the entry doors to the lodge burst open and a lone ranger entered.

Her raggedy cloak fluttered behind her in shredded tentacles. She stumbled through the crowd, trying to catch her breath. Others swarmed her, trying to see what had happened to her.

"Water!" Ven called out. "Bring her some water. Make way," he instructed the others. He met her in the middle of the great hall. "Tinli, are you alright? What's happened?"

When she looked upon him, the room gasped. Her face was covered in blood. She'd obviously taken a slice from a weapon to the forehead, though the cut didn't seem deep.

"Father," she croaked as she slumped into his embrace.

"Hold on," he said, taking water from a ranger. He helped his daughter take a few gulps. "There," he said. "Are you injured elsewhere?"

"No," she said. "Just nicks and bruises. My head took the worst of it."

"What happened?" Ven asked again.

"Jori's dead, Father." She choked on her words. "The wretchlings have crossed the river. They're coming."

"Crossed the river," Ven grumbled to himself.

"What? What does that mean?" Queen Pellad asked, pushing aside any casual attitude she'd brought for the celebration.

The domin ranger eyed her grimly. "It means the battle has come."

CHAPTER TWENTY-SIX

TAKE TO THE SKY

When Karnak had opened the door to Hazkul Bern's room two days earlier, the orc fell to his knees. The window to the room was left open, letting the cool night air in. It was clear to him that, since their conversation in the dark back room of the *High Winds Alehouse*, the assassin had gathered what little he wanted before fleeing. But what he left, struck Karnak's heart.

Dalkeri lay on display in the middle of the perfectly made bed.

Since that discovery, the orc had toiled over the axe, his heart broken. *Firestorm,* Karnak thought, as he held the great battle axe his father had passed on to him, *no more fire in you now.*

Dalkeri was a mangled mess. The axe blades on either side were as sharp as ever, but where the magical orange stone had been encased, only a twisted scar of metal remained. The morning sun behind him glinted off the sharp blades, as he sat on the edge of the cliff looking westward over the Gant Sea.

The sorcerer put out your fire, he thought to the weapon as though to an old friend. He hadn't slept the previous night. Instead, he'd sat with *Dalkeri* under the moonlight, doing everything he could to resurrect the axe's magical flames. He'd gripped the axe so tightly sometimes that his knuckles turned white. He just wanted to feel something from it. A little hum of energy. A small spark. Anything. But *Dalkeri* gave him no indication of life.

His chin quivered with rage as he shifted his tusks from side to side. The axe was yet another thing he'd lost in the war. While it may have still seemed a formidable weapon to others, to him it was a shell of its former glory.

"Karnak?" Orin called gently from a few paces away. The guardian's sudden noise startled the big orc, and his great green shoulders tensed. "Have you been here all night?"

Karnak wasn't sure how to respond, so he brushed past the question. "Are the others awake?"

"They are," Orin said slowly. "The Glain's Griffins are also readying for the flight to Aiden's Dell."

"Very well," Karnak said. "I'll be there shortly."

The guardian was suddenly next to the orc, who still sat in the grass on the edge. "Are you alright?" Orin asked.

Karnak grunted before he heaved a great sigh. He knew Orin to be a caring man who would not relent in his concern—a trait he'd noticed in several of the men he'd befriended. "*Dalkeri* has no magic left in it."

"I can see that," Orin said. "Still a mighty axe."

Karnak grunted a laugh. "I've been debating whether to throw it into the sea."

Orin took a tentative step toward the edge of the cliff, looking far below to the waves crashing upon the rocks. "Why?" The question's tone bore no judgment. It was merely an inquiry.

Karnak thought for a moment. "When I look at *Dalkeri* and this great scar, I think of how far we've fallen. When this axe burst to flame in my hands, enemies trembled in fear. Since I lost it, the only thing we seem to do is run for our lives. Loss after loss."

Orin nodded thoughtfully, weighing Karnak's words. The man always seemed to judge things with due measure. The orc appreciated that about the guardian.

Finally, Orin asked, "Or could it be a reminder of how we've been knocked down, beaten, bruised, and scarred, and yet we remain?"

"Perhaps," Karnak said slowly. He hadn't considered it that way. Though, as he looked at *Dalkeri*, the wind whipping through his long black hair, the weapon triggered only sadness.

Orin gave him a compassionate smile. "Throw it into the sea," he encouraged. "Or don't. But let us move on from this place and rise up to finish this war."

The man extended a hand to the large orc. The guardian grunted as he heaved and helped Karnak to his feet. The gar looked at the smaller man for a long moment, still unsure. Orin merely nodded his encouragement, making Karnak feel as though whatever decision he made, the man had his back.

Karnak rolled the handle of the axe in his hand, feeling the cool metal. *Dalkeri* still felt balanced in his hand. His eyes landed on the twisted metal void where the stone had once been mounted. It was an ugly scar on an otherwise beautiful weapon. He tried once more to set it ablaze, reaching deep within himself and extending every effort toward the axe.

Nothing.

Karnak nodded and stepped into a swinging throw, hurling *Dalkeri* through the morning air. The axe hurtled outward, not flying like the magic missile it had been in years past. The orc turned and thanked Orin as they walked away from the cliffside.

"Let's go and find our people. Hopefully, they made it to Aiden's Dell without much—"

Karnak's words were cut off when cool metal slapped into his hand. Instinctively, he gripped it and raised his hand. *Dalkeri* rested easily in his grasp. He turned to the guardian who looked as shocked as he.

"What in Finlestia?" the orc muttered.

"No magic left in it, huh?" Orin laughed excitedly.

Karnak's face grew into a wicked grin as he turned and threw *Dalkeri* again.

Orin leaned into his griffin, whose name was Olet. A pretty name, he thought. She ripped through the sky, dipping and diving and flourishing as they flew. Orin put her through numerous exercises to see what she could do and found her to be quite capable. As the wind whipped through his close-cropped blond hair and he looked over the land of Kelvur far below him, he couldn't help but grin.

He wasn't the only one relishing a new partnership. Several of the guardians who'd lost their griffins had been paired with new ones in Glain's Shoulder. Like Orin, they had been skeptical about the bonding process. As they attempted acrobatic maneuvers of their own, many of them laughed or smiled broadly.

Being on griffin-back once more was a strange feeling to Orin. His first griffin had been a male, larger than Olet, so sitting upon her felt different. She also had a shorter wingspan, which varied her movements.

They flew until midday, the riders from the Glain's Griffins leading them to a meadow on the edge of a great forest. They landed to drink from the river that snaked through the meadow. Spring flowers were beginning to show their faces to the sun. They painted the meadow in vibrant colors.

Orin patted Olet as she helped herself to some water from the river. He approached Jensen, who was discussing something with Karnak.

"How does it compare to flying wyvern?" Jensen was asking the orc.

"Maxlir's maneuvers are different," Karnak said. "Tighter. Quicker turns and shifts. Less powerful, though. Ker would beat her wings and lift us high with only a few flaps. The griffin needs more with his shorter wingspan."

"Makes sense," Jensen said, turning and seeing Orin. "And how about you? Never thought you'd be on griffin-back again. Must feel great?"

"It does," Orin admitted. "Different, certainly. But it does feel good. I saw you throwing *Dalkeri,*" he said, pointing to the axe in Karnak's hand.

"Just testing what it can do now," Karnak said with a chuckle. "It still won't burst to flame like it used to, and it doesn't fly as fast as it did. But for some reason, it still comes back after I throw it."

Yenklin popped up beside them. The High Seat of Glain's Shoulder had taken charge of the Glain's Griffins for the mission. He'd been a member of the unit for many years before he was designated as the High Seat.

Orin gave the orc a nod and greeted him, "High Seat."

"Yenklin is fine, my boy," Yenklin waved off the formality. "We ride into battle together. Great honor is due to those who fight for the freedom of others. Either of us can fall in battle, thus making us equally worthy of honor."

"Yenklin," Orin agreed. "I wanted to say thank you for sending a contingent of your city guard with our people back to Dorantown."

The orc huffed a laugh. "Well, your people couldn't sail all the way to Far. We haven't had contact with the city in years. Who knows how they would be greeted there? Plus, when we defeat this threat, maybe we can start fresh. It would be good to have friends north of the Palisade."

"Captain Tinothe is going to headquarter from the Shoals for a time while they send regular scouting parties to Dorantown," Orin said. "We're hopeful we can rebuild. We were really starting to build a community there before the wretchlings came. Don't think the creatures would have much use for the town now."

Karnak added, "Captain Tin will be cautious. He won't take them back to Dorantown unless he thinks it's safe. And we're going to ensure it is," he added with a hoist of *Dalkeri*.

Yenklin nodded approvingly before placing a hand on Orin's shoulder. "Well, my friends, we still have a long journey ahead of us. Let's take to the sky and fly toward victory. Show the Glain's Griffins what the Griffin Guard can do."

CHAPTER TWENTY-SEVEN

COUNCIL OF THE MELIOR

T he afternoon sun navigated through the great canopy of the First Tree of Kelvur, glinting off the Alkhoren Mirror in the corner of the room. Nera stared at the mirror and its guard. Renu, the melior assigned to watch the mirror and report what he saw, diligently worked the magic required to shift the mirror's view.

Nera saw many things through the glass as she watched Renu do his duty. He rotated the images amongst nine different scenes—though one was a jagged half scene. Nera assumed it was the view through a broken mirror. Most of the other mirrors sat in rooms. Several of the scenes sported guards, ever watching the mirror. Some of them were in dark places, indistinguishable. Nera thought perhaps they were hidden underground or in a secret chamber like the one they'd found and brought back to Whitestone.

She identified one scene as Whitestone. The canvas cloth tied over it allowed only pinpricks of light through. Even still, she knew the room in which the Alkhoren Mirror had been stored at the castle and imagined it in her mind. While the guards weren't visible through the canvas cloth, she knew they stood vigilantly just outside the room.

The temptation to imagine herself walking through the mirror into Whitestone weighed heavy on her. How she longed to be there again. But the temptation was only that and missed a key factor for her longing. Pernden wasn't in Whitestone. Since she and Shorlis had been at the First Tree of Kelvur for a few days, she thought Pernden may already be in Kelvur. Thus, the urge to work their mission pressed on the guardian captain, who knew time was not on their side.

Among the views of distant places seen through the mirror, two captivated her. One of the mirrors clearly rested in what appeared to be an ancient temple. The stones with which the temple had been built were covered in moss, and plants sprang from seams in the rocks, clinging to whatever edge they could find from which to grow. She'd asked Renu what that place was, but he told her he did not know. The location was a long-forgotten secret, and the dwarves had likely carried that mirror to a distant land.

The other scene that struck her was a dark place with the occasional flicker of orange light. The place seemed as though it were always shrouded in cloud. Every time it appeared, she felt a great sense of dread. The stonework of the room in which that mirror sat looked old. Because Renu spent the most time watching that scene, she wondered if it were where the sorcerer was headquartered. *What if it's in the Fell Keep? Or what if it's in Ventohl, now that Jaernok Tur controls the ancient castle?*

As she watched the melior work his magic to shift the scene, she stepped closer to him. She watched as shadows moved about on the stone walls. She could not make out who cast them, but there were people, or creatures, moving about the adjoining rooms and halls.

"This is the place you've seen the sorcerer?" she asked.

Renu jumped, stepping backward to see her. He clutched at his chest with a strong hand. "Lady Nera," he breathed. "You should not sneak up on people."

"Sorry," she said, swayed sheepishly.

"As you say," Renu answered. "This is the place Jaernok Tur resides. He has used that mirror to travel to Tarrine. It is also the mirror he used to come to Kelvur the first time."

"That doesn't make any sense," Nera said slowly. "Are you saying that Jaernok Tur isn't originally from Kelvur?"

"As you say," Renu affirmed. "The sorcerer's staff is of wood. The monolith stones bond well with metal, weaving their magic into the elements, but wood is different. Only wood from the First Trees can harness their power."

"And the only people who can have a staff from a First Tree are the sovran wizards of each land," the guardian said, piecing facts together. Renu nodded, encouraging her to continue her thread of reasoning. "So, Jaernok Tur was a sovran wizard in one of the other lands of Finlestia?"

"Or he killed the sovran wizard of his land and took the staff for himself," Renu offered.

"Then he came to Kelvur through one of the mirrors," she went on, "where he found Kilretheon the Red."

"Or was called."

"You think the monolith dragon called Jaernok Tur to himself?"

"Perhaps," the melior said. "I do not know."

Nera pondered his response for a long while. She wished she knew all the answers. She had hoped Renu would be able to give her adequate intelligence to make a move on the sorcerer. She realized, of course, that the melior wasn't part of one of the Griffin Guard's scouting teams and was unlikely to have as detailed a report as they were trained to bring. The melior must know something, though. He'd been watching the Alkhoren Mirror for years.

Then it struck her. *If they've been watching the mirror for years, why didn't they help us? Why didn't they stop Jaernok Tur from entering Kelvur or Tarrine in the first place?*

Nera didn't realize that she squeezed *Santoralier* tightly in her hand, sparks of yellow energy arcing from the fierce spear. Frustration built in her, and it took every ounce of self-control she had not to bombard him with the myriad of questions running through her mind. Renu tensed under her gaze, unsure what thoughts troubled her mind.

"Why didn't you stop him?" she asked through gritted teeth.

"I do not understand," Renu replied.

"Why didn't you stop Jaernok Tur before he came to Kelvur? Think of all the lives you could have saved. The people who were enslaved or killed by him here: the orcs of the north, the people of the Shoals, the giants of the Eastern Knolls. Why didn't you stop him before he walked through that mirror?"

Her body burned with raw emotion, though she set her will to hold back the magical energy of the spear, not wanting to harm the melior.

Renu watched her carefully. He took a moment to choose his words before he stated, "He did not come through our mirror."

"What?" Nera cried. "So, because he did not come through this mirror, you let him wreak havoc on others, bounding through the mirrors at his whim?"

"He did not come for the First Tree," Renu said evenly.

The melior spoke as though his reason made the most sense in the world, but Nera could hardly believe what he said. In the past couple of days, she'd seen melior do incredible things. What an advantage they had, she'd thought—with their wings. They were built warriors. She hadn't seen a single one of the melior appear weak, save for the young or the very old. Even the elderly were toned with muscle.

She'd watched their guards spar and train—a force to be reckoned with, to be sure. They flipped and flitted through the air, bringing around great spears at each other in dizzying displays hard to watch, let alone fight against. As skilled as she or any of the guardians were, they'd stand little chance against a melior.

With such great ability, how could they let the world suffer without intervening?

"Lady Nera?" Renu asked tentatively. "Are you alright?"

"No," she said to him. "No, Renu. I am not."

"I can feel your anger from here," Shorlis said. The chelon didn't open his eyes. He sat cross-legged with his hands in his lap. A great branch stretched into a makeshift balcony from the room they'd been offered in the First Tree. Shorlis had sat upon it a few times since their arrival.

Nera expelled the breath she didn't realized she'd been holding.

"Come sit with me," he said.

"How can you sit at a time like this?" she asked, pacing back and forth.

"We don't have a lot of control at the moment," he said, "so, come and sit with me."

Nera gripped *Santoralier* and forced herself not to stomp onto the branch next to the chelon. She laid the spear next to her as she found a comfortable seat. She expelled a great sigh, crossing her legs and closing her eyes.

"Now another breath," Shorlis whispered.

Nera forced herself to slow down, focusing on the air entering her body. She felt the coolness move down her throat and into her lungs, expanding her ribs to the point she felt them stretch. She slowly exhaled the breath, the air warmer upon its departure. For whatever reason, the exercise worked. She was calming down.

"Just be with me here for a moment," the chelon said. "Look at the way the sky paints the branches of this tree. This enormous tree—one I could not have imagined."

Nera looked around. The smaller branches that extended off the one where they sat waved in the evening breeze, producing a ballad of nature that sang calmness over her. When she was in the throes of battle, a strange calmness fell over her—a complete focus—as though nothing in the world existed but her and her opponent. The state of mind Shorlis had coaxed out of her was strangely similar.

"How do you know how to do this?" she asked him.

"My father showed me," he said. "He taught me other things."

"Like how to meditate?" Nera asked. "You've been doing that a lot since we've been here."

Shorlis nodded thoughtfully. "My father taught me many things, but he also left a great many things out—things I've been wondering about. Why would he not tell me about the First Tree? Why would he not tell me about the sovran wizards? He never even told me about *Menthrora*," Shorlis said, jutting a green thumb toward the staff that stood humming nearby.

"I've been wondering a great many things myself," Nera said, her words escaping more aggressively than she'd intended.

She'd already expressed to the chelon her concerns about the mirror and the lack of action by the melior. That unease was part of the reason they had set a meeting with the melior leader, Genuoh.

Momoah had arranged the meeting. His hospitality and efforts to aid them had been a breath of fresh air. He'd even gone back to his hut the first night to bring Shadowpaw to the First Tree. His help had kept Nera in the place. If the other melior would aid them like he had, she imagined a much more even fight against the sorcerer. The mission to find new allies never left Nera's mind, and the only way to get the melior to align with them was through council with their leaders.

Though she and Shorlis had gotten no time with the melior leaders since they arrived, they were far from mistreated. Other melior catered to their every need.

"I think," Shorlis said, snapping her out of her thoughts, "my father didn't tell me of those things because he was trying to protect me. I think he believed he was doing the right thing. Perhaps he thought by not involving me he was saving me from the war to come. And yet, here we are."

"Here we are," Nera agreed, but her mind began to race. *Maybe that's how we can connect with the melior.*

When Momoah arrived to escort Nera and Shorlis to their meeting, the melior's chiseled face appeared sad.

"You don't look like yourself," Nera said to him as they followed him along an intricately carved walkway through the interior of the First Tree.

"I am worried," Momoah said.

Over the past couple of days, Nera had grown fond of the melior, just as Shorlis had. They'd shared all their meals with

Momoah, and discussions had varied widely in topic. The melior was well aware of the situation in the north through Nera and Shorlis's recounting.

"I do not know if the council will give you what you seek," the melior said in his smooth tone, though Nera thought she heard a hint of disappointment. *Maybe apology?*

"You don't think they'll help us fight Jaernok Tur?" she asked.

"As you say."

They walked in relative silence, uncertainty etched on the melior's angled face. A pit grew in Nera's stomach the closer they got to the meeting chamber. Suddenly, Momoah stopped them, just before the entrance.

He turned to Nera, his piercing eyes locking on hers. He gripped her shoulder with his blue hand and gave her a nod with a compassionate smile before nodding to Shorlis as well. For some reason, the act calmed Nera, and she felt she had *his* support, at least.

They stepped through the entry to the meeting chamber where a dozen melior leaders sat around a table. They stood in honor of their guests, though their facial features remained sharp and stoic.

Nera gulped, trying to compose herself. She'd rarely failed at anything in her life. Even when she'd joined the griffin guard slightly later than the other trainees, she'd surpassed them with her unwavering effort and tenacity.

Approaching Aiden's Dell at night had been a mistake. She recognized an opportunity to make up for it by allying with a race of people that could help them finish the war.

Breathe, she told herself, taking a few moments to focus.

"Lady Nera," Genuoh said, "it is my understanding that you wish to address the council?"

"It is," she said. "As you say," she added nervously.

A couple of the council members nodded their heads, seemingly impressed with her use of their phrase. Momoah smiled to her as he took a seat off to the side next to Renu. She wasn't sure why the mirror watcher was present, but she assumed he'd been asked about their conversation earlier that day.

"As most of you likely know," Nera said, "I had a conversation with Watcher Renu earlier."

"As you say," Genuoh responded.

"Which means you know that I asked him why you did not stop Jaernok Tur." She went on, "Why did you not hamper his ability to use the Alkhoren Mirrors to do his evil work."

"It is our understanding that Watcher Renu explained this to you," Genuoh said.

"As you say," Nera said with a nod. "At first, I could not accept his reasoning. How could anyone stand by while the world was being torn and broken? Especially someone with the power to stop it? But then I realized it had nothing to do with any of that. You were on mission."

Genuoh inclined his head, squinting at her. "Lady Nera, I do not know that I understand."

"Your mission," she repeated. "When Shorlis and I first met Momoah, he said the melior are the 'keepers of the Tree.'"

"That is what melior means in the ancient tongue," one of the women at the table said, though all the council members looked as confused as Genuoh.

"I've been on mission my entire life, ever since my father died," Nera said. "See, he was a member of the Griffin Guard. He died, fighting to protect people. And when I lost him ..." Her words stalled as she swallowed the sadness welling within her. A singular tear escaped as she continued. "Well, after that,

I was on a mission to make my life count ... like his. I wanted to protect people. I wanted to help people. I've been on countless missions, and let me tell you, there is no end to missions. Even after we became allies with our greatest foes, we found new missions."

Genuoh brought his elbows onto the table before him and steepled his fingers. Nera took another breath. *Get to the point*, she scolded herself.

"The point is," she continued, "that sometimes while on mission, I forgot about the bigger picture. Tapestries of Whitestone's history hang all over its castle. When you stand close to them, you can see all the intricate threads that make up the tapestry—each one important. But you can't see the greater image when you only focus on the threads. When you step back, you get a grand view of the weaver's intention. You witness the seamless story told as all the threads work together."

"We have paintings like this," Genuoh said, giving Nera a slight smile. "When you are close, you can see each stroke of the brush, but you must step away to see the piece in all its wonder."

"Yes!" Nera said excitedly. "Sometimes we can get stuck on one part of the mission and miss things we shouldn't. You told me the day we arrived that the melior were created when the monolith dragons failed their purpose of protecting and guiding the people of Finlestia."

"As you say," Genuoh agreed slowly. He eyed her again, not sure where she was going.

"Would it not stand to reason that the Maker created the melior then to fill the void where the monolith dragons failed?"

Several of the council members sat back in their seats with disgusted looks on their faces. Others blinked in confusion. Still others glared at her insinuations. Many of them made noises, and some whispered to those next to them.

"Lady Nera," Genuoh said, trying to retake control of the chamber. "It has been the duty of the melior people to keep the Tree since the Maker created us."

"Yes, but was that for the sake of the Tree or for all?" she asked.

The council members stirred uncomfortably again. Shorlis smirked at Nera.

"All I ask," Nera pressed on, "is that the melior rise up from the shadow of the Tree and rejoin the rest of the created while we fight for our lives against a terrible evil."

Her final statement riled the council up, and several stood from their seats, bickering at each other, while others spoke words of the ancient tongue at the guardian.

Genuoh said a word Nera did not understand, silencing the room.

"Lady Nera," he said as evenly as he could, though she could tell he was shaken. "Would you and Master Shorlis please step outside the meeting chamber, so the council may discuss this grave matter?"

Nera and Shorlis stood resolute, the chelon having her back by way of following her lead.

"We will gladly do so, if the council will seriously consider joining our fight." No one in the room said a word for a long moment. Then Nera added, "Have you never even considered opening the mirror? Have you never even considered stepping through it and stopping Jaernok Tur? If his mirror is in Ventohl or the Fell Keep, we could flank him and his forces. We could take him down and end this."

Again, not a soul spoke. Nera shot a glance over to Momoah who watched Genuoh intently. She looked back to the melior leader, wondering if anyone was going to say something or if she and Shorlis were the only ones with any sense.

"Please," Genuoh said, waving an upturned hand toward the doorway and giving her a nod.

Nera scanned the faces of the melior. Whatever Genuoh had said to them was keeping them in check, and none of their stoic faces betrayed any emotion. The guardian inhaled deeply, trying to center herself. Then she nodded gently to Shorlis, who smiled back at her. Without another word, they left the council chamber.

Nera and Shorlis sat in the room with the Alkhoren Mirror. A female melior Nera hadn't seen before actively watched the mirror.

When they'd first entered the room to await the council's decision, Shorlis smiled at Nera and said, "You're going to make a great queen."

She'd smiled back, despite herself. "Only if we make it through all this."

He encouraged her to sit presently with him. For a while, it worked. Hours passed, and the sun was setting.

What is taking them so long? she wondered. Shorlis sat annoyingly quiet next to her with his eyes closed. Nera was unsure whether the chelon was awake or asleep. Judging by his breathing, he was awake.

The guardian fixated on the Alkhoren Mirror, watching as the melior woman gazed upon each scene for a while before uttering words to shift the image to the next scene.

At long last, Momoah entered the room, followed by Renu. Nera jumped to her feet, bumping Shorlis in the process. The chelon stood up next to her, though he halted when he saw the melior's face. Momoah shook his head sadly. If Nera wasn't mistaken, Renu didn't look pleased either.

Genuoh stepped through the doorway behind them, and Nera fought back the urge to lunge at the melior leader.

"Lady Nera, the council agrees that the fire inside you is admirable. But ..." Genuoh hung on the word for a moment. "The council has decided we cannot abandon the Tree to join your war," Genuoh said evenly.

"This isn't *my* war!" Nera raised her voice. "This evil is spreading. If it goes unchecked it will continue to spread. We're not fighting for just ourselves. We're fighting for all of Finlestia. What do you think will happen to the First Tree of Kelvur if Kilretheon the Red makes his way here? You really think he will leave this magical place alone?"

"The vote has been cast," Genuoh said. "It was close; I assure you. The matter was not dismissed lightly."

"So, some of them are scared!" she cried. "You don't think I've been scared during this whole thing? Sometimes it is required of us to overcome great fear to do the right thing."

"Is there any way you can vote again?" Shorlis asked. "Give me a chance to speak to them as well?"

"This is not possible," Genuoh said.

"Sure, it's possible!" Nera yelled. "Go call all of the council members back."

"Genuoh," Momoah said next to the melior.

"This is not possible," Genuoh repeated, more firmly.

Nera's mind raced. There had to be something they could do to change the leaders' minds. Something. Anything. She thought about Pernden. *What would he do? What could he do?*

"Then, let us go through the mirror," Shorlis said, snapping Nera out of her thoughts again.

"This is not possi—"

"Just because the melior won't leave the Tree doesn't mean you can't help us on our journey," Shorlis cut Genuoh off. "You do know how to open the door through the mirror, don't you?" he asked Renu directly.

The younger melior hesitated, looking between his leader and the chelon. Momoah looked at Renu sternly and asked, "You do know how to open it, yes?"

Renu's eyes turned to Momoah in surprise. "As you say," he replied as evenly as he could muster. "But I cannot do so unless by the order of Genuoh. It has always been this way."

"Genuoh," Shorlis started on the leader again, "you must help us. We will fight not just for us, but for your people as well, but you must help us. Give the order and open the portal. If we can flank Jaernok Tur, perhaps we can end this. Sending us through that mirror could save countless lives."

The stoic leader looked between Shorlis and Nera. The guardian said nothing. She was too fired up. She didn't want to say something that could shut down what progress Shorlis was making. Instead, she pleaded with her eyes.

Please! she thought. *You must help us.*

CHAPTER TWENTY-EIGHT

FIGHT FOR THE FISSURE

E erie guttural noises barked and echoed through the night. Queen Pellad had personally taken Kippin back to the keep with her, an act for which Ralowyn was eternally grateful. The halfling would be safer there than anywhere else.

While the wooden battlement she found herself standing atop didn't give her great confidence—especially if a varlek showed up with a dragon—Ralowyn did not intend to let any of the wretchling army get to the south side of the Palisade where they could reach the keep.

The Duskwood Rangers, aided by Javelin, had done everything they could to prepare the northern defenses. The wretchlings wouldn't attack during the day, and the rangers' scouts confirmed growing numbers at the southern edge of Duskwood as evening drew near. Many of the guards and fighting aged men and women from Aiden's Dell were also present, lined up in formations to greet the wretchling army with pointed hospitality. If those gathered in the northern ring were defeated and the wretchlings got through their defenses, the monsters would be greeted by those stationed at the mouth of the fissure and the warriors atop the Palisade.

Night had fallen some time before, and Ralowyn wondered why the wretchlings hadn't launched their attack. She assumed it must have something to do with timing, or maybe they were waiting on the arrival of the varlek. The elf mage couldn't be certain. The longer they waited, the more unnerving the cackling yips and guttural howls became.

Local warriors—those willing to stand and fight for their people—twitched in their makeshift armor nervously. Ralowyn appreciated that most of the lesser trained folk were behind the wall, but the best archers among them stood atop the wooden battlement with the trained warriors skilled in ranged weapons.

Ralowyn eyed a young huntsman, no more than a teen. Merrick stood stoically next to the young man. The teen did all he could to stand bravely next to the elder huntsman, but his face, rumpled with terror, betrayed him. Ralowyn could do little for the teen's fear, but she knew Merrick would fight with vigor, and she hoped the younger huntsman would follow suit.

They stood so long into the night that the raging emotions and tension within them wearied their achy muscles. Warriors along the battlement rolled their shoulders and necks, bounced their legs, and shook out their arms. They began to wonder if the wretchlings would attack at all, but the grotesque noises from the dark were a constant reminder that danger lurked.

A sudden wave of cackling wails rolled in a depressive chorus as the wretchlings echoed each other's calls.

Coal set his war hammer against the battlement's low wall and lifted his bow. "Here they come," he said with a growl.

Ralowyn gripped the Staff of Anvelorian in her slender hands. The humming staff lit up with lavender magic, the swirling pinnacle of the metal staff pouring ribbons of light. Her eyes blazed with the same lavender fire as she watched the first of the wretchlings scurry across the field toward them.

"One arrow at a time," she heard Merrick say to the younger huntsman. "Place each shot."

A short burst of fear rolled over her as the memory of her haunting dream with the wolves came to mind. That fear shortly turned to determined anger. She would not let them take away the future she had planned. She would protect Merrick.

Tonight and forever.

Merrick loosed arrow after arrow, the projectiles spiraling with deadly whistles as they soared to their intended targets. Wretchlings fell in bursts of smoke as they were turned into pin cushions by the swarm of arrows. The teen next to him missed his first couple of shots but had soon fallen into a rhythm. Nock, aim, release. Nock, aim, release.

Heaping piles of smoking wretchling bodies were building up, yet the monsters continued their charge. Some made it to the wooden wall but were quickly struck down by defenders wielding spears and pikes.

Ralowyn lobbed blazing purple fireballs into the field, blasting bunches of the wretchlings and setting the field aflame. The glow made the wretchlings easier to see for those who didn't have good vision in the dark.

An arrow whistled by Merrick's head.

"Archers!" he hollered.

Ralowyn shifted the cantrip she'd been working and raised her staff, forming an arcing shield of lavender energy. Two more arrows bounced off the barrier, just as she got it up.

"Do you see where they are?" she asked.

"Aye," Coal roared. "They're gathering by that big rock over there."

"Aim for the archers," Merrick shouted to the others as a woman nearby took an arrow to the chest and fell backward off the battlement.

The teen huntsman looked at Merrick, his eyes wide with horror. He retched, expelling what little food was left in his system from his last meal.

Merrick said nothing, nocking his arrow and leaning away from Ralowyn's shield. He found his mark, a wretchling standing atop the rock, and let his arrow fly. The bow twanged, and the arrow traveled the distance with incredible speed, striking down the wretchling. Another took its place, but the rangers and other archers were already raining down on the spot.

Unfortunately, as they'd been distracted with the wretchling archers, more of the monsters had reached the wall. Several of them managed to climb atop the wooden battlement, engaging the defenders.

Merrick turned to the young huntsman and growled, "Keep firing. Don't let anymore get to the wall."

"But they're already on the wall," he blurted back.

"Let the others worry about them. You don't let any more wretchlings get to the wall to add to their worries. I won't let the wretchlings on the wall get you."

The young huntsman lifted his bow and began his systematic firing again. Nock, aim, release.

Though the onslaught continued, they seemed to be managing the wretchlings that raced across the field. Merrick knew they couldn't last forever. They were already running low on arrows, and once they exhausted their supply, the wretchlings would make the battlement with ease. That would change the scene quickly.

When Merrick and Coal announced they were nearly out of arrows, Ralowyn scanned the defenders on the battlement. Her elven eyes confirmed they weren't the only ones. A mage on the other end was lobbing more fireballs into the fray.

Ralowyn ceased her own fireball throwing, knowing she needed to shift her focus. As soon as the others ran out of their arrows, most of them would need to fall back. She'd need to create a distraction or a disturbance to slow the wretchlings, allowing the archers to retreat to their designated positions behind the blockades they'd built during the daylight hours.

The elf focused herself. The twang of bows and the sickening *thunk* of arrows meeting wretchling flesh drowned out all around her. She found her center, a lavender bubble of light within her.

She gripped the Staff of Anvelorian in front of her with both hands and felt the power humming through her bones as she connected to the orb. The orb grew. It filled her, then it extended beyond her. She sensed Merrick and Coal next to her. She felt the young huntsman, scared but still following Merrick's lead. She sensed the warriors behind her, waiting for the inevitable moment when the wretchling army forced their way over the wooden wall.

The elf sensed the wretchlings running across the field. She unintentionally snarled at their presence. The orb continued to grow, reaching out into the forest.

There, Ralowyn thought, *and ... there ...* The irony of what she sensed was not lost on her.

She refocused her energy, reaching out to the creatures of the forest. They were all scared, none of them liking the presence of the wicked wretchlings. It was easy to convince them to aid her when she silently spoke to their hearts with compassion, understanding their plight.

A smirk rolled across her face as the lavender flames burned bright in her beautiful eyes, then Ralowyn opened them to watch her play unfold. A great roar echoed from the forest as a bear swung its powerful paws, batting wretchlings all around. Another bear echoed the call and joined the mayhem.

And then ... they came.

The wolves tore through the advancing wretchling army, tackling them then biting their necks to finish the wretched creatures. Savage growls and barks erupted all over the field before them.

"Whoa!" Coal marveled at the scene.

Merrick turned quickly and shouted to the others, "Archers retreat!"

Domin Ven repeated the command some way down the line along the wall, as the archers began their descent to the grass below. More pikemen and spearmen scrambled up the ladders to fill in the gaps. They would hold off the wretchlings long enough for the others to get behind the funneling barricades.

Ralowyn stole another look at the wolves before she climbed down the ladder. She watched them tear the wretchlings apart, the monsters caught completely off guard. She nodded to the pack and thanked them silently.

As soon as she was on the grass behind the wooden wall, she refocused her energy to release all the creatures from her influence so they could run off into the forest once more. They had performed admirably. She knew they'd taken losses, but her hope was that by asking for their help, she'd also save them and their lands. She'd only gotten to see very little of the Crags while Javelin had held Ventohl, but if it was an indicator of what was to come from the sorcerer and his fiends, then every creature in Kelvur was in danger.

She hurried back to the barricades where Merrick was ushering the last of the archers through. Barrels of arrows waited back at the Palisade where many of them would set up, but many others joined the ranks of those waiting to greet the wretchlings with their swords and axes and spears and hammers just behind the barricade.

"Are you alright?" Merrick asked as she reached him, wondering why she'd taken so long. "Did you use too much energy?"

"I am alright," Ralowyn assured him. "I had to release them back to Duskwood before they were surrounded and slaughtered by the wretchling horde. I would not have been able to influence them much longer anyway."

He nodded his understanding, not pressing any further.

She turned to watch the wall. Armor-clad warriors jabbed their weapons downward on the other side of the wall. In her peripheral vision, she saw the nervous twitch of anticipation from the gathered warriors. She still sensed them, a residual feeling that made her keenly aware of all that was around her.

When the first several wretchlings got past or between the pikemen and spearmen on the wall and dove into the grassy area, Ralowyn felt the energy change all around her. At first, she thought it merely the presence of the wretchlings as they clattered between the barricades, struck down with ease by the awaiting forces. She felt their nerves and the exhilaration of finally engaging the enemy. But something wasn't right; she sensed more.

Suddenly, a roar ripped across the night—one that could only belong to a dragon.

"Varlek!" Merrick hollered.

"Up there!" Coal roared with rage.

"Those men have to get off the wall," Merrick said.

The huntsman charged forward, slicing a wretchling with the tip of his spear as he ran.

"Get off the wall!" he shouted.

The spearmen and pikemen who heard him looked up to see the oncoming dragon, followed by death wings, Aiden's Dell set in their sights. The warriors turned back to their duty and continued to fight on.

"What are you doing? There's a varlek coming. With a dragon!"

The ping of a mighty war hammer greeting the skull of a wretchling next to him forced Merrick to turn.

"Come on!" Coal shouted. "We have to get back behind the barricade."

"But the dragon," Merrick said slowly.

"They have their job, and we have ours," Coal said. "As do the archers atop the Palisade. And the mounted bowmen."

The huntsman had seen so much death and destruction. In the woods, he'd been used to death. But it had always been a natural kind of death, an honorable one—the circle of hunter and prey for survival. The death he'd seen in battle had always seemed such wanton violence. The battles had revisited him in his dreams, even though he'd tried to refill his mind with love and joy.

"Merrick!" Coal hollered, shaking the man as though he'd yelled multiple times. "We have to get behind the barrier."

Merrick snapped to action. He'd been lost for a moment but finally had his senses back. Whatever that was, he couldn't let it happen again. Someone could get killed.

Screams resounded as pikemen and spearmen dove from the wall behind them. Merrick turned in time to see fire spew from the dragon's maw.

"Merrick!" Ralowyn screamed, as the dragon's fire exploded the wooden wall into a thousand flaming spears that scattered across the area.

A heatwave followed the dragon as it swooped up from its attack to avoid crashing into the Palisade. The elf heard the clunking of the mounted bows, high above, hurtling large arrows at the dragon. None of that distracted her from her efforts.

In the devastation of the dragon's fire, a lavender orb of light flickered as it pressed against the licking flames. Holding the shield against the dragon fire was difficult. Sweat ran down her face. Ralowyn tried to sense Merrick and Coal. The effort to hold the shield took too much energy, and she couldn't reach out to them. She hoped she'd been fast enough.

Ralowyn held the magic shield in place as long as she could, but death wings were angling their descents toward the burning barricades and the warriors behind them. The death wings hurtled through the air, diving rapidly toward them. Finally, Ralowyn released the defensive orb, hoping it had been enough, and turned her efforts toward forming fireballs to meet the oncoming death wings.

Suddenly, a griffin flew overhead. And then another. And another. A whole flock of them.

Ralowyn's eyes widened as the warriors around her cheered. Dozens of griffin riders clashed with the death wings that had—only seconds before—been bent on their demise.

The Griffin Guard had come!

Orin swung his sword out wide, slicing the wing off one of the foul creatures and sending it spiraling to the ground. His new griffin, Olet, screeched as she caught and tore apart another of the beasts. The Talon Squadron and their new allies, the Glain's Griffins, ripped through the enemy forces, obviously catching the death wings completely off guard.

A death wing exploded as *Dalkeri* crashed through it. Karnak grinned wickedly, pleased to have his axe back, even if its magic was different. Orin spared a quick grin back, but they still had plenty of the monsters to take out.

The guardian soared through the battle with acrobatic ease as though he'd never been without a griffin. A pang of guilt rose in him at how easy it was to bond with Olet when he'd spent years with his original griffin. He brushed away the loose emotion, knowing there was no time for such thoughts in the midst of battle.

Nearby, Jensen skewered another death wing as others tried to swarm the guardian. Orin moved into position, Olet taking one, and the guardian stabbing another with his outstretched sword. Jensen jabbed his spear over the top of

Olet, sticking a death wing that was coming for her jugular. The skilled guardian performed the dangerous maneuver perfectly, downing the flanking monster. The two griffins pulled away from each other, ready to take on more opponents.

"These vile creatures are relentless," Jensen said.

"The reports we've heard of them were not overstated," Orin agreed, as he and Olet charged off.

Merrick pushed himself up from the dirt. The grass around him was charred and, in some spots, still burning. He coughed the smoke from his lungs, dragging himself to his knees. Coal lay next to him unmoving, blood covering his head.

"Coal!" Merrick shouted, shaking the dwarf's shoulders.

Coal groaned and swatted at the huntsman. "Five more minutes, yeah?"

Merrick choked a laugh, despite their dire circumstance. He patted the dwarf's chest and turned to see the dragon's destruction. The wooden wall raged in a fiery inferno, the dragon's fire quickly consuming the length of the wall. A great hole covered in flame created a wide opening in the once gated wall.

Wretchlings jumped excitedly through the flames. They no longer had to climb over the wall. They poured through the fiery hole as if it were a portal to the very depths of Malkra.

"Coal," Merrick patted the dwarf harder. "Coal, you have to get up. The wretchlings are pouring through the wall."

"What?" The dwarf sat up quickly but lolled to the side, clutching his head.

"Come on," Merrick hissed.

The wretchlings sprinted toward the burning funnel barricades, crashing hard into the warriors who awaited them. The clang of metal on metal screeched into Merrick's ears. His own head throbbed. He grabbed Coal by his shoulder armor and hoisted the dwarf to his feet.

Coal blinked several times, trying to focus on the huntsman's intense face. Merrick picked up the war hammer gifted to the dwarf by the king of Galium. He shoved the fine weapon, covered in dirt and soot, into the dwarf's arms and said, "Follow me. Stay close. Can you do that?"

The dwarf's eyes narrowed. "Aye," he said slowly. "I can do that."

The flaming fissure of the wooden wall was growing by the second, allowing more wretchlings to pass through. Merrick stood to his feet and readied his charred spear. Immediately, several wretchlings veered off their course to engage the huntsman.

"Coal," Merrick growled. "Get ready."

The dwarf steadied himself and gripped his war hammer in both hands. The wretchlings raised their jagged weapons as they dashed across the smoldering field. Merrick dug his feet into the ground as he bent his knees, preparing to parry whatever attacks they brought.

Suddenly, a lavender fireball exploded against one of the wretchlings, sending him crashing into the others. They toppled over each other, the monsters squealing at the magic fire as it burned their translucent skin.

Merrick turned to see a tear-streaked Ralowyn.

"Come on!" she called, waving them over.

"Run, Coal," Merrick ushered the dwarf forward, "right to Ralowyn."

The dwarf seemed to be more clear as his short legs pounded dirt. They raced toward the elf mage as she loosed another fireball over their shoulders, striking several more of the smoky fiends. Merrick and Coal dove to the side, out of sight behind a barricade that wasn't fully aflame. They breathed heavily, trying desperately to fill their lungs. The smoke sent them into coughing fits.

"Are you alright?" Merrick asked Coal, inspecting the dwarf's head.

"Took a clob to the head," Coal admitted. "But I'll be alright."

"Sit here as long as you need," Merrick said, patting the dwarf on the shoulder before the huntsman stood to survey the scene.

Ralowyn lobbed another fireball into a group of wretchlings racing to meet the defenders behind one of the blazing barricades.

"We won't be able to hold them off much longer," Merrick said. "Can you sense how many there are out there?"

Ralowyn shook her head, her silvery hair fluttered away from the loose braid. "Too many," she said with a grunt. Merrick could tell she was wearing herself out with her continued efforts. "If the Griffin Guard can finish the death wings and somehow defeat the dragon, then maybe ..."

"The Griffin Guard?" Merrick asked, confused. He looked to the sky and, to his surprise, spotted dozens of griffin riders fighting off death wings. *What in Finlestia?* he thought. They must have arrived while he and Coal were downed by the explosion. *How long was I out?*

"The Talon Squadron made it back to us?" he asked incredulously.

"With some friends, it seems," Ralowyn said quickly. She sucked in a deep breath and coughed. "More griffins than before."

A singular wretchling screamed as it ran toward them, Merrick stepped in front of Ralowyn and parried the creature's jagged sword to the side before sticking it with his spear. A burst of smoke poured out of the wound as it cried, but Merrick pressed forward, ramming the monster into the ground until it stopped moving.

With no other wretchlings in the immediate vicinity, he stole a glance at the sky once more. One of the bigger griffins swooped to attack a death wing that seemed more interested in the ground battle. As the griffin turned, an axe flew from the rider, chopping the death wing and dropping it to the ground. The axe freed itself from the dead creature and flew back toward the griffin.

Merrick's eyes widened. *Firestorm?* he wondered. The axe was not ablaze like he'd seen it before, but he knew the weapon well and recognized its form. The axe was different, though, and the huntsman was having a hard time reconciling what his eyes told him. He knew the great axe had been taken, but when the axe floated back into the hand of the wielder, there could be no doubt.

"Karnak!" Merrick blurted.

As the smooth handle of *Dalkeri* returned to his hand, the orc gar thought he heard someone call his name. He glanced below and spotted his friends. A great relief flooded him at the sight of the huntsman and the elf standing side by side. The relief faded quickly as the dragon roared above him.

The dragon banked wide and angled itself for a strike on the flying warriors, spewing fire through the air at the mass of death wings and griffin riders with no discretion of friend or foe.

A swathe of griffins and death wings alike fell in blazing heaps from the sky. Karnak leaned into his big griffin as Maxlir beat his wings, carrying them high into the sky. He caught up to Jensen as the guardian whipped his spear to send a death wing's body sliding off the end of the weapon.

"We have to take out that varlek!" Karnak yelled to him.

"It'll take more than just you and me to fight that dragon!" Jensen hollered.

"I know," the orc gar said. "Gather as many as you can while the dragon turns around."

They split and took off in opposite directions. Karnak threw his mighty axe, the blades of which sliced through the wings of one of the monstrous creatures near Orin.

"Come on," Karnak yelled to the man. "We have to take out the dragon."

They gathered more than a dozen griffin riders before they chased after the varlek and his dragon. Others stayed to fight the remaining death wings, a diminishing force, but still one requiring their attention.

The griffin riders pursued the dragon, the beast turning high into the sky rather than taking them head-on. Karnak didn't understand the maneuver at first, but when the great dragon leaned into its own weight and barreled down on them at incredible speed, the orc gar braced himself.

The dragon opened its wide mouth, revealing its monstrous teeth and the roaring light of building flame within his throat. The griffin riders quickly scattered to avoid the burst of fire.

Two unfortunate riders were unable to escape the inferno as the dragon turned its head to give chase.

The rest of the griffin riders dove after the great beast attempting to attack it from all sides, though the varlek had other plans. The wicked creature turned on the back of the dragon and whipped a wand from his cloak. The wand shot cracks of energy like miniature explosions.

Maxlir deftly maneuvered sporadically from side to side, making himself and the big orc harder targets. They dove after the dragon, the beast unfurling its great leathery wings to catch the wind.

One of the varlek's attacks exploded into a nearby griffin and his rider, sending them spiraling. The varlek's quick whips of his wand forced Maxlir into the path of their falling comrades. The dead griffin and rider slammed into them, sending Karnak toppling from his saddle. Maxlir screeched, momentarily caught under the momentum of the plummeting bodies. Karnak roared as he hurtled through the air, wingless.

Karnak held his arms out wide, doing anything he could to slow his fall. His eyes locked on the ever-nearing ground.

Talons suddenly gripped the orc's arm, cutting him slightly but slowing his plummet.

"Hold on!" Orin called from atop Olet's saddle.

They were falling toward the dragon, but with Karnak's added weight, Olet could hardly change direction. The orc gar had an idea.

"Get me close to the dragon!" he shouted.

"Are you crazy?" Orin yelled back.

"Just do it!" he roared.

Olet's talons slipped to the leather bracer on Karnak's arm, nearly dropping the big orc. Karnak growled.

Just a little farther ...

They soared over the back of the dragon, Olet barely avoiding several of the varlek's wicked attacks. Suddenly, the varlek stopped whipping his wand, a wicked grin splitting his face as he eyed Karnak.

That's right, Karnak thought. *You remember me, and I remember you.*

Karnak raised *Dalkeri* and struck the leather bracer on his arm, destroying the straps and releasing him from Olet's grasp. The sudden loss of weight sent the griffin careening to the side, but Orin turned her quickly as the guardian yelled, "Karnak!"

Ralowyn's movements felt sluggish. The continued effort of drawing magic from the Staff of Anvelorian was wearing her down. She'd never needed to draw upon its power for such a sustained period of time. In truth, Ralowyn wasn't sure how much more she could help.

The elf mage spun the staff in her hands, striking at an oncoming wretchling. She was too weary to draw upon the magic and resorted to more basic hand-to-hand combat to thwart the creature.

Merrick slashed another wretchling, cutting deep and spewing smoke from the creature's innards. Domin Ven jabbed his sword through another, grunting from the effort. Lidrea spun around two wretchlings and sliced out with her twin daggers, dropping them both.

Between the Duskwood Rangers and the Javelin warriors, the defenders of Aiden's Dell had done great damage to the wretchling forces. Smoking heaps littered the field, signs of the great many enemies they'd vanquished. But wretchling bodies weren't the only ones that marred the field of battle.

The scene folded Ralowyn's stomach over. She closed her eyes, attempting to sense the wretchlings on the north side of the flaming wall. She could not tell how many there were. The chaos of their presence caused much distraction as she tried to focus.

Coal pounded another wretchling into the ground only a few feet away from her. The dwarf looked haggard, a far cry from the combed and braided dwarf she had seen the night prior. He sighed as he lifted his war hammer and said, "You've got to keep your eyes open, lass. They're still coming."

He changed his footing, facing away from her, ready to protect her from the continuing horde. But did she have enough left in her to protect him? What about Merrick?

The orc gar fell through the sky, angling his body so he hurtled toward the varlek on the back of the dragon. The varlek watched the orc in anticipation.

Karnak hit the back of the dragon with a great thud, knocking the wind from his lungs. The dragon was not much larger than the one Gar Nargoh had ridden in Drelek. Karnak grabbed one of the dragon's plated spikes to hoist himself upright. The dragon's whole body moved as it flapped its wings, making it difficult for the gar to gain his balance.

The varlek watched, a despicable smile on its face.

Karnak snarled, gripping *Dalkeri* in his big green hand. He did his best to throw the axe straight. It whizzed past the varlek as the dark creature dodged to the side.

The wicked grin returned after a brief scowl of annoyance, but that time Karnak grinned back. The varlek climbed around several spikes, drawing closer to Karnak as the dragon continued to fly. The dark figure lifted his wand and in a shrill croak said, "Amusing, but not the nemesis I'd hoped for. Perhaps the elf below."

Karnak growled at the varlek's insinuation that he'd go after Ralowyn. As the varlek aimed his wand at the orc gar's throat, Karnak raised a hand. The varlek cackled at what he thought to be a weak attempt at the orc gar begging for mercy.

That's when *Dalkeri* blasted into the wretch's back, bowling him over. Karnak leaped forward, grabbing *Dalkeri* with both hands and bringing the axe down with a mighty swing.

The axe blade buried deep into the varlek's head, before an explosion of smoke sent Karnak flying from the dragon's back. The dragon roared and flapped its wings wildly, the wind of which sent Karnak spinning toward the ground far below.

The orc gar watched the ground rapidly rise to him, hearing Orin call after him and knowing the guardian and his smaller griffin wouldn't be able to save him again. As Karnak fell, he thought of his wife.

Tanessa, I'm sorry.

Suddenly, the talons of an astral falcon dug into his big green arms. He cried out in pain, but the great falcon gripped tighter, doing everything it could to slow the orc's descent.

"Hold on!" Merrick yelled from Valurwind's back.

They continued to plummet but soon *whumped* into feathers and a saddle, meeting Karnak's momentum and dragging him out of his descent. The gar spit feathers from his mouth as he called in elation, "Maxlir!"

The griffin cawed in response as he worked them back into the sky. Karnak turned to see a heavily breathing Merrick, relief lacing his features.

"I promised Tanessa I'd get you home," the huntsman said.

Karnak barked a laugh. He looked past Merrick, something catching the orc's eye.

The dragon, having lost the varlek that was controlling it, didn't seem in the mood to fight the dozen griffins and riders surrounding it. To Karnak's surprise, the great beast flew off to the east. He supposed the dragon didn't like the sorcerer any better than they did, and the beast was not inclined to return to the north and the sorcerer's service.

Great cheers erupted among the griffin riders and defenders below.

CHAPTER TWENTY-NINE

THE SORCERER

The sun was setting on the horizon far to the west, but no one aboard the *Harbinger* gazed upon the spectacular scene behind them. All eyes locked on the great ominous clouds pouring over the sky of Kelvur. Farther up the coast from their position sat Ventohl, tucked back on an inlet. Farther still, as the coast curved northward, red-orange glowing rivers of molten lava poured into the sea. The volatile act resulted in great plumes of steam and perpetual clouds above the region.

All eyes—except for Pernden's—were captivated by the area. The king scanned his sword, *Wintertide*. The inscriptions that Smarlo and Lotmeag had found were from an old dwarven journal that had been recovered in an orc raid generations before. The ancient dwarves recognized the stone mounted in *Wintertide's* hilt for what it was—or at least that was Smarlo's theory. The orc mage seemed pretty adamant that the stone was one of the "monolith stones" created long ago by the monolith dragons. Pernden wasn't convinced.

He'd known of *Wintertide* his whole life. Even before he went to train under Master Melkis's tutelage at the Grand Corral, he'd been told stories of *Wintertide's* might and power. The stories of Melkis and his triumphs and of the wielders of *Wintertide* before him were legendary and recited to many a Whitestone child before bed.

Could all the heroes of the Griffin Guard who wielded the blade really never have known it to be imbued with such a powerful artifact?

In truth, Pernden wasn't sure. Since Smarlo's assertions, the king had thought back to sparring with Nera and *Santoralier*, her magic spear matching the power of *Wintertide* stroke for stroke. In their downtime, he'd inspected her weapon. The golden spear held a yellow stone, much like the one *Wintertide* held. *Could hers be a monolith stone too?* he wondered. Pernden didn't like the progression of his thoughts.

"We're nearing the point where we need to fly you over to the *Wenli,* so you can get Rocktail," Smarlo said from behind the king. "Lehra has offered to fly you while Belguv and I fly Lotmeag and Commander Fario to the *Lentoria.*"

"Very well," Pernden said. He took one more long look at *Wintertide.* He inspected the singular rune on the blade, his eyes landing on the crystalline white stone embedded in the hilt. *Such a strange fate,* he thought, *how it all comes down to a stone so small as this.*

He wished Melkis were still alive, not for the first time. He wished the old master were there, wielding the magic sword himself. He also wished Danner Kane were there. What if the old High Commander had kept the sword himself? Would he still be alive? Would he be standing next to Pernden?

The king pushed the impossible thoughts aside as Smarlo asked, "Are you ready for this?"

Pernden huffed a laugh. "Are you sure this will work?"

Smarlo breathed in deeply, taking another couple of steps to face the king. His short tusks moved from side to side as he considered his answer. "I think it may be our best chance."

"Hm," Pernden grunted.

Smarlo smiled at the noise. "You've been spending too much time with Commander Fario on this voyage," he teased. "That sword of yours may be the only thing that can defeat Jaernok Tur. With him having Karnak's axe, *Dalkeri*, which I believe to have another of the stones, *Wintertide* may be the only weapon that stands a chance."

"Don't you think it odd how it all comes down to something so small as a stone?" Pernden asked him.

"I don't actually," the orc mage said softly. "To be honest, it makes a lot of sense to me. Even the greatest trees of Drelek come from the smallest of seeds. It is the way of our world. The small things can give birth to the great ones. It seems rather fitting. Look at you. Did you ever think you would end up being king of Whitestone?"

"Not in my wildest dreams," the king admitted. "Growing up, all I wanted to be was one of the greatest guardians. One that made a difference. One whose deeds earned him a few pages in the Chronicles of the Griffin Guard."

"Seems like a good dream, but think of what will be recorded in the Chronicles now. A guardian and a king, rising up to defeat the greatest threat our world has known since the inception of the Guard. You'll have more than a few pages after this."

Pernden smiled and shook his head. "Those were old dreams. Now, I find myself dreaming for something different. I want to defeat the sorcerer so I can go home to Whitestone, knowing that the people will be safe. I want to find Nera and wed her. I want to raise a family, filling the halls of Whitestone Castle with love again. I want to grow our friendships, so all of Finlestia know that the peoples of Tarrine stand together. And the only thing standing between me and those dreams is the sorcerer."

"Those, my King," Smarlo said, clapping a hand on Pernden's shoulder, "those dreams are far greater than the old ones. And I will do everything in my power to help you accomplish them."

Pernden nodded to Smarlo, the two sharing a silent moment of mutual respect and admiration.

"We will do our part to hold off whatever forces he has, while you get to him," Smarlo said. "I believe in you."

As the orc mage turned and made his way belowdecks to retrieve his wyvern, Pernden found himself standing alone again with a great many depending on him and his ability to accomplish a terrible task before him. The words of his former mentor came back to him in Danner Kane's voice: *"No one wants such things in their lives. Like so many guardians that came in the long lineage before us, I have no doubt that you are capable of overcoming any challenge that arises. Even one so strange as this."*

The king blinked away the tears forming in his eyes as Lehra and her large wyvern crept out of the *Harbinger's* hold.

"Are you ready, my King?" Lehra asked.

"More than ready," he said, his face shifting to a determined grin.

Nothing was going to stand in the way of the dreams he had for the future.

Smarlo patted Klovur's scaly neck as they flew toward Ventohl. The wyvern clicked at him with nervous affection. She sensed his tension, and even though he'd taken her out of the *Harbinger's* hold for exercise a few times on the trip across the Gant Sea, he wished he'd gotten her out more. "Sorry about that," he said, though he realized she had no idea what he was thinking.

As he looked around them, their force was an intimidating sight. The Scar Squadron flew in no distinguishable formation, granting their wyverns the flying space the beasts preferred. *No sense stressing them out before we engage the enemy.*

Smarlo was pleased to see that the garvawk warriors from Galium had a similar mentality. The winged panthers flying with their dwarven riders interspersed with the other squadrons.

The Griffin Guard's 5th and 8th Squadrons flew wide to either side of the Scar Squadron, staying in designed formations. The griffins appeared to have no problem with the tightly uniformed shapes, making agile adjustments to remain in formation. Smarlo had seen them use formations going into battle before, breaking off in predetermined directions to confuse their opponents. The strategy was clever, though not something the wyvern riders would be able to mimic.

Though the Griffin Guard's formations were impressive, the Riders of Loralith progressed as a singular unit. Their pegasi flew in such tight formation, it was hard to see from a distance where one pegasus ended and another began. Smarlo didn't imagine the creatures were fond of the proximity, but it was a testament to the elves' great ability to train the pegasi. He thought the notion something he should add to his journal if they made it through the battle before them.

When, he reminded himself, stealing a glance at Lehra, the human woman looking small on the back of Galbrish's big form.

Lotmeag and Pernden flew nearby. *We can do this*, Smarlo thought. All they had to do was get Pernden close enough to the sorcerer before Jaernok Tur could hurtle *Dalkeri* at the king.

Smarlo doubted the orc sorcerer could hold off the guardian king in hand-to-hand combat.

"Here they come!" Lotmeag hollered as they flew over the inlet.

Smarlo snapped his eyes ahead. Ventohl looked almost exactly how he'd imagined it. Lanryn had described it to them thoroughly, and Smarlo took a silent moment to thank the elf for all he'd done. It was a short-lived moment, for a cloud rose from the ground around the old city, distinctly different from the perpetual clouds that covered the region in gloom. The cloud moved.

"Death wings!" one of the orcs shouted, holding up his spy glass.

Smarlo patted Klovur again and muttered, "Here we go."

As the allied forces crashed into the mass of death wings, monstrous bat-like creatures the size of a man, the Griffin Guard Squadrons and the Riders of Loralith scattered into the fray. Elves sliced their way through the monsters, death wings falling from the sky like massive fleshy hail.

Griffins ripped and clawed and bit with their talons and beaks, shredding whatever death wings they could grab. Pernden gritted his teeth as the guardians hacked and slashed against the monsters. The king remembered the first time he'd fought the beasts above the Gant Sea Narrows in the middle of a sea storm. The lightning had been a great ally that night. Unfortunately, he saw no lightning, and he realized they'd have to fight every single one of the relentless creatures like they had in Calrok.

The garvawk warriors dipped and flipped, the quick mounts pouncing on death wings and ripping them to shreds while the dwarves chopped down others.

The scene seemingly broke into all-out chaos, but they had a plan.

The front flyers of the Scar Squadron plowed through the death wings, chomping many of the monsters in their great maws. They angled into a dive toward Ventohl, all of the Squadron following suit. Pernden nudged Rocktail into a similar flight path, close behind Lotmeag. The dwarf leaned into his garvawk, following the wyvern-riding orcs. The mass of death wings scattered as the wyvern riders left toppling bodies far behind them.

Pernden gripped *Wintertide* in his hand as his eyes narrowed on their target. Ventohl drew ever closer as they dove, but soon enough, death wings were upon them again, having given chase. Pernden swung his sword in a slashing sideways arc, a blade of ice flying from it and slicing a death wing in half. Rocktail performed a midair tackle, gripping one of the creatures in his talons and tearing it apart with his razor-sharp beak.

Another death wing hit Pernden, clawing and biting at his back. The king attempted to stab at the creature but couldn't get a good hit while Rocktail jostled, engaging yet another. The death wing on Pernden's back exploded into an inferno, launching off of him and careening to the ground far below like a falling star.

"Come on!" Smarlo yelled, throwing another fireball at a nearby death wing. "We have to get to the castle."

Pernden lobbed another ice blade with a swing of his sword. The ice blade pierced the back of a death wing that was closing in on Lotmeag, the dwarf already preoccupied with another of the relentless monsters. A spear blasted another death wing nearby, and Pernden realized that some of the 5th Squadron had fought their way through as well.

Good, he thought quickly. The more allies they could get to Ventohl, the greater their chances. They weren't sure what kind of ground forces they would face.

The answer to that question was revealed soon after, as wretchlings lined the tops of the walls, lobbing arrows at the incoming forces. The Scar Squadron didn't slow their descent. They'd planned for such an attack. The wyvern's scaly hides were the most likely to deflect arrows—though certainly many would stick. The Scar Squadron crashed upon the walls, wyverns ripping wretchlings from their feet and killing them with one bite, sweeping many others from the top of the wall with their tails. The sight of smoke billowing from dead wretchlings in wyverns' mouths made them look more like their dragon cousins.

Vast numbers of the wretchlings of all shapes and sizes waited in the fields surrounding the castle—eager for a chance to kill the attackers. The 5th Squadron was the first to hit the wretchling warriors, griffins scooping and throwing them into heaping piles as the monsters crashed into their own.

Pernden and Lotmeag followed Smarlo as the orc mage threw fireball after fireball, lighting the field of battle ablaze. They swooped low, seeking Jaernok Tur among the wretchling forces. Small plumes of smoke erupted all over as the allied forces fought and killed the wretchlings.

The king gritted his teeth as he scanned the area for the sorcerer.

Where are you?

After a few laps around Ventohl, Smarlo began to think Jaernok Tur was not there. It had been a possibility they'd discussed, though it did little to assuage his annoyance. The sorcerer may be at the Fell Keep in the Crags instead, or worse, he could be with his wretchling armies marching south. If either of those were the case, retaking Ventohl became the priority, killing as many of the wretchling forces as possible.

Not seeing any sign of the sorcerer from the air, Smarlo pulled Klovur back. The wyvern flapped her great wings and angled upward to slow herself. She clambered her two legs onto the side of one of the castle's towers, her wings wrapping it to hold herself upon it. Pernden and Lotmeag flew close enough to hear the orc mage.

"He doesn't appear to be here," Smarlo said with a growl.

"Then we fight," Lotmeag called, "just like we planned."

"Yes," Smarlo agreed, "but keep close to each other. If Jaernok Tur does show up, we'll have to help Pernden get to him."

"Aye," Lotmeag said with a grunt. "Let's start with these ones!"

The garvawk dropped onto a group of wretchlings below.

Smarlo nodded to Pernden. The king returned the gesture before his griffin dropped to the ground, crashing hard on another group of wretchlings.

The orc mage threw a fireball to the ground, the magic erupting into a swirl of flame, sending wretchlings skittering. He took only a second to scan the battle. Members of the 8th Squadron and the Riders of Loralith still fought high in the sky with death wings, but most of their forces had made it to the ground to fight the wretchling horde. The battle raged all around the old city's mostly ruined structures. Many of the structures were nothing more than stone lines in the great field inside the broken walls.

A stream of wretchling archers hustled from a doorway atop a nearby wall. "That looks like us," he said to Klovur, and the wyvern leaped from the tower, crashing hard onto the archers as they started loosing their arrows.

Pernden struggled to hit the wretchlings as he and Rocktail swooped in and out. The griffin tore at the creatures, spewing smoke from the injuries he inflicted.

Pernden dismounted and immediately charged his enemies, feeling the welling magic in *Wintertide* grow with his effort. He cut down several wretchlings, small decrepit creatures, before he ran into bigger ones. The larger wretchlings stood a head taller than he but were brutish, like orcs. He found their dark translucent skin similarly easy to pierce, as he sent ice blade after ice blade soaring at them.

A big wretchling roared in from the side, bringing his jagged axe down with great force. Pernden parried the axe, barely getting his sword up to deflect it as he spun away. An explosion of fire erupted behind the king, sending several wretchlings flying. He faced the brute of a wretchling head-on. The creature said no words, his eyes glowing with flame. The monster stood there, seemingly with no life in him save for the wicked fire that kept him upright. In that moment, Pernden thought the creature no more than a mindless ghoul.

The wretchling sprang forward, swiping his battle axe across his front. Pernden clanged *Wintertide* against the attack while he shifted his stance, dropping his shoulder low. Ice shards sprayed from the impact as the king slipped the sword away from the axe's momentum. The wretchling didn't stand a chance as the axe went wide, opening him up to Pernden's counter. *Wintertide* swooshed into a slashing uppercut. The magical blade sliced through the wretchling as if he were hot butter. Smoke billowed from the brute as the king turned toward another.

Pernden soon found himself fighting next to Lotmeag and his garvawk. The dwarf had also dismounted and was dealing some heavy blows to the wretchlings with his morning star. The weapon was fierce, sporting a long handle which Lotmeag gripped with both hands and a heavy shaped head that battered and cut at the wretchlings caught in its path. The dwarf ripped the morning star into an upward arc, shattering a wretchling's face into a smoky explosion.

Lotmeag's garvawk was a sight to see. The great cat tore through the enemy like it was playing with mice. The garvawk leaped from enemy to enemy, shredding them with its claws and biting the heads off others. It took to the sky again before pouncing on another group.

Rocktail scooped up another wretchling with his talons before launching the monster into one of the castle walls.

As they fought, an enormous wretchling barreled around one of the castle's nearby towers. The monster stomped and kicked other wretchlings out of his way as he hurried toward Pernden and Lotmeag.

"Watch out for the big fella!" Lotmeag hollered. Pernden wondered how he could possibly miss the wretchling giant.

Their friends who'd been in Kelvur for a while had told them giants existed there. Pernden believed their reports, of course, but something in his mind must not have truly accepted it, for the sight of the wretchling giant nearly bowled him over in shock. The massive monster, more than double the man's height, crashed into the space while other wretchlings dove out of the way.

The giant stopped, heaving great strained breaths, looking no more from the land of the living than any of the other wretchlings. Its fiery eyes looked from Pernden to Lotmeag, as though sizing them up. The pair shot nervous glances to each other before readying themselves.

Pernden gripped *Wintertide* in both hands, squeezing with effort to sync his body with the magic in the sword.

The wretchling giant ambled forward, lifting a great wooden beam in his hand. He swung it at the king and the foredwarf who both dove out of the way. He swung and smashed his wooden beam on the ground again and again as Pernden and Lotmeag ran and dove and spun and rolled, doing everything they could to keep from getting smashed.

Several of the wretchlings in the area were caught up and killed by the relentless pounding, bursts of smoke indicating their deaths. The giant's swings pummeled the ground, ripping up the grass and leaving great muddy trenches along the area. The giant roared a sickly noise and angrily stomped his feet.

Pernden tripped as his boot suctioned from the mud. The wretchling giant lifted the great wooden beam again. The man watched in horror, bringing *Wintertide* above himself in a feeble attempt to create an ice shield. He knew it wouldn't save him from the giant's strike.

Suddenly, a fireball struck the giant in the chest, knocking him slightly off balance. Rocktail screamed into the giant's face.

The great wretchling threw his wooden beam to the side in an attempt to pry the rampaging griffin from his face. Lotmeag's garvawk was soon tearing at the giant's legs, forcing the monster to stumble backward to the ground.

A painful screech pierced the air as the giant ripped Rocktail from his face. A sickening pop rang out, as the monster yanked both of Rocktail's wings before hurtling the griffin toward a stone wall. The mighty griffin slammed into the wall with a crunch and fell into a silent heap.

"Rocktail!" Pernden roared, but there was no time to check on the griffin. The garvawk was doing everything it could to keep the giant down, but the great wretchling was already trying to regain his feet.

Lotmeag hustled past the king, yelling, "Come on, lad! We have to get him while he's down."

Pernden gritted his teeth and ran after the foredwarf, knowing he was right. Lotmeag slammed his morning star down on the giant's ankle as he ran past, forcing a great wince from the monster. The garvawk ripped and clawed at the giant before a large hand swung at the cat, and she pounced on the monster in another position. Lotmeag reached the giant's face first and whaled on him repeatedly.

Wintertide's power filled Pernden's hands. His muscles tensed as he prepared his strike while he ran. Another fireball from Smarlo blasted into the giant's face, knocking him back and exposing his massive neck. The king struck true, *Wintertide* extending itself with a magic blade of ice and cutting down hard, all the way to the ground.

Smoke billowed from the wretchling giant as it went limp. Great clouds of smoke covered the entire area. Pernden utilized the cover and ran toward the feathered heap near the wall.

He slid to his knees as he approached Rocktail, unsure what he'd find.

"Watch over him." Smarlo pointed to the guardian king as he hollered down to Lotmeag. "Our forces are engaging another giant nearby. I'm going to help them."

"Aye," Lotmeag said. "We can handle this for a while."

Smarlo quickly scanned the area below. Few wretchlings remained, most having been smashed by their own giant or killed before the monster had arrived. The wretchlings who had survived moved slowly, likely having taken injuries during the giant's rampage.

They'll be alright for a minute, Smarlo thought.

In truth, his thoughts were distracted because the other giant bounded toward where Lehra and Galbrish fought. Her big wyvern crashed upon a group of wretchlings, ripping several of them in his jaws and shaking them apart as smoke seeped from his mouth. The giant also had little regard for his fellow wretchlings, stepping on and squashing many more into the dirt.

Smarlo leaned into Klovur's back. "Come on, girl," he urged her onward.

They flew as fast as they could toward the giant, but the monster would reach Lehra first. Smarlo reached back and loosed a magic missile. The arcane fire ripped through the air ahead of them, aimed straight at the giant's back. The massive wretchling lifted his great club and swung it around at Lehra and Galbrish. Just before the club made contact, the magic missile exploded in his back.

Smarlo didn't see the giant's swing connect, but Galbrish's great cry told him it had.

No ... Smarlo thought with horror.

The wretchling giant had been knocked to his knees. He used his club as a crutch to lift himself to his feet again.

Smarlo and Klovur swooped wide so the orc mage could see the damage the giant had done. When they flanked wide enough, Smarlo saw Galbrish, baring his fangs, his wings stamping at the ground like an eerie spider creature. His rider was gone. Galbrish hissed at the sluggish giant, keeping the wretchling in front of him.

No ... Lehra ...

Smarlo readied another magic missile as waves of grief and rage mixed within him to create a deadly fierceness. He spurred Klovur into an attack pattern headed straight for the giant. The wretchling didn't seem interested in the orc mage as he lifted his club to strike at Galbrish again.

Suddenly, a spear took flight from behind the wyvern, striking the wretchling giant in the chest. The giant's movements faltered, as did Smarlo's own. He leaned over Klovur's side, peering with all his might to see where the spear had come from.

Lehra!

She'd obviously been dismounted, but Galbrish—the big beautiful wyvern—protected her while she regained her seat.

Another wave of emotions flooded through Smarlo, adding to the already dangerous concoction within him. He snarled as he sent all of his effort into the magic missile he'd been forming. He loosed it and leaned into Klovur's back.

The missile whistled through the air, blasting into the giant's chest with an explosion of light just before Klovur crashed hard into him. The wretchling giant toppled over as the wyvern bit and clawed at him. Smarlo rained fireball after fireball onto the giant, whose luck got even worse as Galbrish pounced him as well. The wretchling giant wriggled against them for only a moment before it gave in to death.

Smarlo swiveled Klovur to face Galbrish. Lehra was atop her mount again, leaning over to pull her spear from the smoking giant. Smarlo's heart leapt into his throat as pure joy tempted it to burst.

"Are you alright?" he asked.

The question seemed odd in the midst of the cacophony of sounds that surrounded them—metal on metal and weapons on shields and armor. Battle cries and the cries of the wounded.

"I'll be alright. Thanks for the assist, but this big boy had me covered," she said with a nod, patting the large wyvern fondly.

Her honey brown hair was matted and disheveled, but from Smarlo's vantage, she didn't seem much the worse for wear.

"Alright. I've got to get back to the—"

A sudden explosion erupted near the castle. Smarlo turned on Klovur with wide eyes.

"The king!"

The sudden explosion of energy sent Pernden flying backward. His ears rang with a piercing tone, and his head lolled as he tried to regain his faculties. His vision blurred as he pulled himself up from the dirt. Muffled yells from his side resounded with no distinguishable tones, until a hand grabbed at his shoulder armor and shook him.

Lotmeag stared into his eyes, the dwarf's image sharpening as the ringing in Pernden's ears faded. The dwarf was covered in mud, and his intense eyes squinted as he hollered, "Pernden! Can ye hear me? Are ye alright?"

Pernden wavered to the side again but straightened, grabbing the dwarf's forearm as Lotmeag helped him to his feet.

"I'm alright," Pernden lied, shaking the fog from his head. "What hap—"

Before he could finish his question, Pernden spotted the sorcerer descending the steps from the castle entrance. If it weren't for the sorcerer's black cloak that drifted like smoky tendrils, the king might not have recognized him. The last time he'd seen Jaernok Tur in the king's chambers in Whitestone, the sorcerer's face was still orcish. The enemy that stood before them was rigid, with stone-like skin covering his face and both arms. His eyes were still pitch and his glare just as menacing. There was no doubting the sorcerer's presence.

There was another change in the sorcerer. Instead of being completely black, the grains of his staff glowed with an orange hue.

"He doesn't wield the axe," Lotmeag said.

"He's taken the stone from the axe and mounted it to his staff," Pernden replied quickly.

"That's not good," the dwarf said with a grimace.

"No, it is not," the guardian king huffed. Pernden rolled his shoulders and popped his neck to the side, taking *Wintertide* into his strong hand. "Keep the wretchlings off my back."

Lotmeag hesitated next to the man, shooting a quick glance at the sorcerer and then back to the man he'd just helped up. "Aye. I'll give ye all the time I can. Go, finish this," he said finally. "But make sure ye don't get yerself killed, alright?"

"Fair enough," Pernden said.

Smarlo pressed into Klovur like he'd never done before, hoping to make himself as aerodynamic as possible. *I have to help Pernden,* he thought as they flew. *How could I be so foolish?*

His mind reeled as Klovur whipped through the air. He'd left Lotmeag and Pernden to help Lehra and, in doing so, abandoned them in the very moment the sorcerer had revealed himself.

Did he wait for me to leave? No. Why would a mighty sorcerer worry about a mage?

As he drew closer to the battle ensuing before him, Smarlo looked around desperately to see *Dalkeri* in the orange blasts that erupted but could not put eyes on the axe. Then he saw Jaernok Tur's staff. The black magic ribbons swirled with orange ones, rippling into powerful attacks that careened off of the king's parries.

Maker, help us ... Smarlo gasped as he realized the truth. *He has two monolith stones ... a black one and an orange one.*

The orc mage swooped low allowing Klovur to tear up several wretchlings that were waiting their turn to fight the foredwarf. Lotmeag held them off by bottlenecking them through rubble. Smarlo lobbed a few fireballs to thin the horde before leaping off Klovur and landing next to his dwarven friend.

"The sorcerer has two stones!" he shouted, as he launched a magic missile that exploded into a group of wretchlings attempting to climb over a pile of smoldering stone.

"What?" Lotmeag hollered back, blasting a wretchling with his morning star. The wretchling crumpled into a smoking pile.

"I think he always had one. Think about it." Smarlo lobbed another fireball. "He was always powerful. If the monolith dragon is his master, wouldn't he want to gather all the things that could destroy him? The safest place for them would be under his own guard."

"Sure, but Pernden only has one monolith stone. Can he beat the sorcerer if the wretch has two?"

"I don't know, but I'm not going to leave him to do it alone."

"Go then," Lotmeag growled as he smashed the crooked knees of another wretchling. "I've got these ones."

Smarlo threw one last fireball, making the bottleneck tighter, then turned and ran toward the castle.

Try as he might, Pernden could not get close enough to land a blow on the sorcerer with *Wintertide's* metal blade. He'd launched dozens of the ice blades at Jaernok Tur, but the sorcerer had parried them away with wicked ribbons of magical energy.

Pernden halted, his breathing so erratic that his shoulders heaved. Sweat dripped down his face and off the long tips of his blond hair, half of which was matted to his cheeks.

"You tire, young king," Jaernok Tur said, a wicked grin scrawling across his stony face. His words seemed to echo in whispers.

"Not too tired to defeat you," Pernden said, straightening himself.

Jaernok Tur chuckled, though it sounded a macabre noise. "Do you even know what power you play with?"

"You mean this?" Pernden asked, holding *Wintertide* out, showing the sword to the sorcerer. A greedy—almost hungry—look flashed across the stony face. "Oh, you mean the stone. What are they called? Monolith stones?"

The sorcerer shifted, his stance becoming more aggressive. "You should not be so flippant with a power you do not understand."

"I know more about this sword and its history than you can imagine. I—"

Pernden's words were cut off by the low, patronizing laughter that emanated from the sorcerer. "Foolish young king." Pernden didn't appreciate the tone, but he would take every extra second to regain his strength. He wouldn't admit it to Jaernok Tur, but his exhaustion worried him. The sorcerer was powerful. "The sword does not matter. It is merely a vessel for the stone—the stone which you do not understand."

"Oh." Pernden feigned as if he were finally catching on. "You mean the stone that the monolith dragons created. The stones they wanted to use to ruin the world."

His frankness caught the sorcerer off guard, as Jaernok Tur's stance slacked. "It is inevitable," the sorcerer said.

"I don't believe that. To leave the world in ruin is no great achievement. Why would you go along with this? Once the monolith dragon is finished with you, what use will he have for you?"

"In the wake of ruin there is rebirth," Jaernok Tur hissed. "There will be rebirth. My family ..." The sorcerer suddenly stopped himself.

Pernden caught the movement out of the corner of his eye. Smarlo stood, readying a fireball in his hand. He gave Pernden a quick nod before the king turned his attention back to the sorcerer.

"I think our conversation is over," Jaernok Tur said. "I nearly had the white stone when I first came to your city. A foolish man kept it from me then. I will not let that happen again."

"Go!" Smarlo yelled, as he loosed a fireball that blasted into the sorcerer's face.

Pernden leaped into a sprint, bringing *Wintertide* around for a strike. But the sorcerer was quick as lightning, turning his staff to block the blow. Sparks of orange and black and white sprayed in wild arcs of energy. Pernden tried to pull the sword back, but for some reason he couldn't. It was as if the stone in the sword wanted to join the others in the magic staff.

Jaernok Tur grinned evilly. "And now an even more foolish man has brought it to me."

"Danner Kane was a great man," Pernden growled.

"And what about you, young king? How will you be remembered?"

The question seemed funny to Pernden in that moment. Only a year ago, he would likely have been concerned with the answer to it. As he faced the sorcerer, he cared little. He thought of Nera and Orin and Garron and Smarlo and Porg and all the people he loved. He did not care how history remembered him. He only cared how he could love his friends better.

Suddenly, Jaernok Tur was tackled to the side by a mass of feathers. Rocktail clawed and bit at the sorcerer orc, the hard tackle breaking the connection between *Wintertide* and the sorcerer's staff. Pernden stood, stunned. Only a short time before, he thought Rocktail to be dead. He'd hardly been able to check the griffin before the sorcerer showed up.

Smarlo ran in to help the griffin, but a great blast of orange and black energy erupted from beneath Rocktail, sheering feathers in all directions and launching the two into stone walls nearby. The griffin lay motionless again, while the orc mage slumped dizzily to the ground.

Pernden gripped *Wintertide* in both hands, feeling something in the sword he'd never felt before. *Did its contact with the other two stones unlocked something?* He did not know, but he felt a buzzing power emanating from within.

Suddenly, the words of Danner Kane filled his mind again. *"You are capable of far more than you know ..."*

Pernden closed his eyes, bringing *Wintertide* upright in front of him. He knew the sorcerer was regaining his feet, but the king did not care. He needed to tap into whatever magic the sword had, or they would lose the battle.

A trickle of light pierced his mind, like the first snowflake on a moonlit night. As it drew nearer, it grew. And somehow, Pernden knew the sword. He knew the stone. He knew without any other prompting what he could do.

His eyes opened, and a determined grin grew across his face.

Jaernok Tur's eyes narrowed, and he snarled.

Pernden was not close enough for *Wintertide's* metal blade to bite the sorcerer, but he knew he no longer needed to be. He whipped the sword around and jabbed it forward, as though he were striking a nearby opponent. White light erupted from the sword, shooting toward the sorcerer.

Jaernok Tur seemed surprised but quickly angled his staff to loose his own powerful bolt of energy, catching the white bolt just before it struck him down.

The orange and black ribbons seared into the white bolt. They sprayed great arcs of energy all over the place. Shadow and light danced a dangerous game of hide and seek as the sparks flew.

Pernden leaned into *Wintertide*, feeling the energy and boosting it with his own willpower. He realized shortly that the orange and black energy was splitting the white bolt, drawing closer to him.

No ... he thought with a grunt. *No. I have to do this. I have to.*

The orange and black energy slowed its work down the white bolt of magic but continued to crawl along.

Jaernok Tur leaned into his staff even more, roaring as he put the weight of all his efforts into the magic he dispensed.

Pernden roared back.

The orange and black tendrils of energy continued to send white shards flying as they drew ever closer to the king.

Pernden roared even louder as the orange and black magic crept inch by inch toward *Wintertide's* tip.

No ...

Suddenly, the orange and black ribbons of light retracted as though they were being sucked back into the sorcerer's staff. A translucent bubble wrapped itself around Jaernok Tur as a shield.

Wintertide's arcing beam of light crashed against the shield, shooting sparks and ribbons of magic flying in all directions. Those ribbons began to swirl with red ribbons on one side and yellow ribbons of light on the other.

What?

Pernden thought he was losing his mind, but slowly, he saw Nera step around the sorcerer's left, *Santoralier* in her hand expelling waves of yellow energy. On the other side appeared a man-sized creature that looked like a turtle. He couldn't believe it, and had no idea where they'd come from, but suddenly, they had the advantage.

"Finish him!" Smarlo yelled, having regained himself. "The death wings have abandoned the fight above. They're coming this way!"

Pernden chanced a glance to the sky and found Smarlo was right. The king leaned into the magic of *Wintertide*, not knowing how much longer he could hold it.

Just push, he encouraged himself. *We have to finish this!*

Suddenly, blue people with great white wings emerged from the castle's entrance and took to the sky. They bore spears and met the death wings that swooped to the sorcerer's aid. A few dozen of the blue people flew into the sky. Pernden blinked furiously, focusing himself on *Wintertide*. He could little afford to lose his concentration.

Through the arcs and waves of magical energy colliding around the sorcerer, Pernden's eyes locked with Jaernok Tur's. The sorcerer looked ... sad. Almost as though he experienced a great loss. Pernden had expected fear, but the look of sadness ...

What had Jaernok Tur said? Something about his family?

An explosion lit up the night as the magic barrier failed, and the three arcs of magic energy came together, no longer held apart. Jaernok Tur let out a scream that could hardly be heard over the crashing magic. His body disintegrated into dust as the slashing magic ripped him apart. Another explosion erupted, blasting a wave of energy that sent the three magic wielders sprawling backward, tumbling along the ground.

The night went silent for a long while before Pernden opened his eyes to see Lotmeag hoisting him up. The dwarf's mouth moved, obviously asking the man something. The king could not quite make out what he said. *Have I gone deaf?* Pernden wondered. Shortly, the noises around him came back into his ears, as though his mind needed time to process everything his body was experiencing.

"Ye did it!" Lotmeag cried. "Ye did it!"

"I ..." Pernden started to say something, but in the moment, he had no words.

"Though ye almost got yerself killed," the dwarf grumbled at him. "I thought we had an agreement."

Pernden sat up with a start, glancing around for enemies.

"Oh no, lad," Lotmeag said with a chuckle and a shake of his head. "They're hightailing it away from the castle. Though with those blue folk cutting down all the death wings, I don't suppose the rest of our forces will let the wretchlings escape either."

"Nera!" Pernden said suddenly, jumping to his feet and sprinting toward where he'd last seen her.

Nera shook her head and blinked crazily. She'd taken a knock to the head in the explosion. The castle's stone wall had not caught her softly. She looked across the large stone square and spotted Shorlis. The chelon was slow to get up, but he gave her a nod and a weak wave to let her know he was alright, too.

"Nera!" she heard.

Pernden ran up the steps to greet her. He slid to his knees, embracing her in a tight hug. He grabbed her face in both hands and kissed her, his lips warm with love. She gripped his cape—or what was left of it—and kissed him back.

"Where did you come from?" Pernden asked when he finally pulled his lips from hers. Tears streaked his face, and blood issued from more than one cut.

"That," she said with a slight giggle, "is a long story."

"Well, I look forward to hearing it over and over again in the years to come," he said, wiping at something on her face. "That is, if you'll be my queen."

Nera huffed a laugh. "You know your timing is terrible, right?"

"What better time is there than now?" Pernden laughed.

Nera glanced around. The battlefield and the castle were strewn with smoking heaps. Not too far away, ally forces were still rounding up and slaying the last of the wretchling army. Fires burned heaps of refuse and rubble. And yet, for some reason, she couldn't think of a better time.

"I just can't waste any more time without you by my side," Pernden said with a sheepish grin. Then he looked her straight in the eyes and asked, "Nera, will you marry me?"

I guess I win, she thought for a split second, reminiscing on all the years they'd danced around their feelings for each other. Sitting with Pernden, she balked at their foolishness. She'd loved him for years, and she planned to love him all the years of their lives.

"Of course," she said, kissing him again. His mouth formed a great grin, and soon her kiss faded to a smile of her own. "Took you long enough," she teased.

Pernden barked a laugh.

Smarlo slowly limped toward the charred spot where Jaernok Tur had once stood. Wisps of smoke still swirled from the spot, while scorch marks extended in all directions on the stone ground. The black Staff of Tur lay in the center, neither glowing nor looking broken. The staff lay on the ground almost like it was of no consequence to the world, but the orc mage knew better.

"So, it's over then?" Lotmeag asked quietly next to him, the dwarf also inspecting the scene.

"I don't know," Smarlo said slowly. "The sorcerer is gone, but ..."

Suddenly, the earth beneath their feet began to rumble and groan as if Finlestia itself was waking from a long winter's slumber.

"What's happening?" Pernden called to them as he helped Nera to her feet.

Smarlo didn't answer. He had some theories, but he couldn't be sure. He bent down toward the staff. He'd been right about the stones. As the orc mage examined the staff closer, he saw the orange stone that was previously mounted in *Dalkeri* and a black stone of similar shape and size.

He reached a tentative hand out.

"Be careful," Lotmeag warned. "Ye don't know what kind of curses are on the thing."

"I'm not sure the staff is cursed," Smarlo said. "I think it was Jaernok Tur who was cursed."

Lotmeag grumbled slightly, shaking his head. The foredwarf showed his discomfort with the situation.

"Smarlo?" Pernden asked, as he and Nera joined them.

"It's alright," the orc mage said. "I'm just going to ..."

As his long orc fingers slipped around the magic staff, the earth shook again, and a great roar filled the world, rumbling deep into their bones.

CHAPTER THIRTY

GATHERING STONES

E lrenigeth was like a flying mountain, so large that Garron, Ezel, Ellaria, and Enkeli secured themselves easily between the great ridges on his back. Silverwing and Benley rode on the gargantuan dragon's back as well—though it required much coaxing for the pegasus, who was not thrilled about the situation.

Garron watched the world flash by beneath them. Even as a kid, he'd never dreamed he'd ever see Kelvur. The land far below didn't seem much different to him than Tarrine, but the living map that unfolded beneath them was nonetheless unfamiliar. Garron was particularly struck by a great wall that seemed to crawl for miles across the land. A large split in the wall housed a city, spreading out more on the southern side.

Enkeli spoke to Ezel with earnestness, going over their plan again and again. Garron could only hear muffled bits of the wizard's side of the conversation over the great winds that the monolith dragon produced as they flew. Ellaria was nestled nearby, and he was grateful for her closeness.

Suddenly, Ezel popped up and walked over to them.

"This is our first stop," Ezel signed quickly.

Enkeli watched the deep gnome intently. "You can sense the stones?" the wizard asked.

"At first, I thought it was the token," the gnome responded, *"but I can feel them in my bones."*

"Let's mount up then," Garron said, ready to carry his friend anywhere.

He and Ezel climbed onto Benley. The pegasus stamped excitedly, clearly ready to get off the monolith dragon's ever-moving back.

Ellaria and Enkeli followed their descent on Silverwing's back, the griffin able to carry the combined weight of the slender woman and the skinny wizard with ease. Garron shook his head again at the griffin. The man assumed Silverwing had to like the wizard if Enkeli was able to send the griffin to Galium to save Ellaria and Ezel during that battle. He couldn't help but wonder if Silverwing was an oddity among griffins or if, perhaps in the process of their rearing at the Roost in Whitestone, the guardians had nurtured the fierce exclusive loyalty in them.

Those were questions for another time, however, as they glided toward the city. Soon enough, several griffin riders ascended toward them, and a strange sensation washed over Garron. *The Talon Squadron?* he wondered. Judging by their numbers, he couldn't be sure—that is, until he saw his cousin.

"Orin!" he shouted.

"Garron? What in Finlestia are you doing here?" Orin called back. Before Garron could answer, he asked, "And what is that?"

His outstretched arm pointed toward Elrenigeth as the monolith dragon continued his northward flight path.

"That, cousin," Garron said with a chuckle, "is the one buying us time."

Merrick rushed to hug his sister, a flood of emotions welling and bursting from his face through his tears. As he held her in his tight squeeze, he wondered if he had any more tears left to shed.

"How are you here?" he asked her.

"That's a long story," she said. "We went to the Nari Desert and found the First Tree of Tarrine."

"The First Tree?"

"Aye," she said with a laugh, "and that monolith dragon."

Merrick looked to the northern sky. The sun was warming the sky with colors before it made its morning appearance. The dark silhouette of the massive dragon flew onward.

Coal nudged the huntsman out of the way to greet Ellaria. "My turn," the dwarf said excitedly.

"Oh, Coal," Ellaria said squeezing him tightly.

"I've missed you, lass," he said sweetly.

"I've missed you, too," she giggled. "What have you done to your head? Did you make this big mess here?" she asked, looking around at the aftermath of their battle.

"Maybe a little," Coal blushed. Suddenly, he pushed Ellaria aside and yelled, "Ezel!"

Ellaria laughed as Merrick embraced her again. He was as excited to see her as Coal must have been to see his gnomish best friend.

The dwarf scooped up the gnome in a big hug, while Ezel patted him on the back. "Boehlen's Beard! I thought I'd never see you again. Wasn't sure we were going to make it last night. Karnak and the other griffin riders came in and saved our hides. I think I'm quite ready to get back to boating the

Palori River—carrying goods and good folk. Although, I'm not opposed to running wagons between Whitestone and Kane Harbor. Same basic game, just going from keels to wheels." The dwarf laughed at his turn of phrase.

Ezel smiled kindly at his oldest friend before placing a hand on the dwarf's shoulder. *"I have to finish this,"* the deep gnome signed.

"What do you mean *you* have to finish this?" Coal asked aloud, taking a step back to inspect his friend.

Ezel held up the token he wore around his neck, showing it to the dwarf. *"I'm the only one who can finish this."*

"What is that? Why's it got green on it now?" Coal asked.

Merrick heard confusion in the dwarf's voice. The huntsman looked to his sister. Ellaria pulled at the leather string around her neck.

"Your stone," he said softly, "the one Greggo gave you."

"Merrick," she said. It seemed she hardly believed her next words herself. "Greggo found a monolith stone. One of the stones that the monolith dragons created when they rebelled. One of the scattered stones of power."

Merrick's face scrunched. Her words sounded impossible. Their brother had found a monolith stone and tied the thing to a leather string for Ellaria before he was killed by a plains bear on a hunt?

"Now Ezel needs to gather the rest of the stones," she continued. "He needs them, so he can kill Kilretheon the Red."

"The monolith dragon that Jaernok Tur has been working with?" Merrick clarified.

"Aye," Ellaria affirmed. "One of the stones is here, somewhere."

"What does it look like?" Merrick asked quickly. "Is it like yours? We can set half of Javelin and the Duskwood Rangers searching for it."

"I don't think that will be necessary," Ellaria said.

Suddenly, Merrick realized why it had grown so quiet around them. Ezel walked slowly toward Ralowyn, his wide eyes staring directly at the elf mage. Ralowyn watched him, inspecting the gnome.

Ezel signed to her, but Ralowyn shook her head and said, "I am sorry, my little friend. I do not know what you are saying."

Ellaria moved toward them to help, but Garron rushed forward and translated.

"Ezel says he is sorry to ask this of you," Garron said.

"Ask what of me?" the elf asked, pulling silvery strands of hair behind her pointed ear and leaning forward to direct her questions to the gnome.

Ezel's hands went into a flurry of motion, and Garron translated his friend's words. "I need to take the stone from your staff. If there were another way for me to end this, I would choose it. Unfortunately, there is not."

"The stone from my staff?" Ralowyn's eyes fell on the swirling metal at the pinnacle of her staff. Merrick had never inspected the Staff of Anvelorian closely, but the light that emanated from the staff always originated from its pinnacle. Ralowyn pursed her lips and scrunched her nose. "I do not think it is something I can separate from the staff. This staff is an ancient artifact of my people. It was forged by the greatest of our smiths."

Ezel nodded solemnly. His hands went into motion slowly, as though he were trying to be kind to her, even in his insistence.

"I can separate them," Garron translated.

"This staff is the only magic weapon I have to wield," Ralowyn said hesitantly.

"I know it means a lot to you, but I'm assured that while the magic will be different, the staff has been saturated with the magic for a long time, and it has seeped into its very core," Garron relayed.

"I have seen this," Karnak interrupted. He hoisted his battle axe to show Ralowyn. "*Dalkeri* has no stone, but there is magic in it still."

The elf mage eyed the weapon, having seen Karnak wield it in their recent battle. She shot a glance to Merrick, who was watching with great interest. He knew how much the staff meant to her. He remembered her telling him how long it took for Master Tenlien at the wisdom tower of Loralith to help her find a magical artifact to wield.

Merrick glanced around to all the people gathered. He'd fought and bled alongside many of them. He trusted them with his life. If Ezel believed he needed the stone, Merrick thought it best to make sure the gnome had it.

He looked back at Ralowyn and gave her a half shrug and a nod.

"Alright," she said, holding the Staff of Anvelorian out before her.

"Thank you," Ezel signed and gripped the wooden token in one hand. His other hand extended toward the Staff of Anvelorian. Tattoo runes on his hands and arms blazed to life with blue fire. The staff's pinnacle burst to lavender flame.

The swirling metal spun outward, opening to reveal a purple stone inside. With a flick of his fingers, Ezel called the stone to himself. The monolith stone unseated from the silver staff. It floated through the air and pressed against the wooden token. Ezel clasped his hand over it, squeezing the token and the stone together between both hands. Every tattoo on the little gnome erupted into blue light. Swirling ribbons of green and purple and blue danced around his pressed hands before an explosion of light burst from him.

Merrick raised an arm to protect his eyes from the great light. The light disappeared just as quickly, and the huntsman stared in disbelief.

Ezel held the token up to inspect it, finding that two of the runes were lit with color. One green and one purple. The tree in the center glowed with a hint of blue.

Ralowyn's eyes fell upon the Staff of Anvelorian, a worried look on her face. Merrick walked to her. He wasn't sure what she might be feeling but wanted to be close to her in case she needed him.

The elf closed her eyes and held the staff in front of her body. She stood motionless for a long time, silently working some magic Merrick and the others couldn't see. A smile crept across her beautiful face. She opened her eyes and said, "I can still feel them."

Chapter Thirty-One

Memories & Curiosity

Smarlo's eyes flickered—first black, then orange, then back to his usual yellow. The flickering looked as though someone were lighting a candle in the orc mage's eyes and then snuffing the flame. Pernden and Nera stepped back, raising their weapons tentatively. Shorlis hurried to join them.

Smarlo had the vague impression that they surrounded him, but the staff was all he knew.

Come, a voice said on the wind. *Bring it to me. I will show you power like you've never known.*

Smarlo's gaze was distant, but in his mind, he examined the Staff of Tur. The dark wood of the staff was of an origin the orc mage could not place. The grains glowed with orange light, a spectacle in his hands. His hands ... how powerful they felt. The energy humming into them vibrated into his palms, running through his muscles. He felt it in his bones. The sensation rolled all the way to the tips of his long ears. Was his half ear long again?

You sense the power, the rumbling voice said. *That is only the beginning. Take the other stones from those who would wield them against you. Add them to the staff, and I will show you greater power than you've ever imagined.*

Smarlo's eyes were suddenly able to move again, though they did not see clearly. A fog clouded his mind, extending to his vision. Each of the people around him bore weapons that radiated with strange hues. One of them bore a sword, blazing with white light. Was it a man? He could not tell, for the bearer also glowed with a bright light. Another bore a spear that radiated yellow light that bounced and arced away from the weapon and the bearer's body. Yet another bore a staff whose light burned a furious red.

But then there was another. He was shorter than the others. He had no light. His grey form seemed to fade in and out of clarity as though he were trying to wade through the fog.

"Smarlo," called the smaller figure.

Smarlo. That had been his name. Or had it? It must have been, for he must surely have once had a name. Now he knew nothing but the power of the mighty staff. He felt the waves of energy crashing from the stones. The orange was bright and radiant. Its magic seemed different. Both stones held memories.

Take the other stones! the voice on the wind said. *They will not hesitate to kill you and take the stones from you.*

The orc mage paused, unsure for a moment. The figures around him hadn't attacked yet, though they aimed their weapons at him. Perhaps the voice did not speak entirely true. Another curiosity pricked at his mind. Could he steal a moment to inspect the stones?

His insatiable curiosity won out, and he reached into the orange stone. He saw memories of the stone. He could not say how far back he'd gone, but he watched the memories sail through his mind. Orcs passing the axe that the stone knew so well down to their sons. One of the orcs he recognized, big and strong. He seemed a mighty and noble warrior. And was that … him? Was that the one called Smarlo? Then there was an orc woman and her orcling with the big orc. Inside, the orc mage felt a great sense of happiness and joy as though the mere sight of those people brought light to his existence.

Wanting more and unable to help himself, the orc mage reached into the black stone. The voice on the wind tried to say something, but it sounded distant in the orc mage's distraction.

The black stone revealed memories of another family of orcs, though they appeared terrified. A great pit grew in the orc mage's stomach. For some reason, he could not see the wielder, but the male orc attempting to defend his family seemed somehow familiar. The black staff swiped ahead and struck the orc, sending him sprawling to the ground. The female and the children screamed, ethereal echoes of horror before the black energy erupted from the staff to kill them.

As the orc mage tried to pull back from the black stone's memories, the next one played before his mind's eye. The stone took life after life until one memory—the male orc that tried to protect his family stood over the staff, which lay on the ground. The male orc leaned down and lifted the staff. The next memories sailed across the orc mage's mind, whipping from one murder to dozens more. And then the great head of a monolith dragon rose into view. The male orc turned with a wicked glint in his eye and looked straight at the orc mage.

The orc mage screamed as he pulled away from the memories of the black stone. Is that what the stones are capable of? Are they tools for destruction and ruin? The mage wanted nothing to do with the stones. And yet, the others wielded similar stones. Were they just as wicked?

The orc mage raised the staff and grasped it with both hands. The bearers surrounding him readied their own stances.

The grey being raised both of his hands high. Was he yelling?

"Smarlo!" the short being shouted. He moved closer to the orc mage, his image becoming clearer as he neared. "Smarlo, what are ye doing?"

"I ...," the orc mage said. Admittedly, he was not entirely sure how he'd found himself in that situation. Had he always been here? Had he been born to it?

"Smarlo, ye have to drop that staff," the dwarf said. Yes, the being was a dwarf, and his face was so very familiar. His great brown beard and his rosy cheeks. Though for some reason, the orc mage remembered it slightly different.

No, the voice on the wind said. *You must complete the task. Kill them and take the stones. Bring the stones to me. You do not want to lose the power. I can make you strong.*

A strange sensation washed over the orc mage. He had a vague memory of always wanting to be stronger. But a lingering curiosity wouldn't leave him.

"Smarlo?" the orc mage asked.

"Yes," the dwarf said excitedly, smiling at him. The dwarf's face looked more familiar.

"Lotmeag ..." Smarlo said slowly.

"Yes, yes! That's it!"

Smarlo's eyes narrowed as his brain tried to process true from false information.

"Come now," Lotmeag said to him, his tone compassionate. "This will make a great installment in your *Book of Dangerous Secrets.*"

The name rang a bell in Smarlo's mind.

"And Maker knows, I can't finish *Heroes of the Harbinger* for ye," Lotmeag continued.

Good title, Smarlo thought.

"Ye said ye'd make sure to describe my glorious beard just right. And I have to admit, if I have to finish it, I'm prone to embellishment," the dwarf said with a chuckle.

Something about the dwarf's mirth and the way he spoke to Smarlo made the orc mage lower the staff slightly. The dwarf spoke to him, almost like a friend.

"Besides, I've gotten used to our tea times and eating half your rations." Lotmeag laughed. "Why don't ye put that staff down, and we can get some tea going. Maybe Cook has some blueberry scones on the *Harbinger*, too."

The dwarf stepped closer, slowly nodding at the mage with a smile. Smarlo couldn't help but sense a great trust rising from somewhere inside his chest. He slowly lowered the staff and let it slip from his fingers.

Instantly, clarity returned to the slender orc. He blinked several times, his eyes having a hard time receiving all the vibrant information of reality again. He turned to the side and retched. Pernden watched the orc warily, as did Nera and the turtle person he assumed to be Shorlis.

"Wh-what happened?" Smarlo asked awkwardly, wiping at his mouth.

"Ye had a little run-in with the sorcerer's staff," Lotmeag said, kicking the staff off to the side. "Thought ye were about to go berserk on us."

No one dared to touch it or pick it up.

"We'll have to wrap it for traveling and put it under guard when we get back to Whitestone," Pernden said.

"Agreed," Lotmeag said. "Nobody should be touching that thing."

A great roar suddenly echoed through the world. The ground beneath their feet rumbled again, but that time, it bucked with a greater fervor, as though the earth intended to knock them down.

The sun was just beginning to rise, but something else was rising as well.

When Pernden first saw the flying mountain of a dragon, his heart sank. He'd never seen a creature so massive. The monolith dragon rose from the Crags, molten lava spraying off the edges of its great wings, accentuating red scales as it unfurled and flapped them to fly toward the stunned onlookers.

They'd barely survived their encounter with the sorcerer. How in Finlestia were they going to survive a fight with a monolith dragon?

Pernden chanced a glance at the Staff of Tur, wondering if he'd be able to hold it without succumbing to the monolith dragon's influence. He certainly didn't know much of wielding such a magical artifact. Maybe Shorlis could, but even the chelon was still learning the ways of wielding magic staffs. If one of them did pick it up and couldn't resist the call of Kilretheon, they'd likely be handing their own stones over to him as well.

Not a soul in Ventohl made a noise, every being captivated by the approaching monolith dragon. They stood in awe like statues.

"Smarlo," Pernden called over his shoulder.

"Yeah," the orc mage said weakly.

"Can we kill the dragon with three stones?"

"I'm not sure," Smarlo said. "The text wasn't very specific on that matter."

Great, Pernden thought, *now, we have to fight a monolith dragon and don't even know if we have the power to kill it.*

Another roar reverberated through the air, rattling the onlookers to the core. That roar forced Kilretheon the Red to turn his attention southward.

Pernden followed the monolith dragon's gaze, and his own eyes widened. The guardian king found it hard to breathe. A second, equally immense, dragon of a blue hue flew north toward Kilretheon.

"Smarlo?" Pernden called nervously.

The orc mage stuttered, saying nothing the king could understand. Pernden turned quickly, thinking the orc mage might have picked up the Staff of Tur again, but found Smarlo watching the monolith dragons, completely astounded.

"They're flying at each other," Lotmeag said, his words sounding confused.

"Or to each other," Nera put in.

"You think they're working together?" Shorlis asked. "There were eight monolith dragons who originally rebelled."

"If they are ..." Pernden started to say, but he didn't have the heart to finish the sentence. They all knew what that would mean.

CHAPTER THIRTY-TWO

CLASH OF MONOLITHS

G arron heeled Benley with his boots. The pegasus flew faster than he'd ever done before. Garron gripped the reins and leaned into the pegasus, trying desperately to stay seated. A lavender flame burned in the pegasus's eyes. Some magic that Ezel was performing spurred the noble steed into an unprecedented speed. They flew so swiftly they had regained sight of Elrenigeth, the great dragon flying directly toward Kilretheon. The sight of the red monolith dragon soured Garron's stomach.

Ezel gripped the man's layered armor, holding tightly. Numerous others followed behind them, though Benley outpaced them by some distance—an impressive feat considering the others rode griffins.

Garron's eyes remained locked on the monolith dragons, unable to look away from what he figured would be a clash unlike anything the world had ever seen. Eventually, Ezel tapped the man and pointed slightly toward the northwest. In the distance, Garron saw the remnants of a city and a castle, smoke rising from the area. Were those ships in the water beyond the city?

The man didn't even need to steer Benley in the direction of Ventohl, the deep gnome had already communicated the necessary adjustments to the pegasus. The man felt useless again, like he was only along for the ride. Garron didn't know how, but Ezel seemed to notice the change in his thinking and reassuringly patted the man on the shoulder.

A great cracking boom reverberated through the sky as the monolith dragons collided in midair. Far louder than a thunderclap, the impact sounded like two mountains crashing together.

The beasts fell, slamming into the ground below, snapping trees that had lived for hundreds of years like they were mere splinters. Great mounds of dirt and rock rose as they slid and rolled in their battle, forming new hills and ravines in the matter of moments.

Benley galloped his feet through the air, pressing onward with even greater fervor. Garron worried about the pegasus, frothy sweat beginning to cake his white and brown spotted coat. "Hang in there, pal," Garron said to the pegasus. Benley made no noise back to him, but the man got the feeling he heard him.

"Smarlo, what do we do?" Pernden asked the orc mage again.

"I don't know," he hollered over the great ruckus of the dragons.

The monstrous beasts beat and slashed and bit and rolled and tackled each other, crashing into the ground and shaking the earth beneath them. What could they do against such immense and ancient beings?

"Maybe if we could combine the power of the stones," Smarlo said, taking a few steps to inspect the Staff of Tur where it lay.

"Easy there," Lotmeag said as he moved between the orc and the staff. "Don't need ye getting swept up again."

Smarlo grimaced. "Even if one of us could pick up the staff, do any of us know how to wield the stones together?"

Everyone looked blankly at the orc mage as the earth shook again.

None of us, Smarlo silently cursed himself. If only he'd sought help translating his *Book of Dangerous Secrets* earlier, maybe he would have had time to find something more in the tome.

He scratched at his half ear nervously as he looked toward the rolling monolith dragons, taking their battle to the sky. Suddenly, out of the corner of his eye, he saw riders in the distance.

"Riders!" he called, and all the others ripped their gazes from the clash of the monoliths to see what the orc mage was talking about.

"It's the Talon Squadron!" Nera yelled. As the riders drew nearer, they all knew it not to be so. Certainly, members of the Talon Squadron flew among the riders, but a pegasus led the way and many of the griffins carried more than one rider.

"It's Garron!" Pernden shouted with confusion.

Pernden's eyes welled at the sight of his cousin. He was beyond confused, but he was also completely overcome with joy. For the life of him, he could not make sense of his cousin's presence as the fastest pegasus Pernden had ever seen came in for a landing.

Garron slipped off the back of the pegasus, hurrying over and wrapping the guardian king in a hug.

"Cousin," Garron said quickly. "I'm so glad to see you alive."

"And you," Pernden said. "What in Finlestia are you doing here in Kelvur?"

A loud crack and great roar reverberated through the air. Other riders began landing nearby.

"No time for that," Garron blurted. "Where is Jaernok Tur? He has a monolith stone, and we need it."

"What?" Pernden said, his face scrunching. He felt the grit that caked his face as he eyed his cousin in confusion. "We defeated the sorcerer. His staff is over—"

As Pernden turned, he saw Ezel closing in to grab the Staff of Tur.

"No, don't!" Lotmeag hollered, also seeing the deep gnome.

But Ezel did not touch the staff. Instead, the Staff of Tur flipped upward, standing vertically before the little gnome. His runic tattoos glowed with blue faery fire as the staff's wood grains widened and stretched. The orange stone popped from its mount in the wood, leaving a perfect circular hole in the staff, and floated into the gnome's awaiting hand. The black stone dislodged itself almost as quickly, and the gnome pressed the stones against the talisman he wore around his neck.

Pernden and the others watched in horror, raising their weapons and readying themselves for anything. Another thunderous boom resounded from the monolith dragons' battle, causing Pernden to wince.

Meanwhile, an explosion of light erupted from the little gnome, and he turned to face Pernden and the others, his eyes black as night.

Pernden shifted his feet, ready to strike.

"No, wait!" Garron said quickly, holding out a hand to stay the guardian king.

The black of Ezel's eyes flickered and faded, returning his eyes to their normal blue.

Pernden eyed the gnome's token. Several of the runes were alight, something the king had never seen on the token before.

"What is this magic?" Pernden asked.

"The token was created from the First Tree of Finlestia," Garron explained quickly. "It can harness the magic of the monolith stones. It's the only way to stop Kilretheon the Red."

Ezel signed to him, and Garron shook his head. "What? That doesn't make any sense."

"What is it?" Pernden asked.

"He said he needs *Wintertide* as well," Garron said, furrowing his brow. The man signed and said aloud, "*Wintertide* was the sword of our old Master Melkis. It's not—"

Pernden cut his cousin off with a hand to the shoulder. "I think it is," the king said. He lifted the sword again, still bewildered that the weapon housed a monolith stone all those years and no one had known. "Its magic combined with that of *Santoralier* and *Menthrora* to defeat Jaernok Tur. Believe me, I was as surprised as anyone."

The king walked over to the deep gnome and knelt before him, trying to meet Ezel eye to eye. He held out *Wintertide* in both hands, lifting the sword reverently toward the gnome. "If you need my sword to finish this," Pernden said, "then my sword I give you. Save us all, little one."

Ezel stepped forward with a grateful nod. He signed something quickly and waved his hand over the sword, the runes on his hands bursting into blue flame. The white stone in *Wintertide's* hilt popped free and floated into the little gnome's hand.

"He said he only needs the stone." Garron choked as he watched the display of care the deep gnome showed.

Nera gave up the stone from *Santoralier* with little convincing. The Talon Squadron's captain had always been mission-oriented and was willing to do whatever was necessary to finish the war.

Shorlis hesitated, however, and Nera moved near to help him overcome his trepidations. She understood he was worried about ruining the staff his father had entrusted to him. When Enkeli the wizard stepped into the gathering and assured the chelon that *Menthrora* would continue to be a powerful tool, Shorlis relented.

Another mighty roar was cut short as the dragons collided, drawing everyone's attention back to the great battle. Kilretheon's massive maw was clamped around Elrenigeth's throat. The blue monolith dragon appeared to not be moving as the two hurtled toward the ground in the direction of Ventohl.

As they crashed, the earth reshaped. Dirt and rock and trees rumpled into new hills, rippling toward the decrepit city. The onlookers could no longer see the monolith dragons amidst the dust-filled catastrophe.

Pernden turned to Garron, as his cousin murmured, "Maker, help us."

CHAPTER THIRTY-THREE

RUIN

Garron hoisted Ezel behind his shoulder as the man mounted Benley. He heeled the pegasus into motion. Benley took off at a blistering speed, his eyes flashing with lavender fire. They flew high enough to see over the newly rumpled hillocks, but the dust clouds that rose from the crash of the monolith dragons produced a swirling mess.

The man peered through the shroud, hoping to catch a glimpse of what had become of the immense creatures.

"Are they … dead?" the man asked, more to himself than the deep gnome.

"I do not know …" Ezel said.

A prickle rolled over the back of Garron's mind. He'd just heard the gnome in his head!

"I just heard you in my mind." He gasped, trying to look back at the gnome.

"The monolith stones hold many powers and secrets," Ezel said straight into Garron's thoughts.

The man huffed a quick laugh despite the scene before them.

He heeled Benley to maneuver them into the dust cloud, hoping they'd be able to get a better angle. Other riders drew near as well, though much more tentatively.

Garron pulled back on the reins, forcing Benley to hover where they were, as a great groan vibrated through the air. A massive silhouetted form began to roil and stretch, rising from the dust clouds.

The mountain of a dragon slowly lifted itself from the devastation. Each placement of large clawed feet underneath its monstrous weight echoed with a boom, and though they were not on the ground to feel it, the pair knew each footfall rattled the earth below.

A guttural growl emanated from the rising monolith dragon, paired with snapping and cracking of bony joints slipping back into place. The dark red scales of Kilretheon the Red shimmered in the morning light. His enormous head, wrought with spikes taller than the highest towers of any castle in Finlestia, turned to fix his fiery wicked eyes on the diminutive pegasus and his riders. A satisfied moan rolled from deep within the monolith dragon.

"Very good," his voice boomed. The words permeated Garron's body, sending a shiver through him. "You accept your fate."

Garron's brow furrowed above his awestruck gaze to form a confused look. He sensed something on his back. Ezel stood behind him, holding the man with one hand to keep steady and whipping up magic with the other. Garron felt the rhythmic movement from the gnome.

"Come human," the dragon boomed. "Bring the stones to me. You know you are but a speck, a dewdrop on the leaf to be burned away by the fire of the sun."

Garron suddenly felt even smaller. The monolith dragon was right. Who was he? He was no king or great champion. He was no hero of the bygone ages. He was just a man. A man who'd messed up plenty. His life would pass like so many before. He would be a footnote in the annals of the library of Whitestone as the fallen king, the one who betrayed his people to a sorcerer from across the sea. He wasn't even certain he'd be granted into the halls of Kerathane with his father and the other warriors of the Griffin Guard when he died.

"Don't listen to him," Ezel spoke into Garron's mind. His voice sounded strained from effort.

"I understand that my grandeur can be ... staggering," Kilretheon continued as he slowly moved one foot forward. Even one step lunged the towering dragon ever closer. "Do you resist; or are you so overcome, you are petrified to paralysis?"

Garron knew it to be the latter. Though, there was a tiny whisper inside, buried far beneath the self-doubt, that said, *You must fight.*

With another step forward, bringing the monolith dragon's gargantuan and cruel face within a league of them, Kilretheon growled, "Resistance is fruitless. I am ruin. My vengeance will not be denied."

A guttural rumble sounded from the monolith dragon's throat. His neck began to glow like hot iron, and his shoulders and wings convulsed in a horrific way.

"Fly! Fly!" Ezel cried.

Garron booted Benley, though the pegasus had already bolted into action, sensing the oncoming danger and likely prompted by Ezel as well. They hurtled high into the sky as the monolith dragon spewed his belly fire, lighting the very air ablaze.

The other riders scattered like fluff from a dandelion on a summer breeze.

The monolith dragon roared, a noise which made Garron's body ache. They flew higher to get away from the dragon's reach. Kilretheon beat his mighty wings to give chase. The wing wash whipped up hurricane-strength winds, sending the riders below spiraling away.

"To the Crags!" Ezel hollered in Garron's mind.

The man heeled the pegasus and shouted, "Benley, get us out of here!"

The pegasus dashed through the sky, racing for the ever-shrouded Crags. With the magic Ezel shared, Benley darted over the molten landscape, leaving all others behind. Garron peeked over his shoulder and wasn't sure whether he was pleased or mortified to see the monolith dragon in the distance chasing them.

On one hand, they drew Kilretheon away from their friends. On the other hand, they were being chased by a monolith dragon over inhospitable terrain with no real plan.

"Tell me you have a plan," he shouted to Ezel as the man turned back to search the area below them.

Rivers of molten lava flowed toward the sea to the west. The sun was rising in the east, but the smoke from the Crags painted the sky with muted oranges and reds.

Garron choked on the smoke. Benley snorted, trying to push it from his lungs. The only one who didn't seem uncomfortable with the situation was Ezel. The deep gnome continued his rhythmic hand motions, working up some sort of magic that Garron didn't understand.

"Ezel?" he pressed nervously.

The deep gnome didn't say anything for a long while. Then suddenly, he said, *"Here."*

"Here? What here?" Garron asked, looking around. Nothing seemed special about the area. Several taller jagged crags shot into the air, but that was not uncommon for the region.

The only distinguishing feature the man could see was a strange crag, a wide one, that flattened at the top, as though the rest of its height had been sawed off, leaving only a great tree stump of a crag.

"We make our stand here," Ezel said.

Garron pulled Benley up short, bringing the pegasus around. The sight of Kilretheon the Red bearing down on them nearly stole the heart right out of his chest.

"Ezel …"

The monolith dragon barreled toward them, an evil glint in his fiery eyes.

"Almost ready," the deep gnome said. *"When I am, we're going to have to get close."*

"I don't think that'll be a problem," Garron said nervously.

Kilretheon the Red slowed his approach. The monolith dragon glanced around and back to the pegasus and the riders suspiciously. He eyed them as he circled out wide and around. Garron thought the monolith dragon looked like a curious cat inspecting a piece of fluff—an enormous, blood-thirsty, murderous cat—but the curiosity of the monolith dragon was plain.

The massive beast glided over the sawed-off crag, landing on the flattened mountain with a great crunch, breaking away shards from the rocky cliffs as big as castle walls under his substantial weight. The monolith dragon's massive head turned on them, and Garron thought Kilretheon was smiling—if monolith dragons were capable of such faces. Perhaps it was more like a wicked scowl.

Suddenly, Garron heard a different voice in his head.

I know you. The booming voice rattled the man's brain. Garron grabbed at the sides of his head. *You are the young king. The betrayer of his people.*

Garron groaned in pain, slumping over to shake the voice from his head. Ezel gripped the back of the man's armor, trying to steady him.

You gave up your people so easily, the monolith dragon pressed into the man's mind. *Jaernok Tur merely whispered the words I gave him, and you crumbled. Who do you think taught the sorcerer his manipulations?*

"Stop!" Garron shouted. He growled and panted, spittle flying from his mouth as he breathed through gritted teeth.

Stop? Kilretheon mused into Garron's mind. *You are a curious human. You know I will not stop. You've seen it in your dreams. I am ruin, and my wave of destruction will not be held back.*

The monolith dragon chuckled in the man's mind, but the sound that came out of the dragon's body was a deep resonant growl.

People don't really change, you know. In the end, they always show their true colors. Like you, Garron, Son of Farrin the Just, Beloved King of Whitestone. You were never going to live up to your father's legacy. You were never going to be as great as him. Instead, you killed his best friend and your mentor. Do you remember?

Garron's eyes crossed, and he blinked hard and shook his head to force the memory out of his mind. How could he forget? Even in the manipulated state, under the curse Jaernok Tur had put on him, the gravity of Melkis's death had pierced into something deep within him. It had carved through the fog and touched his smothered being. He would never forget killing his mentor. Garron's chin quivered.

Others may have told you that you are no longer that man. But people do not really change, Kilretheon repeated. *It is folly to think so. You will betray them again.*

A strange tug on Garron's heart pulled at him. Benley bounced, flapping his wings uncomfortably under the man's unconscious pressure. Garron wasn't that man. That man had been a shell, a cage for the man hidden deep inside. He wasn't that man. Was he? Maybe Kilretheon was right. Maybe Garron couldn't change. Maybe bringing the monolith dragon all the stones had been his fate all along.

Benley edged forward slightly, before Garron realized he was leading the pegasus toward the dragon and pulled back on the reins.

Another growl emanated from the dragon, one more perturbed than amused.

It shook Garron with uncertainty. He wasn't sure about anything anymore.

Suddenly, a gentler voice reentered his mind. *"I trust you,"* Ezel said.

Garron breathed heavily. He wasn't sure if the tears that blurred his vision were a result of the smoke in his eyes or the overwhelming pressure.

Come, fallen king, Kilretheon beckoned. *Bring me the stones. The only way to change is to help me rewrite the world.*

"I'm ready," Ezel said, patting the man on the shoulder.

As blue magic swirled around them, Garron stared through teary eyes. He saw the face of his old mentor, Master Melkis. He saw the old man's wrinkles, forming that disbelieving look on his face after Garron had stabbed him in a cursed and blind rage. Then the old man's face softened, and Garron remembered his words, *"I do not know what voice has twisted you against me ..."*

The monolith dragon's wicked glare shifted into what could only be described as an evil grin as he watched the man wrestle.

Garron then saw the memory even clearer, as Melkis struggled to breath his last breaths while he said, *"I have loved you ... like a son ..."*

Melkis had always believed in Garron, even when he hadn't believed in himself. The old master had pushed and challenged him as he'd grown, always telling Garron there was more in him. When King Farrin had died, Melkis had not hesitated in showing his belief in Garron by immediately standing by his side in the younger man's grief.

The reminder that Melkis had died at his own hands was unbearable. Maybe it was better to rewrite the world. Garron wasn't so sure a world in which he'd killed his mentor was one worth saving. The old man had not only been his mentor but also his greatest hero. The stories of Melkis's exploits in the face of impossible odds had made him a hero among the people of Whitestone.

As Garron sat atop Benley, he wondered what Melkis would do, but that didn't matter. Garron wasn't Melkis.

A smile crept across Garron's face, and Kilretheon's great body purred with delight. *Yes,* he said. *Bring them to me.*

"Oh, I'll bring them to you," Garron growled as he heeled Benley into motion.

They flew through the sky, darting directly at the monolith dragon perched on the leveled crag. As soon as the dragon saw the speed of the approaching pegasus, he opened his great mouth, preparing his belly fire. Light erupted from within, a fiery red, matching the lava all around.

"Ezel, now!" Garron cried.

Ezel's light swirled to greater and greater speeds—the ribbons of blue magic dancing around Benley and Garron and the gnome.

Garron felt a wave of relief wash over him. He didn't care if they were going to die as the magic grew brighter and brighter around them. He had made the only choice he could make, the only one he would be able to live with—if they even survived. He rode Benley faster and harder as though he intended to ram the monolith dragon.

The man smiled broadly as Ezel's magic enveloped them, forming into a great lance of light that extended before them. When the lance collided with the monolith dragon's glowing chest, an explosion tore through the sky, and Garron knew nothing else.

A distant voice called out. A warm voice. A kind and familiar tone. Loving, with a hint of wisdom and years. The voice sent colorful ripples of light across his eyelids. They were beautiful.

Garron blinked slowly, hesitant to open his eyes and leave the wondrous dancing lights. There was something so very comforting about them. He did open his eyes, and the world was bright around him. Every surface was limned with white light. The sun was ... well, Garron couldn't find the sun in the white sky.

Great marble terraces filled with burgeoning gardens and fountains surrounded him. The masonry of the place was entirely unfamiliar to him. He stood atop a short flight of stairs that led to rolling green hills. The place infused a great hope and joy in him—a peace he had not known in so long. He took a deep breath and released the most satisfying exhale he'd ever expelled.

He felt free.

"You have done well," a voice said behind him.

He turned toward the great marble structure and nearly toppled in astonishment.

"Melkis!" he said.

"My King," the old man replied.

Though, as Garron looked at his mentor, Melkis didn't appear old. His body seemed strong and sturdy; even his bald head was lush with golden yellow hair. And yet, somehow, Garron knew him to be Melkis.

"I'm so sorry for everything," he began, but Melkis held up a hand to stay him.

"I forgave you long ago."

Melkis's words pierced Garron. How many times had he murmured his apologies in his cell in the Whitestone dungeons—quiet pleas in the night for the old master to forgive him? He'd toiled over it. It had always seemed an impossible evil to forgive. And yet, hearing the words in that place, Garron believed the old master truly forgave him.

"I ..." Garron stumbled over his words. He had so many thoughts running through his mind, but they were all wisps. He mentally tried to reach out and grab them, but like clouds of fog, they rolled through his grasp and flitted away. Finally, he grabbed one—a heavy cloud that loomed. "I thought my fate was to be the betrayer of our people forever."

"And yet you chose to carry the stone bearer to defeat the monolith dragon." Melkis chuckled merrily. "They told some great tales about my exploits, but none so grand as the ones they'll tell about you."

Garron grinned at the notion and his master's youthful jolly. Shaking his head, Garron said, "I thought I could not change. Kilretheon almost had me convinced."

"Change is a part of life, my King. It is not so bad."

"No," Garron said, looking around at the splendor of the place. "I suppose not. I just thought I was stuck in a fate I could not change."

"No person is stuck to a fate that others heap upon them. Changing your fate is not as complicated as people often make it. Even small things can turn the course of a life. Change is inevitable." Melkis smirked and winked at Garron. "You just hope that when you do change your fates, you keep the good qualities as you go onward."

"That's what I was worried about," Garron said with a chuckle. "I wasn't so sure I'd kept any of the good qualities."

Melkis hugged the younger man, gripped both of his shoulders, and held him out to inspect him. "I am quite sure you did. Do you remember what I said to you when your father died?"

"That he saved all of his best for me and my brothers."

"True," the master said, popping his eyebrows and nodding. "But I also said that I knew you. I'd watched you grow your entire life. You were strong. You had a heart for others. I'd seen it. You'd sacrificed yourself for your brothers a hundred times, in the little things and the big ones." Melkis paused to emphasize his next statement. "That does not sound so different from the man I see before me."

Garron stifled another laugh, falling back into the embrace of his old mentor. He stayed in the hug for a long time, not knowing how long, for time seemed strange in that place. He brought his head up when he heard the distant sound of music and great rejoicing. Garron peered past the old master toward a wide entryway leading into the massive marble structure.

Suddenly, one of the wispy thoughts in his mind solidified enough for him to latch onto it. "Melkis, have I been joined into the halls of Kerathane?"

The old master smiled at him and narrowed his eyes. "Not just yet."

"Then what ... where ..." Garron stumbled to find the right question. There were many, but it was hard to pick one. "How is this possible?" he finally asked.

"You have some very interesting friends," the old master said, turning and nodding toward the side.

There stood Ezel, the deep gnome standing quite tall, even though he was half the man's height. His face was bright, despite his greyish skin, and his wide eyes locked on to Garron's.

"Ezel," Garron said, confused to see his gnomish friend. As he looked the gnome over, Ezel seemed strange but wonderful, just like Melkis had to his eyes. The gnome's tattoo runes were gone and the scar across his neck no longer there.

"Yes," Melkis said next to him, "very interesting friends."

Garron strode away from the old master and bent to one knee to hug his friend.

"Told you I didn't misplace my trust," Ezel said.

Garron pulled back, shaking his head. He'd never heard the gnome speak aloud before. Somehow, it sounded … right—as if the deep gnome were whole again.

"Then, we did it?" Garron asked, hopefully.

"That we did."

Ezel smiled broadly at him, and Garron couldn't help but laugh. Seeing the gnome that way brought him great joy. He felt an unusual peace about everything. If they had died during the battle with Kilretheon but had also defeated the monolith dragon, then at least all their friends were safe.

Garron followed the gnome's narrowed gaze to the man's side and found that his layered armor was in tatters, and the shirt he wore beneath was drenched with blood. The sight seemed entirely out of place.

"You'll be heading back soon," Ezel said, a compassionate smile on his face.

"Me?" Garron asked, confused. Clarity began to creep into his mind. The dull ache of pain in his ribs was a long way off, but somehow it seemed to be marching in his direction. Garron did not know how he knew, but he understood he was leaving that place.

"You're going with me, right?" he asked, suddenly concerned.

"No," Ezel said gently. "The power of the stones required everything I had to complete the magic. The blue stone had become a part of me, a part that could not be separated. I could not defeat Kilretheon the Red and destroy the stones without giving up myself."

"What?" Garron said, kneeling on the marble floor. "You can't mean that. You have to come back with me. What about Ellaria? What about Coal?" Garron pleaded. "What about me? I ... I can't go back without you."

"You can and you will," the gnome said, wiping the tears from Garron's cheek. The man hadn't realized he was crying again. Another pain welled within him, not as distant as the last. "This was the way it had to be. I did what I could to protect you from the blast."

Garron shook his head, unwilling to accept his friend's words. How could he? But then again, how could he not?

"How long have you known?" Garron whispered.

"I knew as soon as Elrenigeth combined Ellaria's stone with the token. Enkeli confirmed it for me while you were resting."

"You knew back at the First Tree of Tarrine? And you said nothing?"

"I said some very wise things in the stable; you just didn't want to hear them," Ezel said with a smirk.

Garron searched his thoughts, trying to recall their conversation in the stables at the First Tree of Tarrine.

"Don't worry," the gnome continued. "You'll remember soon. Promise me when you get back, you won't spend all your time looking at the past. I didn't do all that work to save you just for you to miss all the greater things ahead."

Garron's face scrunched. "Why *did* you save me?" he asked quietly.

Ezel snorted a chuckle. "Because you're my friend." The statement was short, but the weight of it hit Garron like a hammer to his chest. The pain in his side grew nearer as they spoke, its pressure a constant reminder that they had little time left.

"And," the gnome went on, "you will be a beacon of love to our friends. They are going to need you."

Of all the notions that had been discussed in that place, Garron decided that one was the most difficult to believe. He had not assumed anyone needed him for anything for a very long time. When he'd first arrived in the dungeons under Whitestone, he'd figured that would be his life until he died. He relied entirely on everyone else. Since his release, he'd done everything he could to help in some way that mattered.

Kneeling next to his friend, Garron realized what the gnome was saying. A wide smile spread across the gnome's face as he watched the recognition on Garron's face. Then he voiced the thoughts. "They don't need you to do anything. They just need you to be—be their friend."

"As you have been to me," Garron affirmed.

Ezel gave him a thankful nod. "If you do that, I think you'll see many greater things in this life—something I think your father would appreciate."

"My father?" Garron asked. He looked up from his kneeling position to see his father, standing next to him with a proud grin.

"That would make me very pleased, indeed," Farrin said.

"Father!" Garron jumped to his feet and squeezed him tightly. "Father, I—"

Farrin cut him off, whispering in his son's ear. "My son, I love you so dearly. There is not a love like this in all of Finlestia. And one day, when you have a son of your own, you will know the depth of which I speak. We haven't much time, so let me tell you this: I never expected you to live up to some shadow of mine. I have only and will only ever want for you a life filled with joy. It is the deepest wish of a father. Even if we are not always good at saying it."

"You did, Father," Garron cried. "You did. I was just too consumed with myself to listen."

Garron felt his father huff a laugh, rocking them in their hug. "Well, make sure you hear it this time."

"I will."

Garron blinked, and suddenly he found himself at the bottom of the stairs. His side ached, and his head was woozy. He lifted a hand to a sharp pain on the side of his head and found he was bleeding from there as well.

Ezel stood next to him at the bottom of the stairs. The rolling green hills looked inviting, but for some reason, Garron didn't think he'd feel the grass under his boot if he stepped away from the bottom stair. Garron looked back toward the great marble structure. At the top of the stairs, he saw Melkis and his father, a picture of their younger selves, like he remembered them from when he was a small child. They smiled broadly at him, and Garron knew he had to leave.

"Onward you go," Ezel said next to him.

Garron shifted, ready to take a step away from the stairs. He paused and turned to regard the deep gnome. Ezel only smiled at him. "Thank you," Garron said. "For everything."

Ezel nodded. His hands swirled, forming words that Garron's mind recognized. *Oh, and Garron, take care of Coal for me. He's going to need you.*

"I will," Garron signed back as he stepped off the last stair.

Coughing the smoke out of his lungs shot wrenching pain into his side. Garron was pretty certain he'd broken a couple of ribs. He blinked several times, his vision not clear. The rock surrounding him was caked with a thick layer of black dust. As his vision cleared, he saw one of the molten rivers of lava flowing not far away. It was then he felt the heat. The ground beneath him was warm.

Something nudged his back. He croaked as he rolled over, the pain from his side forcing the noise out of him. A big snout nuzzled his face, mixing spittle with the black ash and mucking up the white nose.

"Benley," Garron said, reaching up to pet the pegasus' snout and scratch his chin. Garron's hands were blackened as well, and he wondered how long he'd lain there while the ash from the explosion settled upon him. He inspected the pegasus, also covered in soot. Benley appeared only slightly less battered than himself.

He rolled to his uninjured side, attempting to hoist himself up. Benley, obviously trying to help but making the task rather more difficult, nudged at the man. Garron made his way to his knees, finding it much easier to breath in an upright position.

As Garron looked around, he searched for any marker he'd recognize. Maybe the flattened mountain? He saw something that could have been the one, but it was more a shattered remnant. He spotted a hulking mass of scale a few leagues away—the remains of the monolith dragon, Kilretheon the Red.

Benley stepped away from the man, seemingly convinced that Garron was going to be alright. The pegasus dropped his head, bouncing it at something else on the ground nearby. Garron leaned as far as he could with his pained side and dizzy head trying to spot what the pegasus was after.

"Oh, Benley," Garron said solemnly.

The man forced himself to his feet with great effort. He limped to the pegasus, brushing a hand along Benley's flank as he moved to the spot that held the steed's attention. Garron worked his way to his knees again and petted Benley's face.

"I'm sorry, pal," Garron said with a sniff. "He's not going to wake up."

Garron brushed the ash away from the deep gnome's body and gathered him into his arms. He winced as he stood but groaned through the pain. He held Ezel in his arms and let the tears flow, streaking through the soot on his face. The gnome's lifeless body may have been broken, but Garron knew his spirit had not been.

The noise of flapping wings and the calls of searchers pricked at the man's ears. He turned his gaze upward to see Ellaria on the back of Silverwing above them. Her emerald eyes widened at the sight of him and the weight he carried in his arms.

"No!" the dwarf clutching her waist on the back of the griffin wailed. "No. No. No!"

CHAPTER THIRTY-FOUR

THE PYRE

Karnak rolled his big shoulders. They'd spent much of the rest of that day gathering their fallen. The melior had chased the remainder of the wretchlings through Duskwood, hunting them down. They could not be sure that they got them all, but Merrick assured the orc gar that the Duskwood Rangers patrolled the region and would eventually find the creatures.

Night had fallen, halting their cleanup efforts but also forcing them to slow down. It brought a pleasant warmth, a respite from the lingering cold as spring battled to conquer winter.

Karnak stretched his arms out wide and tightened the knot of hair on top of his head.

"Are you alright?" Smarlo asked.

How he'd missed the voice of his oldest friend. Karnak nodded to the orc mage, grateful for his concern. "I'll be fine." He hesitated and said, "It's finally over."

"It is," Smarlo agreed solemnly. "Can I do anything?"

"No," Karnak said. "I will handle this."

"You know, you don't have to handle it on your own," Smarlo said.

"Oh, I know." Karnak gave his friend a weak smile. "We've been here before," he said, stepping out into the crowded area.

Folks had stopped their tasks, gathering in the great courtyard of Ventohl—the same one in which they'd performed the ceremony when they first took the city from the Sons of Silence. Standing at the front, waiting for him, were Merrick and Ralowyn. Merrick seemed to be explaining the proceedings to Pernden who also stood there with Commander Fario of the Riders of Loralith and Foredwarf Lotmeag of the garvawk warriors of Galium.

Good, Karnak thought. *Everyone should be a part of this.*

In the center of the area, were dozens of small wooden stacks. They'd had little time to collect and gather supplies, but the pyres had been constructed with great care and reverence. At the end of the rows sat a singular stack. Karnak remembered the first time he'd seen Vorenna perform the remembrance vigil. He thought she was likely performing one at that very moment in Aiden's Dell.

Beyond the lone stack of wood stood four melior, standing guard over the covered remains of the little deep gnome. Garron, Ellaria, and Coal sat nearby, holding each other as they wept over the loss of their friend. Orin held a hand on his cousin's shoulder, looking equally distraught. A tinge of regret filled the orc gar. He wished he'd gotten to know the gnome better. Seeing Orin, who Karnak had come to call friend, so upset made the orc feel as though he'd missed out on the opportunity to befriend the gnome as well.

When he arrived at the front of the gathering, he greeted the others briefly before regarding the crowd. At his entrance, the crowd's whispering fell to silence, save for the sniffing and stifled mourning.

"It is good you are all here," Karnak said, projecting his voice over all the people. "I must admit, when I first saw the Scar Squadron, I was overcome with emotion. I saw orcs and wyverns from Calrok—from the Scar Cliffs—the very cliffs that watch over my home. I saw my people."

He paused for a long while letting his words sink in. He scanned over all those gathered before continuing.

"I have been away from Calrok for a long time. Home has been a distant memory for me. I very much look forward to going back. But while I've been here in Kelvur, I have learned many things. I have fought and bled alongside peoples that wanted nothing more than to live a life in freedom, like the one we live in Calrok. I have made and lost friends. I miss them."

Several people in the gathering choked out sobs and tried to pull themselves together.

"I realized something else," Karnak said. "As assuredly as I see it now, gathered in this place, I saw it when we flew into Ventohl. I saw elves flying on pegasi, defending wyvern riders that I know by name. I saw dwarves and men fighting side by side, protecting each other from danger. I saw ..." Karnak choked on his words for a moment. Ralowyn reached over and patted him on the shoulder. He grabbed her slender hand, her pale skin starkly contrasted in his big green hand. "I saw my people. I saw *our* people. All of us."

He watched as people of every race, shape, size, and color nodded at his words. They were interspersed, not separated into units or people groups. They were just together.

"As we are in Kelvur," he continued, "let us honor our fallen the way we do here."

Smarlo wiggled his fingers and a flame burst forth, lighting the torch he handed to Karnak.

The orc gar turned and lit the torches of the other leaders at the front.

"Our peoples may have had a checkered past, but we move forward together," Karnak called over the crowd. "Normally, Javelin has the children helping with this so they never forget. But it is wise for us to never forget as well. We can share the stories, so the next generation doesn't forget either. Let us remember."

Karnak took several steps forward, stopping next to the first pyre. "The past lays the path for the future, and the future remembers the past."

"Remember," a few of the people in the crowd responded, evoking echoes from others.

The other leaders walked from pyre to pyre, lighting each one with their torches. As they walked down the rows, the gathered people watched in reverent silence. When they made it to the end of the rows, Ralowyn and Merrick dropped their torches and the others followed their lead, creating an all-new pyre.

Karnak held onto his torch, and Merrick looked to the orc gar. Karnak nodded to the huntsman.

"This is the pyre of the path," Merrick called out. "This pyre is built to remember all those who have fallen in the past. But it is also a promise. As we throw our torches into this new pile, we promise to never forget those who died so we could live. We promise to live our lives for each other, not letting our predecessors' sacrifices be in vain. We are with and for each other."

Karnak pressed his lips together around his tusks, doing his best to nod a smile toward the huntsman. How much he'd seen the man grow.

The orc gar turned and raised the final torch, his own.

"And this," he said, stepping next to the lone pyre. The leaders had all avoided the singular pyre that stood set apart. "This torch is for the champion's pyre. I wish I had the opportunity to know him better. I regret that fact. And because of it, I pass this torch to his greatest friends to light the pyre, that we all may honor him with you."

Karnak stared at Coal, the dwarf hardly able to look at the orc gar. For a long moment, no one moved. Ellaria rubbed at the dwarf's back, trying to encourage him, knowing he needed the support.

After a long while, Coal stood to his feet. He strode a few determined steps forward before he glanced to the shrouded form of his oldest friend. Suddenly, his feet no longer worked, becoming like stone. The crackling fire from the other pyres seemed to mute and fall away as Karnak watched the dwarf. The stall was painstaking. The orc gar knew he couldn't be the only one wrenched by the dwarf's paralyzing sorrow.

Just as Karnak shifted to move toward the dwarf and meet him halfway, Ralowyn stepped next to Coal and leaned down. Karnak was close enough to hear them as she said, "Come. Take my hand."

The dwarf, his eyes glossed with mourning, looked up to the elf and nodded slowly. He took her hand and walked to Karnak.

Coal took the wrapping from his hand, unraveling it and giving it to Ralowyn. She took it without a word. The dwarf held up his hand, revealing the clan mark to the orc.

Karnak nodded and handed the torch over.

Coal stepped up to the pyre, held the torch high for a moment, whispering something to the sky, and laid the torch on top of the wood. The pyre took to the fire, burning bright.

Several gasps rolled over the crowd as the flames of the pyre burned blue.

Ellaria grunted as she tightened the wrappings around Garron's torso. Pernden chuckled as his cousin winced, finding it amusing to see someone else under Ellaria's healing care.

"What is with the men in your family?" she asked, rechecking the bandage she'd already wrapped around Garron's head. "Always running into trouble and getting yourselves nearly killed. Then I have to patch you up."

"We're lucky to have you," Orin said.

"Yes. We just want to make sure you always feel needed," Pernden joked.

Ellaria side-eyed the king and tightened Garron's bandage even more.

"Ow," Garron groaned. "I didn't say it. He did."

Ellaria grumbled something incoherent as she turned and dug into an oiled leather bag next to her.

"I'll leave you to it," Pernden said with another chuckle as he slapped Orin on the shoulder and turned from the room.

Nera leaned against the stone wall in the gloomy hallway of Ventohl's castle, her arms crossed in front of her.

"She does have a point," Nera said with a pop of her eyebrow.

Pernden huffed and smiled at her. "I think it was you that needed saving this time."

"Oh, is that so?" she said, sidling up to him.

"I did bring a whole army across the sea to save you," he said, hardly able to hide his grin.

"As I recall it, Shorlis and I came through the Alkhoren Mirror and saved your hide." She frowned and pursed her lips.

415

"Details are a little fuzzy," Pernden said, narrowing his eyes and drawing her close. When his lips were only inches away from hers, he whispered, "Let's call it a draw."

He pressed his lips against hers and kissed her. He intended to do that a lot more in the future and was glad they had a future to look forward to.

"Everything we built was burned," Merrick said, as he walked into the courtyard with Karnak and Smarlo.

The big orc stopped next to a pillar, placing a green hand on it and feeling the cool stone.

Merrick remembered the courtyard from the last time they'd been there, when they'd faced Hazkul Bern. The huntsman still had never figured out how the assassin managed to slip away without leaving any footprints or sign of his escape.

"We cannot head home without helping them rebuild," Karnak said.

Smarlo clicked his tongue and gave a little sigh. Karnak turned to him.

"You are right," Smarlo said. "Of course. But you have been away from Calrok a long time. Aside from the city ..." The orc mage's words trailed off.

"Smarlo, you've always been able to speak your mind with me," the orc gar said. "Say what makes you hesitate."

"Your family misses you," Smarlo said plainly.

Merrick watched the two. He'd seen them interact many times during his time in Calrok and knew them to be the best of friends, but a strangeness hung between them at the mention of Karnak's family. The silence was palpable and almost insufferable.

Finally, Karnak raised his chin, protruding his tusks, and stood straighter. "Then they will have to miss me for a spell longer." Merrick didn't quite understand the orc gar's words. The huntsman knew that Karnak's family was the most important thing in the world to him. Sure, there were many things to take care of in Kelvur, but certainly they could handle it without him.

"Karnak …," Merrick started to say, but he wasn't certain how he intended to finish the thought.

Karnak chuckled and drew near to his closest friends. He placed a great hand on their shoulders and smiled.

"I miss my family more than anything in Finlestia. You know that," he said, nodding. "However, we have a choice before us. We have the opportunity to do what's easy or to do what's right. Easy never lasts. Right stands for generations to come. We will help them rebuild. Not here. Not in this shrouded place," Karnak said, glancing to the sky. "We'll help them rebuild Dorantown. It will be a symbol of our peoples' unity. Just as Kane Harbor is across the sea. Two port cities that connect our worlds. Do you not see how important this is? It will bring our peoples together for generations to come."

Merrick nodded solemnly. "It will take much to rebuild it."

Karnak bobbed his head in agreement.

Smarlo chuckled, shaking his head. "I think I know just the orc for the job."

"Oh?" Karnak asked, grinning broadly at his oldest friend.

"An orc from Calrok—one of Master Jalko's crew that went to Kane Harbor to help build there."

"Here? With you?" Karnak asked, confused.

"He's quite …" Smarlo searched for the right word. "Fervent. Wanted to help like they did in Kane Harbor. And King Pernden seems quite fond of him."

Karnak laughed. "Well, if he was one of Master Jalko's orcs, then we'll rebuild Dorantown in no time."

"They're not skilled builders, but the Griffin Guard will stay to help," Pernden said as he entered the courtyard, Nera at his side. "And Porg is rather excited to lend his expertise."

Merrick turned to see the king. He looked extra regal as he stepped toward them. The huntsman nodded to Nera, glad to see her alive and well after she'd left Dorantown so long before and they'd heard nothing from her. She returned the nod, seeming glad to see him as well.

After everything the people had been through in Kelvur, they'd been bonded in a way few could understand. They'd endured hardship and fear and destruction, and yet they were still standing.

"High Seat Yenklin has offered Glain's Shoulder's aid as well," Karnak said. "One of their scribes found an old map in their library that suggested there was once a route between Glain's Shoulder and the north through the Palisade along the coast. Yenklin believes it's high time they reopen the road."

Merrick shot Nera a smirk. "And I think we may have secured our relationship with Aiden's Dell."

Nera smiled back, shaking her head.

"Good," Karnak said, patting Smarlo on the shoulder. "With all the help, we'll have Dorantown up and running again in no time. And then …" He paused for a moment. Merrick saw tears welling in the orc gar's eyes. "And then we'll all go home together."

Coal sat near the edge of a parapet, looking out over the battlefield. Soldiers from all the armies removed the last of the debris littering the area. Garron lowered himself gingerly to take a seat next to the dwarf. Coal's black beard waved in the gentle breeze. The day brought more warmth, and the sun felt good on Garron's face. He closed his eyes, tilting his chin to bask his entire countenance in the sun's radiance.

They sat in silence for a long time—neither of them sure what to say. Ezel had done so much for Garron. He'd been the most loyal of friends to the man when Garron didn't think he could have any friends. Coal was Ezel's oldest and best friend. Garron had no doubt the gnome had treated the dwarf with the same kind of love and generosity in their friendship.

"I just can't believe he's gone," Coal uttered, sniffing away the sobs that threatened to overtake him again.

Garron rubbed the dwarf's back and said, "He's not gone. He's just in a better place now."

"Is he?" Coal turned to face the man. His eyes were red from terrible bouts of sobbing, and the skin of his cheeks above his great black beard were raw and red, matching his nose.

"I know it," Garron said reassuringly. "I saw him. He's with my family in Kerathane. And he can speak again. His scars ... his tattoos ... they're all gone."

Coal released a relieved laugh. "I haven't seen him without those in years. He looked even skinnier without them."

"He does." Garron chuckled.

A silence fell between them as they smiled at memories of the deep gnome. Then Coal asked, "Why did he have to go?"

Garron hesitated for a moment, gathering himself. "He said that it was his time. It was his fate. He needed to do it to save us all. The blue stone was a part of him."

"That blasted blue stone," Coal shook his head. "I was there, all those years ago. That blue stone caused us a lot of hardship. I thought when the witch used it to save his life, we'd be done with it, but the trouble followed us to the mountains around Pearl Lake. I thought we were finally done with all that trouble when we were boating on the Palori, but it seems it followed us there as well."

"You had quite the journey before I met you two," Garron said with a chuckle. "I'd very much like to hear the tale."

Coal laughed as well. "It's a long one, but I'd be glad to share it sometime."

Garron said, "Ezel was so kind to me when I didn't deserve it."

"He was good like that," Coal agreed.

Garron added, "He showed me what it meant to be a true friend."

"Aye," the dwarf whispered.

They sat quietly on the parapet for a long while, each content to sit in the presence of the other under the warming sun. After a long while, Garron asked, "So, what will you do now?"

"I don't know," Coal hemmed. "What does a former king do when he's no longer a king?"

Garron laughed. "I'm not sure."

"Aye." Coal chuckled. "Don't suppose I do either. Though, I think I'm quite tired of adventuring for a while."

"Agreed," Garron said, shaking his head.

Orin smiled as he approached his group of friends sitting along the parapet. He heard their laughter as he strode toward them. Their merriment shone brighter than the sun high above. Coal and Ellaria sat on either side of his cousin Garron, obviously teasing him about something. Merrick sat next to Ellaria, chuckling along.

As Orin approached, it struck him how the scene felt very much like the fun they'd had on the *Lady Leila* as they floated up the Palori River when they'd first started their whole journey. That was before everything went wild. Seeing all the people he loved, including his cousin, warmed his heart.

"Hey!" they called as Orin drew near.

"I was looking for you all," he said with a chuckle, "just had to follow all the noise."

"That's mostly Coal," Ellaria teased.

"Me?" Coal said, bringing a hand to his chest and pressing his beard in innocently. "Never once have I been told I was too loud."

"Ha!" Orin laughed aloud. "You remember that one night at the *Weary Whale* in Stalford when you and Ezel were telling the tall tale about the avalanche? Those guys were not buying it, and the owner forced us to leave because you were riling them up?"

"That wasn't a tall tale!" Coal started. "It really happened."

Orin found a seat, and the friends spent a long time laughing and joking. They spoke often of moments when Ezel had done or signed something funny to them. Occasionally, they signed to each other, even though it was unnecessary. The signing accompanied soft and tender moments.

Finally, Orin asked, "So, what is everyone's plan after we rebuild Dorantown?"

The question fell like a boulder amidst them—almost as though no one wanted to think about anything past the fun they were having together. Even stranger, they all had the sense that life would never be the same for them.

Coal broke the long silence. "Garron and I were talking about that before Ellaria and Merrick showed up."

"And?" Orin asked.

"Well, neither of us really had a good answer." The dwarf chuckled. "I loved boating on the Palori with Ezel. Transporting people and goods up and down the river, sharing stories with good folk around campfires along the river. We also loved our time in Whitestone and getting to know everyone. I was thinking when this was all over, we could buy ourselves a wagon or two. There's a growing need for more wagoners between Whitestone and Kane Harbor. And we'd get to do the same thing, just not on the river. But ..." Coal paused, pulling at the singular braid in his big black beard. "I was planning on doing that with a business partner. And with Ezel gone ..."

"Well," Garron said next to the dwarf. "I'm not sure if you'd like my company, but I don't know a lot of prospects for a former king."

Coal cleared his throat as he turned his glossy eyes on the man. "Well," he said with a smile, "it's one of the best prospects I've found for a former clan prince. I suppose it might do for a former king as well."

Ellaria placed a comforting hand on Garron's shoulder and reached past him to grip the dwarf's hand.

"And what about you?" Ellaria asked Orin. "You've got a new griffin now. Will you return to the Griffin Guard?"

Orin thought for a long moment. He'd asked the question originally because he'd been pondering it for himself; and to be honest, he wasn't sure.

"I don't know," he said slowly. "I suppose I could ..."

As his cousin's words lingered in the air, Garron said, "You know, I was recently reminded by a mutual friend of ours that if we spend too much time looking backward, we end up missing the greater things ahead. I don't think we have to have all the answers right now."

"Agreed," Merrick interjected. The huntsman eased back his eager response when Ellaria eyed him. "This whole journey has taught me that we don't know what's going to happen tomorrow, so the only thing we can do is live right now and be present."

"Right," Garron said. "It's not necessarily about doing something but just being."

"Now you all sound like Ezel," Coal teased.

The friends laughed and continued to joke with one another for a long time as the sun arced across the sky.

CHAPTER THIRTY-FIVE

HOME AGAIN

*T*wo months later ...

The wild grass and flowers that lined the road to the house on the edge of town waved in a dazzling display of colors in the warm breeze. Karnak sniffed the air. The myriad of scents that mixed with the smell of the sea brought a sense of great peace to the big orc as he walked up the road toward the paddock gate. His house at the edge of Calrok was surrounded by floral wonder, just as he remembered it.

Smarlo and Merrick laughed about something Lotmeag said as they followed the orc gar up the road. Ralowyn nudged Karnak as she spotted a black tuft of hair running through the tall grass. Karnak smiled, but tears fell from his eyes. The orc was pretty sure that when he left, the orcling wasn't tall enough to be seen over the wild grass.

The wooden gate slammed open, and there stood Gernot. The orcling looked huge. *How much did he grow while I was gone?* Karnak wondered.

The orcling drew in a deep breath as though he were going to yell out to greet them, but instead, his chest wavered and he began to sob. He ran the last several feet to greet them, babbling something that sounded like, "Dada."

Karnak raced to meet his little orcling, sliding to his knees and scooping Gernot into his arms. "Oh, Gernot," the orc gar said as he kissed the orcling on the head over and over.

The rest of the party stopped to take in the scene until someone else called from the gate. "You better save some of that affection for your wife, too, now," Tanessa said.

Karnak stood, holding the sniffling Gernot on his hip. "Why don't you come and get it," Karnak called back with a smirk.

Ralowyn punched the big orc's shoulder and said, "Hand him over," as she took Gernot into her own hug.

Tanessa feigned offense at the orc gar's words, but she could only hold the facade for a brief moment before she began to cry herself. Karnak didn't wait for her to come to him. He ran to his wife and drew her into his big arms, kissing her with great passion.

"I've missed you," he whispered to her.

"I bet you have," she teased, trying to wipe away her tears.

Karnak placed his large hand on her face and wiped the moisture away with his thumb. "Every day."

"I missed you, too, husband."

Tanessa turned to eye the company behind Karnak. The orc gar followed her gaze. Gernot was being passed around, hugged by all. The little orcling even hugged Lotmeag, which Karnak found humorous. "He's gotten so big," Karnak said.

"You were gone for a long time."

"I know. I'm sorry. I got back as soon as it was right to leave them."

"I know you did," Tanessa said softly. She squeezed his hand, pressing it against her face again. "It seems you brought company."

Karnak laughed. "Yes. About that ..."

"More strays?" Tanessa teased.

"No." Karnak shook his head and grinned. "No, I don't think any of them are lost anymore."

As Karnak and Tanessa joined the gathering on the road, Ralowyn hugged the orc gar's wife, glad to see her. Merrick introduced Gernot to Kippin. The little halfling spoke quickly as though Gernot was his new best friend, telling the orcling how he was a mighty falconer in training. Kippin lifted his arm and said, "Up," sending Davir into the sky. The little orc's eyes grew big as he asked the halfling what a falconer was.

"Do you know how to play hide and seek?" Kippin asked.

"I'm the best in all Tarrine!" Gernot beamed.

"I'm the best in all Kelvur!" the halfling exclaimed. "I bet Davir could find us."

"Not if I show you my best hiding spots!"

Tanessa and Merrick shared a glance before she said, "You know, I thought you were going to bring my husband back a lot sooner."

Merrick's face scrunched, and he bit at his lip. "I know. I did, too."

Tanessa chuckled and pulled the huntsman in for a hug. "And what's this I hear? You married this woman, and I didn't even get an invite?"

"Well," Merrick hemmed. "There wasn't a whole lot of time to send word. There was a wretchling army bearing down on us ..."

"I didn't get to be there either," Karnak piled on, not letting the huntsman explain himself.

"I suppose we'll have to have our own celebration then," Tanessa said. She looked past Merrick and nodded to Smarlo. "Thank you," she said softly.

"Of course." The orc mage smiled back.

"How's that ear? I made a few dozen jars while you were gone. Didn't feel like wrestling with worry, so I put my hands to it."

Smarlo laughed. "It's doing much better. The salve worked wonders."

"You do still need some, though? I made so many jars."

Smarlo barked another laugh. "Yes. I would be very grateful for more."

"Tea tonight?" she asked.

"No," Smarlo politely declined. "I've got a date tonight."

"I'm not a date," Lotmeag puffed.

"Not you," Smarlo said, rolling his eyes and shrugging at Tanessa. He jutted a thumb toward Lotmeag. "Though I do owe this one an omelet and some glorb wine from the *Spinefish Tavern.*"

"Aye," Lotmeag said. "Been getting a taste for orcish cuisine. Heard this glorb wine is quite the drink."

Tanessa smiled at the dwarf and turned back to the orc mage. "The pretty woman with the honey hair?" she inquired.

Smarlo flushed. "We're meeting up with the Scar Squadron there."

"Bah," Lotmeag grumbled. "He's smitten over her. Why, half the journey home, he wasn't in the cabin with his books. He was out on the deck with Lehra."

Karnak chuckled. "It's true. Saw it plenty myself."

The orc mage shifted uncomfortably, his green cheeks rosing.

"Good," Tanessa said. "Very good. I was wondering if you were going to talk to her."

"What?" Smarlo asked, his eyes widening in horror.

"Smarlo," Tanessa said in a scolding tone, "after all those months of tea and you talking about that woman and how wonderful she was doing with the Scar Squadron, did you really think I couldn't tell you liked her?"

"Well, I ..." Smarlo stumbled over his words for a moment while they all stared at him. Tanessa was doing her absolute best not to let her teasing grin show as her lips twisted into a wry smirk. Smarlo finally huffed. Then he said, "Tea. Soon."

"Promise?"

"Promise."

Soon after, Karnak watched Smarlo and Lotmeag saunter down the road. He'd overheard them talking numerous times on the voyage home about the orc mage showing the dwarven warrior Calrok's mage library. Smarlo was curious to find out if Lotmeag could help him translate any of the other texts that sat untouched in the library.

The orc gar breathed in and exhaled slowly, taking in the moment.

"Are you alright?" Tanessa asked.

"Oh, yes," he said. "I'm right where I belong, under the sun and breathing in the mist of the windswept sea."

His lovely wife grinned and turned on the others. "And what about you two?"

"Well," Merrick shrugged to the side. "Maybe we could stay for dinner? And a few nights?"

"Only if you regale me with tales of this wild journey you've all been on," she paused and inspected the halfling playing with Gernot, "and introduce me to this handsome young man."

Kippin's ears perked up, and he puffed up his chest to stand taller, looking mighty brave.

"Of course," Ralowyn said.

Karnak lingered as the others went inside. He sniffed the air. It smelled like home.

Lotmeag elbowed Smarlo as the *Spinefish Tavern* went into an uproarious cheer when Belguv announced the next round was on him.

"Close the book," Lotmeag said. "Ye've been at it for hours."

"I know," Smarlo said as he scribbled into his leather-bound notebook. "I'm almost done."

"Ye said that when we left the library to come here," the dwarf grumbled at him. "It'll keep for tomorrow."

"I know," Smarlo said again. "I'm just so close to finishing this section, and I want to make sure I get it ri—"

"Lehra's here," Lotmeag said, cutting the orc mage off.

Smarlo looked up immediately, mid-word. The dwarf was right. Lehra and the last of the Scar Squadron had just arrived—the reason Commander Belguv had generously offered to pay for the next round. Lotmeag reached over and slid the notebook away from the orc mage. Smarlo had the great urge to fight him and dive back into the book.

Everything had seemed so romantic and urgent on their journey. Since they were back home, would she care about him at all? He wouldn't be spending great amounts of time at the Scar Cliffs training anymore. He had lots of duties to take care of at the library, and moreover, he needed to start training some new mages. With everything they'd been through, he thought it wise to train more than one pupil. If something like what they'd experienced ever happened again, it would be good to have a few trained mages on hand.

Lehra was handed a mug as she waded through the crowd, straight for Smarlo and Lotmeag.

"There she is!" the dwarf said, standing from his seat to greet her. They clinked their mugs together and downed them. Lotmeag let out a great belch, and Lehra laughed at him. "Aye. Sorry lass. The glorb wine makes ye belch like a war boar!"

Lehra leaned and whispered, "Me too."

Lotmeag laughed heartily. "I'll take one from that round Belguv's barking about," he called to one of the tavern hands.

"'Ow long is your friend staying?" a goblin asked next to Smarlo.

The orc mage knew the voice of the *Spinefish Tavern's* owner without turning. Smarlo's eyes were locked on the smiling woman before him. "I hope forever."

"I meant the dwarf," Reglese muttered. "He drinks hearty, and when Belguv is tired of buying, I'm guessing the dwarf will take up the mantle."

Smarlo laughed. "Always about coin, you are."

"Not always," Reglese said, sliding two mugs across the table in front of Smarlo. "For you and the lady."

The orc mage eyed the goblin. Reglese shifted uneasily.

"Alright, tell me about the tavern in Dorantown," the goblin said quickly. "Is it taking up all the business, or is there room for another tavern?"

Smarlo laughed and shook his head. "I think the glorb wine would be a hit there, too."

"Good. Good," Reglese said, rubbing his hands together. "Maybe I can spread my glorb wine empire to Kelvur as well."

"Dream big, my friend." Smarlo chuckled.

"You, too," Reglese whispered, as Lehra turned her attention on them. The goblin slipped away quickly, leaving them alone.

"What was that all about?" she asked.

"Oh," Smarlo started. "Reglese was just leaving a drink for you."

Lehra finished what was left in her mug and accepted the new drink. She sat in the chair next to the orc mage, scooting it closer. She eyed the closed leather notebook on the table before pulling it close.

Smarlo reached out to stop her from opening it. "It's not finished yet."

She opened it to the first page and read, "*Heroes of the Harbinger* by Master Mage Smarlo of Calrok. You didn't tell me you'd come up with a title for it."

"It's a working title," Smarlo said quickly.

"That you penned in. Seems pretty permanent to me," she mused.

"Well, I ..." Smarlo fumbled for a moment, but the woman turned her lovely face toward him with a smile.

"I like it. Has a nice ring to it. How do you describe me?"

"Oh, no you don't," Lotmeag said, as he rejoined them. "If anyone gets to see how they're described first, it's me. We had a deal, lass."

She popped an eyebrow and thumbed through the pages as though she were going to sneak a peek. She held it open for a long moment while Lotmeag stared at her unblinkingly. Suddenly, Lehra closed the book and leaned toward Smarlo. "That's alright, I'll just ask you to tell me."

Smarlo swallowed hard, trying to remove the lump from his throat.

"I'm only teasing," she said, nudging him. "What part are you on?"

The orc mage smiled and grabbed at the leather notebook. "Well, you remember when we were sailing north toward Ventohl?"

"Oh, no," Lotmeag grumbled. "Ye've got him going again. I just got him to close that book."

Smarlo ignored his friend's mumbling as the dwarf said something about going to learn an orcish song from Belguv. Smarlo smiled as Lehra leaned in and laid her head on his shoulder while he opened the book, looking for a map he'd drawn.

"You know," Karnak said as he crossed the quiet paddock under the moonlight. "We could build a proper house for you."

Merrick nodded to the orc as he sat in the chair beside him on the small porch of the cottage he and Ralowyn had stayed in the last time they were in Calrok.

"The world is changing. I don't think our peoples will be separate anymore," the orc gar continued. "You'd be very welcome to stay here in Calrok."

"I know," Merrick replied. "And for that I am grateful."

"But you won't be staying," Karnak guessed.

"No," the huntsman whispered.

They sat for a long time, content to quietly soak in the view of Calrok lit by the moonlight. How many times had they sat on the porch and talked late into the evening? Those were some of Merrick's fondest memories with the orc.

"We'll head down to Tamaria to visit my family," Merrick said softly.

"I suppose they'd probably like to see you and your new wife and son." Karnak chuckled.

"That," Merrick said, laughing himself, "and Ellaria said she wasn't going to cover for me next time she was there. Said I needed to make a visit myself before she does."

Karnak laughed again. "I like her," he said. "As fiery as her hair."

"Yeah," Merrick mused.

"But you won't stay in Tamaria."

The huntsman looked at the orc, wondering at the direct statement.

"I talked to Domin Ven. He told me he offered to train you up as the domin ranger for the new Dorantown Lodge. Said the Duskwood Rangers have needed another lodge for a long time but didn't have the manpower. Said they were going to need new rangers to cover the mountains south of Dorantown to help keep the road to Glain's Shoulder safe."

"He told you all that?" Merrick asked.

The orc shifted his tusks and rolled his shoulders. "Yes. He also told me he thought you would be perfect for the job."

"He told me that, too," Merrick said quietly.

"And I told him, he was absolutely right."

"What?"

"I told him I didn't know a better man. I told him there was not a man in all of Finlestia that I trusted more. And I told him ..." Karnak paused and cleared his throat. "I told him, that as much as it would pain me for my friend to be across the sea, I could see him happier in no other job, and that the Duskwood Rangers will be lucky to have him."

The huntsman confessed, "I've not been sure I could lead others well. I worry that I will let them down."

"The fact that you care is what will make you a great leader," Karnak said. "How about that lad in Aiden's Dell? Where is he now?"

"At home with his family."

"You led him and many others that day. You led them with your heart and mind, making the best decisions you could to do what was right—a quality good leaders share."

"One I learned from a dear friend," Merrick said with a nod.

Karnak chuckled. He hoisted himself from the chair and began striding across the paddock toward the main house. He paused and turned toward the huntsman. "You better get some rest. You'll have to tell Tanessa tomorrow. I'm not doing that for you."

Merrick laughed. Karnak was the fiercest orc he knew. The feigned fear amused him. "I will," he said. "I just want to watch the city for a little longer before I go to bed."

Karnak pursed his lips around his tusk and said, "You've always got a place to stay when you visit. Always."

The man nodded to him, and Karnak smirked before he turned and headed back to the house. The huntsman looked out over the city sloping toward the Gant Sea. The moon was bright and illuminated Calrok with a surreal beauty.

Merrick stood from the chair and held onto the knobbled door frame before he entered. He heard snoring inside the cottage from two different noses, and he smiled before he headed to bed.

CHAPTER THIRTY-SIX

NOT SO LONELY

*T*hree more months later ...

Sweat dripped from the ends of Pernden's hair, as he paused to breathe. He gripped *Wintertide* in his hand, mentally preparing his next volley of attacks. Though the sword no longer threw blades of ice, the weapon remained formidable. It often sprayed shards of ice as it clanged against other weapons and proved to be stronger than any other blade. Several of the guardians Pernden had sparred with over the past few months had needed new weapons forged, theirs having been broken by *Wintertide's* relentless strength.

He knew the weapon of his sparring partner in that round would not break. *Santoralier* was of equal ilk and might.

Nera watched him, her eyes narrowed, analyzing every move he made. The guardian king stood in his ready stance, breathing and coming up with his strikes. He shot a smirk at her, which made Nera's eyebrow pop.

He dashed toward her, bringing *Wintertide* in an upward arc, deflecting *Santoralier's* falling strike. He slid past Nera on his knees, planting a foot and popping to standing with a sideways swing. Before, *Wintertide* would have sent a blade of ice soaring at the woman, so Nera instinctively spun her spear to block it.

Pernden, hoping she would make such a move, darted toward her with his sword swiping low. *Wintertide* pinged against her leg guards. Nera attempted to swing her spear to block, but the king was already bringing *Wintertide* back around. It took every ounce of energy she had to roll away from the strike as the sword swiped just past her chest armor. As she came to her knees, *Wintertide* tapped on her shoulder armor.

Pernden smiled down at her, pleased. "I think I won this one."

Nera stood slowly, dropping *Santoralier* to her side. She strode closer to the king as he lowered his sword. She drew so near that no one but he could hear her whisper. Her skin seemed to glisten, something he never understood. He was sopping. *How does she do that?* he wondered.

"You tricked me," she whispered. "Very clever."

"I've been known to be clever on occasion," he whispered back.

"Known by whom?"

"Oh, come on," Pernden whispered. "*You* have to know it by now. How many times have I won? We must have nearly an even split."

"You're getting close," Nera teased.

"What?" he asked sliding his hand around her back. "How close?"

"Pretty close," she breathed.

Before anyone had the chance to interrupt them, the king kissed her.

"Though I'm not going to let you win to get your record better, even if you are the 'Guardian King,'" she said.

"I wouldn't have it any other way, my queen," he said, as they turned and walked across the field of the Grand Corral.

Guardians were training hard and running their drills in the summer sun. Shadows of griffin riders working on aerial maneuvers high above danced on the patchy grass of the training field. Nera and Pernden walked toward the stalls where they'd left their griffins. Rocktail and Shadowpaw clicked their beaks eagerly as their humans approached. Pernden stroked Rocktail's neck feathers, pleased how well the griffin had recovered in the months since the battle.

As the king and queen of Whitestone mounted their griffins, Pernden turned to Nera and asked, "Race you back to the castle?"

Nera pursed her lips and squinted at him. "You do so love to lose, don't you?"

Before Pernden could argue that he'd just won their sparring match, she heeled Shadowpaw, and the pair took to the sky.

Pernden shook his head, unable to wipe the smirk off his face. "This woman," he said to Rocktail as they chased after them.

The road to Kane Harbor from Whitestone had grown wide since it was originally trailed. The wagon industry in Whitestone had more than doubled in size as well. Previously, the wagoners had hauled cargo and travelers between Whitestone and the midway city of Hillstop. With extra trade routes extending north from Hillstop to Ghun-Ra and from Kane Harbor to Calrok, the need for wagoners had grown exponentially, creating all sorts of opportunity for savvy entrepreneurs.

Garron slapped several parchments into Coal's thick dwarven hand.

"Whoa!" Coal started. "How many did you get us today?"

Garron had taken to the wagoner game of claiming job posts. Whenever they were in town, the man went to the morning gathering at the wagon depot where the master wagoner would announce the job posts available for acquisition. Garron learned the game quickly and had a knack at claiming jobs that paid well. Coal had gone with him for most of the gatherings in the early days but found the man quite capable.

The dwarf brought other skills to their partnership. He was a clever logistician, a skill he'd learned over the years he'd spent on the Palori River. He managed the cargo and the distribution of weight to ensure their wagons weren't overloaded or in danger of damage along the road.

Only a few months into their operation, they'd been able to buy a second wagon, larger than the original, and two horses to haul it. Coal took the bigger wagon, where he created a nice nest among the cargo for passengers to ride comfortably. He usually took the passengers, glad to tell someone his tall tales—a fact Garron found quite humorous after Ellaria told him of their experience with Tobin, the halfling wagoner of Galium.

"Seven cargo posts this time," Garron said to the dwarf as one of the wagon depot workers came to inspect the parchments.

"Seven!" the dwarf said, handing them over.

The depot workers quickly set to the task of gathering all the goods and cargo that needed to be loaded on their pair of wagons. It had dawned on Garron some weeks back that since they had two wagons, they could each run their own operation. But neither the man nor the dwarf said anything about it. Besides the facts that their enterprise was working smoothly and it would be a shame to interrupt its flow, he genuinely loved the dwarf. Being on the road with his friend was the perfect amount of adventure for him.

438

"They didn't have any passengers this time?" Coal asked, sounding disappointed.

"Jerro and Larkin took the only passenger posts before I could get them," Garron said apologetically. Aside from the pay being better for transporting travelers, he knew the dwarf enjoyed it. "Looks like it'll just be you and me on this one."

Coal didn't complain any further, though he did start barking at one of the depot workers. "What are you doing, lad? That has to go on the right side. See here what you've done. You'll make my wagon topple if you're not careful. Let me show you."

Garron chuckled as he let the dwarf manage the young depot workers. Most of them were young boys or dwarves trying to get their start. Many of them had aspirations to be wagoners themselves one day. It was a simple life, but Garron soaked it up as much as he could.

The man moved to the front of his wagon, running his hand along the white and brown spotted coat of Benley. "How are you doing, pal? Ready for another trip to Kane Harbor?" The pegasus bobbed his head excitedly as Garron produced an apple from his cloak pocket.

"You'll spoil that beast," Coal called.

"Never," Garron whispered to the pegasus, as he softly stroked Benley's snout.

He knew he seemed a strange sight among the other wagoners, with a pegasus drawing his wagon. But Garron didn't care what others thought. Benley had earned his place next to the man. The pegasus could no longer fly after their battle against Kilretheon the Red had left him with a crippled wing. Garron knew no more courageous steed. Would any of the horses run into battle against a monolith dragon? Not likely.

That made the pegasus the greatest of all steeds in the man's eyes ... and worthy of an extra apple or two.

Benley crunched happily as Garron double-checked the back of his wagon. He'd learned a lot from Coal over their first several months, and while he felt he understood the basics of packing the wagons, Coal always had some minor adjustment to make before they left the depot.

Garron didn't complain, of course, for they had yet to break down on the road, while they'd helped several other wagoners who had. Though unfortunate for the other wagoners, Garron always took it as an opportunity to learn. He didn't suspect they'd break down any time soon with Coal's detailed eye, but it was good to know how to fix things should something happen.

As they rolled toward the edge of Whitestone, they each nodded toward the Grand Corral, knowing Ellaria was in there somewhere, likely already into her morning training.

They saw her regularly. She joined them for dinner most nights when they were at their little house on the outskirts of Whitestone. She'd even ridden with Garron on some of their trips to Kane Harbor and back. He always loved when she joined them. Even if they didn't speak for hours, her mere presence on the driver's bench next to him was welcome.

As they left the city behind, Garron breathed in the crisp morning air. The summer sun would warm everything soon and evaporate the dew from the long green grass, but that time of morning was something to be experienced. The rolling green hills before them were peppered with great white stones that jutted in high towering angles. The mountains of Drelek stood regally to the north, and Whitestone Forest created a wall of green to their south.

Garron loved being on the road.

He chuckled as he heard Coal singing some sea shanty the dwarf had learned years ago. He often sang to himself when he wasn't carrying passengers. Though Garron thought the dwarf a much better wagoner than a singer, he never grew tired of Coal's songs. He considered them a sign of the great mirth in the dwarf's heart.

Wagonrest sat near one of the last great white stones that erupted from the green hills on the way to Kane Harbor. It was conveniently located at about the halfway mark between Whitestone and Kane Harbor. While it had no real town or built structures, the wagoners used it nightly as a rest stop on their travels.

Numerous circles of wagons scattered the area, each wagoner finding a spot among friends. The wagon circles were wide enough to keep them safe from the fires that were built but compact enough to make for a nice break from the wind when it came through the valley.

Garron pulled his wagon next to Coal's as the dwarf found a circle with space for them. Many of the wagons were headed the other way, bringing goods or travelers from Kane Harbor to Whitestone. One such wagoner was Berrit, a burly man with arms covered in thick black hair. His face was almost entirely covered by the black hair as well. If he weren't two times Coal's height and three times his width, Garron would have thought the hairy man a distant cousin of the dwarf.

"Hey, Berrit," Coal called as he hopped down from the driver's box.

"Hallo, Coal," the burly man replied as he spun a spit over the fire.

"Got something good cooking on the spit?"

"Beef," he said bluntly.

Coal chuckled and shook his head to Garron.

The man smiled. He liked Berrit fine, but the man usually had little to say. Garron figured it was the reason the burly man never had any passengers—that or his great size intimidated any would-be passengers.

The evening was just starting to grow dim and the stars began to pinprick the night sky when excited calls went out across several of the other wagon circles. Garron poked his head around the wagon to see what the commotion was and saw a singular griffin rider headed their way.

"Looks like we have a guest tonight," Garron called to Coal.

The dwarf looked to the sky and said, "Aye," while he added another round of mutton to the pan.

Benley whinnied happily, excited to see Silverwing come in for a landing. Garron loved how the two creatures had forged a friendship. Ellaria slipped from the back of the griffin and jogged over to the campfire.

"Hey, you two," she said. "I hope I didn't miss dinner."

"Coal's just cooking up some mutton. And Berrit already had some beef," Garron said.

"Hallo, Miz Ellaria," the burly man said, brushing awkwardly at his ratty hair. "You look lovely as aver."

"Hello, Berrit," she said with a grin. "Why don't you ever greet me like that?" she teased Garron.

"What are you talking about?" he said defensively.

Ellaria winked at him as she headed toward the fire.

"Got here just in time," Coal said. "Trying a new sprig I heard about from a goblin in Kane Harbor. He called it 'rosemary.'"

"Pretty," Ellaria said.

"Just like you, lass," Coal chimed with a wink.

Ellaria shot Garron another look.

Garron rolled his eyes, smiling and shaking his head slowly at her. They'd grown close over the past few months, and while they were still dancing around each other, he knew a deep love was growing between them. He and Coal had a great arrangement, but Garron was saving up his coin to build a house next to their little place—one a little bigger. One he could start a family in. One he hoped Ellaria would live in with him one day.

But those were all plans for the future. He wouldn't stop making plans—for planning paves the way to achieve goals—but he also wasn't going to let moments pass him by while he worried over the future.

The friends sat together, eating their supper and trying to talk to Berrit, as the fire dwindled to embers. Berrit excused himself and went to bed in the back of his wagon.

Stars danced brilliantly in the sky far above them. They were so bright, they painted the sky with light, as though a brush streaked across the canvas of the night. Garron loved that time of night. He and his friends lay back with their hands behind their heads and gazed up at the speckled sky. Coal told them stories of the constellations. Sailors in the southern isles had stories for all of them, far more than Garron had even known existed.

When it was getting late, Ellaria departed from them saying, "I'll see you boys in a few days," and gave them each a kiss on the cheek.

As Garron prepared his bed roll in the back of his wagon and got comfortable, he gazed up at the stars. Coal had told him that Ezel's favorite constellation was one called Lendendor—a constellation of stars that was said to be the shape of a woman handing out bread. The man couldn't quite see it, but the dwarf had told him that the deep gnome loved it so much because it reminded him of his gnomish grandmother back in Lornteris.

Garron's eyes lingered on the constellation, the sight bringing a smile to his face. Though he knew it not to be so, he always felt like Ezel was watching him from the constellation. When he saw Lendendor, the man always took a moment to reflect and make sure he'd lived in the moment that day. Often, he found himself wondering about Jaernok Tur's use of the black stone on the man. It turned out to be the very thing that allowed him to communicate with the deep gnome. Something meant for evil had been turned for good. He still did not completely comprehend how the magic gave him the ability to understand the different languages, and he probably never would. Regardless, he was grateful he had been granted the opportunity to make such a great friend. Though he knew the gnome wasn't watching him from the constellation, Garron moved his hands and signed, *"I won't forget, my friend. Thank you."*

As Pernden walked down the corridor toward the king's private dining hall, he heard the echoed laughter and merriment from within. He paused in the middle of the hallway, smiling to himself, as Dona came around the corner. The round woman carried a plate of steaming biscuits and a jar of honey.

She grinned at him. The last time they'd run into each other in that hallway, the castle had seemed so empty. So lifeless. So devoid of joy. With the raucous laughter in the other room, there was no denying the vibrancy that had reentered Whitestone Castle.

"Not so lonely around here anymore," Dona said to him.

"No," Pernden agreed. "Not so much."

"Well, what are you doing out here in the hallway? Your brother's only here for a few days now," she said. "Shoo. Shoo."

She ushered him into the dining hall where lanterns lit the room with a warm light. Nera and Ellaria laughed about something between them, while Porg excused himself from his explanation of what he and the other engineers were working on in Dorantown. Bilford, the butcher and soon-to-be husband of Nera's mother Netla, also grabbed a biscuit, though he seemed fascinated with the orc's stories about their work in Kelvur. Porg and Orin had ridden back to Whitestone with Garron and Coal, so they had already heard the update.

Coal danced around the room, clacking wooden swords with Devohn, Nera's little brother. He was quite excited to spar with someone his own height.

Garron sat with Nera's sister, Ada, as they swapped books and discussed what tomes they'd recently read from the Library of Whitestone. Pernden knew his cousin took books with him when he left on the wagon road, and that Ada was as avid a reader as he. The king was glad to see Garron happy again.

Netla poked at Orin, asking if he was getting enough to eat out on the sea. She mentioned that he should make sure their quartermaster stocked more rations, and if he needed help, he should come see her.

The guardian king watched his family, enjoying the sight and sound of them while dinner was being brought into the room. The scene reminded him of when he was little. There was so much life in the castle then. He and his brothers and his cousins were always running around, while their fathers discussed matters of importance.

Suddenly, Ellaria gasped, and the whole room fell silent. Nera tried to shush her, but the woman had already drawn the attention of everyone present.

Nera strode over to Pernden and whispered, "Step into the hallway with me?"

"Of course," he said curiously. "Are you alright?"

"Well," Nera hemmed. "I don't think we'll be able to spar for a little while."

"Why? What happened? Are you injured?" he asked, looking her over.

She laughed softly and said, "No. No. Nothing like that. You'll just have to wait for me to beat you in the Corral for say ... nine months?"

"Nine months?" Pernden said incredulously. His face shifted to utter surprise then delight. "Nine months—you mean ..."

Nera smiled and kissed him. "The first child of Pernden, the Guardian King."

Pernden didn't know what to say. His eyes glossed over, making it hard for him to see his beautiful wife. He blinked furiously and hugged her in his arms. He could already see the little tyke, and more to come, running around the halls, filling the castle with the pure sound of children's laughter.

When they finally rejoined the others in the dining hall, Ellaria stood by anxiously while the others watched with confused faces.

"The first child of our house is coming!" Pernden announced.

The room erupted into cheers and applause. The others rushed around the table to congratulate them, ecstatic about the news. As the guardian king looked around, joy and excitement on the faces of those he loved, he couldn't help but smile.

CHAPTER THIRTY-SEVEN
THE HUNTSMAN'S FAMILY

One year later ...

O Merrick flattened out the latest map Tam and Tinli had brought back from their mapping expedition in the mountains south of Dorantown. The pair had become quite a patrol duo and were excited to share what they'd found.

Tinli had all the necessary skills a Duskwood Ranger required, having trained and earned the title after years of experience under her father's tutelage. Merrick was still grateful that Domin Ven had sent some of his best to help the huntsman form the new ranger element based out of Dorantown.

The Dorantown Lodge resembled that of the lake lodge in Duskwood's east, where the mountains separated the great forest region and the Eastern Knolls. The craftsmanship was brilliant with many of the logs shaped only enough for strong building and not so much that it detracted from the wood's natural beauty.

Tam and Tinli talked over each other, trying to explain what they'd seen, and Merrick had a hard time understanding them. He thought back to what Domin Ven had told him during his training at the lake lodge.

"You're going to be establishing a new ranger element. You're going to be exploring wilds that we haven't seen in generations," the domin said. "It's possible you will see things we don't see here in the east. If that's the case, make note. I will set some of our scribes to copying our journals and texts, but you will need to start some of your own."

Merrick laughed at the memory. Since the Dorantown Lodge opened, they'd discovered numerous things in the wild lands that weren't noted in the texts from the lake lodge. Much of the past several months had seen the Dorantown Rangers exploring and annotating the wilds south of them.

Yenklin had the Glain's Griffins scouring the area as well, trying to reestablish the ancient trade road that once extended between their two towns. Dorantown had sent ships down to Glain's Shoulder, though transferring goods from the cliff dwelling to the ships had proven difficult and inefficient. That was none of Merrick's concern, though. He left much of the town's leadership to Ralowyn and Tenzo.

"Alright. Slow down," Merrick said to the rangers. "One at a time. What is this snaking line here?"

"That's what we're trying to say, Domin." Tam addressed the huntsman with his proper title. "From our vantage on the Klate Peak, I think it was an overgrown road, perhaps the ancient road to Glain's Shoulder."

"Really?" Merrick asked, eyeing the map with more interest.

"Perhaps, Domin," Tinli said, with reservation. "However, we were on our way back from our patrol. It would be wise to start our next patrol in the area and inspect it more thoroughly."

"I'm telling you," Tam interjected, "I'm thinking that's it."

Merrick stood straight and looked between the rangers. He squinted at Tinli and asked, "If not the road, what?"

"I do not know, Domin," she said, "but I do believe it worth another look."

Merrick smiled, noting the giant grin on Tam's face. "Fine," the domin ranger said. "How many days were you out?"

"Six days," Tinli answered quickly, as Tam deflated.

"Two days' rest, at least," Merrick said.

"But Domin," Tam started to argue.

"Two days," Merrick said with finality. "Tired rangers make mistakes. Mistakes can lead to injury or even death."

Tam nodded his head and said, "Yes, Domin."

"Good," Merrick said. "Tinli, I was going through this notebook on the flora of Duskwood to match it up with a sketch brought back by another patrol. I didn't see any of its like. I do not know of a plant from Tarrine that matches it either. I thought you might take a look at it for me?"

"Of course, Domin," Tinli said, taking the parchment.

"You see the petals there?" Merrick asked, pointing to the sketch. "If I'm not mistaken, they look to be—"

Suddenly, the door slammed open, and a young female chelon hurried into the large meeting room. She was dressed in a ranger's cloak, the marks on her sleeve designating her as an apprentice.

"Domin Merrick," she cried, trying to catch her breath.

"What? What is it?" Merrick asked, running to her side.

"It's your wife, Domin. The baby is coming!"

The cottage was quiet. Merrick's head lay back on the chair, his mouth open as he slept. Little Aelwyth snuggled in his arms, finally asleep after a long cry. The girl could whip up a whirlwind of tears when she wanted to, and Ralowyn thought it quite adorable to watch Merrick and Kippin try to soothe her.

In the end, it seemed the battle exhausted them all, as Kippin lay in the chair next to Merrick and Aelwyth, drooling on the ranger's shirt.

"That was ... quite eventful," Coal whispered with a chuckle. He handed Ralowyn some lavender tea he'd made from her tea box.

The elf sniffed it and let the steam roll over her face. She sipped the hot tea slowly, relishing its floral flavor. "The lavender I picked for this brew was lovely," she said to the dwarf who sat in a chair next to her.

"I'm so glad I came to see the little one," Coal said, his gaze lingering on the cuddle pile in the chair across from them.

"Only to see Aelwyth?" Ralowyn asked.

"Of course not, lass," Coal said with a wink. "Came to see Kippin, too."

Ralowyn popped an eyebrow at the dwarf but smiled nonetheless. "The blessing you spoke over her was beautiful, by the way. Thank you."

"Bah," Coal said bashfully. "Don't mention it. It's a royal blessing spoken over all those born into the royals of Clan Carraignyk."

"'A life full of peace and joy,'" Ralowyn quoted, "'overflowing with glory and honor, through every circumstance.' It is quite beautiful."

"Ah, well," Coal hemmed, "I'm just glad I could say it over her. When she turns eighteen, we could tattoo the mark of Clan Carraignyk on her hand to make it official."

Ralowyn laughed but shushed herself as Aelwyth stirred on Merrick's chest. "No, I think Merrick and I will agree to forgo that particular tradition."

"Alright," Coal said with a chuckle. "It'll be a really little tattoo if we try to do it tomorrow."

Ralowyn gave him a flat look, and Coal stifled a laugh of his own.

"You know, if you wake her, you will be the one who gets her back to sleep," Ralowyn cautioned.

"Uncle Coal's not afraid of anything," the dwarf said, "but Merrick did just finally get the gem to sleep. Let's say we let them snore a little while."

"I think that would be wise."

Ralowyn watched Kippin roll over, trying to bury himself into Merrick's side. The little halfling's curly locks fluttered as he exhaled.

"Quite the beautiful family you've got here," the dwarf said finally. "Is it what you dreamed?"

Ralowyn thought for a moment. The small cottage home was lovely and cozier than she'd anticipated. The builders had built it not far from the Dorantown Lodge, just inside the edge of the forest. They deemed it appropriate for the domin and his family to have a cottage away from the lodge. A place where Merrick could get away from the rangers to be with his family. Even if he was out on patrol, Valurwind brought him home swiftly—something for which Ralowyn was grateful.

The fields outside danced with summer flowers, and just that day, she'd watched Merrick and Kippin training with the halfling's falcon, Davir. She remembered kissing the top of Aelwyth's soft head, the baby's silvery hair as fine as her own. She remembered breathing in her daughter's scent and thinking there was no place she would rather be in all of Finlestia.

"Better," she said to Coal. "And you? How are things in Whitestone?"

"Just great, actually," Coal said, sipping his tea. "Garron and I have earned quite the reputation about the wagon depot. We're getting requests almost daily now, including passengers. And ...” The dwarf's words fell away for a moment.

"And what?" Ralowyn pressed.

"And, well ..." Coal hesitated for a moment. "The old wagon master of Kane Harbor is retiring for real this time, and I was asked if I'd take the position."

"Coal, that is wonderful," Ralowyn said. When the dwarf didn't immediately agree, the elf leaned forward and raised an eyebrow at him. "Is it not wonderful?"

"Well, it is," Coal said quickly. "But I don't want the job."

"No," Ralowyn said with a smirk.

"No. Garron and I are doing great things, and wagoning has been so much fun. Sleeping under the stars, transporting goods and good people. It's almost felt like when Ezel and I were on the Palori River."

"Almost, but different."

"Aye," Coal said quietly. "But I love it. I don't want to be locked up in a wagon depot for the rest of my life. I'm a young dwarf."

"In your seventies."

"Right," Coal agreed. "I seem to recall a lovely elven lass telling me I had a good 275 years left. That's a long time to be cooped up in a wagon depot."

"That is," Ralowyn agreed.

"So, you see why I can't take that job. I'd be miserable. Maybe they can offer it to me again when I'm in my three hundreds."

"That seems reasonable to me."

"Aye. Very reasonable. Plus, I want to be the one to transport you all the way to Tamaria when you come through in a few months."

"All the way to Tamaria?" The elf mused and gave him a mocking impressed look.

"It's not the usual route, I grant you," Coal hemmed. "But if you're going all the way to Last Town, I can at least get you to Tamaria. I know a few good boaters there who will get you the rest of the way."

"That would be nice," she whispered.

"Small wonder Ellaria met your brother," Coal said, shaking his head as he blew the steam from his teacup.

"Small wonder," Ralowyn agreed. "When she shared the whole story with Merrick and me, I almost could not believe it. I had always thought my parents had taken my baby brother with them into the Nari Desert. I assumed him lost with them. I am very much looking forward to meeting him."

"Family is a special thing," the dwarf said. He smirked at the light snores emanating from the other side of the room.

Ralowyn smiled into her tea. Coal was only visiting for another week. She had missed the dwarf but knew he needed to go back to Tarrine. The elf reached over to the Staff of Anvelorian and gripped it in her slender hand. The cool metal hummed silently, and she could sense everyone in the cottage. She looked at Coal and felt great pride as he watched the ranger and his snoozing littles. Though Coal's pride swelled and filled a small portion of the house, the greatest sensation—the one that permeated every fiber and grain of the cozy cottage—was contentment.

EPILOGUE

The smell of sea salt hung in the air, as mist sprayed from the bow of the *Sellena*. Orin opened his eyes after taking a long moment to bask in the summer sun. The ship glided through the waters of the Gant Sea with a certain ease, as though the vessel and the helmsman were joined with a mutual trust. His hands held loosely to the wheel as the *Sellena* cut through the waves.

"How long do you think the journey will take us?" Shorlis asked. The chelon wore a blue cloak around his shoulders and held his staff, *Menthrora,* in one hand.

"At the pace Mister Orin steers us," Captain Tinothe answered in his gravelly tone, "maybe a few weeks. Maybe not."

Orin smirked at the captain's answer. He would have been surprised if the old sea captain had given the chelon a straight answer.

Enkeli chuckled next to the captain. "It is not how long of a journey we have, but rather how we travel it that matters."

Captain Tin snickered between puffs of his pipe.

Two peas in a pod, these ones, Orin mused.

Orin eyed the chelon. Shorlis was wrestling with something, as he twisted *Menthrora* in his hand.

"You know," Orin whispered to the chelon, "I've found that even if you don't get a straight answer, it's better to get any answer than to let questions burble within."

Shorlis's sea green eyes squinted at the man, and he turned toward Enkeli with determination.

"Master ..." The chelon's words came out less determined than his stance. "I've been wondering. Why did you let them take the Staff of Tur back to Whitestone?"

"Ah," Enkeli said, stepping away from the aft railing. "The king and queen of Whitestone both witnessed the power of the staff and treat the artifact with proper caution. They have it locked away, and it will be safe there."

"I still do not understand," Shorlis pressed. "You said there is only one staff from the First Tree of each land of Finlestia. You have also said that it is time for Kelvur and Tarrine to rejoin the council of wizards. It's time to bring the training of wizards back to our lands. Is that not possible in the land from which Jaernok Tur came?"

Orin peeked over his shoulder, wondering how the wizard would respond. *The chelon makes some good points*, he thought.

Enkeli's face twisted thoughtfully, and he let out a deep exhale. "That would be unwise," the old wizard said. His burgundy hood fluttered in the sea breeze. "Bajoral is a ruthless place with a dark history."

"Would not a wizard's eye be good for them? Is there no one up to the task?" Shorlis asked.

"Not now," the wizard said, placing a kind hand on the chelon's shoulder. "Do not fret. The Staff of Tur will be safe in Whitestone until the time it is needed in Bajoral. They've got it under guard, just as all your friends have placed the mirrors under guard. It will be safe."

Orin became invested in the line of questioning. "You're sure about that?" the man asked over his shoulder.

"I am sure," the wizard said.

"How do you know?" Orin asked.

Enkeli was quiet for a moment, and Orin wondered if the wizard had heard his question. Finally, the wizard said, "A feeling."

"A feeling is not much to go on," Shorlis said cautiously.

Enkeli chuckled. "When you've been a wizard as long as I have, a feeling can tell you a great many things. You will know what I mean one day. I will teach you."

Shorlis nodded at his mentor, completely trusting him.

"Sounds an awful lot like sailing," Captain Tin said, slapping Orin on the shoulder. "I seem to recall teaching you something similar."

Orin smirked at the captain as the ex-guardian held the *Sellena's* wheel in his hands. He looked ahead of the ship's prow and felt the waves beneath them running along the rudder, vibrating all the way into the wheel. Orin didn't know how long it would take them to get to Candara, the isle of wizards, but as long as he could feel the sea breeze on his face, he was happy to be on the journey. It was just the sea, the *Sellena*, and he.

Acknowledgements

Thank you for reading my book! I hope you had as much fun reading the epic conclusion to the *Stone & Sky* series as I did writing it. If so, please leave a wonderful review. Reviews are the lifeblood of indie authors like me. The more positive reviews we have, the more likely it is that others will pick up the book as well.

As with every book, a lot went into *Stone & Ruin* and I've had some great encouragement and help along the way. I definitely need to thank a few very specific people for helping me on this journey.

Crystal, thank you for your continued love and friendship. Thank you for sticking with me even when certain characters met perilous ends.

Joy, thank you for helping me make this series better with each book. You truly make me better as an author.

And finally, my wife Brittany and our kids, thanks for helping me box ridiculous amounts of books. Your support for this dream is the most important and I hope it only fuels your own.

ABOUT THE AUTHOR

Z.S. Diamanti is the award-winning author of the *Stone &*
Sky series, an epic fantasy adventure and the result of his great
passion for fun and fantastical stories. He went to college
forever and has too many pieces of paper on his wall. He is a
USAF veteran of Operation Enduring Freedom and worked in
ministry for over 10 years. He and his wife reside in Colorado
with their four children where they enjoy hikes and tabletop
games.

You can get the *Stone & Sky Preludes Series* of stories for
FREE at zsdiamanti.com

Connect with him on social media: @zsdiamanti

CONNECT

WANT MORE FROM THE WORLD OF FINLESTIA?

JOIN THE
GRIFFIN GUARD
TODAY!

JOIN Z.S. DIAMANTI'S
OFFICIAL READERS LIST
AND GET EXCLUSIVE ACCESS TO NEWS,
SHORT STORIES, EVENTS, AND MORE!

Good reviews are vital for Indie Authors. The importance of reviews in helping others find and take a chance on an indie author's book is impossible to overstate.

If you enjoyed this book, would you help me get it in front of more people by taking a minute to give it a good review?
I can't tell you how thankful I'd be.

Check out this link for the best places to review this book and help me get it to more readers who love good books just like you and me!